I Will Remember Always

Irene Steinhilber

Copyright © 2023 Irene Steinhilber

All rights reserved

The characters and events portrayed in this book are fictitious. Any similarity to real persons, living or dead, is coincidental and not intended by the author.

No part of this book may be reproduced, or stored in a retrieval system, or transmitted in any form or by any means, electronic, mechanical, photocopying, recording, or otherwise, without express written permission of the publisher.

ebook: ASIN: B0BW4TT7ZS
Paperback: ISBN: 9798378369416
Hardcover: ISBN: 9798390066348
Imprint: Independently published

Cover design by: Garry Steinhilber
Printed in the United States of America

Last updated: April 15, 2023

To my mother.
Her courage and faith was a bright light in troubled times.

Prologue

Where the land meets the Black Sea, a quiet whisper, a murmur is heard, of once prosperous villages and fertile fields; of a people that toiled here. Gone—erased is their passage, only their languished saga remains, telling of well fought wars, of captivity and freedom, of gain and loss, building up and tearing down; of love and hate, of birth and death, of joy and heartache and the yearning of peace... peace that was never to be theirs...

1

Katina looked on as her father guided the horse drawn carriage. Being familiar with the history of this land warranted them to be alert of the unexpected. New to this area; she and her family were only few of German descent who dared settle into this sparsely populated region of Romania.

She threw a glance at her father, a tall and stately man, very astute in business, and by the looks, she guessed his thoughts to be on the things of home. She smiled and leaned against his strong shoulder.

"It won't be long," he reassured her, realizing the twelve-kilometer trek to the station had left her weary.

Once there he purchased the fare, then helped carry her luggage onto the waiting train.

"Be careful," he warned uneasy in letting her go alone.

"I will Papa," she acknowledged his concern giving him a quick hug in appreciation.

Upon entering the rail car, she was relieved to find an entire section to herself. Without regard to other passengers, she placed her luggage on top the provided space then waved to Papa as the train started to move.

With her father's concerned look still on her mind, she leaned back to relax. The big flood came to mind when her family alongside neighbors fought to keep their homesteads from destruction. It was then she felt herself ill and out of sorts. Yet not to show weakness she continued to help Mama, especially with the washing of oil stained clothes. Running an Oil Mill was at best a dirty and laborious job, which her father and her older brothers so diligently worked to further the family's standard of living. Theirs was a large family of fourteen and to be self sufficient was a principle taught to them from early age.

Among nine boys and three girls, Tara, her older sister had recently married and moved to Anadolchioi, where her husband Micha ran a modest dairy farm with his father and younger brother.

Anxious to find the cause for her listlessness, Tara repeatedly insisted to have her come for a visit. It was to seek the advice of a well-known doctor in Constanta. The same Auntie Elena, Papa's half sister, had spoken so highly of.

A vague smile crossed her lips recalling the whole ordeal. It had not been easy to convince her parents to let her come alone. Yet after another persuasive letter from Tara their worries dissipated. In it her sister promised to be vigilant and watch over her entire stay.

Her gaze on the passing land, she gave into daydreaming, forgetting for a moment what ailed her...

"Is this seat taken?"

Startled by a somewhat familiar voice, she looked up and found herself staring into the smiling eyes of Stefan, Tara's brother-in-law. She returned a vague smile, indicating it was not.

After her sister's wedding he had surprised her parents with an unannounced visit, asking for her hand in marriage, yet her father was quick to decline. Saying to give it at least three years maybe then he would consider his proposal, but only if she agreed.

She held her gaze upon Stefan as he seated himself, though his questionable almost pleading eyes made her uncomfortable and she felt uneasy about him.

Stefan searched for words. He felt his throat tightening, partly of excitement, partly out of nervousness. How can he make her understand how much he cared for her?

That day when he asked for her hand in marriage, he had tried to assure her parents that he loved her, and that he was more than capable to provide for her; but her father stood firm.

"Stefan," she was the first to speak, hoping to dispel the uncomfortable position. "Tara never mentioned you'll be on this train?"

He hesitated for a moment. "I had some unfinished business to attend to..." He swallowed hard and looked out of the window. How could he tell her what really was on his mind, she might never forgive him... And how could he tell her that he knew about her coming? Also, that he and his friends had worked out a plan to... No, he could not go through with it, not yet. He had to wait for the right moment.

He looked across the aisle exchanging eye contact with a young couple. Noticing him shaking his head, she followed his gaze. Found out, he quickly jumped in.

"Marika and Duza, this is Katina."

She detected a slight quaver in his voice.

"It's a pleasure to finally meet the girl Stefan was raving about. And I must say he did not exaggerate," Duza said in a most charming manner. She felt herself blush, as she was not used to such praise.

"Why don't you join us?" Stefan suggested. Immediately Marika took up the conversation, raving to her about Constanta, her hometown, and even went so far as to invite her on a sightseeing tour. Reserved but collected she entertained the thought of going, but then declined.

"I would like that. But I'm not sure if my sister would agree. I think I'd better ask her first," she apologized. Yet Marika was ready with an answer.

"Oh... I'm sure she would let you go if Stefan was to be your chaperone," Marika coaxed her on, giving Stefan a hint of a smirk.

Realizing the near sarcastic grin did not escape her, she

noticed Stefan's uncomfortable look. Puzzled she wondered what it was all about.

When Anadolchioi came in view she could not believe the trip had ended. She had expected a long ride. Yet with Marika by her side it had been surprisingly the opposite.

Suddenly her thoughts turned to her sister and she became excited to see Tara again. It had been months when last they seen each other and she missed having her sister around.

There was a squeal in the wheels when the train slowed into the station. In eager anticipation she gave a quick look out the window then hurried to gather her belongings.

Stefan politely offered to carry her luggage as they both bid farewell to his friends.

"Katina, you'll have to promise to come as soon as you can," Marika called after her.

"I'll try my best," she said with a quick glance back as she walked on. At that instant she noticed Stefan's concerned face while conversing with his friends.

--

At the station Tara stood anxiously waiting with Micha by her side. She was glad he had come along. It gave them the much-needed time to themselves. Lately she had felt homesick; hoping with her sister's visit her longing would quiet. Now the moment had come, and she could hardly wait.

"Katina!" Her voice rang out in excitement. "It's so good to see you again!" Tara held her in her arms. "Now let me have a good look at you girl. You are thin as a board and a little too pale for my liking. Hmm…" she paused for a moment. "We'll have to do something about that won't we Micha?"

Tara teased as Micha was waiting in line.

"We sure do," he answered with a smirk about his face.

"Stefan, I heard you were on the train together," she suddenly heard Tara asking with a tone bordering on the incredulous.

Silent for a moment, as if contemplating an excuse, Stefan

looked warily toward his brother.

"I had business to attend to in Caraomar with two of my colleagues," he answered in a subdued voice. But it seemed not quite enough to escape his brother's listening ears.

"Oh you mean Marika and Duza? We've told you so many times to quit seeing those two. They're no good. They're only putting funny notions in your head. All this time you should be at home working. Not gallivanting around the countryside."

She noticed Stefan's jaw tighten, embarrassed to be belittled and scolded in front of her. At that moment a loud whistle interrupted as the train motioned to move. She turned to wave to Marika and Duza; both waving back enthusiastically from an open window. The locomotive hissed and puffed, forcing a cloud of steam high into the air. Uncomfortable of being caught in a family argument, she turned to watch till the train was out of site.

Sensing the tension, Tara attempted to change the subject. She was tired of this never-ending squabble and hated to have her sister's visit spoiled by all this.

Quickly she added in a more positive tone, "Well it was good for you to be on the same train."

Tara paused for a brief second, "I worried for Katina being alone and not strong enough for this journey, but now I know she was in good hands."

Tara smiled and gave her a wink, then put her arm around her.

"Now, let's take you home so you can rest. I've promised Mama and Papa to take good care of you and I intend to keep that promise."

Once in the carriage, Tara doted over her, covering her with wool blankets to keep her warm.

"Tara I'm fine, really I am," she protested, but Tara would not hear of it.

"Just listen to your older sister and let me decide what's good for you."

Micha turned and grinned sheepishly at her. "You'd better give up and do what she says. Once Tara has made up her mind about something, there is no way stopping her."

"Now Micha, stick to driving the carriage and leave us be," Tara came back teasingly. Exchanging a smile Micha gave a loud "Ha…" to the horses and for the rest of the way held the reigns loosely, letting them trot freely along the sun-dried country road.

Katina found the warm sun soothing as it penetrated through the blankets and onto her weak body. Closing her eyes for a moment she could not help but wonder about the coincidental meeting with Stefan and his friends. Also, the mysterious eye contact she had noticed between them whenever they thought she was not looking.

She glanced at Stefan who sat slumped in the front seat beside Micha. His head turned slightly as if to avoid eye contact with his brother.

She studied the two for a moment and noticed a distinct difference between them. It was not only in character, but also in appearance. Micha was broad and sturdy in build, matching his forward manner. Stefan, on the other hand, was of smaller stature and soft spoken, featuring a tender look about his face.

She pondered this thought a moment longer then chose to focus on the immediate surroundings, letting her eyes roam freely over the passing countryside. She could feel the tension between the others as no one wanted to converse. Only on occasion Tara pointed out the green grasslands and the fat dairy cows grazing contently in the mid-afternoon sun.

When they arrived, the welcome from Tara's in-laws was cold and uninviting. It left her feeling uncomfortable and unwanted. She wondered why this behavior, but then dismissed it as part of their nature and accepted it as such.

Tara noticed the resentment and quietly took her aside. She thought it best for her sister to spend as little time as possible around her in-laws; opting rather to show her around the garden. Once there she apologized for her in-law's unmannerly conduct.

Suddenly overwhelmed, Tara released all the pent-up conflicts. On the quiet garden path she poured out her heart holding nothing back.

"Life here is not at all what it is in our parent's home, Katina," she spoke with a slight regret in her voice. "There's a lack of respect and understanding toward each other. It's money that rules this house. Everything else comes second. Despite all the riches, Mother Hartic pinches every penny. It is to the point where she denies herself even the slightest of pleasures. While doing so she expects everyone else to do the same. See these flowers," she pointed around the garden. "Early in the morning she is off to the market standing all day just to sell a few. Despite the riches she continually makes herself a slave to her own greed."

Tara paused swallowing the oncoming tears then resumed with a faint quiver in her voice.

"She had told me on more than one occasion to do the same. But Micha spoke up on my behalf saying I had enough to do around the house. He also told her that there was no need for anyone to scrounge. Well, from that day on she left me alone. Yet I can feel her disapproval whenever we're together. More than once she had made a point that she did not approve how I was doing things, mind you not in words, but in action. So you see what I have to live with every day?"

She suddenly stopped and turned to face her sister. All at once she realized how selfish she had been.

"Now look at me, babbling about my problems, while I should've been more concerned about you. You must be exhausted. Come inside and rest for a moment while I prepare lunch."

She did not protest. She had to admit she felt a bit faint. Willingly she followed her sister into the house.

Micha and Stefan, as well as Tara's in-laws, suspiciously

stayed out of the way, only appearing for a bite to eat, and then busying themselves with chores and other duties outside the house. But that was fine with Tara. It gave her the opportunity to catch up on past and current events from home.

By the time evening came around Katina felt herself tired and drained. It had been an unusual busy day and she welcomed the moment she could retire to her room. It was not that she wasn't grateful, for her sister had outdone herself to pamper her.

"Katina," Tara pushed the bedroom door open, holding a glass of milk and a plate of cookies in her hand. "I didn't want my little sister go to bed hungry."

"Tara you shouldn't have. I'm fine and I don't feel the least bit hungry, especially not after that delicious dinner you've prepared tonight."

"Well in that case, you wouldn't mind if we talk for a little while longer, hmm?"

"No, not at all," she replied gesturing for her sister to come and sit beside her while crawling under the cozy feather bed.

"Ah-h," she released a pleasure-filled sigh sinking deeply into the fluffy feather pillow. It smelled of springtime freshness of laundry hanging on the line on a sunny day.

"I had the whole room freshened up just for you," Tara said as she looked around the room with great satisfaction.

Katina searched her eyes. There was something she needed to know of her sister.

"Tara, are you really happy being married?"

A little hesitant Tara thought for a moment. How could she make her sister understand? It was a topic much too sensitive and she was not sure if Katina understood. She began to explain, "Well, it's not a question of happiness. It's about belonging and having a home to call your own."

"But from what you've told me it's not your home, completely," she hastily interrupted her sister.

"Not yet, but it will be one day! I have to admit, it's not easy getting along with Mother Hartig. Her idea of living is far from what you and I have been accustomed to... and Father Hartig? Well, he is certainly not like Papa."

Tara's face took on a sad expression. "Poor Stefan, he is the worst off being the most sensitive of them all."

"What do you mean?" Katina lifted her head up, surprised by the statement.

"Remember the day Stefan proposed?" She nodded and sat up.

"Well that day," Tara continued, "he was supposed to go to town to participate in the annual Easter event. Among other games there was the usual egg gathering contest for single men. All organized by the local Lutheran youth. The Hartigs wanted Stefan to join in on the activities. With that they hoped he would meet and fall in love with one of the local girls, unlike Micha, who had taken on our faith and married me. Well... when they found that Stefan instead had gone to our parent's home and of all things had asked for your hand in marriage; they were beside themselves."

Tara paused for a moment.

"I remember that night vividly," she continued. "It was late in the evening. Micha was talking to his father in the living room, planning for the next day, while Mother Hartig was busy with her knitting. I was not feeling well and decided to retire early to our bedroom. I had walked up to the window, it had rained all day, and I took a quick glance outside to see if the rain had stopped. It was then I noticed Stefan driving up to the house on his bike, his clothes drenched from the heavy downpour.

"Not giving it another thought, I crawled into bed. I listened for a moment to the rain pattering against the window and was just about to fall asleep. All at once Father Hartig's outraged voice startled me. I jumped out of bed and ran down the hallway. Once at the stairway, I witnessed Father Hartig beating Stefan, yelling from the top of his voice. "I'll teach you to listen when I tell you to. And you can forget that ridiculous notion of marrying Katina. We will not allow it! You hear?"

Tara stopped to catch her breath.

Katina could not believe what she was hearing. "I didn't know. Poor Stefan I feel so sorry for him. Couldn't Micha intervene?"

Tara shook her head. "Micha! He doesn't want to say or do anything against his father, scared he might be cut out of his inheritance."

"What about his mother?" Katina pleaded. "Doesn't she care?"

"Mother Hartig!" Tara exclaimed. "My dear sister, she is behind her husband all the way. She was the one who ordered Stefan to enroll in the army to get this notion out of his head."

"Why didn't you tell me this before, Tara?" Katina was upset over the fact that her coming here might cause even more friction between Stefan and his parents. "Had I known how the Hartigs felt about this whole affair, I wouldn't have come."

"Katina, calm down now," Tara spoke quietly. "You're forgetting that I'm living here too and I have a right to invite whomever I please."

She stopped for a moment then continued. "Yes, I knew you wouldn't have come and therefore I didn't want you to know. Your health is more important right now than that silly squabble between my in-laws."

"Can't argue with you there? The only thing that bothers me is why Stefan doesn't stand up against his father and stop him from physically abusing him. I mean he is twenty-one going on twenty-two. He's certainly old enough and should be allowed to make up his own mind who he wishes to marry."

"It's probably fear that holds him back from going against his parent's wishes," Tara said thoughtfully, pausing momentarily.

"Fear of what…?"

"I guess fear of being cut off his allowance. So far his parents have paid all the expenses for the business college in Constanta."

"Is that where he met Marika and Duza?"

Tara nodded. "He graduated from the college last week and was offered a very good job at the port in Constanta starting in two weeks for 800 leu a month."

"So! That is why the sudden interest in marriage. With this job offer he would be free and independent."

"That's true," Tara added. "But up till then he has to abide by his parents' wishes, as difficult as they may be."

"Poor Stefan," Katina sighed. "How will I make him understand that I am not interested in marrying him?"

Tara reached over, patting her sister lightly on the shoulder.

"Don't worry Katina. I'll try and make him understand. As for now I want you to sleep and not think about anything. Remember, tomorrow you have an appointment with Dr. Lepra in Constanta."

Tara glanced over to the clock on Katina's night table; it showed a quarter to twelve.

"Oh, my goodness," she exclaimed. "Is it that late already? I'd better get to bed myself and let you rest."

She bent over and gave her sister a light peck on her cheek.

"Goodnight," She said tenderly as she dismissed herself from the room and quietly drew the bedroom door shut behind her.

"Goodnight," Katina's voice trailed after Tara as she sank deep into the soft feather pillow. She was too tired to think of what they had talked about. A few moments later she drifted into a deep and much needed sleep.

2

The cows lowing sound woke her early the next morning. She felt her nightgown wet and clammy against her skin. For some reason she was incredibly thirsty.

She looked at the clock on her night table.

"It's only four in the morning," she sighed and plopped herself back into her pillow and within seconds was sound asleep again.

Hours later a knock at the door interrupted her second sleep. Tara walked into the room and opened the curtains.

"Good morning," she let the words ring. "Isn't it a lovely day?"

The sun was shining bright through the window illuminating the entire room with its warmth.

"I hope you slept well," Tara said as she turned to look. It was then she noticed the flushed look on her sister's face.

"Are you feeling alright?" she asked.

"I'm fine," Katina muttered.

She certainly did not want to be a burden to her sister, as she had enough to do without becoming her nursemaid.

"Well, we'll see what the doctor has to say about that," Tara said touching her forehead. "I detect a slight fever," she concluded with concern. "We should get you out of this wet nightgown and into some dry clothes before you catch a cold."

Gathering enough strength, she climbed out of bed to get

herself ready. Tara in the meantime took the bedding outside, letting it dry in the warm sunshine.

A few hours later Micha drove both to the train station where they boarded for the short ride to Constanta.

Auntie Elena was already waiting at the station when they arrived and was overjoyed to see them. Being the perfect hostess, she almost outdid herself to make their short stay as pleasant as possible.

With an hour to spare, she suggested to show them around her beloved city. Both had no objection, especially when they were to be escorted in style and comfort of a stately horse drawn carriage.

Auntie Elena asked her horseman to take them to the nicest and most scenic sites including a detour along the sea. It was something neither of them had ever seen.

Katina, in particular, was overwhelmed by the wide streets and the many people that leisurely strolled along the boulevards, shopping or just chatting with one another.

"Don't they have work to do?" she asked puzzled by their seemingly easygoing lifestyle.

"My dear Katina," Auntie Elena chuckled, amused over her niece's candid question. "This is a port town. Most of the people you see here are visitors passing through to other resort towns along the Black Sea. At the same time many also remain here for a few days to take in the sights and scenery of this town. Which I have to say is very famous for its old and historic Turkish mosques."

"Oh, I see," Katina listened with great interest to Auntie Elena's illustrative tour. Her proud demeanor seemed to indicate that nothing was more pleasing to her than to show off her hometown to her two nieces.

The horseman weaved the horse drawn carriage carefully through the bustling streets of the city, then took a sharp turn off the main road. Suddenly a whole new scene opened up right in front of their eyes.

Katina sat in awe gazing over the vast water of the Black

Sea. Mesmerized she watched it reflecting on top its white foaming waves.

"It's beautiful," she said quietly.

At that moment she happened to glance over to Auntie Elena and noticed a faint trace of remorse in her eyes. She wondered what it was that brought about this sudden sadness. But she did not dare intrude in her aunt's private thoughts.

"My goodness," Auntie Elena all at once exclaimed. "We'd better be going. Take us to Dr. Lepra at once," she called to the horseman who did just as ordered.

Katina threw one more glance toward the sea with the thought to return someday. But hopefully it would be under different circumstances.

--

Dr. Lepra took great care in examining her and in no time had found the cause of her ill health.

"Its double pneumonia," she announced with concern.

"It's amazing she had not complained more about pain," She stated again with surprise in her voice as she went to prepare two bottles filled with medication. Handing the package to Tara, she gave strict orders. "I would advise for her to rest as much as possible, preferably out in the warm midmorning to early afternoon sun."

Auntie Elena now felt sorry for taking her niece on a lengthy tour about town. She apologized for not being more considerate. Katina dismissed it and told her not to feel guilty, as she had enjoyed herself immensely despite her discomfort. Yet Auntie Elena insisted to take the blame. "I should have known better," she said.

To make up for it, she invited both of them to her home for lunch. She thought it would be good for her niece to take a little rest before taking the train back.

If the city had made an impression on Katina, Auntie Elena's home did even more. The ostentatious stately villa was painted all in white with beautiful stained-glass windows facing the street. The very same was surrounded by a large rose garden that had a breathtaking view over the Black Sea from the back of the villa.

The interior of the large residence matched the magnificence of the outside. It was decorated in a Victorian elegance. The grand piano standing in front of a scenic bow window was Auntie Elena's favorite piece of furniture. Being talented in music, she spent many hours in her pastime playing for herself or for anyone who cared to listen.

Immediately Katina felt drawn to this grandiose place and could not help but marvel about the beauty of it all.

And since it was a warm and windless day, Auntie Elena advised her servants to serve lunch in the garden. Here they sat in leisure surrounded by fragrant flowers enjoying the warm midday sun.

While they took in a tastefully prepared lunch, Auntie Elena told them of Uncle Gustav's plan to move to Uruguay. And it was then Katina understood the sadness she had detected earlier in her aunt's eyes.

"It must be hard to leave such a beautiful place," she expressed with profound sympathy.

"Yes it won't be easy," the older woman sighed and looked about sadly. "I've become attached to this land. But Uncle Gustav and the boys caught the adventure fever, and there is nothing I can do or say to stop them from going."

She paused at the thought. "I'll especially miss your father. He always had been like a real brother to me…" she wiped a lonely tear from her cheeks.

She chuckled to herself then added, "Did your father ever tell you how many siblings he had?"

"Well, I'm not quite sure," Tara was the first to speak, "but I think he mentioned that there were eighteen all together. Let's see… there were six from his father's first marriage, six from your mother's first marriage and then they had six more together."

"That's correct!" Auntie Elena exclaimed and smiled with

amusement. "What a busy household that was. Your father was the oldest. A lot of responsibility was put on his shoulders. He had to help Mother in looking after us smaller ones. Oh... He tried so hard to keep the peace among us and looking back now it could not have been the easiest thing to do."

Auntie Elena suddenly paused as a frown appeared upon her brow. Her face took on a faraway look as she gazed out into the blue horizon. With a sigh upon her lips, she spoke again, "I'll miss you all, terribly."

"We'll miss you too."

Both reached over to comfort her.

"You know girls," Auntie Elena said with a fond expression on her face. "I always wished to have a daughter of my own, but God only saw fit to give me sons. I had envied your mother for having not one but three daughters. Now after this little chat I envy her even more. Seeing what caring and fine upstanding young ladies you have turned out to be."

Flattered by Auntie Elena's comment, they willingly enjoyed her praise.

Later on the train, Katina was left with a lasting profound impression of the day's events. She had come to love this grand and dear lady. She would always have a special place in her heart.

3

When they arrived back at the estate, Katina mentioned that she intended to take the early morning train home, but Tara would not hear of it. She was persistent in convincing her that she was in no condition to travel. She urged her to stay for at least another week.

Reluctantly Katina agreed. She had enjoyed her stay here with her sister but felt uncomfortable around her in-laws. This was especially true now that she knew how they felt about her.

As advised, Tara made sure her younger sister received the proper rest and care she needed to speed up her recovery. She also wrote Mama and Papa about Katina's condition and she told them that she intended to keep her here until she was strong enough to travel. To this, Mama and Papa agreed.

So whenever weather permitted Tara was adamant in keeping Doctor's orders, and submitting to her sister's pampering, Katina lay covered under wool blankets basking in the warm sunshine. The daily routine in the garden had become a home away from home. Here she felt at ease and she began to treasure this tranquil sweet-smelling setting.

The soft sea air drifting over the land had a soothing effect on her. And within days her pale face had taken on a fresh healthy look.

Tara was proud of herself to have accomplished what she had set out to do. She even managed for her sister to gain a few pounds.

What was intended to be a week had turned into a two week stay. And feeling a little better, Tara had allowed herself to take Katina out for short visits.

Just recently a cousin of theirs had married and moved here to Anadolchioi. Her husband, a Romanian officer, had been stationed here. Yet already stricken with homesickness, Martha was looking forward to having Katina and Tara over for a chat.

Spending the afternoon with much fun and laughter, they reminisced of their growing up years in Cogealac; a city north of Anadolchioi, one, Katina and Tara's family had previously moved from before settling in Girargi, to the south Dobrujan region of Romania. With that move, Papa had given up his father's homestead and instead had gone into the sunflower oil production. It was a time Katina remembered with fondness.

And sitting in the garden the following day, her thoughts went back to that time. She remembered this incident with her older brother Mark. Always full of mischief, he approached her one day with a proposition. Built onto the big kitchen was this cool room where all the perishable food was kept. And for obvious reasons the door to this room was always locked.

The cool room itself had no windows, except for one little square opening near the top. It was much too small for him to squeeze through. Yet he had thought it big enough for her to slip through. Repeatedly he had begged her to go and retrieve some of the figs and dates as well as the delicious cream.

It was not that they were deprived of good food, there was always plenty of that, he just had a hankering for more, and to avoid the risk of being caught he concocted for her to do the job.

At first reluctant to follow through with Mark's suggestion, she finally gave in, but it was only after he agreed to share.

Carefully she had made her way through the small opening, then passed the wanted items to Mark. After they all had their share she slipped back into the cool room and put the jar of cream back in its place. Purposely they had left a portion in hopes no one would detect that it had been tampered with. Recalling it now, a rueful smile passed her lips, she should have never agreed to this. Anyway, all seemed to have gone well, until they sat around the supper table and Papa suddenly announced, "Mama told me that some of the cream had mysteriously disappeared out of the cool room. She thinks a four-legged creature might have slipped through the opening and she wondered if anyone had seen it," her father had jokingly said, but they all knew it was not intended as such.

A long silence followed. No one had dared to say a word. After all they had made a promise not to tell.

She remembered how uncomfortable she felt when she noticed Papa's eyes moving from one to another. Mark had given her a pleading look, when suddenly Papa's eyes were on her.

"Katina, do you know anything about it?" She remembered sitting very still, hoping Papa would give up asking.

All at once Ben, one of her younger brothers, blurted out, "Katina climbed through the hole."

Although Papa was not quick in giving out punishment, what followed was a lesson she would never forget. She smiled now at the thought, but it was no laughing matter then.

She leaned back and closed her eyes. Suddenly a peaceful scene came to mind, one of warm summer evenings at the farm in Cogealac. Mama and Papa would sit on the back porch watching them play among stacks of hay. It was amazing Papa had allowed them to do that, as it did not take long, and the mounds were tunneled through from end to end. But that was just like her father, very patient, and always considerate of his children. When weather did not permit them to play outside, Papa would lay himself literally on the floor and let them crawl and bounce all over him.

As they grew older he would often take them on hikes through a nearby valley. Engrossed with the natural habitat, they learned of the many species of birds, especially eagles that roamed here in large numbers. Yet it was not only birds that were of interest, it was also the plant life she recalled, as every spring wild Peonies bloomed here in abundance.

With memories of bygone days still on her mind she listened to the bees humming. She watched them fly from flower to flower. Her thoughts turned to home remembering all the work that had to be done. She felt guilty not to be there and help Mama…

"Katina."

Startled, she opened her eyes and turned her head slightly toward the direction of the voice.

"Oh! Hello Stefan," she said surprised by his sudden appearance. "I haven't seen much of you lately. Have you been away?" She sat up and moved into a comfortable sitting position.

All this time he had been standing in the garden beside a tall rosebush watching her.

"Yes."

A smile crossed his face. "I had gone to Constanta to look for accommodation."

When he saw Katina's questioning look, he added, "Didn't Tara tell you about my new job at the port?"

She nodded with a smile. "Yes, she had mentioned it briefly. You ought to be congratulated for landing such a job."

He returned a proud smile.

"Katina."

He spoke her name softly as he stepped closer. And for a moment it seemed to her as if he wanted to reach out and touch her hand, but then changed his mind.

She had to admit he looked very handsome in his striped

I WILL REMEMBER ALWAYS

light gray suit, matching white shoes and white straw hat. All at once he removed his hat, turning it nervously in his hands.

"I've found the most darling little home not far from the port," he continued and bent slightly forward. He could feel his heartbeat throbbing against his chest as he lowered his voice, almost to a whisper.

"But what is a home without a wife, one that loves and is kind?" The tenderness in his voice made her feel incredibly uneasy. It caught her completely off guard. She searched for the right words to tell him how she really felt. But for some reason she could not bring herself to say what she thought.

Stefan took her silence as a positive sign. He reached for her hands and took them gently in his.

"Katina, I love you," he pleaded.

Abruptly, she pulled away.

Sensing the rejection, he felt a stabbing pain pierce his chest. His head spun. He could not believe this was happening. He had hoped she would reconsider his proposal and say yes.

This was too much to bear. He struggled to gain control of his emotions. Suddenly he straightened up. His face cold with a distant expression. Like lightning a thought surged through his mind. He remembered the plan he and his friends had concocted that day on the train.

It was an old tradition in this country that a fellow could kidnap the girl he loved and marry her, without her or her parent's consent. And as far as he was concerned, after all the rejections, he was ready to act, if only he could get her away from here.

Maybe if he asked her to come on a double date, she would not be so reluctant to go with him. With carefully chosen words he approached her again.

"Katina, I'm truly sorry if I offended you. It won't happen again." He paused for a moment to see her reaction then proceeded cautiously.

21

"Marika and Duza have invited us to a big boat show, which is taking place this weekend in Constanta. Afterward we'll have dinner at one of the romantic sidewalk cafes by the sea. And in the evening, we'll watch spectacular fireworks..."

She opened her mouth to speak but Stefan continued his pitch.

"It'll be like double dating," he quickly interrupted her, scared she might refuse. "Remember Marika will be there also."

She hesitated for a moment. "I should ask Tara first to see if she has other plans."

Stefan nodded.

"I understand," he said politely, managing a vague smile.

He was surprised by the calmness in his voice.

"Till tomorrow then," he added placing his hat back onto his head and tipping it slightly as he walked away.

4

Confused by Stefan's proposal to double date, she could hardly wait to talk to Tara. Come evening, she told her sister everything.

Tara debated for a moment whether she should agree to let her go, but considering her in-laws, she decided against it and told her to decline.

When Stefan heard of Tara's decision he was devastated. He had tried his best to get Katina on side. Yet again he failed miserably.

In his last attempt, he invited Katina, along with Tara and Micha, to join him in a picture show that was playing in town.

He had chosen this movie to make them understand how serious he was, only to realize after the show that no one understood the meaning behind it.

Arriving home that evening, he made his way upstairs to her room. He wanted to see her one more time, maybe she would reconsider. But Micha was at the top of the stairs before him.

"And where do you think you're going?" he demanded. "If you have any notion of seeing Katina, you'd better forget it. Besides you are much too young -- still wet behind the ears. You can use some growing up first before considering marriage."

"But I have to see her," Stefan pleaded. "Please Micha, let me through. I have to talk to her..."

Micha laughed with contempt and began poking his brother, belittling him. Tara came out to see what the commotion was about.

"Look at this, my little brother thinks he's in love. Well you get those notions out of your head. Leave her be. Turn around and go back down to your room. And do not let me catch you near her again. You hear?!"

Reluctantly, Stefan backed down the stairs and returned to his room. Dismayed he picked up the fountain pen on his desk and started to write, scribbling down all his pent-up emotions.

The letter in hand he stepped out of his room. He found Tara still awake and handed it over to pass to Katina.

After returning to his room he sat brooding. Suddenly his eyes fell upon an old army rifle his father had given him as a keepsake. Taking it off the wall he turned it over and over. His hands were shaky and unsteady. The feel of it made him shiver and go cold inside. He checked it and carefully loaded it.

One way or another he had to do something about this matter.

The night air was calm as he stepped outside. The fragrance of fresh salt air drifted in from the sea. A full moon wandered silently along its heavenly path illuminating the quiet land beneath it.

He stopped for a moment; his loaded rifle heavy in his hand. He gazed heavenward. Tears began to fill his eyes. Breathing became difficult. His heart trembled by his decision. The darkness in his mind was absolute.

He sat down and wept bitterly.

He did not know how long he had been in that position before he decided to take the next step. A bone chilling shiver crept over him as he looked toward the house. It stood strangely distant in the moonlight. A terrible loneliness filled his heart. For a moment he waited, for someone, anyone, to open a door or window; to ask him to come in, letting him know that everything was all right. But nothing stirred, only a dark foreboding silence.

Heavy-hearted, he slowly dragged himself toward the barn. Inside its darkness a single shot pierced the silence of the night.

"Katina!" An anguish cry resounded...

What had he done?

He staggered outside leaning against his rifle using it as a cane. Disoriented he walked in aimless circles around the yard. He felt the warm blood flow down his face. Terror gripped his heart. With an outstretched hand he tried to reach Katina's window.

"Help me... please... help me!" he cried in utter despair, but there was no response... His spoken words fell deaf against the hard surface of the wall. He felt his strength fading. Everything appeared distorted and blurred. He tried to steady himself but to no avail. The straw pile in the middle of the yard seemed inviting. Slowly and with much agony he staggered toward the heap and let himself fall face down into it; drifting into unconsciousness with the moon as his witness.

5

Early in the morning, she suddenly awoke from commotion coming from outside her bedroom window. She got up and walked over to see what it was when Tara hastily entered the room. Her face looked pale, a contrast from her usual rosy complexion.

"What's wrong Tara? What's going on?" She took a step toward her sister. She had never seen her this way.

"Katina," Tara flung her arms around her. Her eyes filled with tears. "Thank God you're all right. If something would've happened to you I could never forgive myself."

"What could've possibly happened to me?" She asked, anxiously waiting for Tara to explain herself.

"It's Stefan..."

Overwhelmed with tears Tara swallowed hard to bring herself to say those dreadful words.

"He... He shot himself..." Tara sobbed. "Micha found him this morning on top of the straw pile. There is a trail of blood leading to your window..." She stopped to regain control of her emotions. "Oh my God, Katina... Who knows what he had in mind?" Tara cried in agony.

She was shocked.

Stefan dead!

The sudden realization chilled her to the bone. "Poor Stephan," she exclaimed with sadness. "It's unbelievable! I had no idea this would happen."

"If we only had known," Tara said with regret. Suddenly

remembering the letter, she reached in her pocket and gave it to her sister.

"He gave it to me yesterday to give to you."

Katina threw her a questionable look and took the envelope.

"After you had retired to your room, Stefan and Micha had an argument. He wanted to come and see you, but Micha as always belittled him and told him to leave you alone. Later on, in the evening, Stefan found me still up and that's when he handed it to me," Tara's voice broke as more tears flooded her eyes.

"Anyway… It was too late to give it to you last night."

She walked across the room staring aimlessly out of the window.

"Micha feels terrible now and can't forgive himself for treating his brother so cruelly."

Katina looked at the envelope. Her hands trembled. She felt uneasy and could not bring herself to open it.

A knock suddenly interrupted their conversation. Micha's head appeared behind the door, his eyes red and swollen from crying.

"I'm sorry for the intrusion but there is someone here who wants to see you." Without further explanation he pushed the door wide open. Both gave a cry of joy.

"Robert!" Katina jumped to her feet and gave her older brother a hearty hug. Attending a ministerial college in Hamburg, Germany, he had come home for his summer break.

"After receiving a letter from home telling me about your illness and that you're staying here with Tara. I decided to drop by and see how you're doing."

His concerned look went from Katina to Tara. "But it seems I've come at an awkward time," he spoke with solemn expression on his face. His head lowered slightly he searched their eyes. He realized the horror of the event had affected them both deeply.

Being older and of a caring nature, he felt accountable for the wellbeing of all his younger brothers and sisters. It was this sensitive and upright character of his that befitted his ministerial goal.

"Oh Robert," Tara cried out. "It's so horrible."

"I know," he answered with sympathy. "I too shuddered when upon my arrival Micha told me of his brother's tragic death. What a waste of a young man's life."

He shook his head with sad remorse. He turned, expecting Micha to be still at the door only to find him gone.

"Oh... If you are looking for Micha, he probably went to be with his parents," Tara replied.

Robert nodded in thought, "They'll need our help, especially at this time."

"Yes," Tara spoke again. "And I think that's where you, Robert, are best qualified."

She paused for a brief moment to control her emotions. Her eyes filled with tears again. "Forgive me for crying," she apologized, "but it's all so painful. I can't control..." Overwhelmed again by tears she could not finish her sentence. Robert put his caring arms around her.

"I understand," he said with comforting reassurance.

All this time Katina stood in silence, shaken and confused by this dreadful ordeal.

Her head lowered. She stared at the envelope.

Suddenly Robert noticed it.

"What's this in your hand Katina?" he asked in a gentle voice.

"Oh, it's a letter from Stefan," Tara quickly answered ,wiping the tears from her eyes. "He gave it to me yesterday to give to Katina."

"May I see it?" Robert held his hand out. She passed the envelope without reservation.

He opened it and started to read in silent. Suddenly a deep fold formed on his brow. Visibly disgusted, he tore the letter into pieces and slipped the remains inside his coat pocket.

"Its better you don't know what was written in it," he said with seriousness in his voice.

Indifferent, she accepted her older brother's opinion. If he thought it was not good for her to read, she was not about to say otherwise.

"It's okay Robert. I understand," she replied somewhat embarrassed.

Her hands pressed tightly together she stood feeling terrible to be entangled in this whole affair.

Confused, she sat down on the edge of her bed and wished she had never come. Maybe then this whole dreadful ordeal would have never happened. She longed so much to go home, to leave this unhappy place.

"I think I'll see if I'm needed in the kitchen," Tara interrupted to ease the tension. "Robert, why don't you join me?"

She smiled and tugged at his arm. "It'll give Katina time to get herself ready to join us for breakfast."

Robert took the hint.

"All right then," he replied returning the smile. "I'll come along and help. We'll see you downstairs Katina." He motioned for Tara to lead the way.

"I don't think I'll be down for breakfast this morning. I don't feel hungry," she replied with melancholy in her voice.

"Well," Tara stepped in firmly, "I'm sure most of us don't feel like eating after all that happened, but we have a long day ahead of us. And whether we want to or not, we all need a little nourishment to see us through."

She kissed her sister gently on the forehead. Then looking at Robert, she added teasingly, "Besides we have to think of Robert. He probably is starving for a good home cooked meal."

Robert smiled in agreement.

"Now that you mention it, I do feel a gnawing pain in my stomach. Let me see," he paused for a moment to think, his finger pursed against his lips. "I haven't had a bite…. since yesterday. That is right! It was yesterday on the boat."

"Then it's about time we get you something," Tara clapped her hands together upset. "Why didn't you tell me? Oh, I feel terrible."

"Tara, please, it's really not that bad," Robert tried to calm her down. But she would not hear of it. Helpless in changing her mind, he lifted his arms up in mock defeat.

"See you later," he called out to Katina and followed Tara out of the room.

She smiled. For a moment she had forgotten the tragedy. But then again, a thought, unlike any other began to torment her. Maybe if... Maybe I should have... Maybe then he would not have...

Her weary mind kept nagging.

All at once she stopped herself. Why was she even entertaining this thought? It was too late anyway.

--

Robert followed Tara down the stairs when all at once he had a change of heart. He thought about the letter and Katina's connection to it. Had he reacted a little too harshly? He had not even asked her how she felt. Had she really cared for Stefan? No, she could not have. She was too young to know the difference. Midway down the stairs he stopped, then decided to return to Katina's room. Upon entering he found her still sitting on her bed. A little hesitant he walked the few steps over to her bedside and sat down beside her.

"I'm sorry, Katina," he said with sincere regret.

"I hope you have no ill feelings about me destroying the letter."

"Oh no, I've almost forgotten about it, especially after watching you two tease each other. It brought back memories..."

A vague smile crossed her face. "I thought about Stefan and how things would've been if he could've had a family like ours."

"Katina, you mustn't torment yourself with thoughts of

this nature. You are much too young. That is the reason why I did not let you read this letter. I wanted to spare you from further pain."

"I'll tell you what," his voice took on a caring undertone. "As soon as all this is over, I'll make arrangements for both of us to go home."

He stood up, assured that this was the best thing to do.

All at once he remembered Tara. "Oh, I'd better be going, or Tara will come after me the moment she finds me gone."

He smiled apologetically and hastily walked out of the room.

Amused, she watched him scurry out of the room. She was relieved by his decision to go home. She walked over to the closet to search for something appropriate to wear. She chose her dark blue dress then tied a white silk shawl around her neck.

All at once she realized that it was not appropriate for her to wear. The shawl was a gift from Stefan the day he had asked for her hand in marriage.

She quickly removed it and decided to give it as a keepsake, either to Tara or to Mother Hartig. Anyway, it held no special meaning for her... or should it?

Looking into the mirror she noticed her pale complexion. Mechanically she applied a few pinches to each cheek.

She walked over to the window and looked up toward the sky; appropriately it was covered in a blanket of gray. It was as if it too was mourning the loss of a friend.

Her eyes caught Micha as she was about to turn. He was still busy cleaning up around the yard, trying to erase the traces of his brother's blood. On his stooped demeanor she could tell of his unimaginable sorrow.

It all seemed like a bad dream, she thought. Abruptly she pulled herself away. It was too unsettling. Quickly she went out of the room to join Tara and Robert.

She had reached the bottom of the stairs, and was about to pass the den when she noticed through a half open door

Mother Hartig. Her body stooped over Stefan's lifeless corpse, as it lay on a makeshift viewing table that Micha and Father Hartig had quickly set up.

At that moment Mother Hartig turned. It was as if she had sensed Katina's presence. With uplifted hands and a sorrowful outcry, she came over and hugged her.

"It's my fault. I should not have been so hard on him... I should have allowed him to marry you... It's my fault," she carried on in her grief.

Katina gazed over to the motionless covered body. She suddenly felt pity for Mother Hartig, who had come to realize too late the wrong she felt she had done.

All at once it hit her, being so close to Stefan's lifeless body made her empathize with Mother Hartig's terrible loss. She fought back the overwhelming sorrow. She tried to find words to comfort Mother Hartig.

"He's gone now and there's nothing more we can do to bring him back... There is no sense in blaming ourselves over something we can't change." Katina surprised herself over the calmness of her voice.

"Oh Katina," Mother Hartig sobbed. "He was too young to die, only twenty-one... my Stefan... my poor Stefan."

She threw herself over her son's lifeless body and wept bitterly.

Overcome by this heartbreaking scene, Katina felt the deep anguish of this woman. A lump in her throat threatened to cut off her air supply, as she fought back the tears.

An oppressive stale odor filled the entire room. Suddenly she was in need of air. She quickly withdrew herself. Moments later she regained strength to join the others around the breakfast table.

--

Robert and Tara both thought it best to send a telegram to Papa, to let him know what had happened. A return telegram from home advised Katina and Robert to take the next train home. It also mentioned that Mama and Papa would come instead to the funeral to pay their last respects. She had no objections about this decision and gladly agreed. Relieved to be going home soon she went to pack her clothes.

Before leaving, she remembered the silk shawl and graciously handed it over to Mother Hartig who was again overcome with sobbing holding this special gift close to her heart.

When Katina and Robert finally said their last farewells, the whole Hartig house had turned into a busy beehive. Relatives and friends, including Martha, had dropped by to help and to comfort.

Lost in their grief, the old Hartigs could not be counted on to help in the many preparations that went before the funeral, and Tara and Micha were grateful for all the help and support they received.

Once on the train, Katina took one last look back. She remembered the day she arrived in Anadolchioi. How different it had turned out to be.

Tired and relieved to be finally going home, she sank into her seat across from Robert. She closed her eyes as if to shut out all unwanted memories.

Robert, sensing her thoughts, gently reached over and touched her hands.

"Don't take it too hard Katina," he said caringly at first, and then added in a joking manner. "By the time we shine our shoes for your wedding this all will seem like a bad dream." Settling back into his seat he grinned when he noticed the flushed look on her face.

Embarrassed to be found out, she wished his comments to be right. Yet in her heart she knew that it would take more than time to erase all the unpleasant memories of this visit... memories she probably would never forget.

6

Two years had passed since that unfortunate event of Stefan's death. Two years since that day on the train. Katina remembered Robert's words spoken to her then in fun had now indeed proven true. She had come to understand and put all that had happened in proper perspective.

Set to meet other young people, she recently joined her brothers in a songfest that would take them all over the Dobrujan region. And it happened, at a large banquet gathering, her brothers noticed a young man watching her with great interest.

Job, the oldest, married and living in Mangalia, took the initiative to investigate. He had seen this young man occasionally accompanying Pastor Hildebrand, a traveling preacher to the Romani people, the gypsies in the region. By further inquiry he found his name was Johann Wendel, a Baumeister by trade, about to launch his own business in designing and building of homes and extravagant villas. He also discovered that he was living here in Mangalia with his father.

When asked, Pastor Hildebrand spoke highly of Johann and mentioned he had known him as a personal friend for many years. He questioned Job as to why this sudden interest in this young man and when told he chuckled, amused over this delicate affair.

7

From the first time Johann had seen Katina, he felt deeply drawn to her. But he did not know how he would succeed in making her acquaintance. The thought of not measuring up was always in the forefront of his mind.

He was not yet established in business. He could never compete with all the rich young men who were in rivalry over her. His fear of being rejected was the reason he never dared approach her when he had the chance to do so.

Back in 1909, when he was but three years of age, his family had ventured to Brazil to seek their fortune. But as fate had it they returned soon after.

His father, gone on business ventures, had left his family alone for days in the jungle settlement. His mother, overcome with loneliness and homesickness, became depressed and despondent. It left his father little choice but to return to their homestead on the Crimean Peninsula in the northern part of the Black Sea.

Yet their hope to resume life as they had left it was soon dampened when they found their homestead had been taken over by the People's Republic. Disillusioned, with only a few personal belongings they fled, hoping to return to reclaim not only the land but retrieve the buried gold and jewellery his father had stowed away before leaving for Uruguay.

Tragically though, during their escape from the Crimean Peninsula, his mother lost her life from heat stroke. A year later his fourteen-year-old sister also died from severe pneumonia, leaving him and his father as the only survivors.

He remembered how hard it was to adjust. Their home, once full of life and happy chatter had turned into a depressive, lonely place. Yearning to once again be surrounded by a loving family, his hope was renewed when falling in love with Katina.

The question was how to become better acquainted. Taking all the courage he could muster he confided in Pastor Hildebrand, telling him of his fears in not measuring up; asking if he could be the mediator between him and her parents.

Pastor Hildebrand, who was like a second father to him, willingly agreed to bring this matter before Katina's parents the next time they met.

--

A month later, on a warm and beautiful Sunday in May he found himself accompanying Pastor Hildebrand and his wife to Girargi. It happened that on occasion, Pastor Hildebrand was invited to preach at the Stack's home.

Girargi, where the Stacks lived was smaller than Cogealac where he lived. Unlike Cogealac, which had large Lutheran and Baptist churches, schools and a town hall, Girargi was the opposite, inhabited mainly by Romanians and Turks with only a few German families. Among those families were Katina's mother and two aunts with their families.

One aunt and her husband previously co-owned the sunflower oil mill, but a year later sold their entire share to the Stacks.

On the neighboring property next to them the other aunt and family operated a dry goods store.

And since there were only a few Germans in this village with no established church, the Stacks had graciously opened their large home as a gathering place. Everyone was welcome to join them in Sunday morning worship. If by chance a stranger ventured into their home he was treated as a friend, no one was turned away. The samovar, a tall Russian tea kettle, always stood simmering on the stove, ready to serve unexpected guests.

On this day Mother Stack was, as usual, greeting her guests when she took notice of Johann. Teasingly she asked Pastor Hildebrand, "And who is this young man?"

Pastor Hildebrand took the opportunity and remarked in the same amusing way, "This is a young man who is still looking for a good wife!"

"Ah!" she exclaimed, giving Johann an understanding nod and welcoming him with a warm smile.

Immediately Johann felt drawn to her. Her tender smile brought back memories of his own mother.

Job, who was also visiting with his wife, overheard the conversation. After his mother had finished talking to her guests, he took her aside and asked, "Mother, what do you think? Wouldn't Johann be good for Katina?"

"Well..." she hesitated and took another glance at Johann, who had retreated into the living room and was engaging in talk with the other men. "Now that you mentioned it... Hmmm..."

Katina's mother stood for a moment in thought.

"I've already inquired about him and Pastor Hildebrand had nothing but praise on his behalf. He had mentioned that Johann had regularly accompanied him on his rallies to the gypsy settlements. I think that says a lot about his character. Don't you agree?"

Job stopped for a moment, his mind busy thinking.

"But before we start something, shouldn't we ask Katina first if she cares for him?"

He waited a moment to see his mother's reaction, yet before she could reply he again jumped in. "And I think, maybe it would be best if you would do the asking."

She hesitated for a moment, but then agreed and quickly hurried off to the dining room where Katina had been busy setting the table for lunch.

37

Job smiled triumphantly and rubbed his hands together in anticipation. He had done his part, now it's up to Mother to complete this matchmaking. He liked Johann very much and could not think of a better partner for his younger sister.

"Katina," he heard his mother quietly call from the door, "Could you come to the kitchen and help me for a moment?"

Unknowingly she did as her mother had asked and followed her into the kitchen.

"Katina...," Mama started, busying herself pouring water into the tea kettle. Job stood behind the door listening.

"What do you think of this handsome young man?" Mama motioned with her head toward the living room and smiled. Before she could respond, Mama delivered another question, "Do you like him?"

She blushed.

"Mama..." she hesitated, a little embarrassed over the delicate question. "I haven't given it much thought... I don't know. What do you think?"

Just then Job entered the kitchen. He would have liked to listen longer, but that had to wait for now.

"Mama, Katina, come we're ready to begin the service."

"We'll be right there," Mama answered as she turned to him, giving him a quick nod. It meant that he could go ahead with the matchmaking.

Katina had seen the funny smirk on both their faces but thought nothing of it as she walked past Job.

As she sat there listening, her mind was on everything else but Pastor Hildebrand's sermon.

She had noticed Johann glancing at her more than once during the service. It had made her blush and lose track of what was said! As the closing hymn was sung, her mind was still on Mama's question. Unsettled by all this sudden attention she quietly withdrew herself. Mama was already in the kitchen and needed her help for last minute preparations. With so many mouths to feed she was always surprised of her mother's ability to get things done.

After a relaxing lunch Job took the plan a step further and approached Katina and Johann. He asked if they cared to join him in a quiet stroll through the garden. To his surprise they both agreed.

He quickly schemed up a plan and told the others, that once he excused himself, they were to stay away and leave the two alone. Everyone agreed.

On their stroll, Job did as planned and told both of them to go ahead without him. It was then she caught on and remembered Job and Mama's mischievous grin. She was sure that even Johann knew what was going on. She had noticed his thankful smile toward Job as her brother turned to go back to the house.

Quietly they went on and after a brief moment of silence Johann started to talk. He told her how much he had enjoyed this day being together with her family.

She blushed whenever their eyes met, and for the first time she felt a warm sensation stir within her heart.

--

Johann had fallen in love the first time he had seen her and now even more so as he walked beside her. As they shared their conversation, her quiet understanding seemed to soothe away all his cares. He wanted so much to reach out and hold her hand. But he knew it would not be proper, especially not on their first date. Besides, it was more than he had expected when he first arrived this morning. Calmed with this thought he was satisfied of what he had accomplished. For a moment longer they tarried in the warm afternoon sun, enjoying each other's company.

When the time came to part, they walked back to the house. And seeing Katina's mother, Johann approached her with concern. "Mrs. Stack," he asked a little hesitant. "Would it be all right if I come again for a visit?"

Mother Stack beamed with happiness. "Yes, my son, you may come again!"

--

After Johann had left, Katina pondered of their meeting and the enjoyable walk in the garden. Never had she felt so deeply drawn to a man. His eyes, whenever he looked at her, portrayed sincerity and true devotion. A delightful smile crossed her lips recalling the moment.

8

Just the other day Mama decided on a whim to accompany Papa to Brasov, a city located in the Transylvanian Alps, where Papa planned to purchase a new oil press for the mill. Mama let it slip out that it was Papa's idea to have her go along. Papa's excuse was that it would be good for her to get away from all the household duties.

Now it was left in Katina's discretion to look after her smaller siblings and some of the household duties. Luckily for the larger part she had the help of a young Romanian couple who worked for her parents in return for property and livestock.

Daniel, one of her older brothers, was put in charge to renovate the old mill. He was to have it ready when Papa returned with the new piece of machinery.

Realizing that the boys would need more help to finish this project, Papa had asked some of the local villagers to help bring in the rocks and sand that were needed for this project. But to his surprise, because of hard times more men showed up than necessary. Confronted with a hard decision and knowing how much they needed the work he employed them all.

The villagers had known Papa to be a very generous man when it came to pay for labor done. That reflected the many helpers who eagerly came to work for food and goods in return.

As soon as dawn broke and the sun sent her first rays

across the land, the workers started out with their horse drawn wagons, driving all the way to Mangalia and back hauling wagonloads of sand. The others went to the nearby hills to collect stones.

She watched the workers from her open kitchen window. She could hear the horses and wagons and shouts from the workers as they called instructions to each other.

She could see that with the effort of the villagers, Daniel would have no trouble getting his assignment done. And having so many men at his disposal, he took the opportunity to upgrade the eight-foot-high stone wall that surrounded the entire property.

It happened that every summer gypsies gathered in countless numbers near the river that divided their homestead from the rest of the village. So, the barbed wire on top the eight-foot-high wall was a warning to all intruders to stay out and that included four legged creatures as well.

Most of all, it was to protect the livestock from wandering wolf packs, that during lean winter months, would descend upon the homesteads in search of food.

Katina recalled one such winter night when the eerie and ghastly howls of wolves pierced the dark stillness of the night. That lost and lonely sound even now sent chills through her body.

She remembered it as if it were yesterday. Drawn by the haunting calls no one in the house had been able to sleep that night. With much anxiety they listened as the wolves drew closer, signaling to each other while circling in on the homestead.

She and the rest of the family watched Papa put on his coat then reach for his shotgun that always hung above the front door. Ever so carefully he had checked and cocked the gun, then gave the go ahead to Job who stood ready with lantern in hand.

Their eyes peeled on Job as he took the lead and stepped out into the foreboding darkness with Papa close behind him. They heard their footsteps crunch on the gravel then diminish as the two crossed the yard. Mama closed the door as they waited.

Fearful, they listened to the fierce growling and snarling, with their own guard dogs joining in the fight to protect the property. Suddenly a painful howl mingled with the terror-filled 'baas' of sheep was heard. Seconds later the bellow of the gun split the night. What followed was an ominous stillness.

She remembered the endless moments as they waited for Papa and Job to return. After a long apprehensive silence, more shots rang out. They peered through the windows into the darkness but could see nothing. Their ears perked for any sound.

Finally, and to their relief, Papa and Job appeared again in the doorway. Their faces showed dismay as they reported the damage. Job was the first to speak.

"Just as we thought, the wolves had jumped the wall and went on a ruthless rampage," his voice broke. "Many of the sheep are scattered all over the farmyard with their throats ripped open."

Papa jumped in and told the rest of their findings.

"It was strange, but the wolves did not take any of the sheep."

He shook his head in disgust. "What a needless slaughter. The sad part is..." Papa had lowered his head at this point, and she had detected sadness in his voice as he continued. "Mamuk..." his voice quavered.

"What a faithful dog. He tried to fight them off but there were too many. As you can guess... he met up with the same fate as the sheep." With this announcement Papa placed his gun at its usual place then added. "We'll clean up in the morning, no use doing it in the dark."

She remembered the somber mood that hung over the house that night. The big German shepherd was her favorite dog and she missed him terribly.

She recalled many more stories that evolved out of nights like these. Stories that were told and retold as family and friends sat around the warm *kachelofen*, a ceramic wall oven, on long winter nights. Everyone, including children, would listen with their eyes wide open as their elders shared accounts that unfolded from own experiences but also were passed on from other sources.

One of the stories was of a soldier who ventured homeward after the war, and despite the warnings of others, he decided to take a shortcut through the woods before night fall. Days later his identification tag was found alongside his boots with the remnants of his feet still stuck inside of them.

A rush of goosebumps, brought on by the fresh spring air from the open window brushing against her skin, abruptly broke her train of thought.

"Uh...! That's too much," she scolded herself. Why was she thinking of these things, especially on a beautiful day like this?

A sudden smile crossed her face, as she remembered Johann's request to come again. Holding her hands against her chest, she released a happy sigh. She was in love and it felt so absolutely wonderful. It was strange, but meeting Johann she had no apprehension; she was actually looking forward to seeing him again.

As for now she needed to help Michaela in cleaning up after the men folk, as they had just finished a hardy midday lunch and returned to work.

A whole hour passed when she finally put the last of the washed dishes away. Now finished with all the chores and her younger siblings playing outside, she relished the thought of sitting for a moment and relaxing over a cup of tea. That was until she remembered all the mending and knitting Mama had put out for her to do. Suddenly a knock at the front door interrupted her intentions. She went to open and was surprised by the unexpected caller.

"Joanna... Come in. It's good to see you." She gestured for

her Romanian girlfriend to come inside.

"I just came by to invite you and your family to my wedding; it will be in two weeks." Joanna announced excited, her face beaming.

"Joanna! That's wonderful news. How come I haven't heard of it sooner?"

"I couldn't, it was only yesterday when Mugur and I decided." Joanna looked around concerned. "Where is your mother? I wanted her advice on something."

"Oh, she's away on business with Papa and won't be back for a couple of days," Katina replied, then quickly added. "But you're welcome to sit and have a cup of tea with me." She shut the door behind her friend and motioned to follow her to the kitchen.

Joanna welcomed the gesture as she had hoped to have a little chat with Katina as well.

"Michaela, you're welcome to join us!" Katina called out, but there was no response. She suddenly remembered that Michaela had told her that she would be helping Mikhail in the garden. Without giving it another thought, she went about to prepare the tea while resuming her chat with Joanna.

"Mama went along with Papa to Brasov to buy a new oil press. Is there something I could help you with?" she questioned as she brought two cups of hot steaming tea to the table.

"Well the thing is I need your mother's advice on sewing my wedding dress, but..." Joanna hardly finished her sentence when Katina interrupted her.

"I can come over tonight after supper and you can show what you had in mind. That is, if you want me to."

"Oh, could you?" Joanna was excited. "It would be nice to have another female's input." Her voice suddenly filled with sadness she spoke again. "You know you're so lucky to still have a mother. I miss mine very much, especially now that I am getting married."

45

Katina reached over and touched Joanna's hand lightly. "I know... But don't forget, I'm always here if you need someone to talk to."

"I know and I appreciate that." Joanna was quiet for a moment then added.

"My father... has found a girlfriend..." she said with a solemn tone in her voice, "and he is planning to marry her as soon as possible. That is why I had agreed so quickly to marry Mugur. I want to get out of the house before she moves in. I know we would never get along. I just can't see any other woman taking my mother's place."

She listened quietly. She was surprised by Joanna's statement, but did not say anything. She just nodded and continued to lend an understanding ear. She reached for her knitting that lay beside her chair in a basket and heard the big wall-clock in the living room strike the passing of time. The simmering sound of the samovar gave a cozy and snug feeling to the room. She was glad Joanna had come.

Her mind wandered back to when Joanna's mother had died. She remembered Mama talking about it to Papa.

After delivering her third child, Joanna's mother had started to hemorrhage profusely. A Romanian midwife who was tending her had tried every method she knew to save her. But nothing seemed to work and the nearest Doctor was twelve kilometers away. Out of desperation she asked some of the ladies from the neighborhood to gather cold water into a wash tub. She then aided the ailing woman into the tub to slow the bleeding. But with her already weakened heart, Joanna's mother could not take the shock of the cold water.

She remembered how hard it was for her friend to get over her mother's death, and how she as a friend tried her best to comfort to her.

"What is it you're knitting?" Joanna suddenly bent over to have a closer look.

"Woolen stockings," she answered bluntly.

"Woolen Stockings...! Katina, summer is around the

corner." Joanna laughed, looking at the half-started project.

"Looks a little bit tight, don't you think?" she teased.

She had to smile; she was used to Joanna's teasing.

"It's Mama's idea. She wants me to learn how to knit stockings before I marry and move out of the house. She's always after me and tells me..." She mimicked Mama's voice. "You never know when it'll come in handy. Bad times may come unexpectedly and then you'll be glad you've learned."

They both burst out laughing.

"That sounds just like my mother," Joanna added jokingly then stopped abruptly. She had distinctly heard Katina mention the words 'marry and move out'. With a smirk about her face, she confronted her.

"Katina! Is there something going on I should know of?"

Katina blushed as she told Joanna about Johann.

"Ah..." her friend smiled triumphantly. "So that's what it's all about."

"Well, it isn't certain yet, but if something will ever become of it..." She paused from her knitting and counted the stitches, then looked up at her friend with an assured smile, "But if it does, you most certainly will be the first to know."

Joanna chuckled, "I'm sure from what you've told me, that this Johann of yours has every intention to go through with what he had come to do. He strikes me to be a very honorable and gallant man. You're so fortunate Katina."

The wall clock in the living room gonged.

"Oh my goodness...! Is it two-thirty already?" Katina gasped in disbelief. "I'd better go and bring refreshments to my brothers. They're probably wondering if I'd forgotten them." Quickly she put away her knitting.

Joanna too realizing what time it was, hastily excused herself.

"I too have to go home and do something, before my father and my brothers come home from the field." With that she helped Katina in taking the dishes to the wash counter.

"Thank you very much for the tea. I really enjoyed the little chat and don't forget tonight! I do so much appreciate your willingness to help me."

Katina nodded graciously and reassured her that she would be there after supper.

--

As arranged, she went for a short visit to her friend's place later that evening. Upon arriving Joanna met her at the door.

"Come in, Katina, I am just about to make tea for everyone."

She directed her over to a seating place where she had set up two cups for the both of them. In the middle of the room on the clay floor, the fire that was used for cooking and heating was still smoldering. And hanging above it on a tripod was a sizzling pot of water, spewing hot steaming droplets onto the embers below.

Katina stood for a moment looking about the room. She suddenly realized how fortunate she was to live in a home where there was adequate space for every member, unlike Joanna's family who lived in a one room home. She was amazed how they were able to get along in such close quarters. She definitely could not imagine herself living in one room with all her family, which even after Job and Tara married and moved away, still made up a clan of twelve. Yet despite Joanna's family's primitive way of living, she found her friend's home cozy and inviting.

"Joanna, I love these woven wall hangings. They are so colorful and bright. And these embroideries are so delicate. Have you just made them recently?" She questioned.

"My mother and I made them together. I had them all this time in my hope-chest." Joanna said with fondness.

Moving closer to study the intricate workmanship, her eyes were suddenly drawn to the handmade pottery on nearby shelves.

"It's been a long time since my last visit, and I had forgotten how beautiful they are," she raved with true amazement.

Joanna filled the teacups and motioned for her to sit down, then added, "The pottery is my father's handiwork. He had learned it from his father."

"They're simply lovely."

Joanna's father in the meantime was sitting in one corner of the room teaching his two sons the art of his craftsmanship. He looked up for a moment. His face showing a gratified smile, pleased over Katina's compliments. Then without further involvement, he went back to work.

Over a cup of tea, the two girls reminisced, recalling one particular time when Mama invited all the neighborhood ladies to help with Tara's trousseau.

Katina remembered how privileged the women felt, to be able to come to the *Klaka*, which means to return a good deed.

Mama always had a large plate of home baked dainties at hand, which she served with freshly brewed mocha coffee, a rare item even in the most prestigious homes. The neighborhood ladies enjoyed it immensely. They thought it a great honor just to be invited to the Stack's home.

She recalled them working late into the evening hours, their hands busy, embroidering and sewing, chatting with one another, telling stories of courtships and weddings. She too had thought it a privilege to be part of these gatherings.

While going over the details for her wedding dress, Joanna proudly showed off the items in her hope chest she and her mother had created. Katina could not help but marvel again over all the fancy stitchwork.

Suddenly aware how little she had, she was inspired by her girlfriend's collection. Eager now, she made her way home with the promise to start as soon as possible, but she had to admit, she could never compete with her friend's elaborate detailed stitchery.

9

It was early in the week when Mama and Papa returned. Daniel had gone ahead with the family coach to pick them up at the Caraomar train station. Mikhail followed along with a large straw-filled wagon pulled by their team of Belgium horses. The straw in the wagon was to protect the new oil press from the rough and bumpy ride home.

Many strong arms were needed to handle the heavy piece of equipment. For this Daniel had rounded up his brothers, Mark, Ben and Josh, who had been busy helping him at the mill. He also had the help of Mikhail as well as a couple of eager villagers.

With much anticipation she watched them leave. After days of running a large household such as theirs; she was more than happy to hand over all the responsibilities to Mama the minute she and Papa came driving through the gate.

At their arrival, she watched the yard turn into frenzy with the many willing hands helping in the unloading. And with the know-how of her older brothers, the mill's oil press was ready for business again.

Papa was proud of them. All along he had made sure that all his sons had a chance to learn a trade. As soon as they had finished school, they were free to choose and go their own way or stay in the family business, as Papa planned to expand it to an even greater establishment soon.

As for the girls, she remembered him saying, that it was

50

important to learn all the household duties and get married. But Mama had different plans especially for her. She always wanted her to go to Constanta and become a hat designer, but now with Johann, this dream was put on hold.

--

It was early in the morning when after hours of tossing and turning she decided to get up. Mama and Michaela needed her help in the kitchen. As she dressed, she wondered why the quietness in the house. All at once she remembered it was Sunday. And as usual on the Lord's Day no one labored at the Stack's home, and that included Michaela and Mikhail as well. Only necessary duties were performed, for as far as Papa was concerned, this was a day of rest for all.

Not wanting to disturb Edwina she walked quietly out of her room. She especially did not want to wake her older brothers in the next room, as they always treasured the extra hour of sleep on Sunday morning.

She heard the faint sound of pots clanking in the kitchen. "Mama is up," she said with a smile about her face. It always surprised her how her mother could stay up till all hours of the night, and then be the first one up again to prepare breakfast.

"Good morning Mama," she announced cheerfully as she walked into the kitchen and automatically started to help set up the table for breakfast.

"Good morning Katina," Mama did not take her eyes off the huge pot of steaming porridge, stirring it occasionally.

"I think you should set an extra place," she suggested as she went about her work.

"Are you expecting a visitor so early in the morning?" Katina asked, stopping briefly to look at her mother.

"Well, we never know... do we?" Not letting on who she meant, Mama walked for a moment into the cool room that lay adjacent to the kitchen.

All at once it dawned on her which visitor Mama was referring too. A smile washed over her face again as she put an additional setting on the table.

A sudden rustle of book pages coming from the living room made her aware that Papa too was up. 'No doubt preparing for the Sunday morning service,' she smiled thoughtfully.

Every time she seen her father stooped over the old bible, it left her with a reverent hush. The large scripture book was a treasured heirloom passed down from his grandfather's father. From what she had heard it had been in the family since their forefathers had immigrated in the late 1700's.

Quietly she slipped past the living room not to disturb him. She stepped outside and closed the door carefully behind her. Without notice of her surroundings she walked towards the garden with the intention to cut flowers for the breakfast table. All around her the crisp morning air was filled with the sweet fragrance of spring flowers and blossoming fruit trees. She took a deep breath lingering in her step she listened to the happy chirping of birds.

'They seemed to be singing sweeter this morning,' she thought wistfully. Watching them for a moment her eyes were suddenly drawn to a peony patch standing in the middle of the garden, on their vibrant red blossoms, droplets of morning dew. She reached for the first one, when a cold nose brushed against her hand.

"Rex! You old rascal you!" she called out with a lighthearted laugh. "What are you up to this morning, Hmm...?" She patted the big black dog, holding his face close to hers, stroking his head.

"Where is Rolf?" she asked, as if the dog understood what she was saying.

"Is he still dozing in his doghouse and letting you do all the work? That lazy wolf hound...!" Just then she heard Rolf's warning bark.

"I guess I was wrong Rex. Your old buddy was on duty after all."

She started to walk back to the house but for some reason

stopped and glanced over toward the front gate. She noticed that it had not yet been unlocked as they always kept the gate locked for the night.

She laid the flowers down on the bench in front of the house and walked over to open the gate. When she did, a surprised gasp escaped her lips.

"Johann...! How long have you been out here waiting?"

He smiled at her as he stood leaning against the stone wall.

"Oh, I've been here... let's see.... about an hour or so," he replied casually. He did not want to tell her; he actually was here before the sun sent her first rays over the grassy plains.

"Oh my goodness!" she fussed. "You must be tired and chilled to the bones." She gestured for him to come in and turned to go.

He was about to follow when she suddenly stopped and looked around puzzled.

"How in the world did you get here?" she said curiously, as she did not see a bicycle or any other transportation."

"I walked!" he said with a proud smile.

"You walked all the way from Mangalia? Why, you must have practically walked all night." She looked at him astonished, bordering on disbelief.

"Well, almost," he said amused over her concern.

Standing so close to her he wanted so much to reach out and touch her gentle face. To stroke her light brown hair that hung softly over her shoulder tossed playfully by a gentle breeze. For a moment he looked at her thoughtfully.

She blushed and looked away. The big black dog suddenly joined them. He had taken to Johann as if he was an old friend.

Johann patted the dog gently, "How come you barked at me earlier? Hmm? You should have known it was me." He playfully took a stick and threw it for the dog to fetch.

"Anyway," he turned again toward her. "I lent my bike to a friend who urgently needed it to go to Constanta, so I decided to walk here instead," he stated so matter-of-factly with a grin, as if it was no big deal.

She blushed again, shaking her head by his determination to be here with her. She gave him a loving glance.

"I can't believe, all this way on foot. You must be totally worn out. Come on in, we're just getting ready to have breakfast," she said caringly.

He was not about to protest and willingly followed her into the house where he was welcomed by the others.

Mama had a feeling that he would show up. But she had not expected him to come walking all this way.

"He must really be in love," she mumbled under her breath, hiding a grin she scooped the porridge into bowls.

--

The rest of the day passed quickly, almost too fast for Johann's liking. He had relished every moment spent in conversation with Katina and her family. When the time came to go away, he took all the courage he could muster and asked Papa and Mama for Katina's hand in marriage. Amused, yet expectantly it came of no surprise as both were ready to respond.

"Well my son," Papa started. "If you promise to love her, respect her and provide properly for her, then we have nothing against it. But before I give my consent, we have to ask Katina if she feels the same way."

He nervously agreed.

Katina was just about to finish up in the kitchen when Mama called her into the living room. Unexpected she walked into the room not knowing why she had been summoned. Papa cleared his voice and gently came straight to the point.

"Katina! Johann had asked for our approval to marry you. And Mama and I want to know if you accept his proposal. Do you love him?

She blushed, giving Johann a shy smile.

"Yes... I do. I do love him very much and I'll marry him if he'll have me," she answered softly.

"Well, that's settled then," Papa announced proudly. "You both have our blessing."

Mama nodded happily, signifying her consent.

Her older brothers, who had been quietly listening in on the proposal, were now in the partying mood. They went ahead and got the best bottle of wine from the cellar to celebrate the happy occasion.

All this time she and Johann never held hands or kissed, and it came as a surprise to her, when upon parting he mustered enough courage and gave her a quick peck on her cheek.

His spirits were high when he made his way home on Daniel's bike. His long-time wish had finally come true. He did not mind the long ride back, not at all. In fact, it was just what he needed to release all this extra energy. He could hardly wait to tell his father the good news.

Katina sank happily into her fluffy feather pillow. This proposal had come so unexpected and she was still in disbelief that it really happened. Although she had felt all along that it would come sooner than later. Her heart gave an extra beat as she recalled his attentiveness toward her. His action had portrayed nothing but deep devotion. His eyes, whenever he glanced at her, had a loving and caring look about them that literally left her helpless. She felt drawn to him the first time she had met him and now even more so.

Restless, she tossed and turned about, her mind going from one event to the next. Sleep did not come easy tonight. Not to disturb her younger sister she quietly rose from her bed and glanced out of the window. The moonlit landscape lay silent and yet disquiet. Her thoughts went to Johann, alone on that long treacherous road home.

"Be safe my love," she whispered thoughtfully.

10

Despite the hard times that gripped the region, life at the mill had been busier than ever this summer. With the new oil press in operation, farmers, wholesalers and merchants had come from as far as Bulgaria to do business with Papa. Many times, the front yard of their property resembled that of a public market, as wagonloads of goods were lined up waiting to be refined.

Because of the long wait and the lack of accommodation, it was not unusual to see the visitors asleep, huddled on top of their wagons within the safety of the property's stone wall and locked gates.

To escape the merciless muggy heat of the hot summer nights, her brothers would often join the caravan of strangers. Yet sleeping outside under the cool night air came with its own demise. Plagued by hungry mosquitoes, most of them abandoned the idea and retreated instead to the summer house near the garden.

The mill was in operation twenty-four hours a day, Papa and the boys had to work in shifts to provide for all their customers. It was only on Sunday the whole operation was halted. Oddly enough the strangers did not mind as they were welcome to partake in family mealtimes and church service as well.

Ever since his proposal Johann too was a regular visitor at the Stack's home. With their wedding date set for the nineteenth of December, he was eagerly looking forward to the time when he and Katina could finally start a home of their own, one that would be filled with the same love he had experienced at her parent's home.

Mark, Katina's fourth oldest brother also was planning to get married to a Romanian girl. He and Maria had set their wedding date to be at the end of August.

All this news put Mama into frenzy as she realized that yet two more of her children would soon leave the house. Her large family was diminishing, and she had a difficult time accepting it, especially when they moved so far away.

Even Papa had misgivings of eventually losing all his sons and daughters to the bustling coastal cities. And now he too considered selling everything within the coming year. So when the opportunity presented itself to buy a prime property in Mangalia, he wasted no time to secure a twenty hectare property right by the shore of the Black Sea.

The purchase was made possible through his lucrative profits that had accumulated from the sale of the processed sunflower-seed cakes. He had shipped them in large boxcars to Brosov and farther on into the surrounding Transylvanian mountains. There the seed cakes were sold and used for heating fuel as well as feed for cattle.

Mama too was in the buying mood and ordered new dress material for herself and the girls for the upcoming weddings. The dresses were to be sown by their regular seamstress in Mangalia, who as far as Mama was concerned, was the best around. Apparently, she had apprenticed in France and was a master in her own field. Each finished dress was proof of her amazing craftsmanship.

--

On the day of Joanna's wedding, Katina wore one of the new dresses. It was a flouncy long-wasted silk dress in a delicate shade of rose, which beautifully enhanced her usually pale complexion.

Johann, who also had been invited as her escort, just could not keep his eyes off his bride-to-be. As far as he was concerned, she was and always would be the prettiest girl around.

Joanna's wedding ceremony was performed with all the usual pomp and customary dances where she and Johann were coaxed to join in on the big hora. It was a folk dance, where men and women dancers held hands and form a large circle round the *lantari*, who sang while the ring of dancers whirled around him. Their arms and feet moved in harmony, advancing and retreating, making the circle smaller and larger.

--

Months later, as her own wedding was drawing near, Katina thought often about Joanna. She had not seen or heard from her girlfriend since the day when they promised each other to keep in touch. After the wedding Joanna and Mugur had moved to a different village and she has lost all contact.

She wondered if she would ever see her girl friend again, remembering the time they had shared as young girls. Thinking back now, she would have loved nothing more than to have Joanna here to chat with and to have her attend her own wedding.

--

Summer had passed by so quickly, and with it, Mark and Maria's wedding. The two had moved to Mangalia, where Mark had planned to open his own tailoring business. Johann in the meantime was put in charge to build a house for them on a ten-hectare property Mama and Papa had given as a wedding gift, with this they also would receive all the necessary livestock to start out on their own. As far as she remembered, it was a standard gift Papa and Mama had given to every son and daughter of theirs.

With Mark and Maria's house still in the building stage, Papa had thought ahead and rented a house for them in Mangalia. But it came with a condition. They were to share it with her and Johann once they married. Then after Mark and

Maria's house was completed the four of them were to share the new house, but only till Johann had finished their own home. Papa had already purchased a beautiful property for them not far from Mark's place. Both properties overlooked the Black Sea.

Johann, at first, was overwhelmed by all the projects, but at the same time excited. She had never seen him so enthusiastic. His dreams of building tourist accommodations had always been front and center in his plans. Ever since he had come to Mangalia and had seen the potential his mind was made up. Now with this property as a wedding gift, had made his dream more achievable. She supported him and promised as much as she could to help him achieve this goal.

11

For weeks now she and Mama had been busy getting everything organized and ready for the wedding. What had made things more difficult was the fact that the actual ceremony was to take place in Mangalia and not here in Girargi. This added to the already painstaking task of all the preparations.

It was a week before the actual wedding date when they finally packed up all the imperishable items, including her entire trousseau. Stacked to the capacity, their horse-drawn carriage stood ready for the transport. Mama and Papa were anxious to be there ahead of time to get everything done and she agreed. The rest of her inheritance, some of her older brothers would bring the day before her wedding.

Robert had volunteered to stay back to look after the younger siblings and the property. She was told he had decided to cancel one year of seminary. He had done it for the purpose of helping Papa in the planning and relocating of the new oil mill in Mangalia. A further plan had also been devised to build a new weaving and dying factory. All this and more was to take place come spring.

With all this on her mind she took a moment to reflect. Deep in thought she stared out of her bedroom window. For weeks she and Mama had been up till all hours of the night preparing. Now that the last item was stowed away in the carriage, she suddenly realized she would never return to live under her parent's roof as a single girl. The carefree days of childhood had come to an end and another period in her life was about to begin. She would have to make her own decisions and take up the responsibility of being a wife, and perhaps soon, a mother.

She had learned all there was to know of being a good wife and mother from Mama, but that was as far as it went. No one had actually sat down and discussed things about marriage with her. It was not that she blamed anyone. Particularly not Mama, who could hardly find time for herself as she was always busy looking after everyone else's needs.

With a deep sigh she glanced around the bedroom she had shared with her younger sister Edwina. A sudden creak behind her made her aware that she was not alone.

"Katina!"

Abruptly she turned when she recognized Robert's voice.

"I thought I would find you here," her brother spoke compassionately, noticing the despondent expression on her face.

"Everything is ready and packed and the only one missing is you."

"Thank you, Robert. I'm ready to go." She tried to suppress the tears that threatened to well up in her eyes.

"And what's this Katina, tears?" Robert took her by the hand knowing that something was not quite right. He sat her down on the edge of the bed next to him.

"Now tell me what's bothering you... hmm? Maybe I can help," his smile was genuine and caring.

All at once she felt embarrassed to tell Robert what was on her mind.

"Oh... it's nothing!" she exclaimed. "It's just that... it's... all of a sudden so overwhelming... getting married... and leaving home and..."

Overcome with emotion her voice left her.

"And you wished there was someone you could talk to?"

She nodded, wiping tears from her eyes.

"Well you can always count on me," Robert comforted her.

"If and whenever you need someone to talk to, I will be there. And do not forget, we will soon be all together come spring and then we can visit whenever time permits. Until then I can assure you that you will be in good hands. I will have you know that in my profession we study people very carefully, and from what I have seen and heard about Johann, he's a good and a very caring man, one, if had to, would give his very own life for the ones he loves, and may I add, we're all very proud to have him in our family."

Suddenly she felt the heaviness lift from her chest as she listened to her brother. There was something special about the way he talked that seemed to ease even the heaviest burden. Quietly, and with confidence renewing in her heart, she listened as Robert continued.

"Now, as you know, I've never had the experience of being married. But one thing I know is that when two people love each other and try to do the best for each other in an unselfish way, their life together will be blessed with much happiness for years to come."

A little fold formed on Robert's brow. His face took on a solemn expression as he spoke again. "Yet, in every married life, sometimes unforeseen troublesome conditions may threaten to destroy even the best of marriages. Then, that same unselfish love will prove itself to withstand even the worst of storms."

He was quiet for a moment looking at his sister searchingly, as if to ask if she had understood what he was trying to say. He got the reply when she gave him a thankful smile, indicating that his little session had done its job.

"Katina! Robert!" they heard Papa calling.

"Coming..." their voices rang out together as they proceeded to walk outside. After many good wishes and all-around hugs to everyone, she gave one more hug to Robert.

"Thanks," she whispered. "Thank you for everything."

She stepped up onto the carriage and found a sheltered

and comfortable spot behind the bench seat that Mama and Papa shared. She covered herself with a warm blanket Papa had placed there for her to use and settled in for what would likely be a long ride. Papa picked up the reigns and soon they were out of the yard and down the road.

For some reason, the weather had remained very dry. It had been like that right through fall and into the early days of December. It definitely made the trip to Mangalia more bearable than it otherwise would have been. Papa now kept the horses in a steady trot, skillfully maneuvering the carriage along the well-worn uneven country road.

Thoughtfully she watched the scenery as it passed. Once in a while she tried to contribute to Mama and Papa's conversation, but she found herself competing with the noise of the wheels as they grated on the gravel. It left her little choice but to retreat into her own thoughts for the rest of the trip.

In a way, this quiet time was refreshing as her thoughts drifted aimlessly from past events to future plans. The sameness of the open countryside began to play with her imagination. All at once a most disturbing thought crossed her mind. She envisioned themselves victimized by a brigand who she heard referred to by the name Varlan. The name itself was not uncommon in Romania. The person she knew as Varlan had made quite a name for himself around the Bulgarian and Romanian border. Probably he had made the forest there his home base. The Turks called the forest the Deli-Orman, and to the German population it was known as the 'Wild Forest.' Anyway, he had been a modern day Robin-hood character in the 1920's by stealing from the rich and distributing it to the poor.

A distant cousin of theirs had actually seen Varlan in person, not alive but dead. He was on display in a town square for everyone to see, clothed only in a pair of woolen pants. Varlan's own brother-in-law apparently did not approve of his actions and had done him in. She thought for a moment, but she could not recall his first name, or in which city their cousin had seen Varlan's dead body.

She did not mind giving to the poor but did not like being robbed to achieve it. Just the thought of losing her precious dowry made her stomach turn. Her eyes roamed the open steppe. There was nowhere for anyone to hide. The land was quite flat with few trees, if any. The fields, which just a few months earlier held corn or flax, now lay quiet as a gusty wind made dust funnels amongst the stubble. It was an empty land. Still she could not keep from feeling concerned.

She had also heard other folks say that there was no relying on the Romanian Gendarmerie, the military police, to come to their aid. They too were known to turn against the law if given a chance to gain riches. For that reason, Papa had tucked his trusted rifle underneath the bench seat to avoid any unpleasant surprises.

To her relief the only passers-by along the seemingly peaceful country road were the occasional farmers with wagon loads of dry goods bought from the city. They were stocking up provisions for the long and cold winter months ahead.

By late afternoon, Mangalia finally came into view, with its crescent crowned mosques standing amidst stark white houses surrounded by acacia and lime trees. In the near distance a familiar sound of a muezzin was heard. He was shouting in a thin high voice exhorting Muslims to the *Asr*, the afternoon prayer as he stood in a tall tower facing toward Mecca.

The sights and sounds were not new to her. She had been here on several occasions with her family including with a cousin of hers. He and his young wife, also from Girargi, occasionally had taken her along on day trips to Mangalia to join them in a refreshing dip in the salty sea water. Now moving here, she would certainly have to try to enjoy the water more often. But for that she had to wait for the return of the summer season and only if time permitted.

I WILL REMEMBER ALWAYS

She was still deep in thoughts when Papa suddenly pulled the team of horses over and stopped in front of a specialty store. One where both, Mama and her, had intended to buy some of the last items needed for the wedding banquet.

"Woah…" he pulled the reign for the horses to stop. "We finally made it." He turned to Mama as he set the brakes and stepped down from the seat. "It's a good place to stretch your legs," he added with a chuckle and walked around to help Mama off the coach. Then he reached out his hands and did the same for her, both a little stiff from the long tiresome journey.

"Papa, you must stay with the coach. Katina and I will be in the store only shortly," Mama said as she tapped her feet to get warm.

"Hello Joshua!" a voice bellowed from across the street as the caller hurried over to greet them.

It was Thomas Backer, one of Papa's business associates. They had come to know each other over the past year through Papa's land dealings here in Mangalia.

"Well hello, Thomas," Papa replied. He returned the greeting with a friendly smile and a good solid handshake. He then went on to introduce Mr. Backer to Mama and her.

Mr. Backer turned to her giving her his full interest. "I've heard folks talk about you and that young fellow you're getting married to," he said now with a smirk on his face. "And some of them are not too happy, saying you could have had any of the rich young farmers around this area. Instead you chose this poor fellow who they say has nothing to show for but his name."

"Well now, is that what they're saying?" Papa chuckled.

She too could not help but smile over this accusation.

"Come Katina," Mama tugged impatiently at her arm. "Please excuse us," she said to Mr. Backer as they turned to walk toward the store.

Well out of listening range, Mama scoffed, "Rich farmers! Once you're married to them, they'll only make you a slave.

65

They'll treat you no better than a servant."

Dismayed, she added, "Don't pay any attention to what they're saying. In my opinion you have done the right thing. Your father and I agree. A man with a good heart is far better than one who is rich and uncaring."

Katina gave her mother a grateful hug, then opening the door, they both entered the store.

12

A pale December sun rose on her special day, reflecting a dim yet captivating light across the sea. Thoughtful, she stood by the window looking over the neighboring rooftops. She watched as the sea swirled and pushed its way around and upward, creating white foaming crowns on each wave. She never tired of this scene as the sound and the movement of the sea felt calming and for a brief moment, she lost herself in a thoughtless daze.

All at once she caught herself. It was still very early in the morning, and as far as she was aware, there was no movement of any sort inside the house. She had plenty of time to crawl back into bed and enjoy a second snooze, but the tasks before her left her apprehensive.

She looked about the bedroom which was to be hers and Johann's. It felt strange and unfamiliar, yet inviting to be explored. A faint smile brushed her lips.

She remembered her sister talk of how important it was to have a home of her own. Now she understood that feeling. It gave her a sense of self worth and accomplishment. One that rested solely now on her and Johann to work toward a common goal in beautifying and fulfilling each other's lives.

The sound of waves lapping against the shore reached her ear, reminding her of the time. The sea did not stand still, and it was in her best interest to do the same.

She felt a little nervous twitch in her stomach when her eyes fell upon her wedding dress. She was indebted to Florica the seamstress. She had really outdone herself in following her instructions on how she wanted the gown to look. Gently she let her hands glide over the soft white silky material. She took the dress from the hanger and held it against her. Standing in front of the mirror a gasp escaped her lips.

"Oh, Katina you look a mess!" Shaking her head, she abruptly hung the dress back to its original place. Quickly she brushed her hair and putting on her house coat she tiptoed quietly out of her room.

Suddenly a familiar clanking sound reached her ears.

"Mama..." she said to herself, suppressing a quiet chuckle. "Who else would be up this early in the morning, working in the kitchen?"

It must be a force of habit with her. After so many years and with so many children, a woman was bound to end up this way. She smiled, envisioning herself falling into the same rut.

As she entered the kitchen she was greeted by the familiar *Kletterwurzel* odor, a root from the burdock thistle. It was said to give the hair a thick and healthy-looking texture. A firm believer, Mama had always added this extract to the water for her and the girls and this morning was no exception.

As she was just about to add water to a tub for Katina to use, she noticed the time, and suddenly in a hurry, urged Katina on.

"Quickly, get in and don't dawdle. We have to have everything cleaned up and out of the way before the others get up." She spoke with haste in her voice then placed another chunk of pressed sunflower cake into the fire. Then took another pot full of hot water from the stove and emptied into the tub. Last she added a portion of scented oil into the bath water.

"Mmm...." Taking a deep breath, she smiled and closed her eyes enjoying for a moment the scent of violets drifting in the hot steam. "Ah... it's absolutely wonderful..." Her voice rang out as she straightened up and busied herself to prepare breakfast.

For a moment Katina allowed herself to enjoy her luxurious bath then remembering Mama's warning, she hurried on. She was glad her mother was here to help her, especially today, as there were too many things to be done.

She was equally grateful to Maria and Lena, her two sisters-in-law. They had diligently helped in the past few days in preparing the wedding banquet. And the men folk, they too had been busy gathering and setting up tables and chairs. They had borrowed them from friends around the neighborhood, to accommodate all the invited guests.

Shortly after breakfast the first party arrived, among them her brothers and Hilda, a younger cousin from Girargi. She was to be her bridesmaid as Tara was her matron of honor. Micha too had joined Tara for this special occasion. Auntie Elena and Uncle Gustav were also among the invited guests.

Tara, who with Hilda, had come up to the room to help her get dressed, told her that some of their brothers were in a rowdy mood and had gone over to Johann's house. They said, 'to give him a helping hand' just to make sure he will be in church on time. They all had good chuckle. She could just imagine what they had in mind.

"Poor Johann," she said with a mischievous grin. "I hope they'll be gentle with him."

Their laughter resounded throughout the house.

--

The big moment had finally arrived when she stood ready in her white satiny dress. Her brother Ben brought the polished horse-drawn carriage around to the front of the house. She and her bridesmaid, as well as Tara, Mama and Papa would be in the first coach. The other guests would follow in several carriages Papa had rented for this purpose.

Her heart fluttered with excitement. It was not easy to stay calm under the gazing eyes of onlookers who happened to be standing on both sides of the street. Word had traveled fast about the wedding and it seemed that everyone in the neighborhood had come out to get a glimpse of the bride. She had to admit that she herself was just as guilty and nosy when it came to other weddings.

She managed a nervous smile toward the crowd as Ben guided the horses around the last bend. Gracefully he brought the carriage to a halt in front of the chapel. Immediately her eyes fell upon Johann. Dressed in a handsome brand-new suit, he stood proud and upright in front of the church entrance. Pastor Hildebrand was beside him equally honored to perform the wedding ceremony. The two were surrounded by friends and some of her brothers who had eagerly awaited her arrival. The sparkle in Johann's eyes as he looked toward her told her that he was pleased by what he saw.

Papa came around to help her out of the carriage. Filled with emotion and pride he escorted her to where Johann stood waiting. Symbolically he handed her over to him.

A lonely tear escaped Mama's eye, as she watched with a twinge in her heart.

"Another daughter gone," she exclaimed. "I'll miss having my girls around me. It probably won't be long and Edwina too will leave."

"Oh! Mama! Don't worry we're never too far away to visit," Tara comforted her. "Besides, Edwina is a long way off from being married."

Katina tucked her arm into Johann's. She felt him tenderly squeeze her arm against him in approval. She blushed, overcome with a happy sensation. When the organ started playing, she walked down the aisle secure and calm on Johann's strong arm.

Her radiant and blushing complexion complemented the white silk ankle length wedding dress. It looked stunning on her slender figure. Gracefully it flowed about her with every step she took. Her thick and wavy light brown hair was beautifully arranged underneath the floor length veil. The girls had adorned it with sprigs of maidenhair fern. All this stood in gentle contrast to the pastel colors in her wedding bouquet.

Standing in front of the altar with Johann by her side, she felt his eyes reach out in love. Solemnly he vowed before God and man that he would love and cherish her for the rest of his life. Promising the same, she had no doubt she had made the right choice.

--

The huge rented house served its purpose well. The celebration continued with plenty of good food and drink. It was filled with the gaiety of laughter, happy chatter, music and singing of songs. Music had always played a big part in the Stack's family. Also included in all this was the reminiscing of times gone by and hopes of future plans aligned with an array of good advice. Freely they shared as they celebrated well into the night.

13

Katina adjusted favorably to her new role and loved every moment of being the new wife of Johann Wendel. His tender caring way made her forget all the fears she once had about marriage. Now in his arms she felt loved and protected, and no one could ever change her mind to think otherwise. Deeply devoted, she believed that nothing could ever separate them.

Her thoughts were of all the relatives and guests that had come to her wedding. Now after three days of celebrating, many had packed up, to return home again, leaving behind good wishes for the both of them. It was hard to say goodbye and she felt a little let down especially when it came to her family. Yet there was one other person in particular that brought a little sadness to her heart. Auntie Elena and Uncle Gustav had planned this to be their last farewell to all the family and friends before departing for Uruguay. She had become very fond of this dear and special lady. As for Mama and Papa, she comforted herself that it would only be a matter of time when they would see each other again.

With all the guests gone her thoughts turned to household duties. As an added responsibility she had promised Johann to include his father in providing meals for him. Johann's father lived not far from here in a small decrepit looking house that stood surrounded by ten hectares of land.

Johann had in mind to tear down that house and build new. But despite all his explanations that it would look more favorable for his personal and business interests, his father stood firm and denied him this wish. His father was a very stubborn man by nature and not easily swayed yet Johann tried his best to get along. It was not in his nature to neglect his father, who suffered from deep depression as well as arthritis and a disabling hernia. For this reason, Johann continued to care for his father. Now Katina also joined in, but she knew it would not be an easy task.

It proved true on her first visit when she tried to get rid of the rancid food her father-in-law stored in a small cupboard near his bed.

She repeatedly reminded him that there was no need for this as he was welcome to dine with them. But he declined the invitation. In a way she was glad that Father Wendel did not live under the same roof with them. But she knew the day would come and she dreaded to think that it may be sooner than later. Yet for Johann's sake she was willing to put up with Father Wendel's strange mannerisms.

--

The Christmas season was approaching fast. The thought of not being able to celebrate with family this year left her a little homesick. To get out of this solemn mood, she arranged a little celebration of her own, inviting Mark and Maria, as well as Job and Lena. To her surprise even Father Wendel was excited, as he and Johann had endured many lonely Christmas holidays without family and friends.

With little time to spare, she, Maria and Lena set out immediately to prepare for the celebration. For days, the whole house was filled with the beautiful aroma of Christmas baking. And coming home to all this brought back heartwarming childhood memories for Johann. He was humming songs his mother used to sing, especially when working around the house. She loved to hear his voice. It was a melodious baritone with an undertone of deep longing that captivated her deeply.

The laborsome work of baking and preparing for the

Christmas holidays proved to be successful. It was all she could have wished for. And despite the cold and frigid temperatures outside, the house felt warm and inviting. In a festive mood with Christmas in the air she did not want the evening to end. It felt good to sit back, for once, and relax. With fondness she and the rest of them reminisced of Christmases past. Each one had stories to tell that provoked laughter or sadness.

Father Wendel, more than once, wiped his eyes, not so much of sad memories, but from the overwhelming joy he felt. As he departed, he mentioned to Johann, who had accompanied him home, "I'll come more often, if you'll have me. I enjoyed the evening, especially the singing."

Johann was moved to tears. He had never heard his father express his feelings to him, especially not happy ones. He mentioned it to her later as they lay in bed, talking about the event.

"Oh Johann, that is good news. Hopefully now he'll be more agreeable."

Johann was amused at her statement.

"My dear Katina that would be a drastic change indeed, for as long as I've known my father, I've never seen him like this. Tonight, he just surprised me. But I do hope you are right. It would make life much easier for all of us."

She cuddled close to him when she heard the wind howl outside their bedroom window.

"Uh..." she said shivering. "It sounds ghastly... I hope we don't get a snowstorm." With that she pulled the feather-comforter higher and snuggled even closer to Johann.

"I hope not! If that happens, it will make it even harder to work on Mark and Maria's house. I want it done as soon as possible so I can start on our home."

"Just think Katina, our own home."

He held her tenderly against him as they listened to the wind. It captivated their thoughts. The sound was eerie yet comforting and soon they both drifted into a deep sleep.

I WILL REMEMBER ALWAYS

--

The next day the winter cold came with a blast. Johann was looking out of the kitchen window assessing the condition as Katina sat near the stove busy knitting a pair of socks.

He measured the fury of the storm and was fascinated but not worried. He had taken extra precautions to stock up on enough dry goods to last them through the worst of winter. Before Christmas he and Mark had worked steady to bring home wagon loads of pressed sunflower cakes from Papa's mill. Considering the cold, it had not been an easy ride on the treacherous road, but he was glad they had worked so diligently in achieving this.

He turned to Katina, proud of what they had accomplished, "We won't have to worry. We have enough to eat and plenty of fuel to keep us warm and cozy. What more can we ask for?"

He smiled and bent down to kiss her. She returned the smile and handed the finished pair of woolen socks for him to wear. She then continued to finish the last pair.

"Oh... I can hardly wait to put them on." He rubbed his hands with excitement. "The cold weather is quite brutal on the feet and they'll keep me nice and warm." He playfully gave her another peck on her cheek.

"Oh, and while you're at it, I'll need a new pair of gloves soon," he said teasingly, chuckling to himself as he was walking out of the room.

"I'm so glad Mama taught me to knit," she thoughtfully admitted, recalling the tedious hours of learning this craft. Luckily, she had stuck to it and succeeded to perfect herself in it.

"Thanks Mama!" she acknowledged again.

14

With the poor weather not allowing him to work on Mark and Maria's house, Johann decided to look for odd jobs. And it was with Papa's help he was able to land a job in cutting ice from the edges of the Black Sea. He then sold it to homeowners for their cold-storage.

His first customer was Herman Grundman, a rich lawyer, who happened to live down by the sea right across from Mark's future home. Papa knew him through business dealings when he purchased the properties here in Mangalia.

Through this contact he was swamped with orders from other well to do customers. With his eager to work attitude he had gained favor with all his purchasers. And because of this he was confident that he would have plenty of work; enough to last him through the entire winter season?

It was the dream to buy view lots near the Sea and build the finest guest villas. That gave him the strength to endure this painstaking and tedious job. To his surprise the demand for ice had soon outgrown his ability to do the job on his own. And to keep up with the orders he had no choice but to hire more workers.

Always a caring sort, it became a habit of his to give those who lived in the same part of town a ride home. Out of gratitude, Costel, a middle-aged Romanian worker invited him for a cup of hot rum tea. "It's just the thing that'll warm you up on cold wintry days," Costel had said with a smirk about his face.

Out of politeness, he accepted the invitation. But upon entering the home he was shocked of their primitive living conditions. Costel's wife was just about to prepare the evening meal. He saw her busy working near a tri-pot that stood over an open fire in the middle of the room. There was no chimney for the smoke to escape other than leaving the front door open.

He looked around amazed how they had survived, especially with this cold weather. Dismayed at what he saw, he felt compelled to help Costel. He presented the idea of building a proper oven with chimney. This way the heat would stay in the house and allow them to cook smoke-free.

Weeks later, he received a dinner invitation from the grateful man. Costel told him that since he could not pay for his services, he would be honored to have him and his wife over for dinner.

Johann chuckled at the thought for he knew what was to be expected. Not sure if Katina would agree to come along, he approached her with little apprehension that day.

"Costel has invited us for dinner. He told me it was the least he could do to thank me for building the stove. What do you think?"

He looked at her with a skeptical grin.

"Why do you smile?" Her eyes narrowed. "Is there something you're not telling me?"

"Oh… nothing… It is just their customs are so different from ours and you might disapprove. And the food most likely will be a basic Romanian meal. I just want to warn you if we go, that no matter how things appear, please accept them so as not to embarrass the hostess.

"Oh, Johann!" she dismissed his warning with a wave of her hand. "I've been so many times at Joanna's house. I know their customs."

She smiled and gave him a loving kiss.

He shrugged his shoulders.

"As you say my love, I only wanted to warn you," he stated with an affectionate smile, hoping she will heed his warning. He knew better as it was not the first time he had dined at the poorest of Romanian homes. In his bachelor years he had been invited on numerous occasions, and he enjoyed the change from the food he and his father had managed to cook for themselves. Now with Katina by his side, he had almost forgotten that time.

--

That evening Johann arrived at Costel's home with little apprehension, still worrying about Katina. To his surprise he found the Romanian couple at their best in trying their utmost to make them to feel at home. Costel's wife proudly showed off the new stove and chimney to Katina. She raved at how wonderful it was to cook now on a proper element, without thick smoke clouds hanging over them.

A little more at ease, Johann was pleased to see Katina interest herself in his project and trying to fit in.

Yet as the time came to gather for the meal, he noticed her perplexed look when the hostess invited them to sit on the carpet next to them. There on the floor on a protective mat stood two large bowls. One filled with *mamaliga*, a cooked cornmeal, the other held a certain type of gravy.

He noticed Katina's eyes going from one bowl to the other.

Aghast she watched, as the host and hostess and each of the children took the lead and dug into the *mamaliga*. Upon retrieving a dollop of cornmeal with their middle fingers they dunked the same into the gravy bowl. Leaving a few droppings along the way they downed the whole lump with great satisfaction.

Reluctantly she tried to follow, but again hesitated. The sight of left behind drippings of cornmeal in the gravy made her stomach turn. She could not bring herself to eat it.

Guessing her thoughts, Johann gave her a big grin. He followed the family and dug his fingers into the cornmeal and retrieved a big clump. He then dunked it into the gravy and stuffed the whole thing into his mouth. She watched him eat. All at once she remembered what he had told her.

The hostess smiled and encouraged her to dig in. She gave Johann another glance then swallowed hard and reached for the *mamaliga*. Carefully she dipped into the partly *mamaliga* partly gravy mixture, then quickly popped it into her mouth. Trying her best not to think of what she was eating.

Amused, Johann watched her struggle each time giving her an encouraging wink to carry on. He felt a little sorry to put her through this. But at the same time, he could not keep the smirk off his face, as he realized how hard she tried to please him.

She had to admit, the meal was tasteful. It was the sight of the way it was presented that gave her difficulty. Yet according to Johann the evening had gone well. On the way home he tried to reflect on the visit, started out by saying... "Next time we are invited..."

Quickly she interrupted. "There will be no next time. I am sorry Johann. I will go anywhere and do anything for you, but not this again."

He drew her close and embraced her tenderly.

"You did well. I'm very proud of you."

15

In the coming months Johann was still very busy, working steadily from morning until night, except on Sundays. She worried that he was pushing himself too hard, especially when she noticed a slight limp whenever he walked. One he so desperately tried to hide whenever he noticed her watching.

Late one evening she questioned him about his work and how he was coping. Readily he admitted that all was not well with him. Reluctant he gave in and showed her the open sores on his knees.

"Johann, why in the world did you not tell me about this sooner," she said disgusted by what she saw.

He shrugged his shoulders and gave her a vague smile.

"I thought it would go away on its own. I didn't want to worry you, but I guess I was wrong."

"Worry me? Johann how could you think this way?" she exclaimed a little upset.

Concerned she quickly set up a basin and carefully washed the sores with soap and water. She had watched her father treat sores and injuries many times.

Johann clutched his hands tightly to the seat. The pain was unbearable.

She felt terrible and it hurt her to see him like this. Tenderly she scolded him.

"Johann Wendel! Do not ever neglect to tell me when you're not well. The first thing tomorrow you're going to see a doctor about this."

She stopped talking for a moment while fussing over him, wrapping each leg with clean cloth. Then she added in a loving way, "I don't ever want you to do such a silly thing again."

He smiled and nodded. She tried to say more. But he tenderly pulled her toward him and gave her a loving kiss.

The next morning, he went to see a doctor at the nearby clinic, hoping to get relief soon. But despite of all the medical treatments, the sores worsened with every passing day. It made every step more painful than before. Reluctant, he was forced to give up his job and stay home.

It was the beginning of March when Robert and Papa had come down to Mangalia and found Johann in this poor state.

Papa, familiar with many natural healing remedies, had another suggestion.

"When all else fails, the juice of a lemon will heal almost anything," he advised.

"Just keep dabbing it faithfully on the sores and you'll soon see results."

Johann thought he would never survive the pain when she first applied the acidy liquid on his sores. He begged her to let him do it on his own. She gladly agreed, seeing how much it hurt him.

With much agony he continued applying the lemon juice to the sores. To his surprise they quickly improved. And after a few weeks they had completely disappeared.

Feeling much better, a restless urgency stirred within his heart. He had been home far too long, and it had bothered him to have wasted so much time. If he wanted his dream to materialize, he had to get out there and work. With much determination and renewed energy, he was once again ready to venture out.

16

With the cold weather behind them, he was in a rush to finish all the jobs left undone. In addition to this, he was also in charge to oversee all the projects Father Stack and Robert had planned to build on their 20-hectare property. The site lay on the south eastern section of the town, close to the sea between the main street and the Limanu River.

Both he and Robert had to work late in the night to complete the drawings for a spacious villa. This time Papa wanted enough space for his family to live in relative comfort.

A layout for the business compound was also at hand. It was to be built on the same estate as soon as the living quarters were finished. As planned, it featured a new oil mill, which was to be bigger and better than the one in Girargi. Added to this was also a large factory for processing and dying wool; and a section for weaving and steam-ironing for larger items such as rugs, wall hangings and woven material for clothing. The colors for the dye would be selected from experienced Romanian artists.

Papa had ordered a rush on all these projects. He had given Johann and Robert instructions to take on as much outside help as needed to get everything done as quickly as possible. He himself had planned to come down in a month and do whatever he could to help. Now even more than before he was anxious to get settled and start his new business ventures which he expected to be very profitable for him and his whole family.

Since the building site was within a good walking distance, she too decided to help along. The thought had come to her to supply Johann and Robert with food. This way no time was wasted, and they could focus on the important things.

She noticed, Robert especially welcomed this gesture and thought it a great idea. Living in a small shack on the property to keep watch over the whole project, he had little chance to cook and provide for himself. Knowing there was a large gypsy settlement nearby, just across the valley, he felt it was his duty to be here at all times. Yet he was not naïve to think them the only ones looting. As they had learned in previous times that others too would not think twice to take what was not theirs. That is why the rush to get everything up and running and ready for the rest of the family to move in. With all of them here they hoped it would be less of a deterrent.

Like Papa, she too wanted the projects done as soon as possible, as with this undertaking out of the way Johann could start building their new home. But aside from that, she longed to have all her family close by once again.

With the food packed neatly into a picnic basket, she set out to meet Johann and Robert for their lunch break. The sunshine was warm and comforting on her back. Many of the young folk passing opted to go barefoot, dressing only in light summer clothing. She was about to take off her shoes when she changed her mind. Somehow it did not seem proper for a married woman, especially with child.

She smiled at the thought. The bright sun seemed to give everyone a cheery disposition. All were busy working and running about. Even the birds had once again returned from the far south, flying about in a frenzy, building their nests. Tenderly she held the area of her body were a tiny life had begun. A feeling of unspoken happiness filled her heart.

Amused she stood for a moment watching a pair of storks squabbling on a nearby rooftop.

Johann had seen her coming from across the valley and signaled to Robert and the rest of the workers to take a break. He walked over to meet her, greeting her with a soft peck on her cheek.

"Mmm... I'm so hungry I was already looking for you!" he exclaimed, taking the food basket from her, walking it over to where Robert was sitting. But before he sat down, he quickly dusted off a pile of mudbricks for her to sit on. Not wanting to eat by herself, she had brought enough to join them both for lunch.

While chewing on a tasty morsel of smoked ham and home baked bread, Robert studied her. For some reason, her usual rosy cheeks looked pale and peaked.

"Are you well?" he asked her suddenly, remembering the talk he had with her before her marriage.

She smiled noticing her brother's concerned look.

"I'm fine Robert, nothing that seven months won't cure."

Robert was overjoyed.

"Johann! How come you haven't told me? Of course, I should have known... the way you fussed over her," he carried on, not giving his brother-in-law a chance to explain himself.

"What do you wish for, a boy or a girl?" he asked teasingly.

"As long as it's healthy, it doesn't matter," Johann said looking caringly at Katina, but she knew better. The first time he had found out that he was going to be a Papa, he aired his feelings. He wished the first one to be a boy, one he could take on special outings, and when old enough he could teach and share the trade of his business with.

In the middle of their conversation, a disturbing cry suddenly interrupted their lunch hour. A man driving on a horse drawn wagon raced toward the building site. With a horror filled voice he shouted from the top of his lungs. Both Johann and Robert jumped to their feet, sensing the dreadful urgency.

The man pulled the reins on the horses and came to halt in front of them.

"Come quickly! The sand-pit collapsed and buried some of the men!" The man spoke with anguish in his voice. Johann quickly took shovels and all the necessary tools then hastily jumped into the wagon. Without further delay they hurried back to the gravel pit.

She stood in a daze watching after them. "I hope, they're not too late," she said with concern.

Robert shook his head in dismay. "They're always so eager to work and don't pay attention to what they're doing." He stood up looking into the direction where the wagon had gone. "So many times we've told them not to tunnel into the sand, for it makes the ceiling unstable." Upset he turned to resume his work, making more bricks.

She watched him as he busied himself, hauling more sand to add to the mixture of mud and straw. Then forming the bricks and laying them out in the warm sun to bake.

"Will they be strong enough?" she questioned.

He chuckled, "They certainly will. This kind of mixture makes a very sturdy building material," he stopped talking, catching his breath. "By the way, thanks for the delicious lunch, Sis."

She nodded in return. All at once she remembered her rendezvous with Maria and Lena. Quickly she gathered her empty basket then called goodbye to Robert. He waved shortly then went about his work. With haste in her step she turned to walk up the hill again toward the market. She had promised to meet them there after lunch.

Straight ahead in front of the marketplace where the main street took a sharp corner to the north; she could see the two waiting, both pregnant and due in about three months.

"Well, well, how are the two beautiful ladies today?" She greeted them with a lighthearted chuckle

"Wait a few months and you can join us."

85

They shared a good laugh as they walked into the market, which on this sunny day was bustling with people.

She had stopped for a moment to look more closely at a brilliantly colored carpet. She was told they came from the Maramures region of Romania. Maria and Lena in the meantime were busy admiring beautiful crafted pottery at the next table.

Deep in thoughts, and dreaming of buying one, she had not noticed the man standing beside her until he started to speak to the lady next to him.

"Which one would you like dear?" he spoke with a snobby, show-off kind of voice.

She looked up and their eyes met. It was Heinrich Schwarz, one of her old-time admirers, his hair red as ever. She could not stand him then, a rich farmer's son, as they were growing up and going to school together in Cogealac; and she could not stand him now. There was a certain kind of arrogance in his tone of voice as well as character that she just could not tolerate.

He gave her a look as if to say, "See what you could have had, if you had married me."

She gave a quick glance to the woman next to him. She looked plain and worn out. At that instant Mama's words came to mind of rich farmers treating their wives no better than servants. The woman suddenly looked at her and she detected a coldness in her eyes. Or was it a touch of jealousy for she too must have known of her husband's one-time pursuit for her affection.

With a polite nod toward them, she turned and walked away to meet up with Maria and Lena. Both had been watching nearby and had not missed the significance of this encounter.

As they walked on, Maria questioned, "Did you see the look he gave you? I could swear he still cares for you."

"Not for all the rugs in the world would I change places with that woman. As rich as he may be, he could never come

I WILL REMEMBER ALWAYS

close to my Johann!" she stated with conviction.

"Good for you," Lena added with a chuckle.

"I'll get a rug someday and I won't need his money to get it!"

Suddenly she stopped herself, realizing how silly and embarrassing the topic was becoming.

"Now you two, let's forget what just happened and not spoil our day, Hmm?"

Maria and Lena had found the whole incident amusing. But seeing how it upset her they dropped the topic all together. Busy chatting, they walked along the many stalls continuing their shopping spree.

--

Johann had come home a little later than usual. Weary and tired he told her about the accident at the sandpit.

One of the workers had taken his teenage son along to help him with the digging. Both had been working in the sandpit and not paying attention mistakenly created a hollowed-out tunnel. The ceiling soon became unstable and collapsed on both of them. It buried the son completely and the father up to his chest. The father seemingly was trying desperately to get himself free to help his son, buried only four feet away from him. But the heavy weight of the damp sand just made it impossible to move.

Johann paused then repeated to her the stricken man's own words.

"I cried out to God to send help, but it came too late. Oh God... what pain! My son! My poor son...!"

"The man had been inconsolable, crying and carrying on. It was hard for all of us to hear," Johann concluded.

He sat quietly his head bowed low, fighting back tears.

Silently she moved toward him, caressing him.

"It must be devastating to experience something so dreadful."

A quiet nod was all Johann could manage, the hurt of this tragedy still fresh in his mind.

87

"What about the man, will he be okay?"

"Well as the doctor said that in time his body will heal, but his heart, well..."

"The poor man," she whispered, gently interrupting him.

Johann pulled her close.

"I hope and pray nothing so painful will ever happen to us and our loved ones. God willing... We'll be together, happy and healthy, until the end of our days."

"Oh Johann..." moved by his statement, she embraced him tenderly. At this moment she did not care whether she had a Muramures rug and all the beautiful things money can buy. Having Johann by her side was all that mattered.

17

In the following days, due to the accident, Johann and the others worked extra hours to make up for time lost. Papa too had come down from Girargi to lend a helping hand. He also brought news from Tara and Micha that they had a baby.

Katina herself was moving into her fourth month of pregnancy and so far, had encountered no difficulty. Although lately she had to admit she felt more tired than usual, she dismissed it as being part of motherhood.

It seemed this year, along with the early warm spring weather, a greater number of tourists had flocked into town. Most had come here for years to take advantage of the hot springs, one located in the southern section of town and the other in the northern section of town. Although the southern hot spring, an indoor bath house at the Limanu River seemed the most favorite of many tourists, others claimed the northern mud bath to be their favorite. It was renowned to aid and cure arthritis as well as several other ailments. And the rest... well they simply came to enjoy the healthy sea air.

Realizing, that with so many people flocking into town, there would be a short supply of accommodations, she and Johann talked it over and decided to take the opportunity to rent out their spare bedroom. It would only be for the duration of the spring and summer season. The extra money derived from this would go toward building materials for their new house.

Excited, she spent hours washing and cleaning the room. Then spreading her best linen sheets over the guest bed, she stepped back for a last look around. The fresh flowers on the table added a cheery and welcoming touch.

"There, I hope all this will make a good and lasting impression, and hopefully it will bring them back year after year," she said with a gratifying smile. It was after all in Johann's plan to build tourist accommodations and what better way to attract them.

She had to admit it was an ambitious goal. But she believed in his ability to accomplish what he decided to do. She saw how skillful he was in making business deals and finding work for himself when others could not.

His industrious ways were contagious even to her, and by getting her first customer, she proved that she could help him in reaching that dream.

Often on warm sunny Sunday afternoons, they would go for leisurely strolls along the main street down toward the cobble-stone plaza. Here wide steps led them down to a large terrace. While yet another flight of stairs eventually brought them further down onto the white sandy beaches.

They both loved to mingle among the tourists and sit in one of the outside cafes on the terrace. From here they could overlook the Black Sea and the seaside town. It was an unsurpassed and breathtaking view with its lovely villas and crescent-crowned mosques in the background high above the beaches. On evenings like these they would sit sipping a cool glass of lemonade or perhaps a cup of the finest mocha coffee. They especially enjoyed listening to the melodious sound of the gypsy's violin as the musicians walked around playing for tourists.

It was a popular gathering place for both tourists and Mangalians alike. The whole plaza and promenade came alive at night, when by soft kerosene lamplight; the local bands performed their lively folk music.

I WILL REMEMBER ALWAYS

During these events, she and Johann would sit holding hands like young lovers listening to music, talking and dreaming of future goals. She loved those moments; they were carefree and happy. These were treasured times she would keep forever in her heart.

--

With the increased workload, Johann decided the following day to start earlier than usual. Quietly he slipped out of the bedroom to prepare his own breakfast. He had noticed Katina restlessly turning from side to side all night and thought it good to let her sleep.

He was only at his work place an hour when Miss Krauber, a German tourist renting the spare bedroom, came running across the valley toward him.

"Please come home immediately Herr Wendel!" she called from afar, gasping for air.

Johann looked baffled, dropping his tools, he hastily walked toward her.

"It is your wife," she called out. "She is not well."

He looked around in confusion.

"Don't worry, Johann," guessing his thoughts, Robert reassured him. "Papa and I will take care of things here. Just go and let us know what is happening."

On the way, Miss Krauber urged him that it would be wise to pick up Mrs. Greta Berg. She was the licensed German midwife who was in charge over all the pregnancies in this section of town. Johann agreed and hurriedly took off in his horse drawn wagon.

Arriving at home he found Maria anxiously waiting for them at the door.

"What happened? Where is she?" Johann asked in a panic.

"We took her back to bed," Maria replied.

Johann rushed toward the bedroom, followed close behind by Mrs. Berg, Miss Krauber and Maria.

"To bed from where..." Johann stopped short at the door.

Miss Krauber, who was standing right behind Maria,

91

started to explain.

"I found your wife laying outside on top the flowerbed this morning with her bed cover underneath her arms." She took a long and shallow breath then continued with a faint quiver in her voice. "My first thought was that something might have gone wrong with the pregnancy. I quickly called Maria for assistance, putting her back to bed and to stay with her, while I went to get you Herr Wendel."

"Thank you," Johann said softly with a slight tremble in his voice. He entered the bedroom and moved closer to her bedside. She seemed incoherent and delirious, stretching herself, tossing about, and breathing very rapidly. Worried, he held her hand while patiently waiting for Mrs. Berg's findings.

"Everything seems to be all right with the pregnancy," Mrs. Berg announced quite relieved. It was when she took Katina's temperature and checked the thermometer that her eyebrows raised with concern.

"My goodness...! She is burning up. I think it would be wise to call the doctor!"

Johann left in a hurry, hoping to find Doctor Pitmeier available. It was not long when the two showed up at the house. Immediately the doctor went to check up on her.

"I'm afraid she has contracted malaria," he announced with concern, then stated. "We should start her on malaria treatments as soon as possible. Only there's one drawback?" He looked questionable at Johann. "The medication might cause her to lose the baby and that won't be good." He thought for a moment. "I think we'll postpone the treatments to the fifth month. In the meant time I put Mrs. Berg in charge to look in on her. And that would be every day," he turned to Mrs. Berg, who gave him a mindful nod.

"It's just a precaution to make sure nothing does happen to her or the baby," he assured Johann seeing his worried look.

Long after Doctor Pitmeier and Mrs. Berg had left, Johann was still reluctant to leave her bedside, despite Maria and

Miss Krauber's reassuring him that they were able to take care of her.

But the fear of losing her consumed his mind as he recalled the illnesses that took both his mother's, and later, his sister's life. Full of anguish he prayed to God. With tears running down his dusty face and onto his dirt encrusted hands, he pleaded for her and the little one.

After a quick clean up and a change of clothes, he resumed to stay at her bedside. With tireless devotion, he carefully attended to her, following all of Doctor Pitmeier's instructions. All at once her fever broke. But in its place terrible chills set in that shook her whole body in a torment for hours. Then the shivering gave way to profound sweating. He watched as agonizing hours later the malaria finally gave way and she fell into a much-needed sleep. In the silence of the semi-dark room, he found himself suddenly overtaken by exhaustion. He sank into the chair near the bed.

--

The next morning, she awoke to the creaking of door hinges. Not aware of what had happened, she wondered what in the world Maria was doing so early in the morning sneaking into her bedroom. Her curiosity grew when she noticed Johann not with her in bed but sound asleep slumped in the chair beside the bed. She tried to lift herself up but did not have the strength.

"Maria, what's going on?" she whispered as her sister-in-law bent over to see how she was doing.

"Why is Johann sleeping in a chair?"

"Shh...!" Maria quietly calmed her. Then explained to her yesterday's events and her illness. She also mentioned that the midwife will be coming later to look in on her.

"The midwife...? Why, did something go wrong?" Shocked she felt her stomach.

"Oh no, everything is all right with the baby. It's the malaria we are worried about."

"Malaria," Katina gasped in disbelief.

"The fever could be dangerous to you and the little one…
That's why the midwife," Maria whispered.

Johann stirred.

"Poor Johann, it must be very uncomfortable for him to
sleep in that chair," Katina spoke in a hushed voice.

"Shh…! I will go and make breakfast for all of us. You just
rest," her sister-in-law calmed her. And with that she made
her way out of the room.

As soon as she walked out Johann woke. He jumped up
from the chair with a worried look about his face, feeling
terrible guilty for falling asleep. But his expression soon
changed when he noticed a faint smile on Katina's face. He
bent over and kissed her tenderly.

"How are you feeling?" He wearily inquired.

"I'm fine, as soon as I can bring myself to get up."

"You'll do no such thing," he said sternly. "I'll stay home
and look after you until you're well enough to do so. You gave
us quite a scare yesterday and I don't want the same thing
happening again today."

He had made up his mind and no one could tell him
otherwise. Not until later when Mrs. Berg assured him that
with her and Maria looking in on Katina, he had nothing to
worry about, did he change his mind and accept her words.

--

Days went by, and after a week of watching Katina suffer,
Johann finally had enough and called on Papa for help. For
Papa had told him when he and Robert had first looked in
on Katina, that he knew of an old but very highly respected
homeopathic doctor; one who might be able to help her with
natural remedies. Taking Papa's advice, he summoned the
doctor to come and see her.

Ruben Yakowich was a white haired kindly old man,
who had successfully treated many people in his time. He
immediately reassured him that he will do his utmost to help
Katina. And after a lengthy examination, he prescribed two
kinds of medication for her to take.

"You start out by taking seven tablets from one bottle, then the next day you take seven from the other. Then rotate every other day." Ruben Yakowich explained. His face showed concern for the fact that his orders were carried out correctly. "It is most important that you take the medicine as prescribed in order for it to work." He commented again as he packed up his medicine case. A polite smile escaped his lips when he bid them both well.

After a few days, and much to his relief, Johann noticed an improvement in Katina. So much so that she was able to carry on with regular duties around the house. But despite her feeling a little stronger, the symptoms of the malaria did not leave her body.

After the fifth month Doctor Pitmeier started his treatments to try and bring the malaria under control. But to her dismay, every time he administrated the shots. She was overtaken with agonizing malaria attacks that left her weak and unable to do her household chores for the rest of the day.

Johann tried to be helpful and did all the necessary household chores for her. But she was desperate to do at least some of the work. In time, she realized she had a few symptom free hours in the midmorning. This at least would give her enough time to straighten out her home and cook all her meals before the doctor arrived. She knew it would be a struggle, but with everyone's help she at least was able to carry on.

With spring gone and summer just around the corner, she was excited to hear that Papa had sold the mill and property in Girargi. They were finally on their way to move to Mangalia. She could hardly wait to see Mama again. Her only wish was to be well enough to enjoy all the excitement of helping her family move into their new home.

Mark and Maria in the meantime could not stand to remain in the rented house and decided to move into their unfinished home.

Not wanting to carry the whole burden of rent, Johann

was now forced to be on the lookout for a temporary place to stay. The main reason, he did not want Katina to be left alone. He calculated their home to be ready by summer's end and it was unfortunate that Mark and Maria had not heeded Papa's recommendation to stay with Katina and Johann. He could understand their anxiousness to be on their own, as he too was looking forward to the same, yet all the unforeseen events had made it impossible to finish their house as well as delayed the process of their own home.

To their surprise, Job and Lena came to their rescue and offered to stay in their home with them. Reluctant at first, they weighed all the options and found they had little choice but to accept and move in with them, livestock and all.

18

It was the beginning of July when both Maria and Lena experienced the final step to motherhood. They each delivered a healthy baby boy, making Job and Mark very proud fathers, and Mama and Papa four-time grandparents.

In the midst of all this frenzy yet another event was in the making. Daniel, the second oldest brother in her family, announced his engagement to Hannah Kranz. Together they had set their wedding date for the first week in October.

Mama and Papa, who hardly recovered from the move, now had to prepare for another wedding. For some reason Daniel's in-laws were unable to host this big celebration. That left his parents little choice, but to have the wedding banquet at their sprawling new villa. With a large family such as theirs, life seemed like a never-ending roller coaster, following one excitement after another.

Heavy-hearted, Katina aired her deep longings to Johann one morning.

"I wish I would be well enough to take part in all the preparation and excitement. Even if I could be there for some of the activities, it would be more bearable than not participating at all. I have already missed too much lying uselessly about. Oh, how I long to ..."

He pulled her close and held her for a long time, not saying a word. He could understand her frustration as he himself felt helpless. What was one to do but wait and hope for the best?

"I miss going down to the beach with you... Remember...?" she whispered, tenderly stroking his face.

"It was so romantic walking along the seashore. To sit together sipping a glass of fresh lemonade, watching all the people and listening to the music," she spoke softly with melancholy in her voice.

"In time my darling when you'll feel a little stronger. For now, we have to be patient," he smiled compassionately.

She nodded in surrender. There was something about him. His quiet and gentle manner had a quality of soothing comfort.

"What would I do without you my love?" She smiled and gave him a big hug. For a long time, they held their embrace.

--

The next morning, while taking a short break from her chores, Katina's mind wandered to the upcoming wedding. It would be wonderful to see everyone again and to hear all the news. She especially was looking forward to seeing Tara. In a letter she wrote that she would be coming down with her two little ones. That alone brought joy to Mama and Papa. Then there was Grandpa Hauber, Mama's father, for whom she had a special fondness and Grandma Hauber, whom she had never gotten to know, for she had died before she was born. Mama, the oldest in her family, was then left in charge to help raise her younger sisters while Grandpa looked after the homestead.

With only girls in his family, nine to be exact, Grandpa recently stated his wish to Mama and Papa. Since he was getting on in age and had no sons of his own, to let him have Daniel as his heir to carry on the family estate. His girls, very talented in music and art, had never developed an interest in farming. And as of now were all married and out of the house.

But Papa, a little selfish about sharing his children, did not like the idea. As for Daniel, now that he was getting married, his heart was set on opening his own business in manufacturing shoes; he had spent three years in learning this craft in Constanta.

She remembered Grandpa Hauber's large estate, especially the spacious house with its beautiful stained-glass windows. She always thought it ill-fitting on a farm, instead envisioning it in a classy neighborhood in Constanta or Mangalia.

Then there was Grandpa's grape orchard and above all his rose garden. One he almost cherishes with the same love and devotion as he did his children and grandchildren. With all this beauty around him, she could understand why he did not want to part from his land, especially now in his old age, as within its roots it held a lifetime of precious memories. Like her father, Grandpa always had time to talk and play with his grandchildren and when it came to stories, he had many to tell.

Startled by the knock at the front door, she suddenly was aware what time it was. With a deep sigh, she pulled herself from the chair. Greta Berg the midwife was earlier than usual, and she was disappointed to see her so soon. She came to hate this time of day, but not because of Greta. Not at all... They had become good friends over the short period of time.

A shiver went through her body by the thought of the suffering that would soon overcome her. But she knew it had to be done. Quietly, but reluctantly, she let Greta inject the quinine into her already sore chest.

Greta tried hard not to show her dismay over this unpleasant task. And she offered her patient as much encouragement as she possibly could.

--

The hot dry summer season progressed parching the land mercilessly. Relentless in its quest; the heat drove even the most seasoned of sun worshipers to look for shadier places. Katina's favorite escape was under large acacia trees that stood in Job and Lena's garden near the Limanu River.

Every day over the noon hour, she came here to escape the overbearing humidity that hung day and night over the land.

The gentle air wafting down from underneath the spreading branches felt refreshing. It was like a cup of water drawn fresh from a cool well. She took a deep breath and slowly released it while listening to the gentle sound of the flowing river. At a glance she noticed it teaming with all sorts of waterfowl; she wished to join them.

For a moment she was lost in this tranquil scene. Forgotten if only for a moment was the illness that would soon drive her back into the house and onto her bed.

--

With Johann busy working, Father Wendel announced one day that he would soon be moving in with them. He told Johann that it would be beneficial for all since Katina was most of the time unable to do her chores. He thought it especially important for the care in looking after the livestock, which consisted of two pigs, a half a dozen chickens, ducks and geese. It also included two cows and two sheep, who for a fee, were picked up every morning by the town's shepherd. Since March the man had rounded up all the neighborhood animals, leading them to public pastures for grazing, then returning them at lunchtime for milking and later on again for the night.

To supply the other animals with the necessary food, whenever he had to build or do work for a farmer, Johann had always asked to be paid in return with wheat, barley, corn or hay for the horses. This way he had plenty of supplies at hand.

When it came to providing for his family, friends and relations alike were amazed how he had managed to save and build a new house so quickly. While in the meantime they were still living in old and cramped quarters, struggling to get ahead.

When confronted, he told them with a twinkle in his eyes, "Its hard work and determination, that's all." But he knew better. It was also his mother's rule that had taught him to always treat others with respect. A practice he kept in his personal life, as well as in business.

19

When the day finally came for them to move into their new home, it was none too soon. For amidst all the commotion of the move, her time for delivery had come. It was to be their first child and Mama and Papa's fifth grandchild. And in spite of all the preparations for Daniel and Hannah's wedding, Mama insisted to be there.

Johann had summoned Mrs. Berg and was anxiously awaiting the birth. He watched the hours pass on the old wall clock his father had given them as a wedding gift. Once in a while Mama came running by to get more warm water from the kitchen, which he so faithfully kept heating. It was the least he could do.

After hours of listening to Katina's agonizing groans and Mrs. Berg's skillful birthing tactics, he heard the cry of the little one. A moment later the door opened and there was Mama presenting him a little girl. Relieved that it was all over he proudly held the tiny bundle.

And even though his wish for a boy was not granted, he was grateful both were well. Tenderly he kissed Katina and showed the little one off to his father, and Papa. Both had come to be part of this occasion. His father especially treasured it as it was his first grandchild.

Johann came to the conclusion that after all the hard labor Katina had gone through, he ought to do his part and name the little one. As it was, he had always loved the name

Rebekka which happened to be his sister's name. He thought it fitting for his daughter. Overjoyed by this decision, his father was moved to tears.

Watching all this Katina was glad to have let him have this honor. Amused, she watched as the baby was passed from one family member to the other. She felt privileged to have Mama and Papa and Johann's father here. Not many of her siblings could boast of this. Soon the room was filled with joyful chatter and all that had gone before was forgotten, at least for the moment. With quiet reverence she stored this special moment into the safe keeping of her heart.

--

Mysteriously the malaria symptoms subsided after little Rebekka's birth. It made her believe that she was finally rid of this terrible disease. But exactly one year later, at Rebekka's first birthday, the malaria returned.

This time Doctor Pitmeier tried to stay one step ahead of the problem. He ordered a much stronger treatment than the previous. Yet after examining her, he was disappointed when realizing he was too late. She was again with child.

To her, it seemed odd the fever surfaced while she was expecting; not before or after. Dismayed, she unwillingly prepared herself to face another nine months of this agonizing illness.

Trying his best, Dr. Pitmeier encouraged her not to lose hope. He reassured her that this stubborn disease had its time. Sooner or later it would gradually be less intrusive. All she could do was to trust and hope he was right.

After this distressing news, she was actually glad now that Father Wendel had moved in with them. On more than one occasion he had helped her with household chores. And also kept an eye on little Rebekka whenever she was not able to do so.

Father Wendel though, was not a talkative man. After his chores were done, she found him retreating to his special corner near the kitchen stove. He claimed it was to nurture his aches and pains he accumulated in earlier years. Yet she never heard him talk of the past. Mostly he kept to himself, brooding, maybe regretting some of the unfortunate moves he had made. And she could only guess there were many, too painful to speak about.

In those moments she retreated to her own thoughts, recalling the events of Daniel and Hannah's wedding. Both Johann and Robert had been chosen as witness to their union. It was a gesture that made Johann feel as part of the family. She had watched him from the front porch of her parent's villa as he stood proudly. His head held high, he posed among others for a wedding picture and she did not realize that she too was included in this picture with little Rebekka squirming in her arms.

On occasions like these, the latest news of loved ones far and near were talked about and passed on. And it was here at the wedding she heard of Auntie Elena's death.

In a letter, Uncle Gustav wrote that Auntie Elena died of a broken heart. Apparently, she never got used to jungle life in Uruguay and succumbed to a deep agonizing homesickness. Most of all she yearned for her lovely home by the Black Sea and all the dear ones there. Uncle Gustav noted that because of what happened to his beloved wife. He regretted the move dearly.

Like everyone else she was deeply saddened by this news, remembering how happy Auntie Elena was in her grandiose villa.

--

As the seasons turned and spring once again transformed the landscape and Easter celebrations passed with all its rituals, Katina carried out the final steps to motherhood for the second time.

Little Julia arrived into the world in the latter part of April, her head already graced by black fuzzy hair. She was a little darling as far as Johann was concerned.

Katina too embraced her growing family. Her hope

renewed that she had overcome her setbacks.

She had dearly missed the togetherness with family. With fondness she recalled the warm summer evenings on her parent's front porch. She remembered the gaiety of laughter and storytelling and the harmonizing of familiar hymns and folk songs. It was told that even the patients and staff members from the neighboring tuberculosis hospital enjoyed their singing, as they would crowd around their windows practically stretching their upper torsos far over the sills to catch every word that was sung.

She definitely was ready and could hardly wait to take part in all the activities. Yet again, Dr. Pitmeier put a damper on her excitement. He stressed that it was in her best interest to start the anti-malaria treatments as soon as she finished nursing her second child. This time he hoped to time it right before the symptoms returned.

20

The evening was late, and the sky was darkening to twilight as Johann guided his horse drawn carriage through the streets of Mangalia. He looked over the town and thought carefully about what this evening would bring about.

Even with their personal setbacks, life in the past three years here in Mangalia had proven to be very prosperous. Business and family had both increased and he finally achieved the completion of his dream. For some time, he had his eyes on a beautiful piece of property overlooking the Black Sea and now was ready to purchase it.

However, upon further inquiry, his spirit was somewhat dampened. By chance he found out that he was not the only one interested in this piece of land. Of the several bidders on the property, there was a man by the name of Heinrich Schwarz that stood out as one of the stronger contenders. He had heard of this man's power and dealings, but he was still hopeful of purchasing the property.

The closing deal was to be finalized at a meeting tonight. It was to be held at the home of Herman Grundman, the same lawyer who had hired him to cut ice for his cold storage.

Now rising in position in the town he was starting to compete against those more powerful in the area. Yet he was not one to be deterred. He was determined to see his dreams through to completion. He had worked many difficult years getting where he was. And this opportunity to purchase this property was just what he needed to reach his goal.

He did not tell Katina the purpose of this meeting, for he feared it would only add unnecessary stress to her already weakened body.

Arriving at his destination he glanced around. In the darkness of the evening he noticed several other carriages more prestigious than his already in the yard. A lone dog barked in the distance as the attendant came to help him with the horses. He thanked the man and strode purposefully across the yard. His figure in the pale moonlight cast a long and ragged shadow on the ground in front of him as he approached the house.

Will he be able to make this deal? It was a perfect piece of property overlooking the sea. It was adjacent to the cobble stoned plaza and entertainment district, an ideal location for luxurious tourist accommodations.

The large familiar villa loomed in front of him. He remembered his humble beginnings delivering ice. A little nervous he knocked at the door. The servant named Mugur, who he had come to know from the ice delivery business, opened the door. Johann greeted him and exchanged a few friendly words. Tobacco smoke filled the reception hall. He immediately recognized some of the men who stood in groups, deeply involved in discussions. The land agent, Thomas Backer, whom he identified from previous dealings, nodded a greeting at him as he moved toward the first group of men.

"So... I heard you are going to bid on this land too Johann. If you are, you had better keep an eye on Schwarz. He has taken a sudden interest in this property and he has a lot of money behind him."

Johann nodded knowingly in reply. He followed Backer's gaze to Heinrich Schwarz across the room. What was his interest in this land? He studied the man through the cigar smoke, a thin haggard man with red hair and hard eyes. His appearance seemed to fit his reputation.

"I think I am well able to bid for this property," he replied coolly. He was getting anxious but made sure Herr Backer would not notice.

Herman Grundman appeared from a side chamber and greeted Johann warmly as he passed. He then paused for a moment, and with a serious undertone, commented, "I'll do what I can Johann, but there is some strong interest in that property here." He nodded to Thomas Backer and proceeded to the middle of the room.

He called the assembly to order and brought out the papers of the property. After describing the legal layout of the land, Herman Grundman asked for their sealed bids.

The tension grew as thick as the smoke as each party brought his bid forward and laid it on the table. In all there were five bids, including Johann's. He offered a little prayer as he walked back to his place beside Backer. He had bid higher than the rumored price and was sure he would get it, yet he could not help his distrust of Heinrich Schwarz. He had noticed an incredible hatred in the man's eyes as he was bringing his bid forward. Why such hatred? For a moment there he wondered what Schwarz was thinking and what he knew.

Before adjourning the meeting, Herr Grundman advised all those present, that he would look fairly at all the offers and within a couple of days would make the results known.

The night air felt cool and refreshing compared to the stale chambers he had just come from. He noticed Heinrich Schwarz turn, throwing a cold hard look toward him before taking off in his stately carriage. Herman Grundman witnessed this little incident and approached Johann, who was the last one leaving.

"Johann, I will give you one advice. Watch out for Schwarz. I have a feeling if you win this bid, it will really stir up trouble. He is a hard man to bargain with."

"I have no quarrel with him," Johann replied calmly.

"Nevertheless, I caution you to tread carefully and watch

the shadows. A man like that cannot be trusted."

"Thank you for your advice, but I have no reason to fear this man other than losing out on the property." Johann tried to play down Grundman's warning, yet something inside told him to heed the lawyer's advice.

With a warm farewell the men parted, while the attendant handed the reigns over to Johann. He hurried his horses on into the night, his eyes trying to penetrate the darkness around him. He had never feared anything. Why was he so uneasy? Was it Grundman's and Backer's warnings? Heinrich Schwarz was just another man who was interested in the land, just like him. Or was there something more behind those cold eyes?

He was glad when he finally reached the protection of his home. He could not believe how a little incident like that would cause him to look over his shoulder more than once.

Katina noticed the uneasiness in Johann as he entered the house but did not ask why. The strain and tiredness on his face told her to hold back with unnecessary questions, rather replace them with an understanding hug.

"Come sit down and relax while I prepare a cup of tea for you," she coaxed him gently.

"Your father and I just had a cup while we waited for you."

"How are the little ones?" Johann inquired when Katina returned with the tea.

"Besides Rebekka complaining about stomach-ache earlier this evening, they both seem fine," she calmly replied and with a smile added, "Father should know. He played with both before bedtime."

His father's face lit up with a broad smile. He loved the children. He did not mind Rebekka crawling all over him, with her constant chatting. It would not be long until Julia joined her as well. Father Wendel stroked his beard with a shy smile as he remembered Rebekka trying to pull at it.

"What can I say?" he said wistfully. "She was very rambunctious as always, doing her best to keep me from resting!" And with a twinkle he added, "But I didn't protest."

Katina smiled over Father Wendel's statement. She thought about the unborn child within her, it was her third pregnancy. Actually, it was her fourth if she counted the miscarriage between Julia and this one. Fortunately, there had not been a repeat of Malaria attacks, for which she was grateful. She believed fully, along with Doctor Pitmeier, that this time they had succeeded in their fight against this dreadful disease.

21

Days had turned into weeks and there was still no news about the outcome of the land deal. Johann tried to be positive and did his best not to lose hope, keeping himself busier than ever. That was especially true today, as two of his men did not show up for work this morning. He went to inquire and found himself confronted by a most peculiar warning.

"*Moarte... Moarte!*" meaning death... death, he heard a woman shouting from behind a partially open door. Shocked and confused by the caller, he asked to see Daniil.

"I've missed him at work today," he called back.

"Daniil... He's deathly ill," the woman replied.

'What's so deathly about a sickness that I can't go in to see him?' he pondered and motioned to step closer.

"*Moarte... Moarte!*" the woman cried out again.

Realizing that it was useless to go any further, he gave an understanding nod.

Bewildered he left the premises, only to find himself confronted with the same at the next employee's house, but this time he learned that it was because of typhoid fever.

"Typhoid?" he questioned in disbelief. "It can't be. There had to be a mistake."

Tired and confused he made his way homeward, only to be greeted with the news that little Rebekka too had fallen ill with the same fever.

"I called Doctor Pitmeier and after he examined her he

confirmed that she has typhoid fever." Katina swallowed hard to fight back the tears as she informed Johann. "They think it was brought in by the tourists."

He was speechless. He remembered the government officials concern at the overwhelming number of visitors earlier in the season. Twenty-two thousand to date were reported to have converged into town this summer, and the fear of sanitation problems arising from the overcrowding had been great. Now the outbreak of typhoid fever had proved their fears true. It was not enough that they had to deal with a large surge of malaria victims in these past years. Now they had the added worry of something far more devastating.

"Our home is under quarantine?" Johann knew the answer yet had to ask.

"Yes," she replied a little downcast. She was tired.

"They say it is to prevent the spreading... God only knows what good that'll do..." Distraught, she threw her hands up in the air and walked over to the stove. "Most of us have been in contact with each other anyway..." she continued but paused as she just remembered. "Oh... Doctor Pitmeier will be here tomorrow to immunize all of us."

He gave a listless nod and walked over to the day bed where Rebekka lay. His face turned white with anguish as he stooped down to touch her small forehead. It felt hot and sweaty. The pain in his heart increased as he stroked her tiny hand.

'This cannot be happening, not to his little girl.' He fought to gain control over his emotions. All at once he heard a tiny voice behind him.

Katina had brought Julia for him to hold, since she was preparing supper.

All this time he had been so consumed worrying about Rebekka that he neglected to pay attention to little Julia. Her arms stretched out; she was begging for Papa to take her. With one quick swoop he lifted her out of Katina's arms and gave her a long and loving hug. In his usual style he swayed her high above his head as the little one showed her delight by cooing in approval.

"How is my little angel today?" he asked in a proud yet tender way. Her dark brown eyes lit up with excitement. For she understood only too well that at this moment she was Papa's little darling and that is all she cared about.

With one last swoosh he sat down by the kitchen table with Julia on his lap. Supper was ready and it looked good. But with his mind still on Rebekka, the food somehow did not go down well. Her pale and almost lifeless body was in full view as she lay just a few feet from him.

To keep an eye on her during the day Katina had purposely laid her on a makeshift bed near the kitchen stove beside Father Wendel's corner bed. He had claimed the corner bed because of the heat from the oven. He said he needed the warmth. It helped ease the pain for his arthritis, especially in the cold winter months.

As the darkness of night approached, Johann and Katina took turns to watch Rebekka. The illness was like a wild animal on the prowl. It lurked in silence preying upon unexpected victims. Slowly it made its way from house to house; without distinction, attacking young and old, rich or poor.

At daybreak, the seemingly peaceful city was disrupted by the sound of a ringing bell. The town crier was proclaiming what they had feared and known all along. Their city was now in a state of emergency. As cases of typhoid and now cholera were being reported in alarming numbers. It was told that extra trains were standing by, and anyone who wishes to leave the city should do so within twenty-four hours.

Never had they seen the town in such an upheaval. Panic-stricken tourists now were jamming the station, all fearful of not making it out in time. The following day the city almost resembled that of a ghost town, only essential stores and businesses were open. The rest of the inhabitants mostly kept to their homes, bracing themselves for the worst.

As promised, Doctor Pitmeier kept his appointment. He showed up with an assistant to administer the immunization shots to each family member. In conversation he mentioned, that in all his days he had never seen anything like this. "It's like fighting an invisible enemy, not knowing when or where it would strike next," he told them and they understood, as he and others in his profession, were challenged to the overbearing endless task to aid the many poor suffering souls. It would be one that required their tireless devotion.

But despite the Doctor's good intention, no one disliked their kind more than Father Wendel. He protested to Johann and Katina afterwards.

"Those guys should be shot," he retorted. "Don't let them near me ever again... They are going to kill me, I tell you. If I ever get another one of those shots, you can bring me to the cemetery for sure."

Never had Johann seen his father so outraged. Yet he had to admit, after receiving the shots he too felt sick as a dog.

News got out that more doctors had been called in from other places to assist in bringing the epidemic under control. But even that did not help the matter. With so many people in need of medicine, they soon found themselves in short supply. The Doctors and staff were left to stand helplessly by, leaving many to die or if lucky find a cure of their own.

Every day Katina counted up to five corpses as they were carried past their house to the cemetery. The disease had struck dangerously close to home. Two teenage boys from the neighborhood were among the victims. It staggered her to think that little Rebekka might soon join them.

But to her surprise within a week Rebekka had become stronger and looked well enough to be out of danger. She went to prepare lunch and suddenly realized the pantry's low food supply. 'Was it any wonder with all that had happened and not being able to go to the market?' She contemplated for a moment how she could manage without taking Rebekka outside.

For some reason Father Wendel had gone to do errands of his own. And there was no one left in the house. Thinking the weather to be warm enough she did not give it a second thought. She dressed her two little girls and walked the short distance to the market. Yet soon after and to her dismay, she found out too late, that the incubation period for Rebekka was not yet over and a relapse occurred.

Now her little one was in much worse condition, as this time she also contracted malaria. The combination of the two illnesses plagued her tiny body in a most dreadful way. Among other complications, she also lost most of her beautiful hair and there was little anyone could do.

She had expected a lot of blame from Johann and the rest of the family that she had not heeded the incubation period. But to her agony no one gave her the satisfaction of making her feel guilty.

The following evening as they sat at the supper table, they noticed Rebekka's tiny body suddenly going into a seemingly endless stretch.

"I think this is it," Johann said solemnly. "I think she is going to die."

In helpless horror they watched as the little one suddenly opened her eyes wide in a stare.

"For the last time," Katina said in a hushed voice, "she is looking around for the last time."

Johann leaned over to stand by and give aid if necessary, when unexpectedly Rebekka started to speak.

"Papa, I want to eat little fishes."

In disbelief they looked at each other. Had they heard right...? Was this her last request? They just had small fried herring for supper, and she had always loved to eat them.

"Should we dare?" not sure, Katina asked both Johann and his Father. The two stood in bewilderment looking at the child and then at each other.

"What harm can it do? Let her have some," Johann gave in.

Quickly she made up a dish and gave it to Rebekka. To everyone's surprise she emptied the entire plate.

With tears in their eyes they kissed and hugged the little one.

"I think she has recovered. Our little Rebekka has recovered," Johann cried repeatedly as if to reassure himself that it was truly so.

--

Rebekka had indeed recovered. And after a couple of weeks she showed no symptoms of the illnesses that had plagued her. Finally, they could get back to normal everyday living. But to their dismay that hope was short lived, as once again the illness struck. And this time it put Julia and Johann onto sick beds. Although it did not affect the little one as hard and she soon recovered. Johann's condition though worsened with every passing day. Soon after contracting typhoid fever he also fell ill with cholera.

This time she and Father Wendel took turns tending to Johann day and night, keeping him as comfortable as possible. They watched over him with much care, continually washing and boiling all the linens and clothing.

After spending another tiresome night at Johann's bedside, she went to prepare breakfast. In passing she gave a glance out of the window, and to her horror she noticed the health nurse with her helpers in tow heading in their direction.

No doubt, she thought, they are coming to administer Johann with another dose of medicine. As it was the health nurse was now calling on Johann on regular basis.

Oblivious that this time they also had in mind to vaccinate each and every family member against cholera. She watched them approach. Suddenly she recalled the painful side effects from the previous shots. And as far as she and her family were concerned, they had gone through enough. Johann especially was in no condition to go through more suffering.

Quickly she locked the door and coaxed Rebekka to stay out of sight. She herself tried to hide with Julia, as gracefully as possible, underneath the kitchen table, which today was luckily covered by a long tablecloth.

Julia did as she told her, but Rebekka thought it funny that Mama was trying to hide. She decided instead to stand by the window smiling and waving to the nurse and her entourage.

"Rebekka…! Get away from the window!" she whispered in a scolding manner. But no matter what she tried; the little rascal did not budge. Rebekka gave an even broader smile. And looked back and forth, giving away her position.

"In the name of the law open the door!" the nurse shouted and pounded angrily at the door, then at the window.

She realized now that her little scheme had been discovered. But with a stubbornness of her own she did not open the door.

"You're not getting in this time," she vowed under her breath.

Father Wendel heard the commotion came to see what it was about. Spotting him from the corner of her eye, she quickly waved him to stay out of sight.

"I'm not going to let them in. Johann had gone through enough. I've made up my mind and no one can force me to change it," she whispered angrily.

"That's good. I agree with you. Don't let them in, otherwise it'll be the death of Johann," Father Wendel was onside, encouraging her not to give in.

The standoff lasted a good ten minutes. And even with the health nurse threatening to bring the authorities down on them, she stayed firm. This left the others little choice but to retreat and come back another day.

Father Wendel and her both knew they would be back. But for the moment they rejoiced over their small victory.

Suddenly, a knock at the door unnerved them. Surely the nurse had returned and this time with more reinforcements, she thought. Quietly, she and Father Wendel listened. Even the children remained silent, fear showing in their eyes.

"Does someone have to wait so long to be let in?"

"Papa...!" she called out with relief. Upon opening the door, she explained the locked door.

Papa had a good long chuckle, and then pulled something out of his coat pocket.

"Here," he said, holding a small bag in his outstretched hand. "I brought you something from old Ruben Yakowich. He gave this to me when I told him about Johann being ill."

For a moment, she stood in thought as she could not place the name.

"Remember the old homeopath who gave you the medicine for malaria?"

"Oh yes," it came to her suddenly, "The one with the long beard and dark eyes that looked twice the size whenever he used his spectacles to look you in the eyes."

"Now, now, don't make fun of him Katina. We've a lot to thank the Old Russian for," Papa scolded her lightly, shaking his finger at her.

"All right, all right," she waved Papa off. "Let me see what you have in that bag."

He handed it to her, and when she couldn't make out the contents, he acknowledged that it was charcoal.

"You're supposed to give it to Johann as prescribed on the bag. It's guaranteed to help against cholera and..." He turned to pick up a familiar contraption from a chair near the door, "I also brought along the *schreppmaschine*," also known as a *lebenswecker*.

Papa's *schreppmaschine* was the ultimate remedy when all else failed. The knowledge how to use it had passed from his father, who in turn had learned it from his father and so on. It was used cautiously and only when every other recourse had failed.

This stick-like device had fine needles attached to its top, used to open pores by puncturing the needles against the skin. After that, the poisonous ointment was rubbed over the area and left to penetrate. The hope was that the patient's body would awake and fight both the poison and the original infection. There was one drawback to the treatment, and a very critical one at that. The patient had to remain indoors and out of drafts for three days. If a person went outside before this time, death would surely follow.

Considering this, she had confidence in Papa's ability to make this treatment work. She remembered how it helped Robert back in Girargi, when after cleaning the premises of the oil mill a rat suddenly jumped out of the rubble and bit him. Not long after Robert developed sores all over his neck and head and soon became infected. Worried, Papa sought the help of doctors from as far as Constanta and Bucharest. After weeks of unsuccessful treatments in hospital Robert was sent home with the doctors stating they had done all they could for him. At this stage, the infected area had become one big open sore.

It had not been an easy decision to try the *schreppmaschine* and the blue stone. The stone was highly poisonous and was mainly used to treat animals. And even then, it was done with caution.

Papa had weighed the odds and with much thought came to this conclusion.

"If it worked... fine. If it did not, at least I've tried," he confided in Mama, and with much prayer, had gone ahead with the treatment. To everyone's astonishment, within three days, Robert had shown improvement. The entire infected area started to dry up and heal.

But there was another time, when the treatment had not worked out the way they had hoped. It was on that cool spring morning, around the time of the Great War. She and her sister Julia had received the treatment against typhoid fever. Papa at that time had been away to fight in the war. And Mama was left alone with eight little ones to look after.

She could not recall whether Grandpa Hauber had performed the treatment or someone else? Anyway, it happened when she and Julia were still within the incubation period. Mama had run outside that morning to catch the latest news as it was shouted out by the town crier. And as she turned to go back to the house; she noticed Julia standing behind her with bedding in her arms and in a delirium.

Right then and there Mama had said she knew Julia was done for. Sadly, as predicted, within a short time her young teenage sister died. Mama told her that she herself only survived because she had not left the safety of the house.

Considering all past experiences, Papa never entered lightly into these things and she knew it. That is why she trusted and respected his judgment.

And to her and everyone's relief, this time Papa's treatment worked, as Johann showed improvement within a week.

It was hard to say which of the remedies made Johann's health improve. Was it Papa's *schreppmaschine* or Ruben Yakowich's charcoal? She came to the conclusion probably all things combined had worked to get him back on his feet. Yes, probably even those dreadful shots from the community health nurse.

She herself as well felt stronger after the heavy dosage of anti-malaria medication. This time Dr. Pitmeier had succeeded.

22

In all the turmoil caused by the typhoid fever, the thought about the land deal had taken last place in Johann's mind. But now with all the sicknesses behind them, he hoped to take up where he left off.

Although the more he thought about the land the more uneasy he felt about it. It bothered him that he had not received news of the outcome. In the past he could always rely on prompt action from Grundman. Yet, this thing concerning the property had taken far too long. Something was not right, and he was going to see for himself what was holding it up.

He hitched up the horses to the coach and started off down the road.

As he approached the familiar grounds of Herman Grundman's estate, it struck him odd to find the yard without activity, as it usually was bustling with customers.

Strange, not even the coachman was in sight to tend to the horses. It was not like him to leave anyone waiting.

He stepped down from the coach, securely tying the horses' reigns around the post. He made his way over to the house. Knocking at the front door, he waited, and then knocked again. There was no answer. He looked around and noticed the un-swept steps and drawn window curtains. The whole place had a deserted look about it and it puzzled him.

Had the disease taken its toll in this house too? Was that the reason why there was no one around? He hated to think that it was so. A creak from the barn door across the yard made him spin around. His heart dropped to his feet. His legs literally shook when he tried to walk.

"Who's there? Anyone in there?" he called out, slowly making his way over to the barn. He was still shaking from the unexpected sound. Just then a terrible thought entered his mind. Why he happened to think of Heinrich Schwarz at this moment, he could not tell.

The barn door was ajar as he approached. He could now see the wind was playing with the large door as it creaked again. All at once a strong gust coming off the sea swung the barn door wide open. Johann stood paralyzed for a second. Why in the world was he so jumpy? He had nothing to fear. He was not doing anything illegal. He was just here to get some answers about the land deal... that was all.

He felt his heart pounding heavily inside his chest. He knew he had no right to snoop around on another man's property, but all this mystery was getting to him and he was dying to find out what had happened here.

He stepped inside and was overcome by a strong odor. It smelled like something had died. He looked around to see if there was a dead carcass of a horse or something. The poor creature probably starved to death with no one here to look after him. His mind raced with questions as he tried to make sense of all this. He searched the surroundings trying to adjust his eyes from the brightness outside to the semi-darkness of the barn. Two small windows let in just enough light to make out some detail.

"Nothing seems to be wrong here," he mumbled to himself as he climbed up to the loft. Scouring around, he stumbled over something. All at once the foul odor was overwhelming. He stooped and let out a gasp. It was Mugur's lifeless body, Grundman's trusted servant. By the looks of it he must have been dead for some time.

His stomach turned. He ran outside, confused and shaken by what he had just discovered. This definitely had taken him by surprise. What was he to do? His mind raced through a dozen options. He could consult Papa or Mark; whose homes were not far from here; maybe they had seen or heard something. Yes, that would be the best thing before contacting the authorities. They might just accuse him of one thing or another. He knew how they could twist events and facts. It would be wise to feel his way around first before asking questions.

Still, after his mind was made up, the unanswered questions remained as to who was behind all this and why?

He left Grundman's premises and was just about to guide the horses toward Papa's place when his eyes caught a glimpse of a man striding across the very same ten-hectare property he had hoped to buy. Without giving it another thought he veered the horses toward the man.

It was then that he realized it was Thomas Backer. Had he bid on the land himself? There was something not right here. He did not expect to see Backer looking at the property as if he was now the owner.

"This is a fine piece of land," Johann hailed Thomas Backer from the distance in his usually friendly manner.

Herr Backer returned the greeting, although he had no wish to speak with anyone who had participated in bidding for the land. He buried his thoughts and managed a smile, all the while stroking his chin. His expression changed and a shadow crossed his face.

"I just came from Grundman's place," Johann started. "But there is no one home. Do you have any idea where he might be?" He was cautious not to mention what he had found.

"Oh, didn't you know? He had to leave town on urgent business."

"But the place looks deserted; not even a servant around to look after things," Johann offered. All the while he was looking at Backer, hoping he might gain a clue.

Backer coughed and looked away toward the sea, pondering on something, his face sullen. After a moment he leveled his eyes again at Johann.

"All I know is what I've told you... and that's all I know."

Johann noticed the change in behavior and wondered. Backer was usually never short of answers or comments. Yet something of this news bothered the man. That Backer knew more was obvious. It was probably best not to mention anything more on the topic.

Johann looked over the property to every side.

"Ah, yes!" Herr Backer came back, "you wonder who the lucky one was?" Backer was his old self again. "You see my friend that is something I cannot help you with, for I, myself don't know."

"But why didn't Grundman send out notices to let us know of the outcome... or for that matter the reason for the delay."

"Look..." Backer was serious again and dark. "I will give you one good advice... Sometimes it's wise to leave things as they are. To probe around would only bring you trouble. I tell this to you as a friend... Don't ask any more questions. Let the matter go and forget about this land deal." He tried to smile but his mood did not let him.

Johann decided it was time to quit. He managed a friendly goodbye and with a tip of his hat toward Backer, he coaxed his horses to move on in the direction he had intended to go in the first place.

After consulting Papa and Mark about this matter. He followed their advice and reported it the same day to the local authorities. They stated the man had died of unknown causes.

Much to Johann's dismay, the local authorities did not take the time to find out more about the old servant's death. As an excuse they said they had enough on their hands with all the typhoid and cholera infestations. They could not be bothered with those already dead.

Old Mugur was buried, without further investigation, in the neighborhood cemetery, taking with him the secret of his death and Grundman's disappearance.

Johann felt upset and disillusioned about the handling of this situation. But there was little he or anyone could do to change matters. All there was left was to put the incident behind him and not think about it anymore.

--

Yet it was not long before he was able to put the event in a new perspective. Family and friends had gathered to hear firsthand reports from Robert. He recently returned from Germany where he had finished his final degree in the pastorate.

His report left everyone in great distress when he told them that many people were arrested and imprisoned for speaking out against the present government's methods of running the affairs of the Fatherland and its people. The government also willfully spread and encouraged hatred against all the Jewish people. All this supposedly was instigated and encouraged from the top, and as a result, the persecution and ridicule was spreading like a mad fire throughout the land. Now all the Jewish people had become open targets.

"Could this be the case in Herman Grundman's disappearance?" Johann thought out loud after listening to Robert. "Now that I think of it, I heard old Mugur mention to me once when I was cutting ice that Grundman was of Jewish descent."

"But this couldn't possibly be the case here," Dad Wendel exclaimed. "We are too far away from the homeland."

"Not far enough as we think we are, Father Wendel," Robert spoke assuredly. "From what I have heard in the Fuehrer's own words, he wants his people all brought closer to the Fatherland. And that means uprooting everyone of German descent. That would include us too, here in Romania and surrounding countries. And while doing so he is weeding out the unwanted. And what I can gather from Johann's account of the Grundman's affair; we probably have spies already working here for the Reich," Robert paused to think. The last words spoken left an ominous feeling in the room.

Troublesome lines formed on Robert's brow when he spoke again.

"In all seriousness now, let this be a warning to all of us to be careful who we're dealing with and calling our friends... Things are definitely not the same as they once were. I have great concern for all of us here especially if the unrest spreads. Another world war will then be inevitable... Just think what all this could mean..."

Papa listened carefully but could not agree. "Now hold on Robert. I think you are exaggerating. How can events happening so far away possibly be a threat to us here? I for one do not think we are in any danger. Besides, I have no desire to have my family go through another war. Let them fight their own war." Papa stopped talking and took a deep breath. Just the thought that Robert might be right left him very upset. But moments later he retreated and spoke with a changed attitude.

"Now please, everyone... let us not panic and worry about tomorrow and its outcome. So far, we have always trusted God for his protection, why should we not this time?"

Katina sat quietly listening to the conversation. Her thoughts wandering back to peaceful, more beautiful days. Where, in their first year of marriage, she and Johann had spent many memorable hours strolling along the bleached white sand dunes by the sea. Aside from the illnesses, she and her family had experienced prosperous and carefree times here. Was it possible all this would suddenly change?

Her thoughts were of her unborn child. It was the beginning of June. She would be due any day now. What was in the future for this little one and all her family? Where would they be in the coming year? All this talk of war left her greatly concerned. But she had to leave her worries to the others and focus on the things before her. Tomorrow was to be the due date and it would come none too soon.

As expected, the following day she went into labor. Johann once again setting his hopes on a boy was disheartened when instead he was presented a little girl. Yet after holding this tiny screaming bundle in his strong arms, his disappointment soon dissipated. He realized anew it was of no importance as long as the little one was healthy.

All along they had been concerned of the effects the Malaria medicine would have on this little one's health, especially after she had miscarried between Julia and Elisa, their third daughter. Doctor Pitmeier also was concerned, admitting the little one into the Hospital for observation, but a month later he confirmed that aside from the colic the little one was in fairly good health.

23

It was three months after Elisa's birth when the realization sank in that Robert's spoken words proved true. They indeed were affected by what was happening in the Fatherland. What was dreaded suddenly became reality. Like an omen, the news of the Polish invasion by German forces left everyone doubtful for their future. Robert had been right all along.

For some time now life for many colonists here in Romania had been unsettling. Especially for farmers, as the scarcity of land suddenly became dominant and the future for their children looked bleak. Only the wealthy settlers managed to survive, those who had accumulated land before the law had passed. It was a law that prohibited all German colonists from buying land. Struggling to make a living, the farmers, who could not survive on just a few hectares, were left to work as laborers in stone quarries.

Katina thought back about the land deals and how they had evolved. She had learned that it was because of King Carol I of Romania that their kind had gained the rights to own land. It was he who had encouraged them to do their best to flourish and make their settlements a showpiece.

And it was he who had brought about the building of new streets, bridges and railroads. The longest bridge by Cernavoda was named in his honor. He also encouraged the building of new schools and brought about new legislative reforms. He had set up lucrative exports for his citizens' thriving economy and had built large silos in the port of Constanta to store all the excess grain.

She remembered the year when she as a young girl stood among other school children with their teachers to welcome the king. Each school assembled according to their nationality, proudly displaying their individual flags. It was then for the first time that she saw him arriving in his stately car. It was the first automobile she ever saw, and she remembered the day clearly.

She stopped in her thoughts. It seemed so long ago.

She pondered why; when things were going good, other forces always seemed to invade the land with devastating results? Why can't good times last?

Now in hindsight Papa had made the right choice at the time when he sold the land in Cogealac. The farm he had inherited there from his father would not have been enough to sustain his large and expanding family. With buying into the sunflower-oil business in Girargi and expanding it farther here in Mangalia, it had definitely paid off.

Although even in this venture if one did not know the language of the land well enough one could be taxed out of his business just as it happened to other mill owners. So, with Papa's ingenuity and calculated move he was able to help all his children to establish themselves with property and businesses of their own. And like him, many of their extended families had done the same and had prospered.

Yet with the cry of war, their future too had become uncertain, as the order soon came down from the Romanian Government that all able-bodied men were now required for work duty. Johann and her older brothers and their cousins were among the drafted. Most of those taken were foreigners, such as Turks, Bulgarians, Ukrainians, Germans and others.

With the younger men gone, the women were left to look after home and family once again. Katina remembered the time when Papa had to fight in the Great War and Mama too was left alone with eight children. It had not been easy for her to take care of all the children as well as house and farm work.

Yes, she could understand now what Mama had to put up with, especially at that time. Safety for family and property was of great concern, as any strangers could come and take what was not theirs. She was glad now that Father Wendel was living with her and the children, but also, that her parents were not too far away to help if need be. The same went for her sisters-in-law, as they had all promised to look out for one another.

With all that taken care of, it was the men they worried most about. The goodbyes had been bittersweet as no one knew how long it would be before they would see each other again.

This action from the Romanian Government brought home again that they were only strangers here in this land, with little rights or privileges. The change had come after King Carol II was forced into exile and King Michael I had taken over to reign with prime minister Ion Antenescu.

She thought back, remembering the history of this land. It had seen many well fought wars, overrun by multitudes of ravaging foreign forces that often had left the land and its people in a desolate state. And by the way things looked, no one knew if the same would happen again.

"Take good care of everything while I'm gone..." Johann's concerned voice still resonated in her mind. Now heavy-hearted, Katina sighed as it had been months and still no news of Johann's or her brothers' whereabouts. This was in late spring of 1940.

--

Johann found himself near Babadag in the northern Dobrujan region. The work in this mountainous area was hard, with little mercy given to them from their Romanian guards. On top of that, the meager food rations they received were hardly enough to keep them going. Their accommodations were deplorable. Sleeping often just where

I WILL REMEMBER ALWAYS

they had stopped working for the night on hard and uneven ground. It seemed to him that all the men working in his group were from other parts of this region. It was hard to know as not much time was given to converse with one another; with the Romanian guards standing over them, slave driving them, watching their every move. He worried for Katina and the children as well as his father. He wanted so much to let them know that he was okay.

Then by chance one day the opportunity presented itself. He happened to overhear that one of the men, because of death in the family, was allowed to go home. And of all things the man was from Mangalia. Taking the opportunity and knowing very well that they were not allowed to tell of their whereabouts, he managed to give the man a message to let Katina and his father know that he was all right. The man agreed and did as he was told.

--

Katina was more than surprised to suddenly see a stranger standing at her door telling her of Johann's message. Asking him as to where and for how long they would be detained, the man declined to give an answer. He simply shrugged his shoulders and told her he did not know.

Well at least she knew that Johann was in no immediate danger. With that she comforted herself. Yet the question remained, for how long?

--

After months of drudgery and to the work group's surprise, one day the Romanian guards suddenly put down their weapons. Johann and the others in their camp were told they were free to go home. Upon leaving he gave one more glance around pondering the purpose of this secret military base.

--

Before the draft he had planned to build rental villas on his father's land. The ten-hectare property located behind the entertainment plaza, in his mind, was just the ideal location

131

for this purpose.

Yet to start a sizeable project such as this, he was told at the time by the Mangalian Authority that he needed a special license. Willingly he had agreed to honor this request. But when he heard of the asking price, he was shocked, his spirits dampened, as all their savings had gone into building their home.

Unable to go further, the draft suddenly came in between, halting all his plans. Now released from his duties he hoped to pursue where he had left off. But there was still the issue with the money to buy the license. Struggling to find ways, Papa agreed to stretch out the requested sum.

Yet later when sitting in front of the notary to make the payment, they were suddenly told to wait. Dumbfounded, they both listened as the man revealed in a hushed tone of voice there might be no need for this as he heard rumors they were soon to be moved.

"Mind you, we rather see you people stay here," he said slyly. "Yet on this matter there is strong opposition from the top German officials..." With that the man suddenly stood up, showing a friendlier demeanor, he led them to the door. "We hope the Fuehrer will have a change of heart. Hmm...?" he smiled again his head lowered to one side to point the way to the exit. He opened the door and gestured for them to step outside.

Still in disbelief by what they had heard, they went home and told the others.

24

It was late fall when the order came. And all families of German descent were told to report to the nearest registration office to be counted for repatriation.

Johann remembered what the official had told, and after some consideration, he and Katina as well as his father, registered with the first order given, but Papa refused. He was not yet convinced that he and the rest of his family should be moving. He even expressed this publicly, whereby he was confronted by an angry Macedonian, saying, if he, 'Papa,' is not moving out of his villa... He personally would slit his stomach and hang him out to dry.

The Macedonians were ousted from neighboring Bulgaria, which had recently fallen under Russian influence. And because Mangalia was so close to the Bulgarian border it had received more than its share of the evacuees. Once here, they lived in crowded conditions among their fellow countrymen or out on the street in makeshift living quarters. They had literally torn their shacks apart and brought them along in scraps and pieces. She recalled them coming with their wagons stacked high, and she was amazed to see their oxen pulling such a heavy load.

Yet with their arrival came the hostilities of war, as witnessed in Papa's case. It showed more and more as the Macedonians waited to take over the soon abandoned homesteads. Their patience wearing thin, many had to be restrained and warned from becoming too aggressive.

On the third of November, SS officers arrived to oversee the final move. They were to make sure everything was going according to their government's wishes. Also, to give protection wherever it was needed to have the process of evacuation go in an orderly and peaceful manner, for this she was grateful, as it eliminated unnecessary hardship.

The thought of moving quickly became reality, when she and Johann witnessed the officers going from place to place. Their job was to estimate properties, homes, livestock, machinery and all such items. It was done in consideration to reimburse everyone, according to their worth.

Their home like all others looked like disturbed beehives, as household goods were sorted and decided upon. Hard decisions had to be made of what was worth keeping or selling, or just leaving behind. Many natives and non-natives alike heard of this. And she had seen them coming from near and far, all wanting to take advantage of the cheap or possible free deals. As for the rest of their valuables, they were told to store them in crates. It was necessary to have them transferred ahead on freight trains and cargo ships.

Yet there was unsettling talk about the command to move. She heard that it had taken most of their fellow countrymen by surprise. And most were not pleased to go. This year in particular some of them had the best crop year ever. Life for most had finally taken a turn for the better. She had seen it even here with her own family, with many were reluctant to leave, especially those who had accumulated a lot of wealth.

Because of this, a group of their own countrymen were trying to resist the move. Some were even willing to get rid of their representatives.

It was becoming brutal and she could see no good in all of this. Suddenly it was man against man, everyone trying to grab and hold onto what had been and was rightfully theirs. It was not only true with the common man, but also with those in government. Why, it was just the other day when she and others heard of prominent statesmen and generals being assassinated in large numbers.

She recalled the day the news of the massacre was publicized. And how, in a most brutal fashion, it had been carried out outside the town of Bucharest near a wooded glen. She shuddered at the thought of the brutality and hoped that it would not happen here.

The task before her, of sorting and packing, was a tedious one and she could not help but feel a deep depressing loss.

"What was all the hard work for, of saving and accumulating more goods and properties, all the hardship, for what?" Words left her suddenly as she was overcome by tears. Quickly she wiped them off her face and grudgingly went about her work. Unfortunately, it had to be done as soon as possible as yet another job awaited her.

It was just this morning, when a second order was announced. And everyone was told to go and buy as many clothing items and linens as possible, since their currency would soon lose value in the exchange.

As she was brooding over all the turmoil and injustice, memories of earlier times suddenly entered her mind. After their marriage they had worked diligently, collecting and buying all these precious items to make their home warm and welcoming. Now parting with most felt utterly disheartening.

"Poor Johann," she sighed. He wanted so much to have this home. Soon it will belong to someone else, no more will its walls resound their laughter of joy. Their home was built of dreams and longings, where peace and love had flourished.

She sighed again. 'What was in store for them out there? Where would their next home be? Would it be a friendly place, or...?' She shuttered by the thought of not knowing.

"Why? Dear God... Why?" she questioned.

Her thoughts turned from the now to the distant past, as she recalled the journey of her ancestors. It had been retold and kept alive; passed on from generation to generation.

In the 1700's, her forefathers had left their plagued and

poverty-stricken homeland. They trekked by oxcart halfway across the European Continent, all for the promise of land.

Included in this deal was a ten-year tax exemption and immunity from military duties for them and their offspring. But what really had drawn them to this far away place, she believed, was the promise of religious freedom.

This package deal had been offered to them by the then reigning Russian Czarina Catherine the Great. In addition, she promised food and lodging as soon as they crossed the Russian border to the time of settlement. Knowing by then many of the settlers would be at the brink of their resources.

--

She sat down for a moment in thought, watching the girls play among the packed parcels and suitcases. Johann and his Father had gone outside to take inventory. They were told the officials would come this afternoon to evaluate their possessions and properties.

She remained a little longer, returning her attention once again to the past. "Where was I now?" she said in a half loud voice. "Oh yes..."

As her father told, the colonists had prospered in the Odessa region of Russia. And to the delight of the Government the almost empty land was dotted with clean-looking villages. The once harsh and barren plains had turned into rich crop-bearing soil.

Yet a century later their bright hopes and dreams of the land ceased. With their privileges suddenly removed. The Russian oppression toward the colonists was at times unbearable. And when after years of crop failures, a powerful earthquake devastated the land, many were left without means and in fear for their lives.

Most of the settlers were ready to abandon their land. She recalled her forefathers were among those colonists, looking now toward the Turkish-occupied Romanian-Dobrujan provinces.

In October of 1842 it was reported that a considerable

I WILL REMEMBER ALWAYS

amount of the Colonist families left the Akkierman region by the Dnieste River. But it was passable only with the payout of 60 to 80 silver rubles per person to the Russian government.

Yet their ordeal was far from over. At their release, the Russian Government also issued for them to be sent back to Germany. But after so many years for most there was nothing to go back to. Left with no home country they wandered aimlessly for six weeks. Hungry and exhausted and their means depleted. They finally found refuge in the northern Turkish occupied Romanian town of Galatz.

She released a deep sigh. She remembered Papa and Grandpa Hauber telling stories, how here in the Dobrujan region, life too had often been unfair and sometimes cruel.

Their start was primitive. The land they had been assigned to was desolate endless grassland. Their first homes were those of in-ground dugouts with reed covered roofs, reinforced with mud. The same was erected for their animals.

With the low-lying homes, these villages were not easily seen in winter, as they looked like snowdrifts from afar. Yet as primitive as they were, the settlers were glad to have these humble abodes. It at least gave them protection from the icy cold north winds; but most of all from the rampage of hungry wolves.

She remembered Grandpa Hauber telling stories how they had to secure their doors and even lock up their dogs and livestock to save them from the hordes of wolves that roamed the steppe in large numbers in search of food.

"It was eerie to hear them scour over the low-lying roofs and hear their spine-tingling howls. By morning you could see the evidence, as their paw prints were all over the place," he had said.

Just to think of it now gave her goose bumps. But wolves were not the only concern, she was told, as the battle with the elements was ongoing. The colonists soon learned that it was wise to take shovels into their shelters before locking themselves in for the night. As with the roofline at ground level it was not unusual to be covered by deep snow.

She could not imagine herself in that predicament. Life must have been hard especially with small kids to look after. She shuddered to think how they could have survived this trying time. As with winter behind them, summer too had its plagues with the merciless heat and torturous mosquitoes.

Grandpa Hauber had often said that life at times seemed like an impossible feat. But no matter what danger or weather condition, work had to be done.

Come spring the old ancient untouched ground had to be readied for plowing and tilling. And because of shortage of workers, even the children had to help, sitting on the horses' backs and guiding them while father held the plow steadily pushing it deep into the soil.

From the wee hours of dawn until late in the evening they had worked hard. The only break they allowed themselves was for a quick bite to eat. In the case of a young family it was not usually that the mother too had to help along, as the sod needed to be dug and dried then stacked and put away for the cold winter months. It was necessary fuel to heat their home and cook their meals. Although in summer's heat all cooking and baking was done outside.

As Grandpa Hauber put it, life at best was trying. But the colonists prevailed and many were beginning to feel at home once again. Yet things were far from over when another obstacle presented itself.

Seeing the accomplishment of the settlers, the Turkish government took it upon themselves and placed a large number of Tartars in between the German settlements. Unfairly, the European colonists were told to give up their best land. And if that was not enough, they were also ordered to build homes for the newcomers as well as barns to house their animals.

She stopped for a moment in her thoughts. It was amazing

I WILL REMEMBER ALWAYS

to her how their people could have survived all this hardship. But then she remembered Grandpa Hauber telling that the lifespan in those early years was low, especially in women.

As it happened the Tartars were not the only ones to encroach on them. In 1864 after years of warfare the Russians succeeded to oust a large group of unwanted inhabitants from the Caucasus region. To the colonists' dismay some wild and work-unfriendly people also came to settle near their settlements, showing themselves to be a dangerous and burdensome lot.

Grandpa told that colonists living closest to these unruly folks were so overwhelmed by the constant plundering and stealing. They had no choice but to abandon their homesteads, with some taking refuge in the much larger settlement of Cogealac. Distressed by this injustice, the settlers sought help from the German Embassy in Istanbul. And after some time of stating their grievances they finally got through to the Turkish officials. Needless to say, it took the might of the Turkish army to cast out these unwanted folks from this region.

Yet peace did not last. She recalled Grandpa saying, that a few years later trouble once again loomed on the horizon.

In 1877-78 when Russia was at war with the Turks, Romania was pulled into the fight. Russia succeeded to win back the land and Romania won back the once occupied Dobruja. Amidst all the warfare the colonists had endured much, finding their properties ransacked again by the same lot of intruders. But this time they fought back and were successful to drive them out of the area.

Years later in 1916 on the outbreak of the Great War, the Romanian Government ordered all able-bodied men to help fight in the war. What were perceived to be peaceful years in the settlers' minds now proved the opposite as deep hatred had developed toward the foreigners and many of the German men ended up in Romanian prison camps.

She thought back. Why some were spared she did not

139

know. Anyway, her father was among those called for war duty. And like so many other women, her mother too was left alone to look after the children and the whole household. She recalled that time when the typhoid fever claimed her sister Julia's life.

During the absence of the men, the more vulnerable isolated colonists' homesteads and villages were again at risked of being raided. Their women left helpless against this, buried in haste what was left of their household goods. They fled with their children to escape the abusive and ravaging forces. Yet, in a hurry to erase the traces of buried goods, they found the last of their belongings taken. It was told, what the Romanian and Russian army left behind the Turkish and Bulgarian troops were sure to take with them.

Then in 1917-1918 under the German rules, when Romania was fighting against Germany the European farmers were forced to give up part of their food production; both to supply the German army and Germany itself. It was not unheard of that German soldiers would come and take from the colonists' farms whatever they needed, be it cows or horses. Many mothers were left in hopeless despair not knowing how to feed their children. Without the horses, the whole process of plowing and planting the land came to a standstill.

Luckily for some, a farmer who was spared from war duty and left with older horses that were unfit for the army, came to their aid and seeded at least five acres. But the yield from these few acres was hardly enough to get them through the winter.

Yet because of this forced collaboration with the homeland, many settlers had to suffer for it later. As a Romanian could easily accuse a German of wrongdoing and get away with it. After the Great War, five hectares of land was promised to everyone who had helped fight on the Romanian side. Papa was among those who had chosen to fight for his adopted Homeland. But sadly, even this promise was not carried out truthfully, favoring the original inhabitants over the foreigners during the land distribution.

Papa had taken it in stride, but not all were as forgiving. He had told of those men who had survived the war and came back to their eradicated desolate homesteads. Many of them packed up and left Romania with their families. Some immigrating to America and Brazil while others made their way back to Russia.

Yet through all the setbacks most colonists who remained had fared well, especially during the reign of King Carol. But unfortunately for them it did not last and now they too were on the move.

She shuddered at the thought remembering the journey of her forefathers. Yet it gave her courage. In faith her forefathers had stepped out and in faith she and her family would follow to do the same. They had to trust that the God of her ancestors would also protect and accompany them, wherever this whole ordeal would take them.

And with this thought in mind she went to finish the overbearing chore before her.

--

The following day Mama and Papa invited her to come along for the shopping spree in Constanta.

It was a beautiful calm fall morning when they set out by coach. Robert had agreed to drive them to Caraomar to catch the train there, and then pick them up again later in the evening. She was glad now she had agreed to come along. It would give her a chance to see Tara again as they were to meet her in Constanta.

Pressed for time, and with all that was going on, Johann had not been able to go along. Now with Mama's and Papa's offer, he had coaxed her to go, while he opted to stay back and look after things at home.

As she entered the half empty railcarriage, she followed Mama and Papa to a vacant window section and took the seat across. Settling in they were soon involved in small talk about the latest events. But when the two started to discuss between themselves of what items they needed to buy, she took the chance to sit back to relax and observe.

Some people around them were talking while others just sat in silence staring out the window, watching as the train rolled northward. It was hard not to see the strain on their faces from all the upheaval.

She leaned her head against the bench-seat and gazed out of the window as familiar towns and villages passed. It brought back not so sweet memories of times gone by. Brief sadness touched her heart as she remembered. In all the years since then, she had not quite been able to erase Stefan's tragic death from her memory.

She wondered now whatever became of Marika and Duza. Would she ever meet them again? A smile crossed her lips when she thought of Marika's sneaky way to get her to go out with Stefan. With the situation they were in now, she doubted she would ever see her again. And soon they would be far from this place.

She was still deep in thoughts when she heard the conductor announce Constanta, their final stop.

Tara was already waiting when the train pulled into the station. It was a happy moment for all, for they had not seen or heard from each other for quite some time now. And there was so much to catch up and talk about.

Among things, Tara told Papa about the SS officials who had paid them a visit a few days ago. Jokingly she added that he too can expect a visit. Like Papa, Micha too had been hesitant to part with the estate. But after the official's visit he had a quick change of heart.

Papa had heard about the SS and their dealings and even after Tara's warning, his decision remained unchanged.

"Well, Tara..." he said assuredly. "I'll deal with them when the time comes. Let it be said just between us now... They have to be very persuasive if they think they can push me off my property."

"Believe me Papa, they are," Tara said in a most convincing way. She decided to stop pressing Papa, after noticing he was not willing to see things her way.

Once in town, they went from store to store to look for the best deals and every possible bargain. Weighing what was absolutely necessary for the journey and beyond.

In all the years from her first visit here in Constanta, Katina noticed not much of a change. It still was the same bustling town. The way she had remembered when Auntie Elena had given her and Tara a tour through the city. She sighed as she recalled that day. She wished Auntie Elena would still be here, welcoming them with open arms. It pained her, knowing it could never be.

So far this whole day seemed one big memory trip into the past, as familiar surroundings kept reminding her of special and not so special events.

Tirelessly now, she and the others kept pushing themselves to finish what they had set out to do. After hours of shopping, Papa was the first to suggest that it was time to take a break. They agreed, as all the walking had made them tired and hungry.

Searching now for just the right place, they sat down at one of the sidewalk cafes. Distracted by the sights and sounds around them, they sat enjoying the atmosphere of the moment. Suddenly, startled by someone calling her name, Katina turned to look and could not believe her eyes.

"Marika!"

Katina jumped to her feet and held an outstretched hand to welcome Stefan's friend.

"How wonderful to see you again, I did not expect this... What a surprise..." She was bubbling over for joy while Marika stood beaming.

"Oh, forgive me," Katina caught herself, remembering that neither of her parents had ever met her.

"Mama, Papa, I'd like for you to meet Marika, an old friend of Stefan's. Remember?" She turned to Tara. "The one, I met on the train that time I came to see Doctor Lepra."

Tara nodded and smiled, while Mama and Papa sat puzzled, for Katina had never told them about her. Just the same, they gave her a warm welcoming smile.

"Come sit down and tell me a little about yourself... Did you and Duza ever get married?" Katina questioned eagerly waiting for an answer.

"Me and Duza... Oh no Katina. There was never anything serious between us. Duza and I were just school friends. He had come here only to upgrade his degree in business commerce. Besides, with him being from Krivoy Rog, he never intended to make Romania his permanent homeland. And I would have been too stubborn to leave Constanta. I love this city and the sea too much to ever move from here. Oh no, Katina... I've married one who shares my ideals and dreams and I'm very happy here." Marika stopped for a moment, dealing with her own curiosity, asked bluntly and without thinking.

"What about you Katina? Have you ever been able to get over Stefan's suicide? Oh... I am sorry... I shouldn't..." She apologized, suddenly realizing from Tara's face expression that she was stepping on a still very touchy subject.

"It's quite all right Marika. No need to apologize." Katina quickly intervened. "It was a very dramatic and sobering time for all. One I hope we do not have to go through again. As for me..." her face took on a fond expression. "I'm married to the most wonderful man, whom I love very dearly, and we've been blessed with three darling daughters..." Her voice trailing, she added. "But I do not know what the future will hold for them or for that matter, all of us. The way things are right now, it does not look very promising. We had so many plans Marika. Now they're..." With a heavy sigh she shrugged her shoulders, adding, "You've probably heard about the evacuation order."

"Yes," Marika said solemnly. "And I can understand how hard it must be to leave a land you've grown up and set roots in. I for one would be very devastated."

"Thanks Marika, for understanding," Mama said appreciably. "Lately not many of your countrymen share this view."

"Yes… it's a terrible thing…" Papa said thoughtfully. "Yet, there seems to be little we can do about it." Releasing a deep sigh, he slowly got up from his chair. "But for now, I think we should get on with our shopping. It's been well over an hour since we sat down."

"Oh, my goodness, has it been that long?" Marika exclaimed and got up suddenly gathering her belongings; they all followed to do the same.

"It was so nice to see you again Marika…" Katina said wholeheartedly and stretched out her hand in farewell.

"Same here," Marika replied with fondness. Turning to the others, she added, "I wish you all God's protection on your journey. Take care of yourselves."

They waved to each other one more time as they parted. Katina watched for a moment until Marika disappeared among the crowd. She knew she would not see her again. Abruptly she turned and followed the others as they continued their bargain hunting.

Tired and drained from the day's event, they arrived home late in the evening. And considering the time, Mama suggested for her to spend the night at their place, and then go home in the morning.

Reluctantly she agreed, as by now everyone at home, including Johann, would be fast asleep, and she certainly did not want to disturb them.

Exhausted, she settled down for the night after Mama had fussed over her and they said goodnight to each other.

It did not take long for her to fall into a deep and dreamless sleep. All that walking around and buying had made her exceptionally tired.

Hours later Mama was at her bedside.

"Katina, hurry… Get out of bed quickly… the house is

shaking... It's an earthquake!" Mama spoke in haste, hurrying her on.

It did not take long, and they were both outside, where Papa and the rest had already assembled on open ground. Everyone was laying flat against the trembling surface.

It all had happened so fast, there had been no time to think. Now laying face down on the ground she suddenly remembered Johann and the girls.

"Johann!" She cried out in desperation and motioned to get up.

"Stay down, Katina," Mama's hand was upon her, pulling her back down.

"But... I have to go... Johann, the children, they need my help," she stammered nervously.

"Don't worry... Johann knows what to do," Mama reassured her, "Besides Father Wendel is there to help him."

She took her place again on the ground, as it continued to rumble and shake furiously.

This whole front beach property, which Papa had built upon, had once been reclaimed from the sea. And she hated to even think what could happen to all the buildings.

The dwellings nearby moaned and groaned as the force of the quake threatened to destroy their very foundation. Again and again, loud horrific thunderous rumbling shook the ground inspiring fear among all. The outcry of her younger sister Edwina joined the terrified gasps of the others, mingled with her mother's whispered prayers, who lay closest to her. She felt a strange tightness in her throat, terrified with fear, her hands grasped tight against the ground. She looked up toward the misty dark grey sky, which at this moment looked just as foreboding as the land and sea around her. She thought of Johann and the little ones and was filled with worry.

"I hope they're all right. I would never forgive myself if..." she quavered. All at once there was an eerie quiet. The quake subsided just as fast as it had appeared.

Still frightened and in shock, they listened, investigating the ground around them. Papa cautioned for everyone to stay put while he and Robert went to inspect the damage.

Over the dark and gloomy sea, the day was dawning along the eastern horizon. It brought a faint light of hope when Robert returned with the report.

"The major structure of the house has been spared. It is still sound, and we can go back inside. There are some things that need repair, but these are minor." Robert looked down. "As for the mill..." his voice left him, he swallowed hard fighting back the tears.

Over the years they had worked so hard to it build up. Now with one blow, the main machinery, a thick heavy steel grinding plate from the oil press, had split in two. There was other damage, but the loss of that plate meant the loss of the mill.

Carefully she followed the others to see for herself. Pulling her mother's shawl tight around her chilled body, she stopped at the doorway to take a peek inside. But the dusty semi darkness in the building made it almost impossible to see. She decided to move closer to the inside to have a better look. When all at once her eyes fell upon her father's motionless figure stooped in front of the broken machinery.

"Come Katina... come into the house..." Mama coaxed her quietly, gently tugging her by the arm. "He needs to be by himself." When they were outside again and crossing over to the house, she spoke solemnly. "I'm sure by now you all know the struggle your father has in giving it all up." She paused for a moment while sidestepping over fallen debris from the nearby buildings. "That's why its best we leave him alone... It isn't easy for me either, but..." she choked down some tears. "So much of him went into this project..." She paused again overwhelmed by the anguish of it all. "Now... it is between him and his Maker."

Katina could not help but feel concern for her father. But her mother was right; at this given moment none of them could do or say anything to help Papa.

The violent force of the quake had left all of them in a daze, unsure of what to do next. There was so much debris in the house that needed to be cleared away. Even the furniture had been tossed about like toys.

Her brothers busied themselves tackling the bigger items in the house. Mama, Edwina and she took charge of the kitchen. They started salvaging Mama's good china. Then they gathered pots and pans and other household items. There was food also that needed to be collected and saved.

Suddenly everyone stopped from whatever they were doing. They had noticed Papa entering the house. A quiet hush fell upon the room; they could see he had been crying. Papa managed a vague smile as he hung his coat on the wooden rack. He cleared his throat indicating to speak, but the words did not come. He needed to show strength in front of his family. Yet again was overcome by tears. Finally, he managed; his words were somber and full of defeat.

"Helena..." He only addressed Mama in this fashion when he needed to say something important. "I think it wise that we too should start packing... Today, I will go and register us for the move," his voice broke by the last word.

Katina could feel the pain her father was going through. She was sure the others felt it too as they sat in silence, their eyes moist, listening to him speak. She realized that deep in their hearts her parents had known all along it was a losing battle and they eventually had to give in to the authorities.

That was the reason why she and Johann had registered with the first notice given. Although she had to admit, it had not been without a struggle. As for Father Wendel, well, he did not care anymore what happened to him. He had lost so much, loved ones included, when they fled Yevpatoriya. Ever since that time his spirit was crushed. It had left him a hollow broken man. Now she feared the same for Papa, seeing how hard it was on him.

Mama suddenly was the first to break the silence.

She walked teary eyed over to Papa and gave him an understanding hug. "It'll be all right Joshua. There's nothing for us here anymore."

"Yes Papa, we... that's all of us here, agree with Mama..." Robert stepped forward to underline the statement. "Besides, if we would stay, I doubt we'll survive, even for one day. Once our countrymen have been moved and the protection of the German officials has gone... need I say more? You've heard it yourself from one of the Macedonians."

"Yes," Papa said thoughtfully. "You're all so right. Things have definitely changed for the worse. God only knows what is best for all of us. You'll probably remember what I had said, that I'll only move if God gives me a sign. Well, after today... I'm totally convinced that he wants us to go."

This conviction brought tears of sadness to everyone, but also deep contentment of knowing the inner battle was over. Now all that was left for them to do was to ask for strength to go on. Also pray they will not be forsaken wherever they had to go.

25

Robert accompanied Katina home in the early morning and upon arrival she learned from Johann that the foundation of their house had cracked. There also was minor damage to the rest of the buildings. Other than that, besides being a little shook up, everyone seemed to have come out unharmed from this horrifying ordeal. Her worries were put at ease, seeing how Johann and Father Wendel had taken every precaution to protect the little ones.

Rebekka and Julia could not help but rattle on, telling her all about the scary sounds and rumblings. How Papa and Grandpa had rushed them outside and how afraid they were.

"We were all worried for you, Mama!" The two girls crowded around her, hugging her.

"Well, I was very worried for all of you too, and I'm very glad you're all safe." Katina hugged the girls lovingly back, giving Johann a thankful smile as he looked on.

"Don't I get a hug too?" he inquired.

"Most certainly." Katina flung her arms around his neck and gave him a hearty kiss. "That's for being such a good father."

"And husband," Johann added teasingly.

"Yes, that you are, my Darling."

"Mama, Papa." The two girls giggled with delight, clinging onto their parent's legs, wanting to be part of their embrace.

--

Father Wendel just sat watching, with little Elisa on his lap. His eyes moistened. Deep contentment filled his heart. He was happy to be part of this union and nothing could sway him to feel otherwise.

Little Elisa especially had stirred up something in his empty heart. In her cute childlike way, she had more than once succeeded to bring a smile to his brooding face. He felt his heart melting by the touch of her tiny hand, whenever she reached out to stroke his wrinkled face. Although it had not been his intention to favor one child over the other, but without noticing, he had come to do just that. He was giving her all his attention, spoiling her more then he should.

Maybe it was that little Elisa had been a colicky baby and he felt more needed than he did with the other two girls. He could not explain even to himself as to why he preferred one over the other. Could it be there was something about little Elisa that reminded him of his own daughter?

Many times, he felt bitter against God. He personally did not understand and never would after seeing what a cruel hand He had dealt him.

He had never understood Johann taking on the baptist belief and why he had been so fired up about going along with that preacher to help convert the gypsy folk. As for Katina, he had to admit he had taken a liking to her the first time Johann had brought her around. And her family, well... they were a nice bunch of people, not pushy, no not at all.

In fact, Father Stack and Robert had a very convincing way about them when they preached. He had heard them on special occasions in their home and on visitations to neighboring villages. Johann had often coaxed him to come along for the ride whenever he and Katina accompanied some of her family, as they all were needed to help along in the singing while her brothers played their zithers, harmonicas and mandolins.

Ah... that music. It could move any heart. That, he could not deny. Maybe, just maybe, he might give their belief a try, but for now, he just could not. There was still too much bitterness his heart.

The house, now almost empty, sounded hollow. He sat and listened to Katina's and Johann's footsteps resounding along the floor. He watched them pack the last of the newly bought clothes and linens. Lucky for them they had stored most of the breakable items in crates before the quake. In doing so they had experienced less damage.

Today was to be their last day in this house. Actually, now as he looked around, it seemed strange and foreign. Not that cozy and inviting place he had moved into. Tomorrow the new owner would come and claim this place, livestock and all.

"I hope they have some decency not to come today and leave us with nothing to sleep on," he said, as Katina took a break to prepare lunch.

"Don't worry Father Wendel, I've been told by our good Romanian neighbors that the couple was in no hurry to claim this place..."

A knock at the door startled her. Johann went over to open it.

She heard his surprised voice as he went from a "Yes?" to "Joanna! What in the world brings you here?"

Katina dropped everything, rushing to the door. Did she hear right? Did Johann say Joanna?

No sooner did she reach the door when she recognized Joanna's familiar face. Beside her was Mugur, both smiling like mischievous kids?

"What in the world are you two doing here?" Katina exclaimed.

"We've come to look around..." Joanna hesitated for a moment, feeling her way. As she realized that this was not an easy thing to deal with on Katina's and Johann's part. "You see...we are the new owners..." Joanna hesitated again to see their reaction.

"What...?! You...?" Katina could not believe such luck, to

run into an old friend, who she thought she would never see again.

"Come in you two, come in. This is truly unexpected." Katina was beaming for joy.

"Ahem." Father Wendel made himself known. "Are you moving in today?"

"Oh no," Joanna said still unsure about this delicate matter.

"You are the new owners?" Katina had to find the nearest chair; this was too much. Johann too could not believe what he had just heard.

"But how...? We thought some Macedonians..."

"Would be moving into your house?" Joanna finished. "We always had the intention to someday move to Mangalia. Now with this whole resettling business..." She stopped and looked again uneasy. "Forgive us if we're intruding. I feel so bad that this is happening... but...we could not help... You see our acquaintances... your neighbors... told us that there is a homestead coming up for grabs next to them..." Joanna hesitated when she realized that she had said 'for grabs'. The very idea of this whole deal was even to her standards a little underhanded. And of all people it had to be Katina's and Johann's property. But there it was, if not them, then others would take it without the feeling of guilt. She took courage to finish what she had started to say. "So, we took the opportunity, and when we saw your name on the list... well the rest speaks for itself."

"Well we were and still are not too happy about this whole situation, but then there's nothing any of us can do about it!" Katina confessed with a hint of remorse in her voice. She looked at Johann who nodded his head in agreement. To stop from going into painful details she quickly went on.

"At first I had misgivings, thinking of some strangers taking over our home and property. But now with you and Mugur taking over...? You do not have to apologize. This whole ordeal is not your fault. Yes... we are sad it had to come to this, and we will miss this place. But nevertheless, we are comforted that you of all people... you..." Tears filled her eyes. "What more could we have asked for, than for a friend to take over something so precious. Now, at least, we'll be content in knowing that our home will be appreciated and in good hands." She gave her friend a hug. "I hope you both will be just as happy in this place, as we were."

After they had toured the house and were ready to leave, she gave Joanna another 'goodbye' hug. "I will always treasure our friendship." She spoke with deep fondness in her voice.

"So will I, Katina!" Joanna returned the hug then hesitated for a moment. "Take good care, all of you and thank you again for being so understanding." With that she followed Johann and Mugur out of the door to see the rest of the property. Katina stood by the door for a moment watching them disappear into the barn. She shook her head still in disbelief, then turned to finish what she had started.

"Did anyone mention the crack in the foundation?" Father Wendel grumbled in passing, still upset about the intrusion. Not waiting for an answer, he walked back to the chair and sat down cradling little Elisa in his arms.

26

When the final day arrived, Katina took one last look around, just to make sure none of their personal belongings were left behind.

Tenderly, as if the house could feel and understand, she walked through the rooms saying goodbye. Each room held a memory of its own. She ran her hands over the window sills and wall features Johann had so lovingly crafted. It was hard to part. She forced herself away and reluctantly made her way downstairs, where Johann stood waiting.

"We're all ready to go." He rubbed his hands in nervous excitement. "Father and the girls are already seated in the coach… I have tucked them under warm blankets to make sure they are not cold. I have also taken care of Puffy. I locked her in the barn with the other animals so she wouldn't follow us."

He had seen the painful expression on her face when he had mentioned the dog's name. But he did not go into detail how she had whined after him with a long-drawn cry. It was as if the animal could sense what was about to happen. It was painful even for him to go through with this, yet it had to be done, besides the dog would be in good hands with Joanna and Mugur as her new owners. At least he wanted to believe that. He had to show strength for now and not let Katina see how he felt. For that reason, he had purposely given her a few minutes to go through the house. This way he hoped she did not see and hear the dog's reaction, knowing that it will hurt her too much. He had enough trouble calming the two girls and explaining why it had to be done.

Without another word he reached for her hand. Then gently led her outside, closing the door behind them.

An unearthly howl, coming from the barn unnerved them all. Katina staggered. He felt her go weak on him and was worried for her wellbeing.

He saw the pleading look on her face, as she motioned to go to where the dog was. Uncertain of what to do he glanced over to his father, who with a shake of his head indicated not to let her see the dog, knowing himself it would only make matters worse.

"Katina no... It's no good. It's best you do not. She'll be in good hands."

Tears streamed down her face. Reluctantly she gave in and let him help her into the carriage. Seeing her like this weakened his spirit. He could not contain his tears any longer. Through clouded eyes he gave one more glance around. He then climbed onto the wagon and gave a loud "Hah!" to the horses.

Torn in mind and spirit he wrestled to gain control over his emotions. Nothing could describe the feeling in his heart. Only God knew the pain and suffering all this turmoil had brought upon them. He felt so helpless. Oh, dear God... it was almost too much to take. It was so heart-wrenching to part. What he had planned to do here could have been the start of something so great. He could have been stubborn and refused to go. But he knew enough that sometimes a man had to swallow hard. He had to accept things the way they are if he and his family were to survive.

Gently, he reached out to comfort Katina, quietly taking her hand and holding it tenderly. He gave a quick glance back to see to the others when he noticed the bewildered and teary-eyed look on both Rebekka and Julia. It made him realize they too felt the pain. It was obvious they could not comprehend what was happening. But, like all children, as they drove on and with a new scene before them, their despair was soon overtaken by anticipation of what lay ahead.

"When are we going to ride on the train Papa?" Rebekka impatiently asked.

"Soon, sweetheart... but first we have to say goodbye to Grandma and Grandpa and the others... then we'll go to the train."

"Why aren't they coming with us?"

Johann and Katina exchanged a smile over Rebekka's nonstop questioning.

"Because Grandpa did not want to move when we did, now he and Grandma and the others have to wait their turn to be moved. But don't worry they'll soon be with us again."

Rebekka seemed to be satisfied with his answer.

Slowly the wagon rolled along familiar streets. It brought to mind many memories, especially when driving past the large entertainment plaza. It now had become the gathering center for all those in need of transportation to the train station. To have everything going in an orderly manner, the overseeing SS in charge had large Army trucks standing by.

Katina recalled the warm summer nights when she and Johann sat on the entertainment terrace, dreaming so many grand dreams. Where were they now?

She noticed Johann looking over the square. She could only guess what went through his mind. He too must be recalling those wonderful and carefree times. They seemed so promising. She suddenly straightened her back as if to forget and wipe away the haunting memories. Too much had changed and there was nothing she or anyone could do to recapture that time again.

A moment later they drove through the front gate of her parent's estate. Enthusiastically they were greeted by the old watch dogs she had grown up with. Gently, she talked to them knowing soon they too will be abandoned. and left behind like all the other animals. A pain pierced her heart anew.

The mill, once the busiest center on the whole property, now lay deserted. Ever since the decision to move, Papa and the rest of her brothers at home had lost all desire. There was no intention to make it work again.

She had always adored her parent's villa and its location, as it had a perfect view over the Black Sea. She measured the mass of water with her eyes. It looked dark and ominous. Was it a sign of things to come? Did it too feel the turmoil and upheaval?

With a sigh she turned her eyes away from the sea. At most times it was a beautiful and relaxing sight to watch. Yet today it felt disquieting; like the future that lay before them.

Drawn by the dog's light-hearted barks, Mama, Papa, Edwina and the rest of her brothers came to greet them. Standing on the front porch of the house, she noticed the surrounding dormant grapevines; waiting for spring to sprout again. Ah... Spring... with its newness of blossoming flowers. Where will they be then? She sighed... Will they ever find another beautiful place like this? Or will they forever yearn to return here to the Dobrujan plains, its milky jade-colored sea and bone-white sandy beaches.

A few days ago, at a farewell party she had promised Mama and Papa they would come by their house before leaving. Now the time was here, and it was not an easy one.

She was saddened at the sight of her parents' strained appearance. The last few weeks had taken much out of them. In her heart she believed that Papa was still struggling to overcome the battle of surrendering, even if he had openly said otherwise. It was only natural; anyone in his position would feel the same.

Like her father, her married brothers had waited for Papa's decision to leave. Now they too had applied to evacuate. This was the reason why she and Johann including his father and the children were the only ones leaving.

After a brief moment of hugs and farewell wishes they

said their goodbyes to each other, each with a heavy heart. It was not easy to part, even though she knew it would only be for a short while, but nevertheless, it hurt. Who was to say they were going to be shipped to the same destination? What if they were ordered to live far apart from each other? No, this thought was too much to bear. She wished for it never to come true.

Papa's prayer over their journey before they parted eased her downhearted feeling. She was also comforted that Robert had taken the initiative to drive them to the train station; it made parting a little easier to bear.

Upon leaving she changed seats, leaving Robert to take the front seat beside Johann. Sitting in the back beside Father Wendel she watched through blurry tear-filled eyes, until her parents and siblings were obscured by a row of sumac trees. Papa had planted them the year they had moved here. She had always loved the breathtaking vivid red leaves they produced so faithfully every fall season. Distraught she looked away. No use remembering. It was of no use anyway. It only made it harder to part.

The road to the station was busier than ever. It was unbelievable to her to see so many of their countrymen along the way. Many native Romanians, among them friends, lined the streets waving, their faces portraying a look of bewilderment. She could only guess they did not comprehend why so many of her people were making this move. As they practically had left everything they had so diligently worked for behind. And not knowing what all this meant for them, many must fear, their land once again vulnerable, overtaken by Russians, Turks and other plundering and rampaging forces; just as it was in earlier years. For a moment she pondered this thought, realizing that she and others of her countrymen were not the only ones uneasy of their future.

She recalled the rumor that entire German villages in the northern Drobujan region had dared resist the SS.

Their orders to leave land and homes to be integrated into the Reich had spitefully fallen on deaf ears. The result of this consistent refusal, they were arrested. The men were separated from their women and children. All scattered into different labor camps closer to the Fatherland.

She shuddered at this thought. It was unthinkable that this was true. She now was glad her family had all agreed to go peacefully. For it was better to all be alive and together, than to lose each other in the process or worse yet, be killed. Yes, it hurt to lose all their earthly possessions, but what choice was there? It was a hopeless situation and one had to make the best of it.

As they reached the vicinity of the station; she looked on as masses of people struggled to get themselves and their luggage checked in and loaded. Overtired and stressed, everyone was anxious not to lose sight of each other.

While Johann and Robert looked after the baggage, she, Father Wendel and the girls quickly went ahead to reserve seats. Then it was time for a last farewell. She had never seen her brother near tears. But all this turmoil had worn even the toughest of men. Unwilling to let go, Robert gave everyone a hardy hug. "Do not forget!" He tried to encourage them as well as himself. "It will not be long, and we will be together again." He said with a hopeful expression.

Once they were all secure on the train, she felt relieved that this part of their journey was behind them. All the turmoil of packing and saying farewell had left her drained and listless. Weak and despondent, she joined Johann and the two girls at the open window. Father Wendel though chose to remain seated, holding a sleepy Elisa tenderly in his arms. From his facial expression she had noticed that he did not care to give one more glance out the window. He had said his goodbyes at the house and she guessed it was good enough for him.

She turned once more to look at her littlest one, who at this moment had no knowledge of what was happening around her. All that mattered for her was to be held and loved. Suddenly a couple of bumps and rumbles resounded from one rail car to another. Then, as if carrying a heavy load the train started to move slowly out of the station.

"Mama... come and look," Julia begged. She took hold of her mother's face and turned it again toward the open window. "The train is moving," she called out. Overjoyed, she and Rebekka hopped and giggled, waving their arms in excitement to Uncle Robert.

With mixed feelings, she watched her brother fade into the distance. She hated goodbyes. Especially this time, for she knew it was the last time their eyes would behold the country they had all come to love. She swallowed hard to keep the painful cry deep within her from surfacing.

But yet, among the sad and depressing feelings, there stirred another. There was within her an awareness of adventure, of new horizons she had never seen. With hope in her heart, she wanted to believe that somewhere was a place waiting for them. A place they could once again call home.

A cool breeze coming from the partly open window gently touched her face. It suddenly made her aware that she was the only one still standing. She felt Johann's hand on her shoulder.

"Come sit down and relax." He motioned for her to sit down while he closed the window.

"From what I've heard, we'll have a long journey ahead of us. The train is taking us first to Constanta and from there we'll be going northwest to Cernavoda. There, I've heard ships were standing by to transfer us further."

Having said this, he leaned back watching the familiar countryside as it lay dormant in front of him. He recalled the laborsome hours he had spent cutting ice from the sea. The bitter cold temperatures he had endured to achieve his dream. The thought made him shiver. He buttoned up his suit jacket. He had no wish to go back to this experience.

--

The train ride up to Cernavoda had gone slower than she had anticipated. As with each stopover to pick up more passengers the train had slowed and fallen behind its regular schedule. Now nearing its destination she suddenly noticed an increase of excitement among fellow passengers. And just as Johann had mentioned, she could see large river boats standing ready for transport.

From what she could gather, and in her own experience, not many people had the privilege of taking a boat ride along the renowned Danube River. This was a luxury that had only been reserved for those who could afford it. Many people, themselves included, had spent most of their lives working and saving every penny for the future. Taking a boat ride along the Danube was never a part of their plans.

And so they had worked and saved money. 'For what?' she asked herself. 'Where was it now?' The little cash they did salvage was not much. Most of their earnings and inheritance went into house and property. 'What good did it do them now?' The officials had mentioned a reimbursement, but will it come to pass? Their lives, like chaff, were tossed by the ideals of those in higher authority with no concern for the individuals.

She took a deep breath to calm herself. It did not matter anymore. She had to put it all behind and forget what was and had been. She smiled at Johann as he glanced at her. It was as if he had read her thoughts. His hand reached hers, softly and with assurance he spoke in a lowered voice. "Don't worry about what was, leave it all behind. We are going to make it no matter what is before us. As long as we're together, we'll survive. Hmm...?" He gave a reassuring smile. "We will survive! We always have!" The last words spoken were directed more to himself than to her.

She gave him an understanding nod, "You're right." And yes, Johann was right. From now on she promised herself to hold on to what mattered most in this life and that was her family. Their love and companionship was, after all, more important than all the houses and properties this world could offer. With renewed hope she readied herself to assist Johann and Father Wendel with the girls and the luggage.

A long line of people greeted them at the dock, all waiting to board the ships. Under the ever watchful eyes of the SS officials, each person young and old was fitted with an identification tag around their necks.

As they stood in line, they suddenly witnessed a man with his family desperately trying to go on board without identification tags, but it was without success. From what they overheard, he apparently had refused to leave his home and property at the first offer given. And having a last minute change of heart, had tried for the second time to register at the dock, but ruthlessly was denied passage.

It was told, that after they declined to board the ship, he and his family had gone back to their homestead and found it occupied. Thrown off the property in a most humiliating way, they found themselves homeless and poor, working for meager wages.

Again it was made clear to her and Johann how fortunate they were to have agreed to go and not to resist.

As they stood waiting, Johann suddenly gave her a nudge. "Look over there..." He gestured with his head. "It's not only the SS who is standing guard. We're also being observed by a Romanian gendarmerie and he doesn't look too pleased... ," he whispered in a low voice.

"Probably he doesn't believe and trust what's going on," she quietly came back, as she too did not want to be overheard. With the things as they are, it was better to keep one's opinion to oneself.

After the final commotion of being checked out and registered, Rebekka and Julia could hardly contain themselves, fidgeting with eager anticipation to explore the ship as Papa had promised them. But just when he was about to carry it out, a Red Cross nurse was there to intercept. With a stern face she took the girls from his hands., then crossed the long boardwalk and delivered them onto the ship.

Surprised, Johann thanked her as they caught up.

"No thanks necessary," she answered with a cold smile. "It's all part of the move. Later, when you've settled in, you can bring the girls up to the deck. We have all sorts of things planned to keep the children entertained," she regimentally excused herself and walked back across the plank to help the next family.

"Well that settles it; we don't have to worry what to do with the girls, or my father," Johann teased Katina. As his father had gone to scout out his accommodation that was set aside for his age group.

"Last I saw him he was very excited when found out that he'll be traveling with old friends from Mangalia. It seems they had thought of everything. You know what that means Katina?"

She gave him a questionable look.

"We'll finally have some time to ourselves," he smiled mischievously at her as they made their way to the individual cabins; reserved only for young families.

As promised he took the two older girls for a walk about the ship, then on the way planned to check on his father, just to make sure he was taken care of. She in the meantime opted to stay in the cabin to tend to little Elisa. After the little one was fed, diapered and sleeping, she took the opportunity to relax. Upon lying down, she was surprised how clean everything was, even the sheets and blankets smelled fresh.

"Katina," Johann's voice echoed into the room a moment later. He lowered his voice when realizing she was resting. "You wouldn't believe who is with us on this ship."

Before she could ask, Rebekka blurted out in excitement, "It's Auntie Hetti and her parents."

"Rebekka," Johann scolded light-heartedly. "Now you've spoiled the surprise for Mama."

"Hetti," Katina's eyes lit up. She abruptly stood up, straightened her clothes and hastily rearranged her hair. She thought back to Daniel and Hannah's wedding when she had gotten to know Hannah's younger sister Hetti. She was a very upbeat and likable young woman, very easy to talk to.

"Why didn't you bring her here?"

"She wanted you to come up to the lounge. She thought it would be more comfortable there," he explained.

With no further comment she quickly bundled Elisa up and followed Johann and the girls to the ship's lounge.

"How could we have missed seeing them on the train?" she questioned him on the way.

"I don't know... With so many people anything is possible. They must have boarded the train at a different time. All we know they might have only been one rail car away from us, considering we never left ours."

She agreed, thinking how many other friends they might have missed that way. So far Hetti and her parents seemed to be the only ones. Just the same, she was overjoyed to know there were at least some familiar faces on board.

Before she could call out to Hetti, Becky and Julia were ahead of her.

"Now girls give your mother a chance to talk to Auntie Hetti. And don't be little pests," Johann said jokingly.

"Oh, it's quite all right Johann." Hetti intervened while embracing the girls.

"Nevertheless, they shouldn't do it." He tried to sound stern, but did not succeed. He knew he had a weakness when it came to disciplining the girls and they seemed to know it.

"Come girls, let's go and see what else there is to find on this ship," he quickly diverted their attention, knowing that they were always ready and willing to go along with him.

Katina and Hetti watched as the two older girls walked, hopped and skipped beside their Papa across the lounge floor, then disappeared through the doorway.

"Katina, you're so lucky to have such darling girls and a gallant, handsome man like Johann. I wish I could be so lucky."

Katina quietly had to agree with Hetti. She truly was blessed to have Johann and the girls. But not to sound boastful she replied gently. "Oh Hetti, you will... Just you wait and see. Someday when you don't expect it he'll be there. For all we know, he might be right here with us on this very same ship. If you've noticed..." Katina smiled and gave a quick glance around, as she continued. "There are quite a few handsome young men around."

"Katina, you're forgetting I'm not the youngest anymore. And if the threat of war keeps hanging over us, they'll probably find themselves drafted. Then what will happen to girls like me?"

"Don't worry Hetti, there'll be someone..." Katina stopped suddenly. "Oh no..."

"What is it? What's the matter?" Hetti panicked for a moment, thinking Katina might be ill.

"It's someone I particularly don't care to meet."

"Is that all?" Hetti laughed. "And here I thought... Who are you talking about? I don't see anyone." She turned to look.

"By the doorway... Someone I had known from Cogealac, an old admirer."

"Ah... that sounds interesting," Hetti smiled. "Now there you see. I can't even boast about that."

"Believe me Hetti, this is not someone you would care for either."

"You want to try me?"

"Oh no, he's coming this way." Katina turned to hide her face.

"I see what you mean," Hetti commented after taking a good look, "A haughty looking character. That must be his wife beside him. They make a good match."

"Is he still coming toward us?"

"Yes, but I don't think he saw you. Not yet at least."

"Oh good, let's hope he doesn't."

"Katina, remember we're on a ship. You're bound to run into him sooner or later."

"Yes, I know, but..."

"But what, he's nothing but an old admirer. Unless...?"

"There's no unless Hetti. I never had feelings toward him, whatsoever."

"By the way, what is his name?" Hetti asked without letting the party in question out of her eyes.

"Heinrich... Heinrich Schwarz."

27

"Mama, Mama," Rebekka and Julia came screaming. "We've seen Grandpa... He was talking with his friend when we got there. He walked with us for a while." Rebekka and Julia babbled in excitement competing with each other to be heard first. Behind them was Johann with little Elisa in his arms, trying his best to keep up.

The commotion of the girls caught the attention of Heinrich Schwarz. He turned. The look on his face told Johann that he had recognized him.

There was a silent moment of measuring up, as Schwarz's eyes wandered from him to Katina and back again. Then without a nod or a spoken word he turned and walked away alongside his wife.

Johann wanted so much to ask him a question or two about unsettled matters from the land deal. But there was something in Schwarz's eyes that prevented him from doing so. Something puzzled him. Why did he look so at Katina? Did he detect a glimmer in Schwarz's eyes or was it just his imagination? Well, whatever, next time he would not let him slip away. There were so many questions that needed answering.

"Yes, I'd better be going to see how my parents are getting along," Hetti suddenly excused herself. "I left them resting and knowing how disoriented they were when we boarded the ship, I have a strong feeling they won't set foot outside

168

their designated area in fear of getting lost." With this she bounced from her seat, adding cheerfully. "I'd like to take the girls along, if you don't mind."

"You sure they won't be too much for you?" Johann inquired, knowing what a handful they can be.

"Yes, I'm sure. Besides, I think you and Katina could use a little break."

"It's fine with me," Katina agreed.

"Then come along girls." Hetti did not have to do too much coaxing. "Let's go and see what Grandma and Grandpa Kranz are up too." The two girls nodded their heads, jumping with excitement, as Hetti lifted little Elisa into her arms.

"Don't forget to meet us back here in fifteen minutes. We'll have to wash up before lunch," Katina called after them.

"We won't forget," Rebekka replied for all of them as they hurried off.

Both she and Johann exchanged a smile over their eldest's friskiness.

"I don't know who she goes after." Johann added with a smile. "To be honest, she worries me at times."

Katina smiled, listening only half-heartedly to what Johann had said. She appreciated Hetti volunteering to take the girls. She had seen the puzzled expression on Johann's face earlier when Heinrich Schwarz had looked at her. So far she had never seen the need to explain. But following this little incident she thought it best to let him know, not to have a misunderstanding between them.

Quietly they strolled, arm in arm along the ship's deck. Still deeply drawn to each other like the first time when they walked in her father's garden. She closed her eyes and took a deep breath. She recalled the beautiful fragrance of the flowering fruit trees.

Abruptly, she was set back into reality by a strong gust of wind that blew across the marshy river delta.

The cool November air chilled her still slender body. But it never penetrated deep enough to offset her unwavering warm affection toward this dear loving man beside her. Hetti was right. She was a lucky girl.

A smile crossed her face. Tenderly she squeezed his arm as they stood soaking in the beauty of the surrounding landscape.

"What was this for?" he exclaimed, while drawing her into his arms.

"Oh, I just thought how much I love you."

"Is that so... Did this by chance have anything to do with Heinrich Schwarz?"

"Johann, Heinrich and I were only school-mates way back in Cogealac."

"So-o-o... that's it... and?"

"And... He liked me... a little."

"A little..." he laughed sheepishly. "From what I could detect, the poor man must have been head over heels in love with you."

"Johann!" she said again scolding, and then had to admit it was true. "Well maybe a little."

"Everything's a little. Well, I don't mind a little," he kept on teasing her. Demonstrating how much a little was by the span between his thumb and finger.

"Come to think of it... a man who falls in love with you couldn't be all that bad... Hmmm?" he said as if trying to convince himself.

Before she could say 'Johann' again, he pulled her up into his arms and gave her a long loving kiss.

"Johann... not here..."

"And why not...? Is a man not allowed to give his wife a kiss whenever he feels like it?"

"Yes, but not with so many people watching," she said, noticing again the smiles on people faces as they walked passed.

"My dear sweetheart..." still in a teasing mood he continued, "The word 'privacy' has gone out of fashion the minute we boarded the train. Now, are you going to let me at

I WILL REMEMBER ALWAYS

least hug you?"

She reluctantly agreed and with a light-hearted chuckle they continued their stroll, taking advantage of the carefree time, if only for the moment.

Not wanting to spoil their togetherness, he purposely kept quiet about his previous encounter with Heinrich Schwarz and the sinister accusations against him. Could it be that it was all a misconception? Seeing Heinrich Schwarz today made him see another side of a man they all had warned him to avoid. How could he be sure though? Can a man love and at the same time be fearsome and cruel? There was so much to know. Maybe in time he will come to see the truth, then and only then will he judge and lay this whole matter with Herr Grundman to rest. For now he will continue to be cautious and feel his way around this unpredictable character of a man.

--

The first meal on board the ship was a big disappointment to all. The watered down pea soup had more black bugs swimming in it than anyone could count.

"Meat substance no doubt," Johann added jokingly, showing the two older girls how to scoop the soup out of the dish without the bugs. Rebekka was easily persuaded and took it as a fun game, but Julia was another matter, knowing how she usually reacted when it came to eating. This was no surprise to him, only this time he had no intention of forcing her either.

He himself was much too hungry to pass up even a meal like this. They only had a light breakfast in the morning before leaving, and the few munchies Katina had packed for the trip was long gone.

"What next?" he heard his father grumble. "It's not enough they took away our houses and land... No! Now they're feeding us leftover pig's slop."

Hetti and her parents were about to join them at their table.

171

"S-h-h-h... Wendel, they might hear you," Father Kranz cautioned.

"Just let them. I'll tell them a thing or two. Who do they think they are? Treating us like scum. What in heaven's name will they have in store for us next?"

"S-h-h-h... Father, simmer down, or you'll get us all into trouble," Johann added. "I agree with Father Kranz, we have to be careful what we say. It's not worth getting in trouble over a bowl of soup."

"Still, I don't like it. I wish they would have left us in the Dobruja. At least there we had plenty of food to fill our stomachs."

"Yes," Father Kranz agreed, "But even there you have to admit things were not the same anymore. Remember the threats against some of our men?"

"Yah, yah..." Father Wendel waved off the truth in protest, shaking his head, while continuing, grumbling under his breath, "I don't know... All that trouble... It's just too much for an old man like me."

Katina could feel with Father Wendel, but had to agree with Father Kranz, there was no turning back. What they thought they once had was no more. The only thing left was to see this thing through and be strong. Strong...? Who was she kidding? The piece of bread she had opted for would hardly keep her strong, if this was to repeat... Nevertheless she could not bring herself to eat the soup and it went against her better judgment to feed it to little Elisa.

Carefully she pushed the distasteful looking creatures to the one side of the bowl. Yet it seemed like a never ending task, for each time she dipped in, the dead bugs found their way back onto the spoon again. To her amazement the little one did not mind, gleefully smacking her lips after every spoonful. But then Elisa was too young to understand about these matters. She wondered... was this a preview of things to come? She hoped not. Oh, what she would give now for a mouthful of that mamaliga and gravy she and Johann had

I WILL REMEMBER ALWAYS

been served that night at the home of the Romanian couple, anything but this.

Her eyes went to Johann, who at the same time looked up giving her an encouraging wink. As if he had guessed what she was thinking. She returned a thankful smile.

She took a glance around the ship's dining room. She recognized some of the people as brief acquaintances from Mangalia and Cogealac. Heinrich Schwarz and his wife had seated themselves on the far side with other Cogealagians. Somehow it seemed as if he was trying to avoid them and this suited her just fine. She would not have wished it any different.

She longed now to have Mama, Papa and the rest of her family here. She wondered what they were doing and relished the day when they would be together again.

Hetti and her parents filled that gap a little and she appreciated having them around. They were mutual friends, thinking and believing alike. It was a big plus in this troubled time, for they stood on common ground. And they did not have to be scared of being misunderstood whenever one spoke what was on his or her mind. It was refreshing and encouraging to be able to lift each other up whenever there was need. Also share a good laugh even when things did not look promising.

When after lunch the children again were cared for, she and Johann spent their time sightseeing soaking in the tranquility of the land and water around them. Passing on the north to them were the scarcely populated marshlands of Romania. It was a complete contrast to the south where the rise of the Bulgarian low heights was crowned with small towns. Here the Danube River acted as a true border, dividing the two Balkan lands. For even if these towns faced Romanian villages, she could seldom see a connecting ferry. She watched and listened to the ever moving river lapping against the ship's hull. It reminded her of life. It too was forever moving forward touching the periods of time, never to return to the same again.

Suddenly at the Yugoslavian-Romanian border the ship was eased through an ancient canal. They watched as the majestic river was racing in rapids through the Iron Gate.

Looking on, Johann mentioned to her that he had heard rumors that a radical group was planning to destroy this lock. In doing so they hoped to hinder the German army from advancing.

Dismayed by this she soon dismissed it, when another gorge greeted them at Kazan. Confined between steep rock walls the river here plunged in a thunderous roar to depths below. Awed by all this, their journey so far seemed to be full of surprises, but nothing in her mind compared with the beauty of the Transylvanian Alps. Here majestic country houses and dreamy fairytale castles stood high on hilltops.

She remembered Mama and Papa coming here on business. Now she understood why Papa had thought it good for Mama to come along. Who would not enjoy a getaway in these surroundings? She was happy for them to have had this time when they could.

It was late in the afternoon when they arrived at a small town not far from Belgrade. And as she found out, it was to be their first overnight. It was also the end of their river journey.

They were just about to leave their cabin, when Hetti intercepted. She had already scouted out the situation on land and came to report her findings.

"You have to come and see what they have prepared for us out there." She swallowed in excitement and quickly continued, "There are tables upon tables filled with all sorts of mouthwatering food. Katina, even you would find it hard to resist. I tell you, there are ham shanks of that size."

She showed how big by indicating with both hands.

Johann, who listened in, had to laugh.

"Well if all is what you say, we'd better hurry and see for ourselves. I'm hungry enough to eat one of those hams shanks by myself." He was playing along with Hetti, believing it a joke. But when he and Katina walked toward the tables, placed in long rows outside on the open ground, they were amazed. What a hardy welcome this was. No one on board the ship had expected this, certainly not after that disappointing lunch earlier in the day. The local's had really outdone themselves in their welcome.

"They must have heard your complaining, Father," Johann mused.

"Yeah, I guess now you can thank me for all this instead of getting more of that soup."

"Father Wendel, please no more mentioning the soup," Katina begged.

As they sat down to enjoy the delicious meal, she suddenly could not bring herself to eat. Patiently she endured as her family enjoyed every morsel served.

After the meal they found themselves grouped in large numbers into long army barracks. Here layers of fresh straw and blankets were provided for them to sleep on.

It was not that she minded sleeping on straw. But she had to admit it was a little degrading, especially from where they had come from. What had happened to their dignity as people, she questioned? With so many people there was not the least bit of privacy provided. What if she had to get up at night? Would she find her way outside without disturbing anyone? Her worries were soon quieted, when she noticed most people too tired to care what was going on around them.

A nurse suddenly entered the barracks with a tray full of medicine. Amidst the dust of the straw of people trying to arrange their sleeping quarter, her voice suddenly rang out.

"Who is sick here?"

About a dozen hands came up. Johann lifted his hand for Katina. She realized now she wasn't the only one feeling ill.

Long after the lights had gone out and everyone had settled down, she lay awake thinking...

Quietly she listened to the girls light breathing. To the left of her, Johann now too had fallen asleep. His hand was slightly over her as if to protect her.

She reached beside her, tucking the blanket tighter around Elisa's tiny body. The air in the room was cool and it gave her concern, whether or not she was warm enough.

Because of the unfamiliar surroundings she had thought the children would have difficulty adapting, but to her surprise they were asleep faster than expected. Slowly she turned and closed her eyes, forcing herself to do the same, but so much was on her mind. One thought after another surfaced. What will tomorrow be like? She wondered. Would there be more nights like these? Everything seemed to be done in a massive scale by groups and units. This was not the most pleasant thing to be tossed into. It was hard enough to live together with ones in-laws, let alone with strangers.

The thought of losing one's identity crossed her mind, if this situation was to prolong... Nevertheless she vowed not to let it get to her. For now at least she would try her best to comply.

Curious of what the next day will bring she settled back. She hoped this nightmare would soon end.

28

Early the next morning, she suddenly awoke by heavy snoring. At first she thought it to be Johann, thinking herself still at home and in her own bed. Disappointed, she realized that it was not so.

Slowly, not to disturb anyone she crawled out from underneath the cover of her blanket. She carefully checked on the girls, pulling their blankets up, tucking them in gently. She was surprised but glad to see them sleep through all that noise.

'The excitement of the previous day must be catching up.' A smile crossed her face by that thought. Quietly she walked the few steps over to look out of the window above their bedside.

She had no idea what time it was. But from the faint light across the horizon she guessed it to be between four and five in the morning.

The surrounding landscape lay peaceful and silent in front of her. From where she stood she could see the river rushing along in the cool November air. Here and there a bird flew over the misty grey-blue water in search for food. She noticed the ship gone. It probably had left during the night, only to return again with more fellow countrymen.

She smiled, wondering if they too would get the same surprise for lunch. It certainly was awful. Just thinking about it made her stomach turn.

But despite feeling a little weak, she was actually doing

far better this morning. It must have been the medicine, whatever it was, it helped.

A quiet prayer escaped her lips, asking for continued protection and renewed strength for the upcoming day.

Chilled and tired she turned to slip back under her blanket beside Johann. But before doing so she took a glance across the primitive looking barrack. Her eyes scanned over the many sleeping strangers who lay like sardines alongside each other. Here and there she could detect a stir, as some pulled their blanket tight around them. 'Army blankets no doubt,' she thought, as they all looked the same.

Hetti too was fast asleep, lying curled up next to Rebekka. Her oldest had insisted last night that Aunt Hetti had to sleep beside her.

She was amazed how the girls had taken to her. In a way she was glad for Hetti, knowing how much she longed to have little ones of her own. With a prayerful thought for Hetti, she closed her eyes and curled up beside Johann.

Some time later she was startled by a baby's cry.

With that the whole place suddenly came alive, as everyone rushed to get ready. A sunbeam found its way through the window, promising a cheery outlook for a brand new day.

Rebekka and Julia, for a moment engaged in a game of hide and seek under the blankets with Johann, and squealed with delight whenever he caught them. But soon this little game had to come to an end as the line up for the morning meal was announced. She was amazed by the efficiency of the servers, with the effort it required to look after so many people.

Soon after the delicious breakfast they were once again on the move. This time they found themselves on a westbound train to Graz. With that they had left the Danube River behind them to the north, and when arriving in Graz, everyone, especially the children, were happy to get off the train to stretch their legs. Johann carried the luggage and little Elisa while she followed with the girls. Hetti was right behind them with Father Wendel and her parents in close pursuit. In what seemed an endless stretch, they were led from the train to their temporary quarters. Here again there were tables laden with all sorts of delicious food. Lucky were those who could enjoy all the bounty that was laid before them.

But for her and others who had come down with dysentery, a temporary hospital base was all they could look forward to. She hoped it would be a quick recovery as she missed being with family.

An hour later Hetti came by to check on her with little Elisa in her arms. She had dressed the little one in a white overall lace-trimmed apron. She said to have bought it from the local women who were peddling their homemade crafts to the refugees. Katina could not help but marvel how cute her little one looked. It cheered her to see her so well cared for.

"Johann will be here shortly to pick you up," Hetti informed her.

"We were told to be ready in about twenty minutes to leave again."

"So soon. I could have easily stood another hour of rest," Katina said dismayed.

And just as Hetti had said, she found herself reunited again with family and friends. This time they were on a westbound train toward Austria. The train-carriages again crowded and cramped. She was glad when by evening they finally arrived in Seidenstaedt. Here a huge monastery was their temporary stay. It was to be till the cold winter months had passed, so they were informed.

To her the structure looked foreboding, the way it stood in a U-shape. It was like a fortress surrounded by a high unscalable wall and an impenetrable gate. The small windows faced only to the inside of the courtyard. It reminded her of a prison.

She noticed the nuns, the inhabitants of this place, kept well out of view in a section of their own. She could never understand how they could live day in day out shut away from the world. Why not share their lives with others, to feel and see the beautiful things this world had to offer? Although she had to admit, things right now did not look so promising and beautiful. But despite it all she would still choose who she was, a devoted wife and mother. She just could not picture herself in any other way. 'Well... to each their own...' she thought, 'as long as one felt content in what he or she is doing.'

Soon the last days of December came rolling by and Christmas was before them. She especially was not much in a festive mood, and she had seen it in others too, as each family pretty well kept to their own, celebrating quietly.

--

All in all it felt good to stay in one place for a change. Even though they had to share their living quarters, she had to agree it was far better than those uninviting and drafty barracks. This time all families with small children had been sectioned off from the rest, always two to a room. The older people stayed together on a different wing away from the noise. Hetti, ended up with all the single women, the same with the young men, also in separate quarters.

At first things seemed to be going fine, but soon after some of their friends got wind their kind was treated unfairly as far as food rations were concerned. Johann and some of the men concocted a plan to intercept the food baskets before they were distributed. He had talked to Katina about it and she agreed he should go ahead and find out the truth. As rumor had it, their Catholic countrymen always ended up with more and better quality of food than the rest of them.

The following day, before they went to pick up their food baskets, Johann and the men with him, hid in the corridor of the monastery.

They did not have to wait long before they heard footsteps

I WILL REMEMBER ALWAYS

approaching. With one swift motion they all jumped out in front of the others, blocking their way.

"So now, let us see what you have in your baskets," Johann challenged the other group of men. At first it looked as if a fight was coming on, but one look made clear to the opposite party that they were outnumbered. Reluctantly, they handed over their baskets, only to confirm the accusation was true.

"You know what we're going to do my friends?" Johann talked to them in a very friendly fashion.

"We're going to switch baskets. Don't you all agree?" In saying this he looked at his friends, who thought it was a marvelous idea.

"You're not going to get away with this," one of the men from the other group protested. "We'll see the superintendent about this."

"You go right ahead," Johann encouraged them. "As a matter of fact, we want to have a little talk with him too."

Nothing though became of that threat, but Johann thought it best to talk to the superintendant anyway. He approached the superintendent the next day about this mistreatment. He and his friends were peaceful men. And fighting over food was the farthest thing from their mind. As far as they had seen it there was enough misfortune to deal with every day.

When confronted, the man did not know what to say. Obviously he had been in collaboration with the other group.

When Johann told Katina of this, she was saddened that this was indeed true. Needless to say, all this injustice spoiled their stay in Seidenstaedt. And she was not surprised, when not long after, the two groups were separated.

March rolled around and with it came their departure. It was to their liking. She and Johann as well as the rest of their people did not want to stay where they were not welcome. Most of all the boredom of not working made the men agitated.

In Stockerau, near Vienna, another monastery was to

181

be their next temporary residence. And as far as she was concerned it was by far a more pleasing site than its counterpart in Seidenstaedt. The high and free standing structure, built in an L-shape had no walls or gates closing in around them. And invitingly, there stood a little chapel off to one side. She was convinced she would like it here; it was a much friendlier place.

Soon after settling in they went through the process of immunization and being sworn in as German citizens. In addition everyone in her family, except Elisa, was tested for blood types. The results where tattooed underneath their left arms. She was told it was to prevent unnecessary delays for blood transfusions in case of emergencies. But she and Johann wondered why and what it really was about. Nevertheless, she was relieved when yet another ordeal was over and behind them. With this she hoped to settle down, even if only for a short while, to resume a somewhat normal lifestyle.

With the citizenship in hand, Johann and the rest of the men were allowed to look for work. He especially welcomed this as he needed to regain his losses. Upon leaving Romania they had been told not to take money along because of the currency exchange and deflation. Yet in order to establish a business here in Stockerau, he needed money. He was now again questioning where he could get it. After talking it over with Katina the decision was to talk to Hetti's father.

Before the move Father Kranz had thought it wise to buy small gold coins, secretly stashing them in several of his suitcases. This move had served him well now putting him ahead of all the others who had spent their money on clothes and linens. Johann thought it very clever and wished he had done the same. Willingly Father Kranz borrowed him the money. And in turn Johann promised to pay it back as soon as possible.

Ready now, Johann went to scout around. He gave his bids and estimates wherever possible. Hopeful with the extra

I WILL REMEMBER ALWAYS

income he could pay off the money owing and put a little aside for the future. It would be good to take charge again and provide for his family.

--

Besides looking after the children, Katina and the rest of the women found themselves sectioned off into groups of eight. They were told with a large crowd as theirs it was a necessity to help along with the chores of cooking and cleaning. They had no choice but to agree.

At first she thought it not an easy job to prepare meals for 600 people, yet after working together in this fashion she found it half the task. She actually enjoyed mingling with the women. It reminded her of the klaka back home in Romania when the neighborhood women gathered in her mother's house working on projects for Tara's hope chest. Like then, happy laughter was heard now, intermixed with a lot of chit chat.

With Stockerau being so close to Vienna, she and Johann thought it to their advantage. And what better way to make life more bearable than to make use of all it had to offer. Living together in close quarters with another family was at best very hard to take. And even though it was a relative, it did not make matters easier.

When first they arrived at Stockerau they met Octavia, a cousin of hers on her mother's side of the family. At first it looked good to share a room, but now she wished it otherwise. The reason was the way Octavia carried on with her step daughter Jobina, a frail-looking six year old.

One could not help but observe a visible dislike on Octavia's part toward the child; forever she was harping on that little girl. From early morning to late evening she was yelling and punishing her over minor things.

They had tried to mind their own business, but could not, and it was wearing on them. Johann had talked to her husband Edmund to intervene. Yet he replied there was little he could do.

183

Just to get away from it all, she and Johann purposely went for long walks with the girls, strolling at the nearby banks of the Danube River. To help the situation they often coaxed Octavia into letting Jobina come along. And luckily Octavia agreed.

This close contact with her cousin brought memories of earlier times when she overheard her mother talk about Octavia's father who happened to be a heavy drinker that often viciously beat his wife in front of his children. The brother of Octavia's father, after witnessing his brother's violent abuse had taken his nephews aside and told them a solution.

"Boys," he had said to them. "When you get to be a little older and stronger; take your father, when in a drunken state, tie him to a chair and let him sit there till he's sober. Then let him make a promise never to lay a hand on your mother again. And tell your mother when you're not around not to give in or feel sorry for him until he is ready to keep this promise."

Katina remembered how anxious she was to hear the outcome of this incident. She was relieved to hear in conclusion that a few years down the road the boys had done just that.

Uncle Karl had been furious at first and protested, her mother had said. Even went so far as to curse them all, but they stood firm. Their mother, reluctant at first, decided to do as she was told, and no matter how her husband fumed and yelled to be untied, she would not give in. Not until he had spent a couple of days tied to the chair, did he finally realize he had no choice but to promise to change his dreadful habit.

Katina recalled her mother saying, that from that day her brother-in-law was a changed man. He knew if he ever slipped up and went back to his old ways, his sons would not hesitate to step in.

Maybe, she thought now, that might explain Octavia's

behavior. But who was she to say? It might be something deeper than that. Maybe the blame lay on Edmund. Maybe Octavia was trying to let out her frustration on little Jobina, over unspoken marriage problems. Come to think of it she had never heard Edmund say or express a loving word or gesture toward Octavia. Could it be that he could not get over his first wife who had died at Jobina's birth? In that case she pitied her cousin. She could not even begin to imagine how it felt to be in her position.

She thought of her mother, who had been in the same predicament when she married Papa. She also stepped into a marriage as a second wife, as Papa's first wife too died during childbirth. But here she knew and had witnessed her father's deep and unwavering love for her mother. He was always the loving and giving kind, like her Johann. Was that maybe what her cousin craved? Only God knew the answer. She hoped in time Octavia and Edmund could resolve their problems, for Jobina's sake.

For now, she had made up her mind not to meddle, seeing that it was not her's or Johann's place to do so, besides, next week both Becky and Jobina were to start school. That, she hoped, might eliminate some of the bickering, knowing Octavia would not be together as much with Jobina.

--

In the midst of all this she received timely and welcome news, of Mama and Papa and the rest of the family's whereabouts.

Daniel and Hannah had arrived in Stockerau after a request to be transferred and reported that Mark and Maria were about to do the same. The work opportunities apparently were much better here, since Stockerau was so close to Vienna.

Another reason for Daniel and Hannah's move was to be closer to her parents; Mother and Father Kranz and also her sister Hetti.

She was overjoyed to have at least some of her family close

by. And even though she was not able to see the others, she had Daniel's assurance they were all doing fine.

In the meantime Johann's search for work had paid off, and he proudly announced his findings to her.

Apparently his new job involved a large building project for which he had been chosen to be the overseer. His knowledge and credentials were finally recognized. That was great news to her remembering the struggle he had back in Mangalia to gain recognition in his trade.

Yet with this job came the need for transportation and after some discussion they both agreed on a new bike.

After purchasing it, the first thing he did was to take the girls for a test ride along the premises and over the nearby bridge. He rode proudly showing it off to the girls.

Rebekka intensely and quietly watched her father, observing all the steps to ride this two wheel contraption. Johann thought it great that his oldest showed so much interest in bike riding and like any father, proudly took time to teach her everything there was to know.

The following day after work, he had intensions to take the girls again for a ride after dinner. Trusting it would be safe, he left the bicycle standing at the front entrance.

Upon entering the premises, he had seen Rebekka and Julia playing games with the rest of the children, calling both to come in and wash up for supper. But as usual they pleaded, and succeeded to have at least one more round.

After he had gone inside, Rebekka all at once noticed the bicycle. It looked so inviting, especially when challenged by others to ride it. And despite Julia's pleading that, "Papa will be very upset if he ever found out." She did it anyway.

Off she went running alongside the bike, all the while trying to jump onto it as the others cheered her on. After several attempts she finally succeeded. Down the trail and over the grassy slopes she went; her hair and clothes flying behind and about her.

A great sensation rushed through her, as the evening

breeze brushed against her face. She was confident that if Papa could do it, so could she.

But before she knew, she lost control. Desperately she tried to steer the bike away from the pillar. In all the excitement she had forgotten how to brake. It was too late. She felt herself flying over the handle bar and hit hard.

She dared not to look. She moaned in pain knowing she would feel worse after Papa was through with her.

"Becky, are you okay?" Julia's concerned voice came from beside her.

"Dad will be very upset."

"You needn't remind me." Becky groaned again in pain, when suddenly an idea came to her. "Julia, you have to help me make up an excuse."

"Uh-Uh, not me, I'm not the one who took the bike and wrecked it." Julia stood firm.

"If you don't help me, you can't ever come along and play with me."

Tears streamed down Julia's face, as she ran off crying.

Johann was just on his way to get the girls, when he saw Julia running across the yard.

"Where's Rebekka?" He called out to her.

"Down by the water, under the bridge."

"What happened? Why are you crying?"

"It's Becky! She... She..."

"What is it Julia... Did something happen to Rebekka?"

Julia nodded as more teardrops ran down her cheeks. She dared not to say anymore, remembering Rebekka's threat.

"Tell Papa, what happened."

"She... She took..." Julia cried. She just could not bring herself to say it. "I told her not to, but she didn't listen... She took it anyway."

It suddenly dawned on him, as he looked over to where he had parked the bicycle. His face turned pale, realizing and knowing what Rebekka was capable of.

"Go inside and wash up, we'll be along shortly," he called

over his shoulder as he took off into the direction of the bridge.

Julia looked after him with mixed feelings. She had no intentions of telling Papa, but somehow it had slipped out. She was convinced now that Rebekka would never ever let her play with her. Upset she ran inside, crying even more.

It took Johann the rest of the evening to straighten out the bike. As for Rebekka, she had to promise never to touch the bicycle again and, if so, only under his supervision. When told, Katina just shook her head in thought, 'What will their oldest be up to next?'

29

The warm days of summer slowly came to an end. The early signs of autumn showed as the foliage started to change colors. Katina especially noticed it among the vineyards that graced the slopes along the winding Danube River.

She enjoyed the changing of the seasons. As with each new transfer it brought renewed awareness of how beautiful nature really was. There was not a season she could single out as her favorite. All were beautiful in their own right.

She had been extra busy these last few days in getting Rebekka's clothes all sorted out and ready. For her oldest, the first school year was about to begin. And there was so much that needed to be done. With all the moving around she had hardly a moment to look after things. Now she was trying to catch up in the little time left to her after the kitchen duties.

But before school started, Johann thought it good to take the girls to the big exhibition grounds in Vienna. It was a year round attraction which they had visited more than once this past summer and the girls enjoyed it enormously.

She in the meantime stayed back with Elisa as it gave her the much needed time to catch up on all her mending. But not to worry, Rebekka and Julia assured her, as they would fill her in on all the happenings as soon as they arrived back home. She had to smile as she watched the three riding off on the bike. Johann had Julia sitting on the handlebar while Rebekka sat on the carrier clinging tightly to Papa. On their faces was the anticipation of the upcoming adventure. She could already picture them on the giant Ferris wheel, called "Das Riesenrad", screaming and giggling with delight, while Daddy held them close. She remembered it said that this Ferris wheel was claimed to be the biggest and tallest in the world, as once on top, one had a breathtaking view over the whole city and beyond.

Then there was Rebekka's favorite. It was a ride through a dark tunnel where scary characters popped out from nowhere. In fright the girls screamed whenever these objects came toward them. Katina herself did not care for this particular ride and she was not too keen for the girls to see it either. But to her and Johann's surprise, both girls enjoyed it immensely and always begged for more. The same with the Hansel and Gretel and the Kasperle theatre, which she had to admit were a lot of fun. Some of those shows were a first even for her, as they had not been around when she was growing up. Their entertainment was of a much simpler nature.

She recalled again the warm summer evenings in Cogealac, when they played a game of hide and seek among the haystacks...

Now, that she thought of, she was amazed again over her father's patience and how he allowed them to mess up the neatly stacked heaps of hay.

These were special memories she wished to instill in her children as well. Someday soon, she hoped, when once again they could call a place their own. With that thought she went about to finish Rebekka's clothes, amazed again, why her oldest's clothes were always in need of repair. She chuckled, amused, yet a little concerned over Rebekka's lively spirit.

--

The school year began full of excitement and expectation for her oldest and Jobina. Both seemed to enjoy their time in school and this she could see made Julia jealous. And no matter how she and Johann had tried to tell Julia that she had to wait a year, she was inconsolable, especially after Rebekka announced their teacher had planned a special field day.

The day came and went. And after Rebekka's return they noticed their oldest sitting very quiet and withdrawn. Realizing something was wrong, as seldom had they seen her this way, only when sick. At the supper table when Rebekka hardly touched her food, Johann became concerned. It was her favorite food, goulash and spaetzle, a type of homemade noodle.

"Rebekka, are you not feeling well?" he asked. "It's your favorite... and you've hardly touched it. Tell Papa what's wrong."

She always was a good eater and he knew that it was not because she was finicky. There was something else that seemed to bother her.

Katina reached over to check if she had a temperature, but shook her head. "She doesn't seem to have a fever."

"Papa, do we have enemies?" Rebekka suddenly disrupted her parent's concern over her.

"No, not that we know of... why do you ask?" he asked, now curious how she came to this question.

"My teacher... She said the people behind the fences were our enemies."

"What people?"

"The people we saw today, Papa..." Rebekka stirred impatiently as she hurried on. "They looked so thin and hungry, especially the children. The teacher told me not to feel sorry for them. But I threw my sandwich over to them anyway when she wasn't looking. And you should have seen them all fight over it."

Her eyes were wide open now and her voice full of excitement.

They both looked at each other, shocked by Rebekka's statements.

"Rebekka what people and what fences are you talking about," he coaxed her on.

Tired to repeat the same story again she ignored the

question. "Can I take my food over to them tomorrow Papa?"

"Yes Rebekka, but first tell us more about the people you saw and what they looked like?"

"No different than us... except..." Rebekka's eyes suddenly lit up. "They all had a star sewn to their clothing. Papa, why are they behind fences? Did they do something bad?"

"I don't think so..." he looked to his father and the others for help. He was lost for words, but they too seemed speechless and perplexed from what they just heard.

There was talk about Jewish people being rounded up into camps. That was all they knew of their situation, but it did not make sense, they were starving, unless there was more to this than they knew.

As it was, they themselves were looked down upon by their own countrymen. The Germans here were the Reichs Deutschen, so called because they were born in Germany. Whereas people like themselves were referred to as the Volks Deutschen. They were people of German descent who had immigrated to and born in other countries. The class difference was real and distinct.

For this reason they kept mostly to themselves. They had always hated the wrongdoing. The distinctions were made from one race to another and from one group to another. But often, as it was the case here, there was not much they could do. Even if they dared to raise their voices in protest they knew very well their own lives were at stake.

She and Johann, like the rest of their family and friends, felt saddened by this situation. It was unfortunate their children had to grow up in such a society oriented around hate. For that reason they vowed even more so, to instill in them the true meaning of 'love thy neighbor as thyself'.

This whole situation suddenly changed their outlook on life. It put a damper on all their expectations for a better future.

As for Rebekka, she had to learn early in life that not everyone thought and felt like them. In some incidences the only course was to leave things alone. No matter how much it went against what they believed to be right and just.

As parents they had tried to honor Rebekka's wish and smuggled some of their food to the hungry people. But after the first trip they became aware that their meager morsels hardly made a difference to so many. They would have loved to continue to share their food but realized that this too was not advisable, as it was, their own rations were barely enough to keep them fed. Beside this, it was also hard to watch the people fight each other for the little bit of food. Witnessing this was heartbreaking. They were left helpless against such an incredible need and injustice. Suddenly, she remembered Robert's warning. Was he right? What they had witnessed here was inconceivable. She dared not think about it as it scared her. What was in store for them as a people, as a family? What they had experienced along the way, there was no telling if their future was safe. No one was sure of the outcome. She shuddered at the thought. All she and others could do was not to lose hope.

30

The days of fall had gone by quickly, and with the heartbreaking experience with the Jewish people still fresh on their minds, she and Johann often wondered how they managed to survive. It was significant, especially now that winter was upon them and the preparation of Christmas was before them. They hoped that even there in that camp, God would in his own special way, take care of all their hurts.

They knew that even for themselves Christmas would be a meager one, but at least they had warm beds to sleep in and enough food to survive. Only on the privacy issue both she and Johann had complaints. It was wearing them down, both mentally and physically. Yet on that subject there were no answers or changes.

With the holidays approaching, she had warned the girls ahead of time not to expect any presents. For days the girls walked around with glum faces over this unpleasant prospect. Yet it all changed when on Christmas Eve, not expecting anything, they and all the other refugees were surprised beyond their expectations. The locals had outdone themselves and had prepared a Christmas party in their honor.

The big hall of the cloister was decorated with boughs of evergreen. And a huge Christmas tree stood at the far side, all lit up with brightly burning candles.

Upon entering, they could not believe that all this was for

their enjoyment. Ushered to their very own table, they were awestruck by the Christmas goodies and gifts for the whole family. This was indeed an unexpected and most enjoyable event. The evening was filled with singing of Christmas carols and the presentation of the Christmas story. After that they all unwrapped their gifts and enjoyed the wonderful tasting goodies before them.

It was a heartwarming experience they would not soon forget. With this kind gesture the future suddenly looked a little more promising. At least she wished it so.

--

The sun rose with a radiant brilliance the next morning, awakening everyone with cheer. Overnight a thick blanket of snow had fallen, adding to the anticipation of the day. Rebekka and Julia were excited and could hardly wait to go outside to play. Forgotten were the new dolls. They had to wait for the evening hour or a rainy day.

Today the nearby slopes beckoned them for a trial run. But first they had to attend to the Christmas Day service and a special lunch, after that they were free to go.

Katina searched for warmer winter wear for the girls and Johann, who at this moment was busy fixing the two old sleds the nuns had kindly lent them.

She had to admit they were a friendly group of women and seemed to enjoy the children. But that's as far as they went. Seldom did they mingle or take time out to chat with the rest of the inhabitants in the cloister. She had watched them going for prayer to the nearby chapel. And often longed to go there, but had refrained from doing so. She felt a little squeamish going uninvited into a different place of worship, not knowing how she would be accepted. Leaving this thought she busied herself to retrieve the rest of the winter clothes.

After hours of fun on the slopes, Johann and the girls were ready to come inside again. With red cheeks, the two girls entered the room babbling on and on, telling her all about their adventures in the snow.

"We built a gigantic snowman!" Rebekka shared with excitement. Julia tried to cut in, but Rebekka hastily continued. Yet not wanting to miss out, Julia fought her way to stand in front of her and shouted over Rebekka. Quickly she blurted out, "And we built a big fort... and had a snowball fight with Papa." She gave Rebekka a triumphant look. Katina and Johann laughed with delight, listening and nodding in acknowledgment. Satisfied, the girls then settled down to play as their clothes hung over the bunk rails to dry.

She stood for a moment by the window, daydreaming. The gentle snowfall had brought about an awe inspiring fairytale look. It was so unlike the Dobrujan plains, where heavy snowfall and harsher bone chilling temperatures were the norm. She recalled the stories of wolves and remembered their spine chilling eerie howls as they descended upon their homesteads on cold wintry nights. No one had dared to go after dark visiting a neighbor or travel by sled to other villages. It was done only when necessary and not without a burning torch or lantern to ward off the animals.

"Katina!" Johann put his arm around her, "A penny for your thoughts."

"Ach...! Johann! You scared me!" She held her hand against her chest and took a deep breath. "I was just thinking back..."

"Ah..." he exclaimed, in thought for a moment. "I think we ought to make our way down to the mess hall. My stomach tells me it's time to eat."

She laughed at his sorrowful expression. "Well in that case... I think we should make our way down, what do you think girls?"

"Yes Mama!" the girls' voices echoed in unity.

"I'm so hungry I could eat one of those ham shanks they served in that town near Belgrade. With all that playing in the snow, a man works up a mighty appetite." She chuckled, nodding in agreement.

"Then you'll love what we're having for dinner tonight."

I WILL REMEMBER ALWAYS

He looked at her, waiting in anticipation.

"All the women agreed that we should have potato dumplings with pork roast and sauerkraut."

"Mmm..." he smacked his lips. "Now we're talking. I can hardly wait. Come girls, we'd better hurry on down."

She smiled with satisfaction to see everyone so eager to eat.

A faint pang stirred within her. Suddenly she longed to have her own home again. How peaceful that would be. To live undisturbed, free from dictatorial authorities. She wondered would they ever succeed. Or was this it? She suppressed a heavy sigh.

"Don't lose hope Katina..." she encouraged herself as she hurried to catch up with the rest of her family.

Once at the dining area she left this downcast feeling behind. For her family's sake she had to make the best of the situation. Uplifted by this thought, she settled in to take part in the delicious supper and as expected, the dinner was exceptional, even the children dug in and enjoyed every morsel. They had not had such a hardy meal in a long time. Their menus usually consisted of soups and stews, as they were easily produced in big quantity. But today was special. It was after all Christmas Day.

She thought back, remembering Christmases past. They seemed so long ago and yet it was not even a year since they had left their adopted homeland. She suddenly felt as if it all had been a dream, even their stay here. She looked around the mess hall, with its stark and austere facade. The only adornment was a single picture of the Fuehrer with an overbearing swastika underneath it. She found it a foreign and unfamiliar presence.

The only comfort and welcome she felt came from their countrymen. People they had known and lived with for so many years. They understood each other as they had experienced the bad as well as the good times. For decades there had been a bond between their forefathers. That had continued on through the generations as they struggled and searched for a second homeland, then fought to build it up only to lose it again. Then once more they strived to build, to gain, to work hard, to survive, to live. But yet again to be uprooted, disowned and degraded.

She thought back, two centuries had passed from the time her forefathers had dared to venture into unknown territory to the present, when they as their descendents where abruptly uprooted, ordered to be moved back again to where their forefathers had come from. They were transposed with no regard of the emotional, physical, and financial upheaval, and the stress they had to endure.

One thing she had to admit. They were survivors, seasoned and hardened to the core. But will they as a people continue to withstand what was in store for them? Again she could only hope it will be so.

--

The last day of the festive season had passed uneventful. And once again everyone resumed to their everyday mundane duties. With the older children back in school and the men out at their various work places, the halls and rooms of the cloister echoed a serene quiet, with the odd exception of a baby's cry.

The older generation welcomed it, as theirs was now the time for quiet walks around the cloister grounds, or just stand or sit and chat about trivial everyday things and reminisce of old times. Katina treasured this scene. It gave her a sense of community, a reminder of days gone by.

Father Wendel especially enjoyed the company of other old timers. He never seemed to tire of conversing with them.

She was glad about it, knowing that without it he would slip back into his old moody self again. It kept him from brooding over the misfortunes life had dealt him.

--

Days turned into months, and before she realized, winter too was on his way out. The snow was melting and running in little rivers down the slopes. Battling with the overflow she watched the Danube River stand to flood levels. Yet this too passed and nature, as time, had a way of rejuvenating, as once again spring flowers greeted them on their daily walks. And, just as nature, she too felt revitalized, hoping the New Year would bring only good things their way.

With all the business before her, she failed to watch her own health and felt more tired than usual. Johann coaxed her to go to the health clinic for a check-up.

After a thorough examination, to her surprise, she was told she was in her second month of pregnancy.

Johann was ecstatic and even though the odds of having a good future were against them, he knew no matter what outcome, this little one was welcomed just the same.

She agreed, yet at the same time was a little weary of going through another pregnancy. Would she again be agonized by the symptoms of malaria? And would she stay strong to deliver a healthy baby?

She knew that Johann still had his heart set on a boy. For his sake she prayed that it would be one with blue eyes and blonde hair, knowing that it was possible, since half of her siblings fell in that category. It would be a complete contrast to the girls, as all three of them had brown eyes and medium to dark brown hair, like her and Johann.

She did not know if the long winter months had anything to do with it, but suddenly there seemed to be an explosion of pregnancies. Besides her, there were eight other women expecting, among them Maria and Hannah.

All this pregnancy business seemed to be contagious, as a couple of months later Octavia too reported to be expecting. Maybe now, she hoped, with her own baby on the way Octavia would ease off on Jobina, knowing that a lot of her time would be dedicated to look after the little one.

Lately to her and Johann's surprise, little Elisa had become attached to Octavia. She followed her around and often requested to be picked up by her. She and Johann could not figure the little one out. And seeing this attachment Jobina quickly thought out a plan. In her opinion, it would be great to trade places with Elisa. Yet she was deeply disappointed when this plan of hers was rejected. She was told she was welcome to join their family, but not at the expense of little Elisa. As expected, this conclusion was upsetting to Jobina. Octavia on the other hand might have agreed to this, but it was not her husband's will to do so.

The summer slipped by uneventfully when the time came for Julia to go to school. To be prepared, she had sorted and put out her second oldest's clothes ahead of time. Julia was anxiously waiting for that day to arrive.

Yet all this did not sit well with her oldest. It meant she had to watch over her little sister and have her tag along. It was simply too much for the free spirited Rebekka.

Katina shook her head in thought. She hoped so much for the two to like each other. Maybe in time... Her mind wandered off to Rebekka's teacher. She had taken the children more than once to special outings before the summer holidays had started, but never again had her oldest mentioned the people behind the barbed wire fences.

She wondered if the same were still there or if they had been moved. Ever since they were warned, they as a family had not been back. It bothered her not to know the outcome.

All this time, Johann had kept busy in his work, and faithfully saved to pay off the money he owed Father Kranz. Now he was desperate to put the rest of the earnings aside for future use, as once again rumors surfaced that they would soon be on the move again.

31

The time was drawing near and so far she considered herself very lucky, as this time around, no major problems had interfered with the pregnancy.

She had been up several times at night walking the corridor floor. Purposely she avoided to stay in their designated room, for fear the creaky bunk bed would wake everyone in the room. The only place left for her was the lounge area, of which, one was available on every floor. But even here she tried to be extra quiet, as the doors to the day room rattled every time she opened and closed them.

At times like this she longed for her own home, where she could be free to go and do as she pleases. Living here, in such a confined area with so many people, was more than she could take. She was sure it bothered not only her and Johann, but others as well.

For a moment she had leaned back to rest when the overseer of the compound peeked in through the half open door; knowing of her condition.

"I heard the doors and wondered if everything was all right? Is it time? Can I help you with anything?"

She managed a vague smile.

"No. There is still plenty of time. I just came out here... not to disturb the others."

"Well... fine... let me know if you need anything."

She nodded and sank back onto the chaise lounge, as the overseer closed the noisy doors behind him.

She never liked him much, as when he smiled, his dark eyes and black hair added a sinister look to his face. It gave her goosebumps.

She did not know why she felt like this about this man. For as long as they had been stationed here he had always worked in their favor. He had shown himself a perfect gentleman.

Tired, she waved off this unseemly feeling within her. For as much as she knew, he probably was a kind-hearted and loving man, one that could not help but look the way he did.

She directed her thoughts toward her immediate problems, as now the labor pains had started to be more predominant.

A few hours later Johann came looking for her. "I missed you beside me in bed and wondered if you're all right," he said sleepy eyed, very much concerned. It was early Saturday morning and all the others were still asleep.

Tenderly and caring he fussed over her, covering her up with nearby blankets, then sat next to her planning to keep her company.

"Johann, please go back to bed," she urged him on. "It'll be a while... I'll let you know when the time comes."

Reluctant he gave in. He could see there was not much he could do, but to hold her hand and be sympathetic.

"Be sure and call me if anything develops," he bent over kissing her forehead, hesitantly leaving the room.

'He is such a dear and thoughtful man,' she smiled briefly in thought, then battled on.

--

Hours later, in the early evening hours, a healthy baby boy finally made his debut into this world. Seconds later the nurse attending came out holding the screaming little one by his feet.

"It's a boy... Herr Wendel. And by the sound of his voice, he's a hearty one at that."

The nurse had remained just long enough for him to have a glimpse, then just as quickly she disappeared with the little one still in hand.

He did not know if he had heard right. Was it really true?

Minutes later the door opened again.

"You can come in now and see your wife and son."

He took a deep breath and entered. Katina smiled a little tired, but very pleased.

"It's a boy, Johann, just what we had hoped for."

32

As she and the little one remained in the hospital. He was out there proudly telling everyone about their newest arrival. He marveled over the fact that at least now he had a boy who would carry on the family name.

This time though the honor went to her to name the little one, and the more she thought the more she favored the name Stefan. Although she did not want to admit it, but deep down and after all this time she still felt sorry for what had happened to Stefan Hartig. In character he had almost matched that of Johann's. Maybe this was the reason why she liked that name. Or was it?

She had never told Johann the full details of that time, and she had no intention of ever doing so. Besides, that period in her life was in the past. Now she had Johann and the children and she could never imagine herself without them.

The day before she and little Stefan were released from the hospital, Johann came with the news that the nuns had kindly cleared out a room for them. It was on the same floor, not far from their original room, and she was told they could move in as soon as she and the baby arrived back to the cloister.

All along she and Johann had been concerned on how they would manage once they brought the baby home to their already cramped quarters, but now there was no cause to worry.

'A private room,' she smiled at the thought. It had been a

long time since they had left the privacy of their own home. She wondered of Joanna and her husband, were they still the owners? If so, were there any children of theirs running through their home?

In her mind she wandered through the house, picturing how it had looked. She remembered in detail every room and every corner. She recalled the sights and sounds from the open kitchen window, with its limited yet tranquil view of the Black Sea.

It was lunch time here at the hospital. Was Joanna also standing in the kitchen preparing food or washing up after the meal? Was she listening to the same ageless sounds and gazing at the same timeless view? Her eyes moistened. She had to stop thinking about all this. It only brought sadness upon her heart, knowing there was no turning back.

"What's this? Are we feeling a little glum today?" On her usual daily rounds, the head nurse stopped to look in.

A weak smile escaped Katina's lips.

"Oh it's nothing... I was just thinking back," she tried to apologize.

"Well now..." the nurse smiled down at her. "With a fine looking boy like yours, there is all the more reason to focus on the future. Don't you think?"

Somehow she had a feeling that behind that robust tone of voice and the stark looking uniform, hid a warm and caring heart. She returned the smile with an understanding nod to the question.

"From this report..." the head nurse continued, not letting down her shield of professionalism, "I can see that you are ready to leave us tomorrow..." She paused for a moment. "If there's anything you wish to know or talk about before leaving, feel free to ask. If not, I hope your stay here with us was a pleasant one."

"My baby and I have been well taken care of. Thank you," she responded. "I am sure we'll be fine."

As the nurse proceeded on her rounds, she sank back into

her pillow. The nurse was right. She had a lot to look forward too. And Johann... well...? A warm smile crossed her face. He was so proud of his little boy. Oh... it was not that he thought less of the girls. Oh no, but to finally have a boy was special for him and she understood that. For this reason she had to look ahead and not give in to depressing thoughts.

She was amazed how that little chat had changed her mood. She felt a lot better. She might as well relax and make the rest of her stay a pleasurable one. For all she knew, this could very well be her last chance for a long time. She could relax and be a little lazy.

A warm feeling rushed through her as she thought of going home soon. She could hardly wait to see the girls' reaction to their little brother. From what Johann had told her, they had been asking for days when Mama was coming home with their little brother. It had been ten days since she had seen them. She smiled and closed her eyes in anticipation. Longing now to hear their childish chit-chat and laughter and feel their little arms around her neck.

Johann had made mention of the many volunteers that had offered him a helping hand ever since she had left for the hospital. "The girls are all fine and well taken care of. No need to be concerned. We're all like one big family." He had said, to reassure her not to worry.

She understood well. They had been together with most of these people for quite some time now. That alone would allow this special kindred spirit. In a way they had no choice but to bind together. She longed now for the rest of her family. She had not seen her parents for such a long time and it felt strange to be so separated from them. Back home in Romania they were a huge part of her world and her security. Even after she had married Johann, she had remained close to her family. She yearned for the day when she would see them again.

--

Upon her return to the compound, she was overwhelmed

by all the hugs and kisses. The girls and Johann as well were overjoyed to have Mama and the baby back. Proud, and with much care, they held the tiny one, sharing him with much admiration. Johann was still in disbelief. He finally had his boy. Father Wendel looked on with his eyes moist at this happy occasion.

Tired from all the commotion, she sat down on a chair near the window. The room was suddenly quiet. Johann, his father and the girls had gone to show off their newest addition. She looked around the new premises. The stillness felt soothing to her mind. She could not believe they were finally alone as a family.

33

It was the end of fall and the weather outside had turned chilly and wet. She could feel the cold penetrating through the walls of the huge stone structure. The hot water system coming up from the basement was barely enough to heat their room. Inquiring about it, they were told it was turned down to conserve fuel. Dismayed, they had to accept.

It was not that she was concerned for herself and Johann, but for the children, especially the baby. Ever since his inoculation against smallpox, he had become cranky and sickly looking. Concerned she bundled little Stefan up and took him to the nearest health clinic.

As she arrived at an old brick building near the center of town, she noticed the doctor seeing her was exasperated, hardly taking time to listen to what she had to say. She was only another of those Volks Deutsche. He would be glad when they all went on their way. He quickly examined the child then looked directly at her.

"I am very sorry, but this child is emaciated and will probably not survive the winter. There is not much I can do." He turned and wrote something in a log book.

She felt sick to her stomach. How could this man sit there cold and unfeeling and tell her something so awful.

She fought down the bitterness inside of her, mustering enough strength to talk. "Is there anything, anything at all that might help him?" She could not and did not want to give

208

up. There had to be something.

"The only thing I could suggest is dextrose and apple powder. But I must warn you not to put your hopes too high. In my opinion, there's not much that can be done for him."

It was then he paused and just stared at his log book. Who was this woman to him? He looked again at her and the child as if seeing them anew. He was getting tired of complying by the rules, of living inside the rationing and allotments.

There was a noticeable change in his tone of voice when he continued, "How is your milk intake? Have you been given extra rations to breastfeed?"

"No, none whatsoever..." she answered. "There was never any milk given to any of us pregnant women. There was hardly enough for the children, never mind us."

"There lies the whole problem." The doctor shook his head after confirming the cause. He paused to write something down on a piece a paper. "Here take this and give it to the administrator of the compound." After a moment in thought he looked up at her. "I'm afraid this is all I can do for you and your baby."

He handed her the prescription as she pulled herself up from the chair. It was not the first time she had to fight for what she believed in. She had been there before, recalling Rebekka's and Johann's illnesses, as well as her own. She could never give up. There was that little glimpse of hope within her. As then she was determined to make it work, even if all the odds were against her child's recovery.

Returning to the compound, she faithfully followed the instructions; also handing the doctor's note to the administrator. She was adamant, not missing a day in feeding the dextrose and apple powder to little Stefan. And to her surprise, she and all the other pregnant and nursing mothers also received extra rations of milk. Yet for Stefan, even after all this effort there was no visible remission in his condition. Still she refused to give in and faithfully continued to feed him the advised formula.

All along Johann stood by her side, and whenever possible, looked after the girls and tended to Stefan. He especially thought it important when he noticed Katina tiring. Concerned that with the extra strain she too would fall ill, and that, in his opinion would make matters even worse.

His fears proved him right when soon after the Malaria symptoms resurfaced and if it were not for family and friends standing by him, he hated to think how he possibly could have managed.

As long as he remembered, life for some strange reason had always been an uphill battle for them. Why? Often he had questioned if it was fate. Or was it something more? Would their life together always be a continuous struggle? Why little Stefan? Why him too? What was the purpose?

He longed so much for a peaceful and worry free period in their lives. Would it ever materialize? Maybe at their new destination, he hoped. Maybe then all this ill, will turn. A deep sigh escaped the heaviness in his chest.

His thoughts went back to the time in Mangalia. If things would not have turned out the way they did, he probably would have kept on building. Oh, he knew it would not have been without problems, but... He suddenly recalled the land deal with Thomas Backer and Heinrich Schwarz. Where were they now? He had not heard anything, nor had he seen Backer ever since that time they met on that property. Now he wondered if he ever would find out who had won the bid. Did it matter now? It seemed all those of German descent had lost their land in this relocation. Still he wondered about it.

As for Heinrich Schwarz he had not seen him since that brief encounter on the boat. Had he purposely requested to be located to a different place of holding? Would he be someone with power and connections to be able to side step this relocation process. Sometimes he felt they were just a herd of sheep being directed here and there by those above them.

And Grundman, will he ever find out whatever made him

leave that beautiful villa? A man does not just leave a place like that without good cause. Maybe one day...

Katina stirred beside him in bed. He heard the wind outside their window. He hoped it would not wake her or the children. He himself had just crawled into bed after tending to little Stefan. He had walked and carried his son until he had fallen asleep. Now he prayed that he would stay sleeping for the rest of the night.

He felt Katina's hot and sweaty body beside him. Her fever must have broken as she seemed to have fallen into a deep sleep. He wished they could have provided him with another bed. He hated to disturb her by crawling in and out. Luckily this time the girls had their own bunk beds. Quietly he nestled in beside her. It felt good to lie down. His tired and aching body welcomed the warmth of the comforter. Listening for a moment to the sound of the wind, he soon fell fast asleep.

--

After weeks of slow recovery, Katina hoped she had seen the last of this agonizing illness, as again depleted of strength she found it hard to carry on.

'Poor Johann,' she thought regretfully. Being sick had left all the duties of motherhood as well on his shoulders. She had noticed the strain showing on his face and it worried her. She had to get better soon to take charge of all her duties.

To her delight she noticed little Stefan had put on weight and was looking much better. The dextrose and apple powder had helped. She gave credit to Johann for taking such good care of the baby and the girls.

Since she had another doctor's visit coming, she thought it good to take Stefan along. About six months had passed since the doctor had last seen him, and she could not wait to see what his reaction would be.

Her guess was right. Upon presenting little Stefan to him, saying..." Doctor this is the little boy, whom you said would die within six months." The man looked at her perplexed.

211

At first he did not seem to recall, but then...

"Oh..." squirming around, he tried to excuse himself but could not. Admitting he had been wrong, he finally said.

"Yes, one should never give up on a human being, no matter what is the case."

34

The month of April was almost coming to a close when the order for another move was given. But along with it came heartache and grief, when Mark and Maria were not included in the transport.

The reason, Maria was of Romanian descent, and only pure German descendants were wanted for resettlement. Not knowing what to do, as going back to Romania was out of the question, Mark and Maria opted to stay in Austria. At present he was working at a prestigious tailoring outfit, and being trained in this field, it gave him hope to establish his own business, preferably right here in Vienna. Yet they all knew this would mean separation from family and friends and for that they were sad.

But who was able to argue against the authorities and their rules of classification.

She thought of Mama and Papa and the rest of her family. She had not heard from them since the time Daniel and Mark, with their families, had arrived here in Stockerau.

What will Papa and Mama think about Mark and his family having to stay behind? She knew it would not be easy on them, knowing they were used to having all their children within visiting reach.

For the next few days there was a lot of commotion. Everyone was busy packing, making sure nothing was left behind. She had a suspicion the nuns were counting the days and hours when they could have their beloved monastery all to themselves again.

But they would not be the only ones, as she and Johann, and most of their countrymen, were glad to leave. Hoping with this their final move, they would once again have a place of their own. If it were not for Mark and Maria, saying goodbye to Austria would have been easy as they had felt unwelcome right from the start. Thinking back now she recalled an incident in Seidenstadt when the girls attended Kindergarten. Because of their girls' beliefs, they had been beaten while the other children received bags of candy. They were told that the beating was to drive out the evil spirits. Both Rebekka and Julia were forced to repent and convert, but they had refused.

She and Johann were saddened when they had heard of this, but chose to keep quiet. It was best to keep the peace. And knowing this, she could not help but feel concern for her brother and his family.

She thought for themselves, who's to say it would be different at their next destination. Their only consolation was that they were not alone.

Loaded to capacity, the train rolled on toward Kirschberg. From there they were told they were to be relocated to various destinations. But arriving in Kirschberg, they were made aware again that the brutality and ugliness of war was still very much alive, as on their way to their own holding place, they passed a familiar compound, just as they had seen in Stockerau. Crowded behind barb wired fences, desolate people looked back at them, their eyes portraying hopelessness and despair. What stood out again was the star on their clothes.

She and Johann as well as the others were saddened by this. But again feeling helpless as there was nothing they could do. Who were they, to go against such a regime that condoned such acts of cruelty? It suddenly dawned on them that they and their families were just as vulnerable. Easily they could find themselves on the other side of that fence.

Rumors had come around again, that more of their Dobrujan people, who refused to take on the German citizenship, ended up in these camps. They found it difficult to understand. Gripped by deep fear they dared not to go against any of the German authority's commands. Even the slightest discontent or complaint could land them in trouble.

Bothered by all this they could not forget the faces of these poor souls. Yet despite the danger, she and Johann and the two older girls made a habit of collecting leftover food. Soon some of their friends joined them. Purposely they took their evening strolls past the nearby fenced compound. Playfully, the girls pulled a small wagon after them. Concealed on the wagon under a blanket were various morsels of food. And inconspicuously when they thought no one was watching they threw them quickly over the fence.

Sadly though, these few bits and pieces of food were not enough to satisfy the hunger of so many. Yet despite it all and the danger it involved, they willingly took their chances. Faithfully, they kept showing up, thinking if only one living soul was spared from hunger, all their efforts no matter how small were worth the risk.

Their short and heart rending stay here in Kirshberg was topped by another disappointment. Katina found out a little too late, she had missed Mama and Papa and the rest of her family by a day. Apparently they had come through a day earlier, en route to Pabianice near Lodz. Daniel and Hannah had found out and given her this news as they had also asked to be sent there. She was told that Papa was to take over a spinning and weaving factory there. So it was in Daniel's plan to be employed at the same.

All she could hope now was to be placed not far from them, as she and Johann, along with most of their friends, had requested a home with acreage in a smaller community.

A little downhearted, she sat looking out the window as the train rushed on to their final relocation site. It would have been good to see her family, at least long enough to find out how they are doing. Now, who knows when that will be?

Deep in thought she watched the landscape as it changed before her eyes. In conversation she started to share her hopes and doubts with Johann and the others. Centered on what their new adopted land held in store for them. Will it be all they had hoped for? Will they find peace and happiness there, which they all so desperately yearned for? She hoped it would be so. She and Johann, and all the others in their circle of friends and relations, were tired of roaming. She could see it on their strained faces. They all longed to settle down, to have a place they could call home again. But, she wondered, will any place ever come close to the one they had left behind?

35

It was the middle of July and the beginning of an early potato harvest when they finally arrived in Quadenstadt. It was a small town which lay about 35 km north of Lodz, with Pabianice not far, where her parents had settled. Quadenstadt was known to be a good crop bearing area and that especially pleased Johann. He had big dreams for this new place.

Yet arriving at their destination was a big disappointment, when they beheld what was to be their new home. Awestruck, Katina fought back bitter tears. All her dreams and expectations of a new beginning were shattered. The house, if one could call a two room shack that, looked filthy and in disrepair.

Johann too felt let down and disheartened by the sight. Speechless, he walked alongside the German official in charge, to have a closer look.

She unwillingly followed holding Stefan as Father Wendel stayed back with the girls and their belongings. "What do they think? This isn't even fit for pigs," he retorted as she walked away.

She shared his sentiments. What a place... They had left a beautiful new home behind and what did they get in return? She could not believe how anyone could call this a home; it did not even have a solid floor. What if it rained heavily and the water seeped into the place? It would most certainly be a muddy mess. She knew that when someone encountered change there would be a time of adjustment, but this was huge. In all her life she had never lived in a place in a condition such as this. For an instant she remembered her new home in Mangalia and tears welled up in her eyes.

She had heard rumors of the SS's ruthless and uncaring tactics, but to call this a home? She could not believe the audacity. Yet she dared not protest. Johann felt the same. He too did not say much. Numbed by what he saw he just looked around. When the quick tour had finished, he thanked the official as they walked back. Sitting among the crates and luggage with the girls playing around him, Father Wendel looked after the official with disgust. "Not even a helping hand. What do they think we are? I'm an old man with health problems. The least they could do is to provide someone to help us with this mess. Hmm! And they call this a welcome? The Fatherland has to do better than this to convince me!"

"Father...! Sh-h-h... Not so loud!" Johann shushed. He looked around just to see the official turn slightly then walk off the property. "You'll get us in trouble and right now I don't think we need any more of that. I mean, I agree with you and I'm just as upset as you. But let's face it. We are nothing to them. If we but buck a little they do away with us. I guarantee you this. Remember what we've seen and heard?" He was angry and disappointed too at the way they were treated. But what could they do? Nothing!

"I know! I know!" his father raised his hands in defeat still put out. "I understand what you're saying, but this whole situation... Ach..."

Disappointed, he waved it off not wanting to discuss this matter any further. "You know what I mean...?" he added in defeat. He realized it's best to let it go. "Well I better get off this crate and give you a hand then. But you'll see me hobbling around in pain after this. And then I'll be no good to anyone," he kept grumbling on.

Johann knew all too well his father's health issues, so he tried to do most of the hard work himself. Unfortunately, this was the situation they were in, and as much he wanted it to be different there was no way around it. So unwillingly they banded together to go about cleaning up the place despite the foul odor that greeted them at the door.

After all they had gone through this was the lowest. It could not have been more disappointing. It was definitely not what they had expected and were used too.

Looking around Katina wondered out loud. "Where does one start to clean up a place like this? There is no end to this."

Johann gave an unwilling smile toward her and just nodded.

After about two hours in trying to clean and set things in place, she looked wearily about. In all this time of working hard at it, she still had done little to give it a homey feel. Will she ever succeed? Startled by her youngest cry, she left the cleanup and busied herself to prepare a meal. She put Rebekka and Julia in charge of the two little ones, while Johann and his father kept up with the cleanup and moving in.

She had noticed a fine garden growing behind the hut, and went quickly outside to gather some of the vegetables. They had managed to purchase some of the staples needed to cook the basic meals. It would be enough to carry them through till they were settled. For now everybody had to be satisfied with what they got. Luckily someone had left some firewood beside the old clay stove that stood in the middle of the partially walled two room hut. In no time she had produced a good size pot full of vegetable soup. Soon the entire hut was filled with a mouthwatering aroma. A proud feeling came over her when she served the meal in her own dishes. She had found a tablecloth between the dishes. She spread it over one of the crates, using it as a table. Her dishes looked invitingly clean and enjoyable to eat from. Satisfied, she looked around, it had been a long time and it felt good to be in charge again.

By nightfall Johann managed to construct makeshift beds out of straw for themselves and the children. Father Wendel claimed the only bed in the hut. It seemed to have been left there by someone. After everything was done and the dust had settled, everyone was ready to retire. They had pulled it off despite all the unpleasantness around them. For the time being, wanted or not, it was their home. She sighed, as she slipped into bed. The children had fallen asleep and beside her Johann too had dozed off. It was no surprise to her as he especially had worked hard. She closed her eyes, tired and weary, still uneasy about where the future would take them.

Suddenly in the middle of the night she woke with a start, scratching herself profoundly. In the adjacent room she heard Father Wendel cursing. Johann too woke up in aggravation. All at once he jumped up. Fumbling around in the dark, he searched for the kerosene lamp. He had placed it earlier near their straw beds. After a few attempts he managed to get it lit. Shining around, they both were horrified at the unbelievable sight of swarming bedbugs. Not just a few, the bed was alive with them. They had been warned to expect this, but they never thought to see so many. What could one do? They had nothing at hand to get rid of these ugly night creatures. Apparently they loved to come out under the cover of darkness and pester anything warm-blooded.

Quickly she tried to brush them of their makeshift bed, to lessen the numbers, but gave up. It was useless. Worn-out and tired she curled herself up at the lower end of their straw bed, thinking it to be less contaminated. In an attempt to get relief, Johann joined her, leaving the lamp burning. As he had heard these kinds of bugs were shy to light. With that he hoped to lessen the numbers.

Beside them, the children too were tossing. "Poor dears," she said with profound pity. She rose again and Johann joined her. Tirelessly they searched in the semi-darkness to get the bugs off their little bodies and blankets. Helpless and discouraged they gave up. It was futile. All they could do was to wait out the night and pray that dawn would come soon.

The long awaited morning finally arrived and never was it more welcomed. As soon as possible, Johann set out to report their unfortunate encounter to their group leader. Before the day was over the whole place was fumigated against lice and other crawling creatures.

It was then during the day, while working around the house, Johann noticed an old man looking scared and forlorn from behind the nearby barn door. Inquiring about him, he learned to his dismay that this had been the old man's home before their takeover.

Compassionately, he and Katina tried their best to befriend him. They felt bad to have taken away another man's home and livelihood. They despised the orders that had been pushed on them to do so.

Now Johann wanted nothing more to do with this. Determined he went ahead to find and purchase his own land. Defeated, he was told that there was no other home to be had. They had to stay where they had been assigned to.

Caught in the middle, he tried to make the best out of this situation and showed kindness toward the old man. It did not take long and he came closer to talk.

With a lot of gestures and strange talk he made them understand. He had grownup children living in the near vicinity. And he'll be leaving shortly to live with them.

Johann tried to make him understand there was no hurry for him to leave. He was welcome to share everything that was growing on the land. But he also made him understand that he should do so only in secret. As their group leader did not look kindly upon anyone aiding the enemy in any shape or form.

Most grateful, the old man understood the situation and remained living in the barn for a little while longer.

36

After he had made the shack as livable as he could. Johann drove with the owner's dilapidated wagon and worn-down horse into town. He had run out of much needed supplies and besides that had to catch up on the latest news. He realized that it was important to build a connection to this community. Opportunity and security were significant benefits of the Dobrujan German community back in Romania. Now he hoped with some luck to make connections here. Although he understood very well that it was a different place with different rules. As it is he was unknown and it would take some time to be recognized and accepted. With that in mind he set out in good faith.

It did not go unnoticed that the Poles were strongly oppressed under the present German authority. He also discovered that many families, Polish and Jewish, had been removed from their homes and land to make room for them. And it gave him no pleasure, knowing how they and their countrymen had felt when it happened to them. There were rumors that Quadenstadt was once a big Jewish center, also that some of the Polish inhabitants had been sent to Germany to work as cheap labor. Of the Jewish families, he remembered the ones he saw behind the fences in Austria and at Kirshberg. What this regime had in store for all of them, he shuddered to think.

There was another thing he found troubling. It was the German authority's growing intolerance for any religious belief. He thought at the many freedoms lost, just to satisfy ideology. He just shook his head. They would have to remain careful with what they said and did. As he drove on he remembered Robert's words. How quickly they had come to pass.

As he arrived at the market he found some German officers standing with a large ledger style book. He realized they were making tallies and dividing out the portions of supplies to the men gathered there. He gave a quick glance around the group to see if there were any familiar faces. But as far as he could see there were none. Either his friends had come here before him, or they were also still struggling with what was dealt to them.

"Well, this is as good a time as any," he encouraged himself and left the wagon standing nearby. He approached the officers. The one with the ledger gave a sharp glance at him.

"Name?" he snapped crisply.

"Johann Wendel," he replied as he glanced at the others.

"We have your supplies in the yard. Bring your wagon around. A future portion of your crops from that property is required for the troops on the eastern front. We will make available some Polish labor to help you with your harvest."

'What crops?' he thought as he did not even have a chance to look around the place.

The officer paused as he looked at the ledger before him then turned to another page.

"Quadenstadt has been selected for the construction of a new and bigger hospital, and we are hiring workers to build it. We are in need of a construction supervisor. It says here that you are a Baumeister. Would you be willing to put your name forward?"

"Yes, although I will still be needed at home to manage..."

"We will provide laborers for your farm," the officer interrupted him a little impatient. "Do not worry about that. The building of this hospital is of great importance."

After discussing a few more details about the construction

project, the German officer wrote his name in the ledger book for the construction supervisor position. Johann walked away in a daze.

"Well that went well," a faint grin covered his face. "I can't believe it, what luck. Wait till Katina and Father hears about that, or better yet, our friends. With the extra money coming in, I probably can afford a better home with a much larger property."

Just as he went about to get the supplies, his attention was suddenly diverted by a loaded wagon leaving the yard.

It was Heinrich Schwarz!

And he was here in Quadenstadt.

Heinrich saw him as well. His eyebrows raised then lowered as his face showed the shadow of a scowl. Almost immediately the scowl left. And in its place was a composed pleasant civility, even a twinkle of humor in his eye as if meeting an old friend. He nodded at Johann and continued driving the wagon out onto the street.

Johann watched him go, puzzled as to what he was thinking. When he was finished loading his supplies, he followed the man as he was going in the same direction. He realized when passing that Heinrich's property had a much better location. In the first place it was closer located to town with a much better house. Theirs, on the other hand, lay on the outskirts of town with a poor boggy mosquito ridden property and an old dilapidated shack. Something did not add up. It was as if Heinrich Schwarz had been given a chance to choose where he wanted to go. He wondered again at the power that man had. Even in Romania with the land deals, he seemed to always gain the upper hand.

Of all places to end up, they were in the same small town together. This was something he had to consider, someone he needed to watch out for.

--

Soon after, Johann got the news that he was chosen to be the construction supervisor for the new hospital. Katina was beside herself.

His father tried his best to show pleasure. "Now maybe we'll be good enough to get a better place," he said still nursing a grudge. "A place like this is not fit for a supervisor. You should tell them Johann."

"In time Father, everything in time," he smiled, shaking his head about his father's comment.

Katina threw him a proud look as it gave her great satisfaction to see her husband in such a good position. "Well who would have thought? Maybe this Quadenstadt is not so bad after all?" she looked around the room. "Maybe in time we can build us a better home. Wouldn't that be nice?" she smiled wishfully.

"Now you two, you just have to be patient a little longer. As for now I've got some inspecting to do," she looked at him puzzled. He came up and gave her a peck on the cheek, then turned toward his father. "Are you willing to walk with me across the land? I was told to give part of the crops toward the troops. Well, I haven't even seen all there is to this place. Maybe you can help me plan next year's crop... Hmm?"

With that the two walked out.

She looked after them a little giddy. Her mind filled with happy anticipation. "Let's see, we do need new beds and a real table and enough chairs. And, oh yes, we desperately need a china cabinet."

She looked around a little dismayed.

"Oh... what's the use, all this would have to wait? There is not much I can do in this place anyway."

With that she unwillingly went to do her chores. She looked up for a moment from what she was doing, watching the children play among the crudely erected straw beds. Of one thing she was grateful, at least there were no more reoccurring instances of bed bugs, that alone was a good thing.

But then just when she had thought to have conquered one problem, another one surfaced. They were into the first week of autumn now and she had noticed a familiar weakness coming on ever so slightly. She blamed it on all the extra stress they had encountered, but it should have been a warning to them when they first had landed here. This, of all places, was a low lying swamp land, a perfect breeding ground for mosquitoes.

Sure enough the malaria struck again, but this time, to her and everyone's relief, it was not as severe. After a short time of convalescing in the local hospital and good medical care, she soon recovered and was sent home.

All this had left her feeling guilty, as Johann was left to look after the children. But when she heard that Hetti once again had come to his aid, she was grateful for her thoughtfulness. Yet Hetti, a nurse by trade, always brushed it off saying that it was only natural to help a friend in need.

Upon her release, the doctor in charge suggested to Johann, that for her sake it would be best to leave this place and to move to Breslau. The town lay southwest from Quadenstadt, where the land was higher and less infested with mosquitoes. Yet seeing how much Johann struggled with the idea of leaving his new friends and a good paying job behind, she put his mind at ease and dismissed the recommendation, reassuring him they would stay in Quadenstadt.

Hearing this, the doctor, still concerned for her well being, kindly reported her condition to the local authorities. He asked them for help to at least provide better living conditions for his patient.

The next day the town's top SS official was at their door. He ordered them to come and look over some of the available homes he had lined up for them.

The possibility of getting a better home seemed very inviting, and both she and Johann were overjoyed at the idea.

But this opportunity of house hunting soon left them disillusioned, when they realized the heart rendering task of taking what was not theirs. Especially when witnessing the

SS official enter with force into a woman's home, and he did it with little respect for her or anything that stood in his way.

Katina was shocked at the scene. She could not take her eyes off the Polish woman, who stood near the door. Bewildered and scared she kept her four children close around her. Being a mother herself she did not blame her for being terrified. She would have felt the same in this predicament.

There was a sudden outburst of swearing coming from the SS official. She looked around just in time to see him stabbing and slicing away at a picture as if he was possessed. Her heart raced when she realized what he was destroying. It was a religious picture of the Madonna and child.

"What an idiot," she mumbled just loud enough for Johann to hear.

He reacted quickly and signaled for her to hold her tongue. Experience had taught him that it was best to keep one's mouth shut. Definitely he did not agree with the officer's behavior. But speaking up now, again would label him and his family as siding with the enemy. And that he knew could mean their persecution and possibly death.

He was just as much angered by all this. Under normal circumstances he would have dealt with this sort of behavior in a different manner. He was not scared to defend what was right. But knowing that he would not only be taking on one man but a whole establishment made him hesitant to act. He had always been proud of his heritage, but after witnessing this, it made him feel ashamed and sad to be part of it.

"Johann, I don't want to move into this house," Katina whispered beside him, her eyes filled with tears.

When he related this to the SS official, he expected the rage and profane swearing that followed. Embarrassed by all this he took Katina by the hand and with a look of apology toward the woman they both walked outside.

The official still angry came out after them.

"This is what I have. If you do not accept it, there is

nothing I can do for you."

As they were coming back near where their search started, Johann saw an abandoned woodworking shop. Considering it, he saw the potential of having it transformed into a comfortable home. They found the owner had two other homes with property so they did not feel as guilty claiming it. At least no one would have to be thrown out to make room for them.

"We will take this wood shop as our home," Johann said to the officer who by now had enough of this house search.

"As you wish," the officer replied indifferently, "My work here is done. I will fill in my report that you have found a place." The SS officer looked skeptical at the dilapidated shop. He realized there was a lot of work to be done to make it livable. His demeanor suddenly changed. "There is a possible grant for some of the building material. You can forward a list to one of the officials. Do you wish to have help moving?"

"No, thank you. We can manage," Johann replied.

With that the officer turned on his heels and walked briskly away. They both watched him go with relief. For a moment they studied the place then began to make plans. As it was, this property was located much closer to town, and of all things, as he found out, it was surrounded by friends of theirs. There were the Rucks across from it and the Kranzes next to the two barns. On closer inspection and to their amazement, the new property had a considerable large frontage along the street. It was double the size of their friends' properties with a small creek running between the two grounds. But the existing barns of that extended property lay right across from none other than Heinrich Schwarz's property.

'Well now that is an unexpected surprise,' Johann mused in quiet. It had not been his intention to choose a property so close to Schwartz's place. But here it was, despite of this unfortunate drawback he was happy to have this piece of land.

"Just wait and see Katina..." He put his arm around her as they walked toward the old wood shop. "Soon we'll have a proper home. One we all can be proud of and feel comfortable in. I promise you this." He drew her close and gave her a loving kiss. For a moment longer they stood still in an embrace their eyes gazing over the land.

"Thank you Johann. I think we'll be happy in here. I feel it. The land is absolutely wonderful."

He felt proud to have secured this place. The start of the day had been anything than promising and very distasteful and ugly at times. Seeing the property in front of him, he was glad not to have chosen the other homes. They would have always felt guilty in doing so. It was indeed much different here. A feeling of great satisfaction came over him. Now finally things were coming together and he could hardly wait to start.

37

Before the woodworking shop could be made livable, he had to cover the six foot hole that existed in the middle of the shop's floor. Yet no sooner had he thought to close it he quickly changed his mind. 'It would be perfect as a root cellar to keep the winter vegetables close at hand and out of the cold,' he thought, proud to have come up with this idea.

With this behind him he decided to secure and winterize all the walls as well as the roof. Then constructing a wooden floor he planned to paint it for easy cleaning, but before he could paint, he had to build two kachel-ovens along the inside walls; then install connecting heating outlets to the bedrooms for cold winter nights. Next, he and his father built a good sized clay stove for the kitchen, one that featured a large cast-iron top for easy cooking.

To get enough daylight into the house he put two large windows in every room. Another task was to bring electricity into the house. It would eliminate the use of the insufficient kerosene lamps.

All in all he managed to get three large rooms out of the remodeled workshop. The first was a good sized kitchen-living room area. The other two, planned to be their living and dining rooms, for now were designated as bedrooms. In time he planned to extent and build proper bedrooms.

The entire house lay in an L-shape, with the two bedrooms facing the front of the yard toward the street. The kitchen-living room was connected to the carriage house all under the same roofline, stretched out toward the back yard. Here not far from the building he had in mind to construct a good sized vegetable garden; perfectly located and within easy reach. From there farther to the back to the property there stood an existing fruit orchard, one he thought to make good use of.

With their home happily situated to one side of the yard, it left a considerably larger grassy slope on the other, where two barns stood close to the street; one smaller in size than the other. The two properties were connected by a narrow bridge that spanned over a slow flowing creek. It was, in their eyes, an idyllic setting.

All the properties in the surrounding neighborhoods were long and narrow with the houses close to the street. So it was unavoidable to see or meet one's neighbors on a daily basis. To the left were the Koenigs and across from them the Greises and the Rucks. To the right, next to the barns, were the Kranzes. And beside the Kranzes were the Eberts, who owned and managed the flour mill. Most of these were friends from Mangalia who made it a habit to stay in close contact with one another. Yet there was one neighbor she and Johann, for obvious reasons could not warm up to.

As another school year had started, both Rebekka and Julia were called to attend. By chance, Julia was in the same grade as Schwarz's daughter, Eva, and the two had become good friends. It was not to their liking, but seeing how good the two girls played together, they agreed not to interfere in their friendship.

As for Heinrich and his wife, she remembered well the few times they had met. They would certainly not warrant a good friendship. But nevertheless she was resolved to be neighborly, so one fine afternoon when Julia was at their house playing, she decided to walk over and call on her daughter to come home. At the same time she would introduce herself and take it from there. She knew it would be an awkward situation, yet she was determined to do her civil duty.

On the first knock Olga opened the door, she seemed more worn than she remembered and the conversation was short and to the point. After that brief visit she realized the woman's hesitation to connect on a regular basis. That was fine with her as she had no wish to become friends with Olga.

Later she told Johann of this meeting, and he warned her not to make it a regular habit to visit with Heinrich's wife. For as far as he had seen, there was too much about that man that left Johann a little uneasy.

On the way home from work Johann had often seen Schwarz sitting in the local bar. It seemed to him, he liked joining other men there for an evening drink. He liked discussing current events, as well as the relocation and the war effort. Many times Heinrich had tried to coerce Johann into joining them in a drink or two, but he had no interest in spending every night in the bar drinking away his hard earned money. He would rather sit at home sharing a drink or a cup of tea with his Father and Katina. No, he definitely was not the drinking kind. Besides that there was still too much work that needed to be done at home. Katina had mentioned to him of Heinrich's wife not looking too happy. "Hmm..." he wondered. Was it because the man was never much at home?

As it was he had heard that Heinrich Schwarz was taking the relocation hard. He had lost much in property and power. But he also knew of the man's ambitions and efforts to gain it back here. Even now he had signed up with the German authorities to work his way into the political structure. And he had a hunch it won't be long.

--

She had noticed a visible change in Johann ever since they had moved to this place. To be able to provide and be in charge, had given him once again pride in his achievements, and he was harder at work than ever before.

She had to admit the new surroundings had boosted all their spirits. The location of the house, as well as the land, had a beauty of its own. She especially favored the twilight hour when the evening fog rose off the brook. Often she stood and watched it move over the meadow and then onto the open land that backed their property. She treasured this quiet peaceful scene. It made her forget, if even for a moment, the turmoil of war.

She and Johann hoped so much to live in peace, to establish a permanent home here for their children. But with every passing day they were made aware they were only strangers here, occupying enemy territory. No one could guarantee them this was the end of their journey. The cry of war had not been laid to rest. The hate and injustice against one race to another had not subsided.

This very feeling struck home again when they were ordered to take Polish inhabitants as laborers. She and Johann found this obligation very oppressive, as it went against their nature. They both detested it greatly, but seeing again they were powerless against it, they had to accept.

A family by the name of Slovak was brought to them the following day. It was an older couple with three grown sons and a daughter, who had been stricken with polio when young. Marianka was to take over her household chores while her father and brothers had to look after the outside chores.

It was hard in the beginning to have a stranger sharing her chores. But seeing no way out of this situation she came to accept it. Besides, now it gave her the much needed free time to do other things. It was not that she was not used to having servants around the house, she remembered the time in Girargi, when Michaela and Mikhail had worked for them, but then it was under different arrangements. They had been treated with respect and as free human beings. She definitely did not want Marianka and her family to feel as servants.

Come mealtime she and Johann coaxed Marianka to sit

with them at the table. At first she was reluctant to accept this special treatment, but then gave in. Father Wendel though cautioned them not to let anyone of their neighbors see this. He feared the German authorities had spies among their own countrymen. Not taking chances they locked their doors and pulled the curtains shut and opened them only after they had finished eating.

At first Marianka did not understand why they would do all this for her, but soon realized, they lived by different rules.

38

It was days later, in the early darkness of night, when Heinrich Schwarz stood at the front of his property. He was not happy most of the days, but today was different. He was put in charge over this part of town. He was told to make sure rules were followed. With this promotion it gave him control, but also favor from the German authorities.

He still harbored deep anger and resentment toward his neighbors in front of him. Katina and Johann, here of all places and on a much bigger spread of land. In the shadow of the house he continued watching the street. He was brooding over things lost and over what he may gain back.

He was angry when Johann got the good paying position building the hospital. He had put his name in for the same and was sure he would have it. Yes, Johann had all the credentials, but still it was not right. Now he would gain power to get the next best job. He had already noticed him getting praise and recognition for this recent one. Heinrich scowled in the dark. He would just love to knock him down... someway... somehow. He had to find something to pin on him, something that would blemish his record.

He waited and watched the entire street, but all was quiet tonight like it was most nights. But he had to stand watch as this was after all one of his duties. Would it be another night with no gratification for his efforts? Oh, he had showed the authorities that he was able to push around the Polish people, but he was hoping for something larger.

He had noticed Johann slip up once in awhile. He had seen him a little too lenient toward his Polish servants, treating them kindly, not as expected. He had a hunch that if he was patient enough, Johann would play right into his hand.

The air was cool and crisp and he felt the coldness penetrate through his clothes. "Just a little while longer," he muddled to himself. "The old man should be finished soon and be on his way home." He had calculated right. Always the last to go home, the old Slovak closed up the barn and walked across the property toward the street.

It was a moonless night and he had to strain his eyes to see. The darkened figure came closer. There was something different about the way Slovak walked this evening. He was sort of bent over, as if carrying something on his back. Triumphant, Schwarz jumped out from behind his hiding place.

"Halt!" he demanded with authority. "What are you carrying in that sack?"

Terrified the man dropped the sack of potatoes. "My wife and children are hungry," he begged. "Please do not report this."

"You know what the penalty for stealing is?" Heinrich ignored the plea and took the sack of potatoes. He sent the old man on his way with a scuff and a kick.

"Get going you old fool. You'll be in big trouble when I report this to the Group Leader."

"I beg of you..." But Slovak's plea went unheeded.

"Stop your whining you old fool and get out of my sight."

Slovak felt another kick, falling face down into the dirt.

"That's where you belong you scum." With a haughty laugh, Schwarz took the sack of potatoes and walked off, disappearing just as quickly as he had appeared. He had exactly what he wanted. This was the advantage he was looking for.

39

"It's going to be a cool night," Johann commented as he came in from the outside with an armful of broken twigs and wood shavings. He had just finished making his rounds to check up on the animals, as he had done every night. Closing the door quickly behind him he carried the kindling over to the wood box. Then he carefully placed it on top of a pile of dried cow dung. There was a wood shortage and the cow dung served as fuel in these parts of the region.

"Here, now that should be enough for tomorrow's breakfast," he brushed himself off and removed his jacket hanging it at its usual place behind the door.

"Has everyone gone?" Katina asked looking up from her mending that lay in front of her in a basket.

"The old man was still in the barn finishing the last of his chores," Johann rubbed his hands to warm them. "I told him to leave it for tomorrow, but he insisted on doing them tonight."

In saying this he walked over to Rebekka and Julia. Both of them were sitting in front of the warm kachel-oven already dressed in their night gowns. Patiently they sat waiting for the usual ritual of reading bedtime stories before being tucked into bed.

"So how are my girls?" he called out louder than intended, reaching his arms out toward them. Then with a swoop he lifted them up as they came running toward him squealing

237

with delight.

"Sh-h-h... Not so loud," Katina reminded them gently. "You'll wake up Grandpa and the little ones."

"Oops," he signaled for the girls to hush. All at once Grandpa's sudden change in snoring sent them all into suppressed laughter.

"Sh-h-h..." she hushed them again, including herself.

At his usual request Johann had placed his father's bed right in the corner between the kitchen stove and the kachel-oven; as he claimed he needed the warmth for his arthritis. Now the coziness of the same had made him fall into a deep and comfortable sleep. His mouth wide open, he lay on his back his feet crossed and hands folded.

"Rebekka!"

Suddenly frustrated with the job before her, she addressed her oldest in a subdued but noticeably irritated voice. While doing so she held one of Becky's dresses up for her to see. "How do these long tears get into here? I've told you so many times not to climb trees when you wear your good clothes."

"I don't Mama."

"Well, then how do they get there?" she looked at Rebekka, scolding.

By the tone of Mama's voice, Rebekka knew it meant trouble.

"It's not me, it's Butch," she tried to wiggle out of this uncomfortable position, knowing she was guilty.

Butch was a midsize black haired Mongrel; Johann had brought him home not too long ago to train him as a guard dog. Yet by the looks of it, the dog took more to playing with the girls than guarding the property.

"How in heaven's name does Butch get to do this?" Katina kept insisting to find out what really happened.

"Well..." interrupted by a sharp knock at the door, Rebekka was relieved for the moment not to provide further explanation.

"Don't people know that it's night time and there are

children sleeping?" disturbed by the abrupt awakening, Father Wendel grumbled angrily to himself.

Not sure who would be calling at this late hour, Johann went to open the door.

"Heil Hitler!"

Perplex by the greeting, he greeted the late visitor back in the same fashion.

"Heil Hitler, Herr Siegheimer!"

Katina looked over to Father Wendel, her brows raised questioning in silence. 'What was the head of the Gestapo doing here at this hour?'

She had often heard Johann mention his name in political conversations with his friends. And from what she had gathered, Herr Siegheimer was not as much a radical as his fellow comrades. For some reason or other Johann seemed to have found favor in his eyes, as it came around that he was admired and sought out for his leadership ability and skills. It all seemed very flattering at the time. But the more Johann had seen and heard what the Gestapo stood for, the more he wanted to distance himself from them.

"Come in please." He offered politely for Herr Siegheimer to step inside. Yet he sensed by the man's expression that this was not a friendly visit.

Noticing Katina and the children, Herr Siegheimer excused his late visit.

"Sorry for the interruption at this late hour, but we've received complaints. One of your Polish laborers was caught leaving your place earlier this evening. He had a sack of potatoes on his back."

"What...?" Katina jumped to her feet looking from one to the other.

"Have you any knowledge of this Herr Wendel?" Herr Siegheimer's probing look went from one to the other. He walked back and forth in an upright and precise manner.

"No, Herr Siegheimer," Johann, daring to defend the loyalty of his laborers. "I know my people; they are honest workers and would never go behind my back."

The commander's face turned red in anger. "You cannot and should not ever trust them. They are nothing but filthy scum, Schweinehunde, I tell you."

After a moment of silent pacing, he seemed to calm down a bit, speaking with an almost pleading tone of voice.

"I have tried to defend the accusations against you., because I know that you are an upstanding citizen and a much-liked man, but I must warn you Herr Wendel, if there is any truth to this..."

He interrupted his pacing. "I personally, and that I can assure you, it won't be pleasant for either of us. I will have to carry out the punishment. So I advise you in all earnestness not to let this happen again."

He looked around, to see if he was understood.

"Yes, Herr Siegheimer," Johann made it clear that he understood.

Satisfied, Siegheimer gave a quick salute and bid them all a goodnight. He left the house, keeping the same precision in his walk.

A quiet hush lingered. No one dared to speak. Johann stood in a daze, not knowing what to make of this visit. One thing he was sure, he had to get to the bottom of this. He had to find out who was spying on them. He could not believe it. His own countrymen were watching and betraying each other. They had to be careful, more than ever before.

He listened to the Gestapo's personnel carrier roar out of the yard and onto the street.

"Katina, tuck the children in for me tonight. I'm going quickly over to see old Slovak. The poor man, I hope he's all right." With a shake of his head he reached for the lantern and his jacket, and before she could say otherwise, he had disappeared closing the door behind him.

He stood for a moment at the gate, contemplating if it was wise to walk over to Slovak's house. Who knows, the one who snitched on him might be waiting for him now to make this very move.

The street was dark and silent in front of him, almost foreboding. The light shining through the windows of the neighboring houses did little to help the darkness.

Now that he was thinking about it, how much did he really know about some of his neighbors? For instance, to the left of them, he had only gotten to know the Koenigs when they had moved here. It was different with the Kranzes, who lived to the right of them, next to the Eberts. Across the street were the Rucks and to the right of them the Greises. All four were old friends from Mangalia and none of them would do him in. Of course then there were the Schwarzes, whose property lay parallel from their barns. Actually he did have the best view over their whole property. It could be possible, but why...why would he be doing this now and for what purpose or reason?

Was it not Heinrich Schwarz who had invited him to join him in the village pub after work? Yet he had always refused, telling him he'd rather drink his beer at home with his wife. Maybe he wanted to befriend him, and with his refusal, disliked him for that reason. But to Johann, home life was and always would be more important. Actually, he disliked hanging around all night in the pub. Already for the reason that he did not want to drink away all the hard earned money. He had better use for it. He wanted so much to build up his equity. His wish was to make life easier for Katina and the children.

The promise he once made, when they were first married, still prevailed in his memory. He vowed as he had done then, not to rest until he had brought their standard of living up to what Katina had been accustomed to before her marriage to him.

Lost in thoughts, the cool evening air suddenly made him realize that it actually was foolish to go and see Slovak tonight. He could be doing it tomorrow without drawing a lot of attention to himself.

He was just about to turn in when he heard Butch growling; giving out a high pitch bark. The dog must not have noticed him being outside.

'This is odd.' he thought, wondering what had caught the animal's attention. Was he chasing something, or better yet someone? What could have engulfed his interest so much that he did not notice him stepping outside? Slowly he made his way past the house and then to the woodshed. He listened. All at once he heard a man's voice speak softly to the dog in Polish.

"Shoo, go away, go away." But instead of going, the dog let out another high pitch bark.

"Who is there? Butch, who do you have there?" The dog, recognizing Johann's voice, gave out another bark. Something rustled in the dark in front of him. "Who is there?" Johann demanded with an aggressive tone of voice.

"Please, Pan Wendel, it's me." A scared voice uttered from out of the darkness.

"Pan Slovak?" Johann asked, not sure if it really was him.

"What in heaven's name are you doing here? I was just about to go and see you at your house." He had learned enough Polish in the short time they had been here to make himself understood and to understand.

"I did not dare go home. I don't want my family to get in trouble. If they come searching for me and can't find me, they will leave them alone," the old Slovak rattled on. "Then I see the Gestapo come to your house..." he gasped scared to ask. "Were they looking for me?"

"Slow down my friend. They did not come for you, they came to warn me, so don't worry." After comforting the old man, Johann changed his tone in a discerning manner. "Next time, Pan Slovak, ask me first before you take anything."

"But I was scared you would not approve."

"Pan Slovak", Johann lowered his voice. "I say it here and now to you in all confidence, I would never let you or your family go hungry. Not if I can help it and that's a

I WILL REMEMBER ALWAYS

solemn promise. Just next time ask me and we'll do it in an inconspicuous way, okay...?"

Still shaken, Slovak promised. Bidding good night, he quickly vanished around the corner of the house.

Johann stood for a moment, listening and then turned in.

Katina and his father were still up, turning questionably toward him as he entered.

"Before I sit down..." Johann requested. "Is there some hot tea left? I'm chilled to the bone."

She quickly went to prepare a cup for him and then set it down on the kitchen table. She pulled a chair for Johann and for her, while listening to the details.

The next day upon Johann's and his father's instructions, she told the Slovaks in confidence, that if they ever wish to take food home, to do it in broad daylight and under the cover of their clothes. It proved to be no problem for Marianka and Pani Slovak. They usually wore a big sprawling shawl wrapped around their shoulders. It would be easy for them to hide food among other things. And it could be done without anyone suspecting it.

So it was agreed upon.

40

With Marianka and Hetti taking care of the children and Father Wendel to look after the outside activities; she and Johann took the chance to pay Mama and Papa a short visit.

They planned to leave early Saturday morning for Pabianice, then return early Sunday evening. He had to be back to see his men get the new hospital finished. It had to be done before the cold weather set in. The structure consisted mainly of brick and would make it difficult to work on in sub-zero temperatures. He knew the visit would be rushed, but that was all the time he could allow himself.

The streets lay in silence in front of them as they pulled out the following morning. Bundled up in a warm wool blanket, Katina sat huddled against Johann in the front seat. She listened to the even trot of the horses as they drove along the stretched out road before them. Her thoughts drifted to a similar time when she was escorted to Mangalia for their wedding. How long has it been? She did not care to count the years. Most of them were hard and difficult. But the memories of the good ones still remained strong in her heart.

Moving closer to Johann she gave him a loving smile. "I love you," she whispered, feeling his strong arm around her. He answered her back with a tender hug and kept that position for a good part of the way.

Once in Pabianice they did not have to search long for her parent's place. The Stack's name had become well known and well thought of. Knowing her father, as in times gone by, he probably still had an open hand to anyone in need.

She suddenly realized how long it had been since they had last seen each other. Her heart began to race. She wondered now how everyone was doing.

She did not have to guess how much this surprise visit affected her family. Seeing her and Johann drive up so unexpectedly was more than they could have anticipated. It had indeed been a long time. There was so much to catch up and talk about. Hugging each other, they all shed a few tears of joy.

"How have you been and how are the children?" Mama asked with excitement in her voice.

"Yah, how are they? They must have grown quite a bit since we've seen them last." Grandpa Hauber interrupted before she could answer.

Leaning on his walking stick, she could see this whole resettlement had taken a toll on him. She wondered if he was still into planting roses.

She could still see him in her parent's garden showing off his roses to everyone. Yes, even to the little ones, who mostly did more harm than good to his prize roses, especially Rebekka and some of the older grandchildren, who would go into things they shouldn't have. What had surprised her, in spite of it all, Grandpa never had ill feelings about this. Never did he tire of his grandchildren. He had always been ready to show and teach them; especially about roses.

"Yes, Grandpa, they have grown," she answered with a smile. "And you'll be happy to know Rebekka is as lively as ever; just as you remember her. Right now she is into tearing her dresses and blaming it all on the dog."

Grandpa Hauber laughed at her last statement. "Well Katina, children will be children. In a few more years, she'll be out of it. Believe me I know. I've raised seven daughters of my own. Your Mother can vouch for that."

A faint smile on Mama's lips told her that it was so.

Robert had stood, patiently waiting his turn. "We've heard from Daniel that you have another addition to you family." He smiled in approval. "I guess congratulations are in order. Now you will have someone to carry on the family name."

"Yes, he is our little Stammhalter. If it wouldn't have been for the long drive we would have brought him and the girls along. But..." Johann shrugged his shoulders, "maybe next year."

"That'll be wonderful," Grandpa beamed. The others agreed.

News of their arrival had spread quickly and soon Daniel and Hannah came to greet them.

After saying hello to everyone, it felt strange not to see Edwina among them. She had known of her sister's marriage, but not in detail of when and where.

"Where's Edwina and how is she doing?"

"Well after her wedding, shortly before we left Romania, we haven't seen or heard much of her or her husband. Just a short telegram, telling us they're now residing in Leslau," Mama said lightheartedly.

She had been looking forward to seeing Edwina. But now, who knows when that would be?

"How about Tara and Micha, have you any knowledge of their whereabouts"?"

"Oh..." Robert was quick to answer. "They were settled together with Micha's parents on a dairy farm. I think it's east of Lodz, not far from Job and Lena."

It was later around the large dining room table, she realized how few in numbers the family had become, as Ben too, one year younger than herself, had married Rosanna shortly before leaving Romania. Now the two had settled with her family somewhere in the Danzig area. That left only Robert, Josh, Matthew, and Daniel assisting Papa in the factory. It was almost like old times. She sensed how proud they were in working together. Jonas and Nathaniel, her two younger brothers were still attending school.

It felt good just to sit and reminisce and exchange old and new happenings. The subject of war came up on occasion, as they all had seen the injustice and cruelty, but for most of the time they cheered each other on for they all knew how precious this time of togetherness was. No one could tell in this turmoil of war what could happen next.

Her family, just like she and Johann, had witnessed and seen things that had left them disillusioned about their ancestral homeland and its leadership. But as Papa put it, there was no giving in and letting despair and hopelessness take over.

She admired Papa's strength. Through good and bad his faith had kept him. Yet, even when it had wavered, at the end it always came out strong.

Just like her father, she tried to rely on that strength.

The following day she and Johann joined them in a Sunday morning service. It was heart-warming to all be together in her parent's home. She loved her brothers playing their zithers, mandolins and harmonicas, as they all sang old familiar songs. It brought back memories of happier times. They seemed so distant now.

After one more gathering around the dinner table, it was time to part again. She had dreaded this moment of goodbyes, but to her surprise she managed to stay light-hearted. It seemed to make it easier on the others.

All in all it had been a good visit. She would relish it for months to come. Satisfied, she set her heart on home, where she knew their little ones were eagerly awaiting their return.

Driving along, she had to laugh at Mama's concern to not have them go hungry on the way. Like most mothers, she had packed all sorts of goodies for their return trip. And knowing they would not be together for Christmas, she had also slipped special gifts for each of the children.

"Come back soon..." Mama's words still resounded in her mind. The smile upon her lips grew faint. She felt a little twinge in her heart. She realized now it will be quite some time before she would see Mama and the others again.

Johann, sensing her thoughts, quietly pulled her close, comforting her. "Don't worry. Time has a way of flying by and before you know it we'll be back, heading down the same stretch of road."

She swallowed back an oncoming tear and with an agreeing nod she cuddled closer to him.

The weather had been deteriorating fast after they had left Pabianice. With Johann at the reigns, the horses set out for home, battling a stiff north wind most of the way.

"Looks like a storm," he commented, pointing toward the gray sky. Before them they could see storm clouds towering like fortresses above the desolate grassland.

"I hope the wind will drive it away. It would be disastrous to have it happen now. Just imagine working in weather like this... unthinkable..." Johann carried on.

Taking a glance sideways, he suddenly realized, beside him Katina had drifted off into a well deserved sleep. Lovingly, he tucked the blanket tighter around her, then kept in his thoughts the rest of the way.

Not knowing what kind of winter weather to expect, he will have to talk to Pan Slovak and his boys as soon as they arrived home. They had to help him dig up more of the peat moss from the moor behind their property. He had to make sure the woodshed was filled to its capacity. He wished to have the house cozy and warm for the cold days ahead.

Weeks before the visit to Katina's family, they had held a Shlachtfest. With the help of the Slovaks he had managed to butcher a couple of large pigs. He had stocked the attic with all sorts of smoked ham, sausages and fried meats. The latter they had stored in large milk cans topped with lard to keep from spoiling.

In all this, the Slovaks had fared well also, just like he had promised. It gave him great satisfaction all the important tasks had been taken care of beforehand. Everything as far as he seen it was under control.

Soon Christmas would be upon them, their first here in this land. He had plans to give the children a treat and disguise himself as St. Nicolas. He wanted to keep up with the festivities of the season. That, he had told Katina earlier and she was in full agreement.

A smirk crossed his lips as they drove onto the property. He could already envision the whole event. In the following weeks the whole household would be filled once again with the spirit of Christmas. Pani Slovak and Marianka had offered to help in the baking. And he was sure with their help the pantry would be quickly filled with all sorts of cakes and cookies.

"Mm-m..."

He could already taste Pani Slovak's special sugar-beet buns, of which he and the children could never get enough of.

41

Christmas Eve arrived and with it all the festivities of the season. Everyone seemed in a good mood, including Father Wendel. Usually when it came to eating he would remain sitting at his bedside. Today he went out of his way and made the effort to sit with the rest of the family.

The roasted goose on the table with all the trimmings looked mouth-watering. He was proud to have had a helping hand in getting it to its plump delicious size. He recalled the many hours he had spent force feeding the bird. Katina was happy when he had offered to take over that task; she had never been too keen on doing it.

He gave her an appreciating wink after tasting his first morsel of goose-meat. "Mm-m... good... This is a meal fit for royalty," he smirked sheepishly, smacking his lips. Rebekka did not have to be coaxed twice. Even Julia, who usually sat pouting, dug in and did not complain. Both knew why the girls were behaving like they did. They had been told earlier that St. Nicolas only brought gifts to good children.

"Maybe we should have Christmas the whole year round... Hmmm? What do you think Mama?"

He gave a glance around to see everyone's reaction. Little Stefan sitting on Katina's lap was already eating by himself. Though at times he was a little messy, but that did not matter to him. Elisa, as always, sat beside her grandfather eating what he had put in her plate. She was his father's favorite.

250

He realized this long ago and was a little dismayed about it. Knowing too well how much the older ones needed his father's love also. But no matter how he tried to find ways for his father to like all children equally; it did not materialize. Well maybe tonight he hoped, since it was Christmas, his father might catch the Christmas spirit and change.

"Papa, when is St. Nicolas coming? I can hardly wait for him to come," Rebekka sat impatiently in her chair, sliding back and forth.

"Oh you have to be patient just a little while longer, besides we're not through eating yet. I think Mama has dessert for us." he spoke and kept eating. He told them that St. Nicholas always started his round on the other side of town. And that naturally would take time... as he did not want to miss a single home.

Rebekka tried her best to sit still, but when Mama started to clear the table, she quickly took the chance to help her set out the dessert dishes. Her eyes lit up. "Vanilla pudding with raspberry syrup...! Mmm! Oh, Mama... That's my favorite dessert!" She remembered helping Mama make the syrup this past summer and that made it extra special.

Later, as Katina and the two oldest were busy cleaning up, Father Wendel took time to play with the two little ones. This was the cue for Johann to excuse himself.

After all the dishes were done and put away. She told the girls not to forget to set out a plate of cookies for St. Nicolas. She in the meantime busied herself to make a pot of coffee, as St. Nicolas might be very thirsty after all the hard work and might appreciate a warm drink with his cookies. Rebekka and Julia were beside themselves with anticipation.

She had just finished when she heard a commotion outside the door. It was the signal she had been waiting for. Quickly she gathered the children around her, while Father Wendel opened the door to ask St. Nicolas inside. A gasp escaped Rebekka's lips. The switch in his hand looked terribly threatening. She moved closer to Mama and tried to hide behind her. She followed Julia who already had claimed the spot. Looking on, Katina could hardly contain herself; Johann looked so funny wrapped in a blanket, wearing a black fur cap and fake unrefined sheep's wool on his face. He disguised his voice, speaking low and raspy.

"I've heard there're children here waiting for St. Nicolas to bring them goodies and presents... Is this true...?"

Rebekka and Julia nodded shyly, scared to speak out. Elisa and Stefan just looked bewildered at the strange man in front of them.

Watching the little ones, he felt almost sorry, he certainly did not want to scare them. But now that he had started he had to go through with it. Deepening his voice even more, he continued.

"Before I can give each of you a present... I have to ask... Have you been good...? Have you been listening to Mama and Papa...?" Seeing the expression on their faces made him smirk. Luckily he could hide it behind the fluff of sheep's wool.

The girls nodded again, their eyes still fixed on that dreadful looking switch. All at once Julia asked the unexpected. "Mama, why does he have our blanket...?"

He could hear his father chuckle behind him and it was hard for him not to follow. Ignoring Julia, he quickly directed his questioning toward Rebekka. He hoped to get through with it before he was found out. "Well Rebekka, I've heard things about you that are not too pleasing. What have you to say...? Hmmm...?"

The pleading look on Rebekka's face told him that she remembered her short-comings. "Will you promise to be good from now on and listen...?"

"Yes..." a scared Rebekka replied.

"You heard Mama, she promised to be good... Oops..." He looked at Katina, now the girls will surely suspect something. But so engrossed with what was in the sack, they had paid little attention to what he had said.

I WILL REMEMBER ALWAYS

"Let's see..." He searchingly looked into the sack. "What have we got in here? Scrambling around, one by one he came out with presents for all of them. And reminding them to be good, he made his way out the door, laughing under his breath.

Upon returning, he did not hear the end of it... How he had missed St. Nicolas... And that he had worn one of their blankets, because he was too poor to afford a real coat... Mama had told them. His disguise seemed to have worked. Satisfied he settled in to sing Christmas carols with Katina and the children, while his father hummed along. All at once Rebekka exclaimed. "Mama... St. Nicolas forgot to eat his cookies."

"Well in that case, let's eat them ourselves. I'm sure he won't mind." Johann grinned and pulled the plate closer to them. After that it was bedtime for the two little ones. And since it was Christmas Eve, Rebekka and Julia were allowed to stay up for a little while longer.

"Please... Papa, tell us the Christmas story," Julia begged.

"All right, I will if you sit very still."

Eagerly both girls nodded, snuggling cozy in beside him.

"Long... long ago..." he began in a hushed voice and told them the story of the first Christmas. Katina gave a glance outside, as she drew the curtains to the bedroom window. She could hear Johann in the next room. Quietly she remained by the window, watching the snow fall. It had started this morning and had kept falling. Now in the dark it gave the countryside a fairytale appearance. She sighed... It was hard to imagine there was a war going on. All at once she fixed her eyes on the barn across the yard. Did she see someone... or was it just the snow playing tricks on her? She strained her eyes to see better, but nothing stirred. It must have been her imagination. She turned to check one more time on the little ones.

"Sweet dreams my darlings," she whispered, not daring to think what tomorrow might bring.

After the children had all gone to bed, Johann played around with the radio. He was trying to tune in on the underground messages he and his father had lately been listening to. Suddenly there it was, not clear, but it was enough to make out what was said.

"The Russians..." the radio crackled, "had begun a series of offensives today..." more crackle, "against the Germans in the southern Russian front..." the message came through the loudspeaker. He could hardly believe his ears.

"Even on Christmas Eve..." he whispered to his father, who moved next to him to listen in. "I hate to think what that could mean."

Father Wendel just shook his head, not knowing himself what to make of this whole war business.

"I don't like it... I do not like it at all..." Johann turned the radio off, speaking in a low and solemn voice. "If this keeps up..." He stood up and paced back and forth. "How could I and others like me escape from being drafted? Maybe that's what was on Hitler's mind all along. He probably needed more men to fight for the Fatherland? He stopped pacing and sat down beside his father. "That could be it, Papa... and now he has us right where he wanted us. Oh... how could we have been so stupid?"

"There was nothing we could have done about it, even if we would have known. Remember... we were all forced to leave. Even staying in Romania was not an option. There was no other way out," Father Wendel added.

"Oh, Papa... I worry about you and Katina and the little ones. What will happen to you all, if something should happen and I'm not here to help and protect you?"

"Don't worry about it now Johann. We don't know if it will come to that, so it's no use to fret about it now..."

"Sh-h-h..." Johann hushed his father just as Katina entered the kitchen. He did not want her to know of his worries.

"Rebekka and Julia are tucked in and waiting for a goodnight kiss from Papa."

"Oh, I had better go then and not let them wait."

Katina walked over to the stove, pouring herself a cup of coffee.

"Want one too?" she asked Father Wendel, but he declined and went instead to sit beside the stove to warm up. "It looks like we're getting a lot of snow."

"Hmmm..." Father Wendel acknowledged. "I could feel it in my bones for days."

She had noticed upon entering, that she had interrupted a conversation between the two, and from the distraught look on Johann's face, she knew it could not have been something pleasant. She wondered what it was about. She went to check the fire in the stove and in both Kachel ovens. She threw in each a few more pieces of dried chunks of peat moss. "There, that should keep us warm for half the night," she said to herself, as Father Wendel sat in thought.

After saying goodnight to the girls, Johann joined his father and Katina beside the stove. In contemplation, he took a sip from his cup of coffee. Quietly, they remained there for some time, engulfed in small talk.

Later in bed he lay awake for a long time, thinking. Beside him Katina had fallen asleep, breathing light even strokes. A warning one of his co-workers in Vienna had mentioned, kept gnawing on him. It had haunted him ever since they had set foot here in Poland.

The man had told him of stories, of what had happened before the Polish invasion. In order to gain more living space for the German people, Hitler had sent his men into Poland. With that he wanted to stir up trouble between the Poles and the Germans that had lived here for centuries. Many of the German people wanted no part in this. As they said, we have coexisted for so many years here in peace so why should we suddenly do otherwise? But the rise of nationalism was strong and the Nazis had no intention of letting the matter go. They stirred up discord and division in the once peaceful communities. Some Germans got carried away and mistreated the Polish people badly. That in turn, made some of the Poles retaliate in a most gruesome way. Hitler then used this as an excuse to invade, broadcasting their countrymen needed rescuing.

He thought for a moment. He had heard the man say that this happened in and around the Bromberg area, a city to the north of Quadenstadt. Maybe some of the Germans there had deserved it, but then not in such a brutal way. He shuddered. Just thinking about it made him weary and gave him great concern for his loved ones.

Was the man right? Predicting from what he had heard of the SS dealings and how they had been treating the Polish inhabitants, if Germany ever came close to losing this war, the revenge from the Polish would be unspeakable.

He did not dare to think it so, but recalling tonight's underground message, a shiver went through him and he was again consumed with worry. It did not look too promising, but then there was always the unexpected... He tried to comfort himself with this thought.

Should he have taken the same approach as that man and rather stayed back? The thought left him with mixed feelings. There were no easy answers. They were here now and there was no going back. For now he had to set aside enough money for his family to live; just in case he was drafted.

Determined, he set out the next day. He had to recruit more work for himself and, if possible, for some of the men who had worked under him at the new compound. Due to the freezing conditions it now lay unfinished under a thick blanket of snow. Because of this, work had become scarce. The only job he could think of was to go back to the ice delivery business.

Katina had protested in the beginning, worrying about his health, but to no avail. He was determined to go through with it and work until the spring thaw. Beside their little creek, there was another into which their brook emptied. That river ran right behind the Ruck's and Schwarz's land past an old partially existing fortified wall. It was considerably wider and a little deeper in some areas than theirs. Satisfied he made the decision to go ahead with this venture as soon as possible.

Again the business took off. To everyone's surprise he had customers from all over town; even from surrounding outskirts. It was to the envy of many who could not believe how prosperous this venture had become.

All in all, Johann's hunch had paid off, just as he had anticipated. And to his advantage, they happened to have one of the coldest winters on record. Because of this there was plenty of ice to match the steady demand of incoming orders. It was the key that kept his business going.

This good fortune irked his neighbors, the Koenigs, and Heinrich Schwarz as well, who of all people had tried so hard to compete, but never made it, that is except in one job. Johann had found out, after Johann himself refused a position in the local German authority, that Heinrich Schwarz was now the new official for the area and he haughtily flaunted it whenever and wherever he got a chance to do so.

Johann, in the meantime, had never neglected to listen in on reports that were secretly broadcasted every night. It was important for him to keep up with the newest developments on the frontlines of the war. He was sure all his neighbors and countrymen were guilty of doing the same, but no one wanted to admit it openly. They all knew too well it was prohibited and highly punishable by law. Not to let it leak out, he had warned everyone in the house, including the Slovaks, not to talk, not even to their friends, for some of them too had become informers. He was very troubled now about Julia's friendship with Eva Schwarz. Was Heinrich Schwarz asking Julia questions, or listening in on their conversations while at play? He had to warn the children never to repeat anything that was discussed at home.

He was puzzled why the real news about the war had been kept from the general public. The SS propaganda minister only reported what they thought was necessary for the mainstream German people to hear. They were mainly passing on news they could brag about. Why?... and for what reason were they hiding the truth? Often they were seen driving along the streets with their supposedly fully equipped detection truck. It was no secret they were scanning every house. It was for the purpose of finding out who was listening in to the underground radio. On top of that they had their emissaries like Herr Schwarz who secretly reported who was disobeying their rules. And Johann for one had plenty of experience on that.

He recalled Christmas day when Schwarz again confronted him about old Slovak. This time it was about taking firewood. To get the old man out of hot water he had told Heinrich that he had given him permission to take it. That day he had expected the Gestapo on his doorstep, but to his surprise no one came. Was there a glimmer of kindness shown on Schwarz's part because of Christmas? Was this the reason he failed to report him? Or were Schwarz and the Gestapo in on getting him on a more serious offense? Maybe it had to do with listening in on the underground radio, or better yet labeling him with more than he was guilty of. He had to be careful, for all he knew his whole household was under surveillance. It worried him and he decided to be even more on guard.

--

It was February, two months later, when another significant message came through the black-box. "The Russians had almost succeeded in surrounding a large German force at Krivoy Rog... And at Cherkassy the Russian Commander Zhukov had captured about 30,000 Germans. Another 30,000 apparently escaped after the German Army South employed all tanks to the rescue..."

Just to hear how many had been captured on this offensive

alone, it told him that he and others like him would soon have to join. Were they losing? Why the slow but steady retreat? The more he heard about what was going on, the more concerned he had for his loved ones. This whole business with this war sickened him. All this senseless killing, he wished it were different. But again, and with much regret, he realized there was no way out of this maddening circle.

42

In March, the German army had retreated to the Panther Line, a prepared fortification on the Russian front.

It was there Johann had pictured himself fighting. And his hunch came true when all able men were ordered to put on the grey uniform to fight for the Fatherland. But instead of going to the Russian front he found himself on the way to France.

The idea of having him gone again for months on end was hard on Katina. Yet knowing that it was equally hard on him she tried to hide her true feelings. And like any other soldier's wife, she accepted the unavoidable fate.

In order not to dwell on this unfortunate plight, she turned her thoughts to the things left in her care. Looking now for ways to keep up the equity Johann had so painstakingly worked to build up. She wanted so much for him to be proud of her when he returned.

Immediately after his departure she began her strategy. She planned to work over the huge piece of land behind the house. Johann had often mentioned to her in conversation, that he wanted to make use of it. He wanted to try his hand at growing herbs and vegetables for the purpose of selling. Now his idea made her think.

She counted on Pan and Pani Slovak's help in giving advice on when and what to plant or seed. As neither she nor Father Wendel knew the climate well enough to know what grew best here.

The operation proved profitable and was in full swing when summer came around. With Slovak's help she had managed to employ eighteen women. Eager to work, they all showed up every day knowing they would be rewarded fairly and justly; in secret of course. She could not believe how well the produce business was taking off. Her supply of vegetables went far beyond the circumference of their little town. Daily a transport vehicle came by to pick up produce, mainly to supply the occupying armed forces.

It was the last weekend in June when she decided to accompany Pan Slovak to the public market in town. This time, it was with the intention to do some shopping for their household.

Eagerly she walked through the market in search of good bargains. For even though business was good and they had plenty of money; it was always on her mind to save.

On her return to their designated stand, she noticed Pan Slovak already engaged in the last bit of cleanup. He had boasted beforehand on how quickly their produce usually sold. Now seeing it for herself she was astonished. Indeed he had not over exaggerated.

'Oh, if only Johann could see this. He would be so proud,' she thought to herself.

With a little time to spare she scanned the neighboring stands. The market square was busy, with people walking every which way. Squinting with her eyes; she looked aimlessly over the crowd. All at once her eyes were fixed on a figure coming toward her. Was it wishful thinking or did her eyes play tricks on her? Was it really him or was she mistaken? But his walk... transfixed she stood for a second, wanting to be absolutely sure. Then her heart raced in excitement, she ran toward the soldier.

"Johann!!!" her cry resounded.

Within seconds she felt his strong arms around her. Forgotten was all the pain of separation. She clung to him, never wanting to let go. Not minding the onlooker's glances, they kissed and held each other for some time.

"Where in heaven's name did you come from? Why didn't you write... to let me know you were coming home?" she suddenly let loose.

He smiled, "I thought I would surprise you." He looked at her lovingly. "Oh Katina... I was so much looking forward to this moment. Just to hold you and be with you and the children. You wouldn't believe how lonely it gets out there on the battle field..." His voice trembled. "I've missed you so much." He did not dare relate to her all the terrible things he had witnessed. It was best to leave them out there. For now he would do his utmost to enjoy the little time that was given to him.

She backed up a bit, noticing tears in his eyes. Poor Johann, she too had missed him more than words could ever tell. "Oh my darling, I can't believe you're really here." Over and over she hugged him.

All at once she remembered Pan Slovak. She pulled Johann gently over towards him. The old man stood with a grin on his face, happy over the reunion.

"Pan Wendel, it's good to have you back." Slovak spoke in a hushed voice.

"I'm glad to be home again, dear friend..." Johann smiled warmly and shook the old man's hand heartily. All at once his eyes met the cold stare of Heinrich Schwarz. Where did he suddenly come from? Was he, after all this time, still watching his every move? Had he known of his coming? Did he have knowledge of the position that was offered to him right here in Quadenstadt? Puzzled, he gave Schwarz a short, but friendly greeting. Without further delay he helped Katina onto the wagon and gave Slovak the go ahead to drive home.

Seeing Heinrich Schwarz again sent chills down his spine. He felt uneasy about the cold and relentless look in Schwarz's eyes. But the joy and anticipation of being with his family soon won over his fears. He had been looking forward to being with them for such a long time, and he wanted nothing, not even Heinrich Schwarz, to spoil this moment.

He held Katina's hand not letting go of it. He listened intently to both of them, telling him of all the newest happenings. The thought of being home again stirred excitement in his heart. Out there on the battlefield his thoughts had often been of her, the children and his father. What would ever become of them if something should happen to him? He could not bear the thought. Over and over he had tried to put it all behind him, but to no avail. The thunderous noise of gunfire and images of wounded and dying comrades were still vivid before him. Constantly they were reminding him how uncertain the future was.

His furlough though had another twist. He had received an order before his leave, to join the SS at the home front. SS Leader Siegheimer had put in the request. And he was to respectfully accept this position as soon as possible.

He had to admit the offer was very tempting. It could mean being close to his loved ones and being exempt from fighting on the front line. Yet all the while his conscience and the awareness of what was required of him at this position, made it very difficult for him to accept. Deep down he knew he had no choice but to decline. But refusing an order meant severe punishment. All this lay heavy on his heart. He worried about the anguish and affliction it would cost him and his family. What future would then be left for them?

No matter how much he pondered to find a way out of this predicament, he could find none. He knew what he had to do. It bothered him to burden Katina and his father with his dilemma. Yet he had no alternative but to let them know as soon as possible. For the moment he thought it wise to wait and make the best of the time with his loved ones.

--

"Johann! Oh, are they ever beautiful..." Katina burst out in excitement; before her lay an opened parcel with two soft silk nightgowns. "Where did you get these?"

"I got them on my stopover in Germany. I thought you might like a change from the heavy flannel ones." He grinned with exuberance. He was proud of himself to have chosen something so exquisite.

"But..."

"No buts."

He knew what she was about to say. "Nothing is too expensive for my wife," he said with assurance. "You deserve to be spoiled a little. Isn't it so Father?" Johann laughed by his father's indifferent shrug, knowing how tightfisted he was when it came to giving. He could not remember his father ever buying fancy things for his mother. He probably thought it sheer foolishness to spend money on something so frivolous. Even when there was plenty, he would still scrounge and eat rancid butter and stale bread. Many times he had talked to his father about it, but he was set in his ways, thinking it could save him a penny. Knowing this, he had not expected any other reaction from him.

"Well no matter what..." Johann added in a more solemn manner. "I only wish I could have done more."

"Johann..." Katina swung her arms around him and kissed him lovingly. "What more could you have given. Look around you. We have each other and a warm and comfortable home and money. Enough to buy all the things we need. The only thing I wish for is to have you home more often. I miss having you around." She gave him a tender hug. "The children... they're growing up so fast. They often ask for you. They can't understand why Papa has to be away so much. But there's nothing we can do about that, is there?"

"That's just it Katina. That's just it."

Rebekka and Julia broke the heaviness of the moment with an outburst of jolliness. All this time eagerly engaged in opening their parcels. They now danced with delight, holding beautiful new dresses up against them.

Johann shook his head with contentment. 'How innocent and carefree,' he thought.

"Thank you Papa," they both echoed in one accord.

"When can we wear them Mama?" Rebekka asked wistfully, turning herself in circles.

"Well, as soon as there's a special occasion."

"Why not right now? Please Mama, please..." Rebekka begged.

"All right, but just to try them on, not to go outside, you hear? If you do, Butch will tear on it, unintentionally of course, as you say, whenever you wear a dress and turn in front of him."

"I promise it won't happen this time. I'll just walk nicely," Rebekka replied.

"Rebekka..." Katina waved her index finger at her. "What did I just say?"

"She only wants to show off to all the kids in the neighborhood, that's all," Julia put in her say.

"No. I don't," Rebekka defended herself.

Katina was about to protest, when she caught Johann's wink to let the girl go, this time.

"Well all right then," she said unwillingly. "But only for a little while, then you're coming in to change." Her voice had softened. Maybe she was a little over concerned.

"You listen now to what your mother had said and take care, alright?"

"Yes Papa. I promise," Rebekka was quick to answer. She knew that it was Papa's doing to let her go.

"Johann, you're spoiling them," she said shaking her head after both girls had gone. Father Wendel agreed.

"I know, I know," he replied with the wave of his hand. "I'm an old softy when it comes to the children. What can I say?" he laughed it off.

"Truly spoken my darling and don't you ever change. Well, maybe a little, when it comes to situations like these."

Father Wendel shook his head, listening to the two. "I don't know whatever happened to the old ways," he said. "When no, meant no."

"Oh, come on father, don't you sometimes do the same thing?" Johann said in a teasing way.

"Like letting little Elisa get away with practically anything she wants to? Taking her side whenever she does not want to sit with us on the table and rather sit with you and eat your food?"

"Well that's different," Father Wendel smiled.

"Oh…" Johann replied laughing.

"Well, she's special," Father Wendel looked lovingly at the little one sitting beside him on his bed. Torn pieces of wrapping paper all around her, she sat staring. Still in the box in front of her lay a doll dressed in pink satin and white lace. It seemed too beautiful to be picked up.

Touched by the special moment, Johann smiled warm heartedly. "She says 'Mama' too. Just pick her up and you'll see."

Carefully, Elisa picked up the doll and held it toward her, "Ma… ma."

"See, just what I've told you," Johann laughed and swooped the little one up into his arms. He had to admit he had just as much fun in giving these gifts as he had in picking them.

"Oh… Father! There's something for you too. It's in my coat pocket."

Johann walked over to the rack behind the door and reached into his army coat pocket.

"I thought you might like these."

He held in his hand a special brand of the finest pack of cigarettes, knowing how his father liked a smoke now and then, but it was from his own home grown tobacco leaves, which he dried and stored in the attic above the big barn.

"O thank you Johann. Thank you so much."

Johann could detect a special glow in his father's eyes. "I'll save them for a special day."

With that comment, Johann watched him store away the pack into the chest drawer next to his bed. The same he kept his rancid butter and his moldy bread in.

I WILL REMEMBER ALWAYS

The next morning Katina awoke to the aroma of fresh baked bread. Thinking she was late to rise she rushed to the kitchen. She was overwhelmed by what she saw. There was Johann with an apron wrapped around him, baking and cooking up a storm.

"The children have all been fed including little Stefan," he announced proudly. "Oh, and while I was up shining my boots, I did Rebekka's and Julia's shoes also. So they're all ready for school."

"Johann," she stood in disbelief. She had never known her husband to be so self sufficient. "When in heaven's name did you get up?"

"Oh early enough, it's part of army life," he grinned. "We rise early and we have to have our boots shined and our guns cleaned and polished at all times. On top of that our clothes had to be wrinkle free. How do you achieve that you may ask? Well step right here and I'll show you."

He lifted his father's straw mattress. "Tada... there you see a pair of pants and they look as if they had just been ironed."

She had to laugh at her husband's ingenious ways.

"Don't laugh," he defended himself. "I had to learn this the hard way."

He poured her a cup of tea and motioned for her to sit down.

"You see it happened when I'd first arrived at the training base. After a long hard day of training I'd neglected to look after my clothes. So when the time came for inspection, they caught me for not having my boots shined to their expectations. As punishment, I had to do forty pushups and report for kitchen duties. I tell you, after that I vowed never to let them catch me again. In the army you learn fast, or else."

"Oh my poor Johann," she teased.

"Well at least the army is good for something," Father Wendel commented lighthearted. "After all this is over... I mean the war..." He stopped talking for a brief moment,

267

moved off his bed and shuffled over toward the coat rack. Then taking his jacket off the hook he resumed talking, pausing here and there while he was dressing. "You can always... if all fails... go into the baking business." He chuckled at his own comment and then turned to open the door. "I'll be up in the barn if you need me," his voice trailed after him as he stepped outside.

"It's good to see Father in a good mood and moving about the place," Johann said positively.

"Yes," she agreed. "And if you ever have to look for him, you can be sure to find him up in the barn loft. He's been busy for quite some time now, working with his freshly harvested tobacco crop. You should see how many bundles of tobacco leaves he has. He has them all neatly hanging from the rafters ready for the drying process. It seems to have been a good year for him. He has eked out a good business for himself. Orders are coming in from all over. You can be very proud of him Johann."

"I guess I should look in on him a little while later." He stood quietly for a moment by the kitchen window. Deep in thought he watched his father trudge across the property and over the little bridge toward the barn. No matter how grumpy and difficult his father was at times, underneath it all he sensed a warm and caring spirit; which he had a hard time showing.

"It's so good to be home Katina," Johann's voice took on a solemn tone suddenly. "You have no idea how much it means to be here with all of you. I wish..." He stopped to fight down a lump in his throat. "I wish I would not have to go away again... I wish this war would be over and done with," His voice trembled. The thought of what was before him pierced through his whole being.

"Johann, what's wrong?"

He remained facing the window, fighting desperately to regain his self composure. He could not bring himself to tell her, but then...

"Katina..."

Before he knew, it was all out in the open of his decision not to join the SS. When he finally stopped, he turned, waiting for any remarks, but there were none.

"Do you understand what this could mean?" he remarked again.

She nodded understandingly. She had seen and heard enough to know.

"I have to report to Herr Siegheimer tomorrow morning... I will have to tell him that I can't accept. There's no way I will accept," he retorted. "It goes against my beliefs."

Quietly and without accusation she put her arms around him.

"I know my darling, I know," she spoke softly, trying to ease the intensity of the moment. She knew very well the seriousness of this situation.

43

His steps echoed through the long hollow corridors of the SS Head Quarters. For some reason he thought it inappropriate for the sun to shine so happily through the long narrow windows. It did not befit the task before him, or justify the friendliness and warmth it portrayed among these walls.

He noted the place to be in a disturbed state. Things were not going all that well at the front lines and it showed. The daily propaganda speeches, coming through the people's receiver, had slackened off considerably.

He had kept up listening to the latest news, despite repeated warnings from the top not to do so. It was reported again that all the front lines were under heavy attack. Undeniably, there had been heavy casualties on all sides. And everyone listening to the underground radio had knowledge of this.

His confidence grew weaker the closer he came to the main office. He fought to stay calm, but to no avail. He felt his heart pounding with increased heaviness against his chest.

"Johann Wendel reporting for the interview with Herr Siegheimer," he saluted. He was surprised at the calmness of his voice. If only he could keep it up throughout the interview, but this he knew would be virtually impossible.

"Herr Siegheimer will see you now."

With the usual military precision he walked in, saluting again in front of Siegheimer.

270

"At ease," Herr Siegheimer replied and motioned for him to take a seat. Siegheimer studied a stack of papers a staff member had handed to him a moment ago.

"Your records have shown good reports Herr Wendel. As I see, you meet all the requirements needed for this prominent position. You have also shown yourself to be a good and loyal citizen. We, as well as the Fuehrer, would be proud to have you in the SS. All there is left for you to do is to sign and to be sworn in."

Johann had listened quietly and as planned, with reverence, declined the position. The final moment of truth had come. It was out and over with and he was awaiting the consequences.

The SS leader's face turned from pale to purple red. His anger was obvious.

"*Donnerkeil nochmal!* Do you know what can happen to men who disobey the Fuehrer?"

"Yes, Herr Siegheimer. I have knowledge of that," Johann replied respectfully.

"I have the power to punish you severely. Do you know that, do you?"

"Yes, Herr Commandant," Johann answered short, but firm.

"Do you have any reason why you don't want to accept this position?"

"Yes, Herr Commandant, I have."

"Well go on then, speak up."

Johann took courage. "It goes against my beliefs, Herr Commandant. My conscience does not allow me..."

"Your conscience? Why this is outright treason! *Donnerkile... verflixed nochmal!* That's disloyalty in the first degree! I can't believe I'm hearing this! *Schweinehund nochmal!*" Siegheimer raged on, cursing and swearing viciously.

"I tell you what..."

There was a sudden change in his voice. He paused for a

few minutes trying to gain control of himself, seeing that he could not get anywhere with Johann. Deep down there was a spark of respect for his stand, but he could not acknowledge it openly. A man like that if won over, could be of great service to the cause and he knew that. He hastily wrote something on a piece of paper and handed it to one of his staff members. "I'll give you another chance to think this over. I'll send a letter stating my request to the head office, and by that time, I'll expect your final answer on this."

He waved to have Johann ushered out.

"Jawohl, Herr Siegheimer... Heil Hitler..." Johann saluted respectfully and walked out.

All the way home the whole meeting with the SS Leader kept gnawing at him. He felt terrible, like a deserter, just like Siegheimer had said. He wanted to serve and do everything for his Fatherland, but this was beyond the call of duty. He had struggled for some time now over this issue. There was no way he could take up the duties required in the SS establishment. It went against his nature. Above all there was a Higher Authority he had to answer to.

He knew very well that after today his life and that of his family would never be the same again. By refusing, he was blackmarked. The authorities would now be more than ever watching his every move. They would suspect him in the slightest way of treason against the Fatherland. Yes, they had been told to hold no high regard for the enemy, to treat them like scum, worse than animals. But he had seen enough to think otherwise.

Katina had noticed a change in Johann the minute he had entered the house. But she was scared to ask about the outcome of the meeting. Tenderly she put her arms around him to greet him back.

"Oh Katina, how I wish this war and all it brought us would never have happened."

He broke down. "Maybe things would be better if we would have stayed in Austria."

"Johann, you don't know if things are any different there than they are here." She tried to comfort. "Besides, we probably wouldn't have had the opportunity of owning our own house and land. Remember? We would most likely still be living in the Convent or who knows where."

"I know, I know." He gave a long and heavy sigh. "It's just... the whole thing... it's so frustrating. Oh how I long for the times when life was not so complicated." He looked wishfully at her.

Quietly she held onto him. She understood. She too had moments when she thought back. Every time unlocking the treasure chest of special moments in her heart, drawing from it whenever she had a down day.

"I tell you what..." she confronted him. "Let's both make it a point to make the remaining days together special. Let's not worry and fret anymore. Who knows, maybe they'll even pardon you from having to join the SS."

"That's wishful thinking Katina. Once they have you on the list, that's it." He paused for a moment. Maybe he should let her believe that this could be so. He now regretted that he told her. He should have never burdened her with all this. She will have enough to worry about with things once he was gone again. Hmm... Gone again sounded so cold and distant... so disconnecting...so lonely and haunting. He had to get into a different mindset for his family's sake.

"You're right on one thing though," he resumed speaking. "I'll take you up on the first part... might as well," he smiled again, "What harm can it do, hmm...?" He gave her a big hug. Then suddenly remembering, he added. "Oh, by the way, there's a dance given Saturday night. It is in acknowledgment of all the soldiers and their families and we were told to be there. So what do you think? We could go for at least an hour or so," he coaxed her on. "At least this way they see we were there and after we can go home again. What do you say?"

"Well..." Katina stood thinking. "I'll have to see if Marianka can watch the two little ones. Your father might also want to come along to visit with his old pals. And then there is the question of what dress to wear."

"I'm sure you'll come up with something," Johann replied upbeat. "As for the girls... I think they'll be thrilled to wear their new ones, especially Rebekka."

Both had a good laugh, just thinking about their oldest.

--

Saturday came and Johann proudly took his place at the designated table with his family. There was excitement in the air, seeing everyone dressed up for the occasion. He was glad they had come and he was sure Katina was too. The army orchestra was playing and that alone seemed to ease the tension.

Looking about he discovered their neighbors all seated next to them on the surrounding tables. Hetti too had come with a young handsome looking soldier, which she had recently met. Even Heinrich Schwarz and his family were present and that was good news to Julia.

Both he and Katina could never understand what Julia saw in Eva as a friend. According to Rebekka, Eva only used the friendship to get help with her schoolwork. In the end it was Julia's choice as far as he saw and it was not for them to stop the friendship. He was puzzled the Schwarzes tolerated Julia as Eva's friend. He wondered again... 'Was there another side to the man?'

Tonight, for the sake of the two girls, he had tried to show himself friendly toward the man. But still there was no motion on Heinrich's part. Not even the slightest of confirmation that would contribute toward better relations between them. As before, he was confronted with the same cold, spine chilling stare. Schwarz's behavior puzzled him to no end. He just could not figure the man out.

The orchestra started again, playing the "Blue Danube" medley.

"Oh Papa, can you dance with me? Please, please..." Rebekka was begging him.

"I actually had in mind to ask Mama," Johann said with a broad smile on his face.

"Go on," Katina waved him off. "Take her. I'll have the following turn."

"Oh thank you Mama," Rebekka was off her chair and waiting for Papa to join her. Johann gave Katina a quick peck for being understanding. Then off the two went, swirling along the dance floor.

Watching the two, she had to laugh. Considering Johann's height, Rebekka was airborne half of the time, but that didn't seem to matter. Her eyes sparkled with excitement as they twirled around the dance floor.

She shook her head in wonder, smiling as the two passed by. Both girls, Rebekka especially, had learned quickly when it came to dancing. It seemed to be in the family, as she and Johann had no problem. In the earlier years back in Romania, they had plenty of opportunities to learn, especially by participating in social folk dancing.

44

Days after, when Johann was gone again, she recalled that evening with fondness. Now life was back to the same old routine. She had found Johann's leaving harder than ever before. She was tired of carrying on without him. She too was weary of the war and all it had brought them. She worried over his well being, it was forever in her mind and did not leave her, but... that was part of being a soldier's wife and there was little she or any of the other women could do about it.

The last month of fall had been rainy and cool. All the crops had been harvested and stored for the winter. The attic chimney was stocked with a supply of cured smoked meat, and nearby a number of tall milk cans stood filled to the brim with fried pork, covered with a layer of fat to keep from spoiling.

She took a long deep breath. The rows of apples, dried herbs and vegetables filled the attic with a wonderful aroma, and she could not help but feel content and proud of her accomplishment. Naturally, it was not without the help of Marianka and her family. Pan Slovak and his two older boys as well had worked hard in providing plenty of heating fuel.

'Now winter can come,' she thought. 'If only the circumstances surrounding them could be of a more peaceful nature. Life would be rather pleasant, but...' she sighed as she turned to leave the attic. She missed Johann so much. His letters had been few lately and she longed to hear from him. From what she read things did not go well out there at the front line. And knowing this all played a part of her being downhearted.

She had woken early the following morning. Her sleep had not been restful. Between tossing and getting up for the little ones, she could not have slept more than four hours. After the two oldest had gone to school, she sat, still in a daze, by the kitchen table drinking a cup of tea. She had put little Stefan down for his midmorning nap, while Elisa was playing quietly beside her. Father Wendel had just stepped out to check up on things. He had said he needed to finish cutting and rolling his tobacco leaves. She had watched him walk over the yard and had noticed his arthritis was bothering him. She could always tell by his pronounced hobble. The weather was not helping either. It had been rainy and cool for a couple of days and there was the smell of snow in the air.

A repeated knock at the door made her rush over to open. Worried it might wake little Stefan, she answered quietly.

"Good morning Mrs. Wendel." The letter carrier greeted her in a friendly manner as always.

With a short "Thank you", she took the mail. There was nothing from Johann, just a letter from her parents. She was hesitant to read at first; scared it might be bad news. Her eyes lit up with relief to find only an invitation. She was requested to come down to Pabianice for a special family gathering. It had been her father's wish to have all his sons come home for Christmas. He had fought to have his two sons-in-law attend this special gathering, but to no avail. Only his own flesh and blood was allowed this once in a lifetime grant. This had only been possible on the basis that he had eight sons serving the Fatherland.

Her feelings were mixed. Excitement stirred in her to see all her family again. At the same time she felt an overwhelming sadness that Johann was not allowed to come. She was sure that Edwina felt the same; as her husband too was excluded. Tara was lucky to have Micha home, as again he had been exempt from serving because he managed a large dairy farm. The reason was, their product was needed to supply the occupying German army. Nevertheless she thought it unfair, yet she was happy for her sister. At least Tara's family life was not interrupted like theirs.

Mechanically she went about her work, her thoughts still on the invitation. She was glad to have Marianka around. She could always rely on her to look after the housework and help Hetti to take care of the children. Yet it bothered her to leave the children at Christmas time. But after a time of careful consideration she changed her mind and agreed to go. 'Well... it would be only for a few days at most. And besides, Father Wendel was also around to look in on things...' she reassured herself.

Mandek and Wiktor, Slovak's two oldest boys, eagerly volunteered to drive her to Lodz. From there she would take the electric rail car to Pabianice. Then after her visit they would pick her up again at a prearranged time and place and drive her home again.

--

Johann sat quietly on the train. Destined for the Russian front, it was filled with fellow soldiers; some in his eleven men artillery unit were friends from Mangalia and now, Quadenstadt. His hunch that he would end up fighting on the Russian front proved true. This thought renewed his worry, that he might not make it out alive. He looked around at the other men. For all he knew all of them might share the same fate.

His thoughts went toward home, to Katina and the children. He had sent ahead a telegram, like the rest of the men who had loved ones en route. With that he hoped to meet her and the children at the train station in Kutno. He was so much looking forward to holding her and the little ones in his arms. Oh what he would give to be home again.

For days they had been on this train. And he could see

on the faces of his fellow comrades what he himself felt. A reflection of desolation and despair, tired of all the fighting. News about the war was not very good. Heavy casualties had been reported in almost all front lines. Everyone here dreaded the Russian front, which above all was said to have the lowest survival rate.

He knew very well why he was among those traveling eastward. He had been summoned and was questioned again about the SS position. But his answer had been the same as before, as he still believed in the same principles. He felt terribly helpless about this whole dilemma. The feeling that he might not make it out alive was overwhelming. And he fought hard within himself to overcome it.

It was Christmas Eve morning, when they finally reached Kutno. It was one of the main train terminals on the way to Warsaw, and Quadenstadt lay about twenty kilometers to the south from here. The sky was overcast with a hint of snow clouds hanging on the eastern horizon. Excitement grew among those who expected loved ones. He felt his heartbeat racing every time someone came through the gates. Anxiously he watched every entrance, pacing nervously along the station boardwalk; in hopes he might spot Katina and the children. But every time he was disappointed.

By afternoon the station was in a big bustle with people coming and going. He observed his comrades and other fellow soldiers with their families, as they kissed and hugged with each greeting. It seemed to him he was the only one left standing without his family. His heart began to sink. Did Katina not get his telegram? Was she sick again? What about Hetti or Marianka, or his father, could none of them come… at least to bring the children? Was there no one that could tell him? Oh how he wished he could go and see. But they had strict orders not to leave the premises.

"Come on Katina!" he muttered and prayed. "Please dear God let her show up. I need to see her and the children. I can't go away from here without seeing them…."

"KATINA...!" he sighed heavyhearted in despair. With tear-filled eyes he walked back to his rail car. Disappointed he sat in the corner of his booth. He had brought gifts for all of them. He had hoped to see them opened with much laughter and excitement. Now they lay up in the baggage net. The only thing he could do, if no one showed up, was to find someone who was willing to deliver them. The thought brought more tears to his eyes. He swallowed hard to keep himself under control. But the disappointment was too overwhelming.

He sat in his seat, counting the hours as they passed. The slight glimmer of hope that had remained up to this point was growing fainter. It was late afternoon now and there was little chance of Katina coming. He slumped lower in his seat. His spirit was crushed. Dejected, he watched the commotion around him until the last of the visitors had said their good-byes. Overall the spirit was solemn among all when the train finally continued on its long trek toward the Russian front. No one, as far as he could tell, was looking forward to the fighting. Tired and listless he settled back. His eyes glued to the familiar country side as it passed in the semidarkness. Home was so close, yet so unreachable. An agonizing emptiness filled his heart.

--

Katina tried her best to contribute and be part of the happy reunion, but her heart was not in it. There was something gnawing at her inside. All weekend long she had an uncomfortable feeling. She should have rather stayed home with the children. After all it was Christmas, a time for families to be together. Johann would have wished it so. It did seem so right at the time to take up Papa's invitation. Now she wasn't so sure. If only Johann would have been allowed home, how different things would be."

"Katina." Edwina had come into the guest bedroom where she had retreated to freshen up. "We're ready for picture taking."

"All right, I'll be right there." She took one last hurried

look in the dresser mirror. Her hair seemed to have lost its wavy bounce. Probably from the gusts of wind they had encountered on the way here. And there was not a thing she could do to make it sit right. Disgruntled, she gave up and followed her sister to the living room. Edwina, like her, was feeling glum and incomplete without their husbands. In Edwina's case, she especially had been looking forward to have him here, to spring the good news that he was becoming a papa soon. But now she had to resort to a written message only. At picture taking they both tried to put a smile on their faces, but to no avail.

Later around the supper table they reminisced again and talked about the war. To everyone's surprise Robert did the unexpected. He announced that he had made arrangements to take Daniel's place at the front line. His reason, it was better for Daniel to stay home since he had his large family to consider, as he himself had no one. "Just in case something should happen," he told everyone. At first Daniel protested. But Robert's unwavering stand reluctantly made him give in.

Katina thought it very noble of Robert, giving himself for his brother. But then it should not have surprised her. Had he not always put his family's needs before his own? He was that sort of fellow and for that she loved him dearly.

Departures were somber and full of well wishes for each other. Everyone hoped the next reunion would bring them all together again, including Johann and Edwina's husband.

--

Mandek and Wiktor had not forgotten their rendezvous place in Lodz. She was actually glad to see them. She was looking forward to going home. For some reason the boys acted peculiar every time she asked how things were going at home. They seemed to avoid looking at her, only giving her short but general answers. She thought it odd, as they usually were lively and talkative. Seeing she couldn't get a straight answer, she left them talking amongst themselves, while she retreated to her own thoughts.

There was one request Edwina had made at the reunion that gave her great concern. She had asked for Rebekka to come and stay with her while her husband was gone. She had said it would be nice to have her there for company. Also if ever the need would arise, to also watch over the baby once it arrived. She herself felt uneasy about the whole idea and had told Edwina that she would think about it. Edwina had said to take her time, since she had planned on staying with Papa and Mama a while longer. Reluctantly she had mentioned to Edwina before leaving, that if the answer was yes, she would meet her with Rebekka at the Kutno station. There, Edwina told her, she would be waiting in two days, on her stopover to Leslau.

Once at home, the girls welcomed her back with open arms. There was so much they had to tell her. Especially about the beautiful presents Daddy had sent along with a hastily written letter.

Katina read the letter over and over. She felt sick to her stomach, why in heaven's name did no one contact her. She had waited for this moment for such a long time; now that it finally came she had to be away. Suddenly she understood Mandek's and Wiktor's odd behavior on the way back. She broke down sobbing. She was overwhelmed by the pain and anguish she felt for Johann, by not being there when he needed her. The letter revealed it all. What especially hurt were the last two lines. In it he begged her to take good care of the children, just in case he did not make it.

She recalled the sad songs he sang the last time he was at home on furlough. Had this been on his mind all along? "Oh Johann..." she sighed in agony. Oh how she wished she would have stayed home to meet him at the train station. To reassure him how much she cared, to tell him not to worry about the children. Tears rolled down her cheeks again and again. Her heart was heavy. She felt torn and so terribly guilty.

The telegram apparently had arrived just after she had left

for Pabianice. No one, not Father Wendel, Hetti, or Marianka had thought it necessary to let her know, or at least have taken the girls down to see him. All the apologies from the others and all the blame she gave herself, the harm could not be undone and that, she felt with utmost despair.

45

S he had spoken to Rebekka about the prospect of staying with Auntie Edwina for a couple of months. It was just to keep her company and to help her, if possible, with the baby. Also, that she would have to attend school there in Leslau for the time being. To her surprise, Rebekka was all fired up about going. She danced around the table babbling on and on about her new endeavor. It got to the point where she got Julia all upset of being left out. The truth was, she even felt a little hurt by her eldest's outbreak of joy. Not even a whimper escaped Rebekka's lips. None that would indicate she might miss them, at least a little. If that would have been the case she would not have let her go. And in a way, she had hoped it so, but seeing how excited Rebekka was made her give in, although it was with much sadness on her part. She entrusted Rebekka in Mandek and Wiktor's care to drive her to Kutno. The two had shown themselves trustworthy and loyal. In fact, she could rely on the whole Slovak family. They were more than friends. Over the years they had become like a second family to them all.

--

Julia took the separation from her sister very hard, especially after school when the two would take off visiting school friends, or just plain romping around the property. Seeing how Julia felt made her sorry she had agreed to Edwina's proposal. But it was too late for regrets. To get Julia out of this mood she decided to involve her in the daily chores. She let her help around the house and take care of the little ones. Within days Julia was her old self again eager to do whatever needed to be done. She acted like a little mother toward Elisa and Stefan. She had to admit, that by keeping busy with the children, she too found the separation from Johann and Rebekka a little easier to take. Yet it was in the stillness of the night when she missed them both terribly.

Father Wendel had busied himself in keeping daily track of the events at the front lines. To keep him company, she usually joined him after the children had gone to bed. In silence they both sat, their ears perked listening to the people's receiver. Hoping and waiting for positive news, but there was little of that these days. The casualties, especially at the Russian front, were heavy. That left them both with great concern for Johann as well as other family members.

The uncertainty of the war and its outcome gave everyone, who was listening to the underground messages, an uneasy feeling. She felt the tension whenever she came in contact with her friends. There was no sense of planning ahead. Day in and day out it seemed to be a waiting game. Only the work that was needed to be done was done. Lucky for them, the attic was filled anew with prepared fried meats and smoked ham hocks; as well as preserves and fresh fruit. There was also plenty of fuel for cooking and heating, thanks to the Slovaks. Life would not be all that bad if... She caught herself again. A deep sigh escaped her lips. Mechanically, she went about her work. She had felt like this a lot lately, as if in a daze, she rose in the morning and after the day's work was done, she fell into bed the same way. She had been waiting anxiously for a letter from Johann, but none came. But then she excused it, especially when she heard the reports of heavy fighting at the front lines. If only she had a way of knowing that he was okay.

--

It was the beginning of January 1944. For a couple of days now the sky was overcast and there was a hint of snow in the air. Father Wendel had just come in from his daily walk across the yard to check up on all the livestock. "Ah... it is nice and warm in here" he exclaimed, while taking off his boots and jacket. "I think we're in for a good snowfall. I can tell," he added while moving close to the warmth of the kitchen stove. "My bones are aching quite fiercely."

She had noticed him having a lot of trouble moving about. "Come sit down and have a cup of tea with me," she said caringly. "It'll do you good." She had just finished her morning chores and the little ones were quietly playing nearby.

After drinking her first cup, she got up to stoke the fire. She was about to pour more tea for herself when she heard a knock at the door. As she opened the door a gust of wind followed, sending a chill across the room. "Telegram," She dreaded to receive them. She quietly thanked the man and shut the door.

"Who is it from?" Father Wendel interrupted.

"It's from Daniel," she read... then paused for a long moment fighting back tears. "They say Robert was killed... by friendly fire." She sank into her chair next to him.

"Friendly fire...? I don't believe that?" Father Wendel exclaimed, reading the telegram for himself.

"Robert... my dear brother... I can't believe it," she sobbed.

It was all too much for Father Wendel. He was never much for showing sympathy. "I had better go and check on the livestock." With that he put on his boots and jacket again and disappeared out the door.

She was alone in her grief...

--

Marianka had slept overnight in Rebekka's bed, as she had trouble walking on the icy road. Early on, Polio had left her one foot crippled. Katina welcomed her company, but Father Wendel did not agree having her here. He had become a little more intolerant of people in general and at times even towards her. Many times he sat in his corner of the kitchen brooding and very depressed. Was it all this turmoil of war that brought this on again? She could not figure him out and it gave her great concern.

Poor Julia got her share of being yelled at. It seemed he forever found faults with her, especially when roughhousing with Elisa. Then there was the moving of the ladder whenever he was up in the loft of the barn. She had to admit Julia deserved a scolding for things like that. But on the other hand he had brought it on himself. Calling her an adopted gypsy and not part of their family, understandably it made the girl upset.

'Maybe… just maybe… It was because she let Rebekka go to her sister. Maybe that made him act this way,' she thought, for he had always favored Rebekka over Julia.

Well… no matter what, she could not let that bother her now. She had more important things to do than to figure out Father Wendel's mood swings. She welcomed the time more and more when he was out and about, and she was left alone with her children. The rest of the time she just stayed out of his way and she cautioned Julia to do the same.

Marianka had busied herself with the two little ones. And seeing the two were cared for, Katina took the opportunity to step out for a few minutes. She had to send a telegram back to Daniel as soon as possible. She had let him know that she had received the news and also to send her condolences, especially to Mama and Papa. 'What a blow,' she thought, fighting back tears.

"Oh Daniel," she suddenly remembered. He of all people must be beside himself, knowing that his brother had taken his place. "Friendly fire, how could that have happened?" Robert had been in the rescue division, stationed in Saberje. "My poor brother," she sobbed again. He had always been such a loving brother to all of them and such a big help to Papa. Oh Papa! How he must suffer, knowing there were more of his sons and sons-in-law, out there in the battle field. Who would be next?

Her eyes filled with tears again. Where were they now? Where was her Johann?

"Oh God, please keep them all safe." She prayed, wiping the constant stream of tears from her face.

46

Things did not look all that well at the Russian front. As soon as Johann and his comrades stepped on this godforsaken ground, they were reminded of the harsh task before them. The endless convoy of fresh supplies and manpower, pushed ever forward over the bleak and merciless frozen Ukrainian steppe. It lay cold and uninviting, far into the vast and endless distance in front of them. Even under the cover of its wintery blanket, the land could not conceal the evidence of destruction. Everywhere he looked were burnt villages and desolate farms, as well as abandoned, broken down equipment. The frozen road to the eastern front suddenly left him disquiet. But there was no turning back. The panje horse and cart, native to eastern Europe, lent itself to be useful. It seemed to be the best transportation on this unforgiving long and tiring trek. The closer they came to the front the more the evidence of upheaval. It was certainly not an encouraging sight to behold.

Once at their destination, he and his artillery unit immediately were engaged in endless days and nights of combat. Of all the previous battles they had encountered, there was no comparison to what had awaited them here at the eastern front. The fighting was relentless. In the autumn, the conditions of the trenches and bunkers had been wet and rat infested, so they were told by others who had been here before. Now they had to deal with this miserable freezing cold.

It was so bitter cold, they all found themselves ill-equipped against it. They were desperate now for warm winter clothing and proper boots. But most of all, he and the others wished for an extra pair of homemade woolen socks. It would keep their already numb feet clear from frostbite. They were overwhelmed by the lack of sleep and the hunger from deplorable food rations. He and his comrades would have given anything for a good home-cooked meal.

To keep their spirits up, they relied on each other's support and encouragement, as at times it seemed so hopeless and disheartening to fight on. But fight on they must, all for the 'Fatherland, family and home.' Yet he found in spite their constant attacks, the Russians held their ground and were not easily flushed out from their hideouts.

Amidst all the heavy sound of thunder and crackling of the artillery he could hear the moans and groans and crying of the wounded and dying around him on the battlefield. The Russian artillery relentlessly pounded the trenches and there was nowhere to run. The Stalin Orgel, a device that added an eerie deafening noise, he found more than anything, wore down their morale. It devastated them mentally and physically, as the shells did a lot of damage. And one agonizing thought kept repeating in his mind.

'Now it will get me... Now it will get me...'

It was heart wrenching and spine chilling, but through all this turmoil, he and his comrades held their ground and stood firm. Their motto, 'either them or us', kept refueling them to keep on fighting. They had to shoot in order to survive. He noticed some of the younger soldiers had to be coaxed to do their job. They were scared to shoot and face the enemy. He felt sorry for them when he seen them hiding in the trenches crying for their mothers.

To him, the artillery guns looked like monsters. Their mouth raised wide open against the heavens; they spit devastating shells all over the icy surface. It was hell listening to their never ending sickening sounds. Forget trying to see through the heavy smoke, as the frozen dirt was flying everywhere. It made it hard for them to see what they were shooting at. They had to rely mainly on their commander for directions and signals. To add to this problem, their hands had become red and stiff from the relentless and merciless cold. It contributed to the stress of maneuvering any machinery. It made even the simplest task aggravatingly difficult to perform.

Many of the soldiers around him looked thin and haggard. Plagued with dysentery, they all found themselves surrounded by the whiff of death. It hung heavy in the air.

At a short break in the fighting he tried to warm his fingers. Heavy-hearted, his thoughts were of home. Quickly he pulled out his paper and began to write.

--

My dearest Katina, January, 22, 1944

I can't even describe to you the emotional and physical upheaval and devastation that surrounds us here day and night. I write this letter to you in haste, as the fighting is relentless. There is little time for personal matters. I'm still in shock... for today, just after I had gone for a bite to eat, the location where I and my comrades were stationed was totally eradicated by heavy Russian artillery. All of them had perished in an instant... Only I remained. I must tell you... it was a very sobering and devastating experience.

My Dearest... I must confess to you... although I do not wish to burden you with this. But I knew at that moment... There was little hope that I... and so many others of my fellow comrades, should come out of this hellhole alive... The fighting is extremely intense and there is no end in sight. The whole sky is in a constant blaze of fire. And the many cries of the wounded laying among mangled masses of dead dismembered bodies is gut wrenching.

O God... My heart is heavy... and I'm so worried for all of you. My darling...it pains me to write this... But if I should not survive, I give you my blessing to remarry... But please... my darling, please... think of the children if you should ever do so. Make sure they're not pushed aside or mistreated. I wish to God... the circumstances would be different and all this did not have to be said...

Should I dare to hope...? Oh God... What a terrible plight...

My dearest there is so much I want to say, but time is short and I have to go... I love you all, so very much... May God have mercy...

Love always, Johann

P.S. I waited for you at the train station in Kutno, but you did not come...? Did the telegram not reach you? What happened...? Oh Katina... It still pains me not to have seen you there and to hold you in my arms... Oh darling I miss you all so terribly... Please write soon...

--

With all that said and done, he knew after committing this letter, it would be some time before she would receive it. With him coming here to the lower Ukrainian region, he had hoped to reach Yevpatoriya; where he was born. In going there he wanted to search out his father's estate. His aim was to find the hidden treasure they left behind when fleeing the Bolsheviks. His father had talked to him about it again on his last furlough home and he had laid it on his heart if possible to retrieve it. But seeing the situation first hand, all he could hope for now was coming out of this hellish inferno alive.

Left without his artillery team he immediately was grouped with other fellow soldiers in the same predicament, ready again to keep on fighting.

Again and again the sky lit up from repeated explosions. The ceaseless monstrous mouths of heavy artillery were never quiet. And there was not an inch on this unforgiving frozen ground for him or anyone to crawl into and hide. Only one thought was on his mind, to stay alive, to counteract, and shoot, hoping he'll be spared from the raining blaze of shrapnel.

He turned for a moment to help reload the heavy artillery. All at once a hellish ear-deafening sound of the Staling Orgel pierced the night sky. He felt himself suddenly hurled through the air. And with great force he was thrown hard against the icy ground. Stunned for a moment he lay there in shock. He did not know what had happened or where he was. Suddenly an indescribable, unbearable burning pain pierced his whole body. Pain so intense, he had never felt before. He screamed in agony, but to no avail. The pain was his and his alone to bear. Like so many other wounded, his cry was drowned out by the screaming sound of the Stalin Orgel and the rumbling thunder of heavy artillery. He drifted in and out of consciousness calling out for help. He needed to be rescued and released from this excruciating hellish ordeal.

"Oh God..." he moaned. "Help me... Oh God... I don't... I don't want to die..." He cried bitterly, "Please God... Help me..." His hand dug into the frozen soil to hold on. He had to brace himself against the hellish convulsions that wracked his pain ridden body. The winter night was coming. If he could only hold on if he could...? Maybe then his comrades could rescue... If only he could hold on... 'Cold, it's so bitter cold...' Fragmented sentences ran feverishly through his tormented mind. Suddenly, the night fell, with the blaring fire of artillery lighting up the dark sky. It kept on resounding thunderously over the hellish foreboding icy cold battleground.

--

The following day rose with a grey blue cloud covered haze. The smell of gunpowder and smoke lay heavy in the air, as the fighting raged on in a violent relentless fury.

Amazed that he was still alive, he assessed his condition as much as he could. The torturous and horrendous pain had never left his body. And as far as he could see it did not look all that well for him. Here he lay in a pool of blood amidst other comrades, some in the same predicament as him, others did not move at all. His left arm had been torn part way off, leaving in its place a big ugly gash on the one side of his chest. This and the many other injuries the shrapnel had inflicted on his body left him totally unable to move. He tried over and over, but to no avail. He felt so cold... so bitterly cold... and extremely helpless.

Along other wounded and dying he called out again and again in hopes someone might hear. The pain had become more and more unbearable and he felt his strength fading. His thoughts, whenever his consciousness would allow, went to his loved ones. Oh... the agony never to see their faces again and to hold them in his arms tore deep into his heart and soul. He felt so alone. He cried out to God repeatedly to help him, not to let him die. Katina, the children, his Father... they needed him. There was too much uncertainty and he feared the worst for them.

"Not yet dear God..." Again and again he pleaded with his Maker, calling out the names of his loved ones.

"Katina!!!" His cry came from the depth of his soul, but there was no answer... He felt so terribly thirsty and cold... so utterly cold... "Please help! Dear God! Please help! Anyone... Please Help!" his cry pierced the frozen, unforgiving, noise stunned battlefield.

Daylight faded and once again the night consumed the sky. It intensified the unrelenting cold and the exploding blazes of gunfire, multiplying the thundering noise level of heavy artillery. He was amazed that he had made it through another day, but the night cold started eating at him again. Could he survive another night? He had to. He needed to. He hoped that his cries would be heard. He knew that he lay in the crossfire. For someone to rescue him, they would be exposed to enemy fire. But he called again with all his remaining strength. Surely someone would hear. Someone would come. What came instead was a dark night... a cold night of creeping death.

He thought of Katina. If only he could tell her again how much he loved her. He had to survive. He had to tell her.

47

A loud bang woke Katina. In bewilderment she looked around. It was as if someone had lifted the cold storage trap door next to her bed and slammed it shut. She jumped out of bed and lit the kerosene lamp that stood on her bedside table. She sat back down again trying to decipher what just happened. She was careful not to disturb the two little ones sleeping in their cribs next to her near the warm kachel-oven. It was amazing they did not wake, for she was sure they must have heard it too.

She had a strange dream that Johann was sitting on a coach, dressed in his long leather coat, reaching out for her to join him. As she was about to approach him he vanished and that's when the sudden loud noise had occurred.

Marianka, who had been sleeping in the front bedroom with Julia, came running. She too had heard the noise and was curious what had happened. Quietly, the two were talking not knowing what to make of this. They inspected the trap door, but all seemed to be in order. Katina looked at the clock; it was 4:00 in the morning. The night was cold and as forecasted the temperature had plummeted.

"Go back to bed..." she coaxed Marianka. "I'll quickly check the fire in all the ovens... Then I'll be doing the same." But Marianka would not go. With the kerosene lamp in hand she followed Katina. She watched her adding more dried peat moss to the existing kachel-oven in their bedroom. It actually was planned to be their future living room, as the

296

extension for another bedroom was still in the making. The second kachel-oven, also serving as a bake oven, ran along the connecting kitchen wall. It was serviced from the kitchen side of the same. With a little ingenuity Johann had managed to heat all rooms, making the whole house nice and warm.

They were just about to refuel the second kachel-oven and the massive cook-stove, when they heard Father Wendel. "What was that noise?" He confronted them as the two came into the kitchen.

Katina tried to explain, but was at a loss why it happened.

Marianka then could not hold back anymore. She told them that she and her family, both at different times had seen what they thought was Johann.

"He was walking yesterday evening along the street toward our parent's house. Then he was standing outside our living room window, moaning in pain. Then again I had seen him here at the front bedroom window, doing the same. It must have been a vision." She paused not sure if she should have mentioned it, knowing it would upset Katina and Father Wendel.

"We didn't want to alarm you, so we kept the whole incident to ourselves. We are very worried for Pan Wendel," she added shivering.

Katina was shocked and speechless.

"Something is wrong, something is terribly wrong," Father Wendel added with a distraught look about his face.

They sat huddled close to the warm kachel/bake oven in silence, no one saying a word.

"I'll make us a cup of tea," Marianka got up from her chair, realizing that no one felt like sleeping anymore.

Father Wendel, in the meantime, busied himself to tune in on the underground radio, while Katina and Marianka moved closer to hear. There it was, the message was a little unclear but enough to understand... 'There was fierce fighting... at the eastern front ....and there were heavy losses on both sides.'

Solemnly they stared at each other. Father Wendel just shook his head. He tried to listen for more, but suddenly the reception was interrupted by a steady crackling noise. Annoyed, he shut the radio off.

"No use listening to this. Have to try a little later, maybe then we can hear the whole report," he sat for a moment beside them trying to make sense of it all, then he pulled himself up and, with a defeated slumped-over posture, walked to his bed. "I'm going back to bed. It's warmer under my blanket," he said dejected.

Katina nodded in acknowledgment, but remained sitting. She herself did not want to go back to bed, uneasy that she might have another reoccurring episode. She reached for her large shawl that hung on her chair. She wrapped it tight around her shoulder and moved closer to the warmth of the oven.

Marianka got up. "Might as well fill up our cups again, it'll help us keep warm," she said as she poured more hot tea into each of their cups.

"Would you like some more?" she asked Father Wendel. But he declined pulling his blanket close around him, moaning in pain, while getting himself comfortable.

"Maybe you'd rather stay close to the oven where it's warm." Katina encouraged him, knowing that his arthritis was bothering him again.

"Ah, the bed is softer," he said with melancholy in his voice.

Marianka sat down again, taking a small sip of tea from her cup. Katina did the same, both remaining in their own thoughts. 'It was good to have Marianka here to keep them company,' she thought, as it did feel comforting and she appreciated it. And she was sure Father Wendel felt the same, even though he did not say it.

The weather outside matched the mood inside with the wind blowing fiercely over the snow covered yard. Her thoughts went far beyond to the eastern front, where she was sure the weather was more intense.

At least they had the safety and comfort of a warm home with plenty of food to satisfy their stomachs, but what about Johann? She could not even imagine or comprehend what he and all the other soldiers were going through out there on the battlefield.

"Oh God please be with them all, especially my Johann... Please God protect him and bring him safe back to me..." she prayed, anxious and confused over not knowing.

Suddenly she felt so tired, but she still refused to go back to bed. She looked at the clock, which hung not far from Father Wendel's bed. It showed five-thirty in the morning. It would give her a little more than an hour before the children would wake. She got up and placed her cup on the table where Marianka had left hers. Both she and Father Wendel had dozed off and were now sound asleep. Quietly she moved about to check on her children. Satisfied that they were still sleeping, she once again resumed her place by the oven. Crossing her arms tight against her body to stay warm, she dropped her head forward and closed her eyes.

--

Startled by Father Wendel's heavy snoring, she suddenly woke, noticing Marianka's chair empty beside her. Thinking herself to have overslept she jumped up. Then glancing at the clock, she realized that she had dozed off for a good hour. Her body felt stiff and painful from sleeping in this awkward sitting position.

In an instant all of last night's happenings flooded her mind with such ferocity. It left her fearful and deeply troubled again, worried for Johann's well-being. Desperately she tried to suppress the dark thoughts that kept rising inside her anxious mind. What had happened here seemed so real and it scared her. It was like a bad omen that was resolved to happen no matter what. But then again there was always hope.

"He probably is injured and laying somewhere in a

field hospital. Yes, that's it..." She calmed herself with this thought. "Oh dear God be with him." She prayed again weary and tired.

All at once she turned, aware of the rustling noise behind her. Marianka was already at the stove preparing breakfast. Quickly she got up to help her in setting the table, but Marianka was already at her side.

"No!" She shook her head and took the cutlery and dishes out of her hand. "I'll do this; you relax and get yourself ready."

"Thanks Marianka, I appreciate it," she said quietly, glad that she gave her the time to come to herself. As she was about to go into the bedroom, she noticed Father Wendel stirring then lifting himself up with a sudden jerk. His face showed the stress from the night's happenings. Without saying a word he got up and put on his jacket and fur hat. Slipping into his boots he opened the door to the outside, letting a cold gust of wind escape into the room. Realizing it he quickly closed it behind him.

"Ugh," she shook herself from the frigid air. "Is it ever cold!" she said to Marianka, who busied herself to add more fuel to the stove.

Standing by the kitchen window she stared for a moment after Father Wendel. She watched him cross the snow covered bridge. His forward stooped walk indicated he was deeply troubled.

"I hope he's alright," she turned to Marianka who stopped for a moment in passing.

"Is Pan Wendel eating with us?" Marianka asked.

Katina shrugged her shoulders.

"We'll leave him some porridge on the stove. He'll eat it when he comes in, and if he doesn't, well he probably still has butter and bread in his cabinet. We'll leave the jam out on the table for him."

Marianka nodded, knowing how difficult Father Wendel can be when it came to eating. "It's good for Pan Wendel to have his tobacco business, yes?" she said it in a questioning

I WILL REMEMBER ALWAYS

manner.

Katina nodded. "Yes, it is a good thing. It'll keep him from brooding too much. Right now I think we all have to guard ourselves from troublesome thoughts," she said it mostly to herself, for she more than anyone else needed to stay positive. She was reminded why, when she heard Julia and Elisa giggling through the half open bedroom door. She was glad the children had slept through the night and were not aware of the night's happening.

--

The next day Hetti had dropped by for a visit and as usual there was a lot to talk about. Mainly it was about the latest news from the front. As again, everyone listening to the underground radio knew, but only talked about it in secret.

And it was after lunch, when Marianka had gone out and Father Wendel had retreated to the barn; Katina confessed in quiet all the strange occurrences to Hetti and her worries about Johann's well being.

Hetti listened in silence, shaking her head in disbelief.

"You know, if it's all right with you? I can take a few days off from work and stay here with you for a while. Marianka can sleep at home, while I sleep in Rebekka's bed. What do you think... Hmm? It might make you feel better.

Katina agreed and had to admit; with Hetti here she would feel more at ease. And Julia too would be thrilled to have Auntie Hetti sleep in the same room with her. All along she had purposely held back and not told Julia about this whole incidence. For she knew it would affect her deeply.

And as it turned out, she had done right to agree to have Hetti here. With her lightheartedness she brought a lot of cheer into the house and the children enjoyed playing with her. But she noticed it was not only the children; as of all people, Father Wendel's mood also lifted considerably.

Two nights had gone by without any recurrences or unusual happenings. It suddenly was as if it all had been a bad dream. Like all nightmares they profoundly linger in

301

your mind for a while then fade into sub consciousness. At least that's what she wanted to believe.

--

The weather had calmed and the sun was shining brightly on the snow covered surfaces, reflecting glaringly against the eyes. She and Hetti sat down to have a cup of tea while the little ones had their afternoon nap. Father Wendel, as usual, had gone out to work for a while in the barn. Julia had just come home from school and was busy doing her homework.

Suddenly a sharp knock at the door startled them. Katina got up and opened the door. Her face turned pale when she noticed two army officers standing in front of her. Across the yard, Father Wendel came running as fast as he could, not to miss out on what was said, managing just to hear one of the officers say to Katina.

"We're sorry to report to you that your husband, Johann Wendel, had died in battle..." Katina did not hear the rest of what was said. Suddenly her head was spinning and everything went black in front of her. The attending officers just caught her as she went down, carrying her to the bedroom, where they desperately tried to revive her.

Little Elisa woke from all that noise, crying over the commotion of people fussing over her Mama, who lay motionless on her bed. Julia on the other hand understood all too well what was going on, as she was sobbing uncontrollably.

"Dead... My God... Johann dead...?" Father Wendel was in shock. He just buried his face in his hands in disbelief and wept. It was too much to bear. His only son, now his whole family was gone.

"Father Wendel, can you hold Elisa? She's crying, maybe you can calm her down. Marianka is occupied with Stefan and I need to be there for Katina," Hetti pleaded.

"Elisa...? Yah... sure... I can do that."

As he held the little one he suddenly realized that he was holding part of Johann on his lap, something so precious and

I WILL REMEMBER ALWAYS

dear, Johann's children, and his grandchildren. His heart was heavy, but warmed by the thought. His tears flowed as he held the little one.

--

News traveled fast. It was a sad and sobering day for family and friends including the Slovaks, for they had come to respect and love Johann. Many times he had gone beyond his limitations to help and protect them. The same went for Katina, as she too treated them, Marianka especially, like family.

Hetti volunteered to stay a while longer and Marianka did not protest. She was happy to sleep at home.

A few days later Katina finally got her strength back and she attempted to look at Johann's letter which was dated January 22, 1944. It had arrived the same day the officers brought the sad news. Along with it there was also a letter from his army chaplain. In it he described the twenty four hours they desperately tried to rescue him.

The chaplain wrote:

'Johann and the other wounded were caught in the crossfire... We heard their calls and we had desperately tried to reach them again and again... But unfortunately it was impossible as the fighting was relentless. It was four days later, when after a ceaseless battle, a truce was finally declared and we were able to collect the dead and wounded... It was heart wrenching not being able to get to them in time... '

She broke down many times. She could not bring herself to finish reading the letters in one sitting. It was too much to bear. Among the chaplain's letter that lay in front of her, there was a small snapshot of a graveside with wooden crosses erected on a worn torn landscape. Johann's was among them with his rank, name and date of birth and death on it. In the background, faintly visible, were the ruins of Krivoy Rog. A city the chaplain had mentioned in his letter. It looked so desolate, so distant, so removed. She stared at it

303

dejected, remembering Johann's smile and his loving strong arms around her. Now, he lay dead in this God-forsaken place, so far away. Suddenly she was again overwhelmed by the hopelessness of it all. My poor Johann, how much he must have suffered, twenty four hours, torn apart in mind and body. She broke down sobbing uncontrollably. It touched her deeply when she read about him calling their names. The agony of it all was too much, it pained her so.

"God, why did you allow this to happen?" she cried in despair. They had only a few happy years together. The two little ones had hardly gotten to know him and now they were without a father; and she only thirty-one and without the love of her life. He was and always had been the pillar she had leaned and relied on. Now she would have to go on alone, without him by her side.

She remembered how eager he was, when they first started out in Mangalia. All the dreams and expectations he had. How happy those years had been. Why was this happening? Their lives now shattered and their dreams gone. Tossed about by a force in which they had no say over their lives. What will happen to them now? 'Oh my dearest Johann...' How he must have agonized over the hopelessness of it all... Overtaken again by tears she began to understand why these strange occurrences had happened. It was all because he cared so deeply for all of them.

The guilt for not being there at the train station in Kutno now multiplied her burden. It made it doubly hard to take, especially when she read his letter. She would give anything to undo events and be there one more time to hold him in her arms. Again and again she was overcome with heavy sobbing, remembering the last time he had been here on leave. How he had sat outside on the front steps polishing his rifle, singing songs he had learned in the army; while Julia stood behind him combing and playing with his hair. One song in particular came to mind, it told of a soldier telling his comrade, as he lay dying, "Take this ring from my finger...

take this ring from my hand... hold it against her white forehead... as a solemn vow and last farewell."

She could barely contain herself, tears clouded her vision. She thought back how hard it had been for him to say good bye. It was as if he had felt he would not return.

48

It was at night she let her sorrow run free, crying herself to sleep. And it was on one of those nights when her sadness reached its peak, that again a loud noise woke her. This time she felt her bed end being lifted and then dropped. She saw Johann standing by her bedside. She reached out into the darkness and cried out his name. But just as she was about to touch him, he disappeared.

Hetti had heard her cry and came to investigate.

"What is the matter Katina is everything all right?"

"Oh Hetti...He was here, right here..."

"Who was, Katina?" Hetti spoke in a quiet voice.

"Johann! Hetti... It was Johann and he looked so happy and peaceful. He told me not to cry for him anymore and that he was all right..."

"You want me to stay with you for a while?" Hetti asked concerned.

"No, I'll be okay," she answered with tear-filled eyes. But Hetti was reluctant to leave her. She went along with her to look in on the two little ones, as it was her nightly ritual whenever she woke.

"I'll go and reload the other two ovens for you," Hetti commented and went out into the kitchen.

Katina stood for a moment in disbelief, thinking about her dream and Johann. What did it mean? Why this message? Did he come to comfort her? It felt so real.

"Oh Johann... I miss you so much," she sobbed quietly.

Hetti entered the room again. "All ovens are restocked," she quietly informed Katina. Seeing she was crying, she put her arm around her to comfort her.

"I think you should try and lay down again to get some rest before the children wake. I'll do the same. But if for any reason you need me, just call," Hetti spoke in a hushed voice.

Katina lay awake for a long time. Too much had happened and her mind was going from one thought to the next. She felt sad, but calm now to have seen Johann so content. Yet within her heart stirred a deep emptiness, a terrible loneliness... She was now truly alone.

She made a promise to herself and to Johann that she would respect his wish. She will always take care of the children and nothing could change that, for this she was certain. They were all she had left now and she loved them too much to let any harm come to them. Life could have been so beautiful if it would not have been for this ugly war. So much pain it had inflicted on so many lives.

Quietly she unlocked the special memories in her heart. She recalled the good times they had shared. Then she locked them back deep in her heart, where no one could take them away from her. They would always be there ready to reach for them whenever the need arose; and she knew it would be many times... many, many times. For now she had to be strong for her children. They were her only comfort and the closest thing to Johann. They were part of him and that would be reason enough to get up every morning; to keep on living.

--

The following day Hetti was such a help in sending out the telegrams to family and friends. Especially to Rebekka, for she wanted and needed now all her children by her side.

Marianka and her family too were so devoted. They practically took over and ran the whole household, helping inside and outside with all the chores. Marianka's grandmother even baked their favorite and delicious pumpkin buns for them. 'What an angel.' No one could make them better than her. When she was not baking she would be found behind her spinning wheel spinning flax. They had harvested it from the fields behind their 18 hectare land. There, in water filled ditches, it had been soaked and processed for spinning. She recalled with fondness the hot summer days when the children played there, swimming in the small creek nearby. What happy times... A deep quiver escaped her lips... She dearly missed Johann. Life would never be the same without him by her side.

49

T he months that followed were like a blur, as she went about to help the others with household duties and taking care of her children. She especially noticed Julia taking her father's passing very hard and missed having Rebekka around. So she and the others decided that it might be good for her to go and visit Rebekka and Auntie Edwina in Leslau. They were soon coming here anyway to take part in the memorial service. It was held in honor for all the fallen soldiers.

In a cheerless mood, Katina picked out a beautiful black dress with white polka dots to wear. Johann had given it to her as a gift on his last furlough. She was reminded again of the tragic and bittersweet state she found herself in. Her heart again was filled with profound pain.

When the day of the memorial service came, she stood proud but broken in spirit like so many other soldiers' wives. Their children all huddled close around them, some with other family members in support. Marianka had lent her a black shawl to go over her shoulders as the weather was not quite warm enough to go without. For some reason she had never thought it important to own a black jacket nor a black coat. It did not matter anymore anyway. The rest of the day passed with much somberness. And it was good to have Rebekka and Edwina here for support.

The day after, Edwina had planned to take her and the two older girls to Pabianice. It was to visit Mama and Papa and the rest of their family. In doing this she hoped it would bring her sister out of her depression.

As predicted it was comforting to see everyone again and be surrounded by so much love. But the visit went by much too fast. And before they knew it was time again to part. She had always hated goodbyes, and this time it was especially hard. For no one knew what lay ahead and when they would see each other again.

What made it more difficult was to see Rebekka go again with Edwina. She had tried to persuade her oldest to come home, but Edwina was relentless in begging her to let Rebekka stay with her. To her and Julia's dismay, Rebekka chose again to go with Auntie Edwina. Despite her and Julia's pleading, Rebekka was unshakable in her decision. With an uneasy feeling, she finally gave in.

Now standing in the Kutno train station, she blamed herself for letting Rebekka go in the first place. It felt so utterly painful to be so totally rejected. Why would Rebekka do this? And seeing how much it hurt her, why did Edwina not decline taking her daughter with her? Why did she have to lose yet another member of her family? This, on top of Johann's death, was almost too much to bear, but the damage was done and there seemed to be no way to change Rebekka's mind. She especially felt sad for Julia, as again she took her sister's leaving very hard.

Rebekka had taken one more glance toward them as she waved goodbye, when she suddenly noticed the sadness in her mother's eyes.

Watching the train leave, Katina felt an overwhelming inconsolable grief rise up inside of her. The loss of yet another member was almost too much on her already grieving heart. Disheartened she reached out to Julia, who was still gazing in disbelieve after the train.

"Mama, why does everyone have to leave?" she asked teary eyed.

She had no answer. She just quietly took her daughter's

hand and they both made their way to the waiting carriage.

50

Summer went and fall had come. Katina had tried her best to keep busy with the harvest to make preparations for winter. She felt detached from life, yet again she needed to remain strong for her children. She especially appreciated the help of those who had remained by her side. It made this difficult time pass.

--

Father Wendel had retreated even more in his own world of grief. He was now the last of his family. His wife and daughter and now Johann were gone. He could not comprehend the cruelty of life for him and his family. Why this struggle? Yet despite it all he managed to keep going. Looking around he could not give up. Katina and the children, they needed him now more than ever. Each morning after he woke, he would go and check on the animals and help Pan Slovak and his boys whenever they needed a hand. But as far as he seen it, they had everything under control.

After breakfast he would give Katina a break and watch the two little ones as they played around him. It was this that gave him strength to go on. And as before, every night he and Katina would do what they had always done for the past year. In quiet they sat in dim light and behind drawn curtains listening in on the underground radio. For especially now it was urgent to know what was happening with this war.

It was one night in October when he and Katina

heard the shocking news that the Red Army had crossed into East Prussia and had reached Nemmersdorf. The German propaganda machine had constantly told them that they were winning the battle, but this time they reported atrocities from the Red Army in Nemmersdorf. Nemmersdorf was just over 300 km away from where they were. Could the German Army protect them?

Realizing now how vulnerable they were, Katina suddenly became very concerned for what lay ahead. Like the rest of her friends, she too had tried to make the best of every moment and each day. Yet this news left her greatly unsettled.

--

The sky again had turned to gray with a forecast of snow. Wintertime had come and was upon them. This time Christmas was just not the same without Johann and Rebekka. But for Julia's, Elisa's and Stefan's sake, she went about the usual holiday activities and celebrations. Father Wendel and Hetti as well as the Slovaks had tried to help along. Yet they all felt the joy of celebrating was not there. What had happened and the uncertainty of not knowing what was coming left everyone uneasy.

After Christmas, the fear in all of them magnified. The outlook on winning the war looked bleaker by the day. All the latest propaganda speeches could not conceal the truth from those who secretly kept vigil around the clandestine radio.

The Red Army was massing troops along the front line, now within 160 km east of Lodz along the Vistula River, outnumbering the German military five to one. The Germans had no choice but to retreat.

On the twelfth of January the report came over the black box that the Russian Army was crossing into Poland. The pact Hitler and Stalin had made to share Poland equally was now broken.

Panic spread throughout the region as all German people feared now for their lives. Most who had lived under the

Russian regime or had heard stories from their fathers and grandfathers, who themselves had experienced the oppression during The Great War, knew what was awaiting them. Many men at that time had been killed or dragged away to labor camps deep in Siberia. Their families, left vulnerable to all kinds of abuse and raids, fled to hide, leaving their properties exposed to ruthless ravaging forces.

Now this news, and the fright of falling into the hands of the approaching Red Army, left them all in a frenzy to escape. Many set out to flee westward to the safety of their ancestral homeland, only to be stopped in their tracks and threatened by the occupying German authorities here in Poland. If anyone tried to escape they would be shot for cowardice. Stunned by this order many were left undecided on what to do.

Despite the warning there was talk among their friends to go against the authorities, to pack up and leave. One good neighbor advised Katina to do the same and not wait, but when she confronted Father Wendel, his reply was, "They won't do anything to me. The Russians are my friends!"

She was torn. For obvious reasons Father Wendel did not like change and was hesitant to go. It was winter and the journey would be treacherous, something one could not undertake lightly. Out there the possibility of freezing to death was very real. Here was food and shelter. And for this she knew it would not be easy to convince him.

Hetti's parents though, went ahead and made their escape. Not to make it too obvious, Father and Mother Kranz left quietly one day without arousing anyone's suspicion. They planned to send for Hetti later; who was working as a nurse here at the home front. But when more of their friends tried to follow suit they were confronted with strong opposition from the home group leaders. They were warned if anyone was planning to flee, or found fleeing, they would be severely punished.

It was a time of whispers and secrets. A family was seen

one day and not the next. Each family made their decision in secret and left in secret. Others waiting for permission or consensus remained behind.

Katina felt trapped; it was not just about convincing Father Wendel to change his mind, but Heinrich Schwarz was still watching their every move and threatening to snitch on them by the slightest sign of departure. He was following official orders. If all the German population fled, the German resettlement would have failed in Poland. And that meant the failure of the Nazi ideology and vision, their cry for Lebensraum, living space for the Aryan nation. All their efforts would have been in vain.

As it was, Katina had no one to talk things over with, no one to help her decide. She missed Johann's decisiveness. She missed Papa's advice. Father Wendel was comfortable here and with his Russian heritage he was comfortable with the Russians.

--

Some of the older German men, who were able to fight, were now enlisted to take up arms and join the home front. Bravely they did as they were told. Only to meet up with opposite advice from other German military leaders who were on the retreat with their battalion to escape the oncoming Russian Army. As one of them put it... "Go home and don't think twice. Pack whatever you can rescue on a wagon, take your family and leave as fast as you can to get away from the Russians." But as soon as they arrived home and tried to do just that, they were told again by their own Party leader to go and fight.

"If you disobey you'll all be shot," so they were warned. Out they went again to fight, only to be confronted again by fleeing German armed forces. Again they were told to forget the fighting, but to hasten and rescue whatever they could and run with their families to safety. This time many did just that.

--

315

In Pabianice, Papa had all along listened to the news and was aware what had to be done. Talking it over with the rest of the family, they all agreed and decided to take the chance and run. Together with Mama and the entire family, including in-laws living in and around the Lodz-Pabianice area, they slipped away in the night. Taking a chance they made their way west across Poland en route to Germany. They had not dared to send any messages to Edwina, or for that matter to Katina, to let them know what they had planned, or tell them that they also should leave, as they were afraid by doing so they would risk being caught and punished.

--

Hetti who was on leave from duty had told Katina that she would be visiting friends up in the Bromberg area. "I'll be back in a couple of days." She had said when she had come by in their coach. One of their assigned Polish workers had been driving her to catch the train in Kutno. That was the last she had seen or heard of Hetti.

--

Edwina with her newborn baby boy and Rebekka, chose to flee by train. With multitudes of German civilians crammed into straw filled boxcars, the overcrowded freight train made its way northbound, stopping only once in a while for bathroom breaks. Most of the destitute used this opportunity to quickly search out the surrounding neighborhood, and beg for food and water.

Rebekka did the same and jumped out of the train, begging for milk for her little cousin. On numerous occasions the train had already started to go. Edwina was left watching out over the crowd worried, looking for Rebekka, thinking that this time she might not make it back. Then just in time, there she was with milk and food in hand, jumping triumphantly onto the moving train.

As any other train on this route, it also was heading toward the designated Baltic port of Gotenhafen in Danzig.

Here among other ships, a former KdF cruise liner, the Wilhelm Gustlof, converted to a 500 bed hospital ship, was standing by to transport wounded soldiers and other Army personal as well as many refugees, Germans and non-Germans alike. They all were fleeing to escape the terrible fate that awaited those left in the wake of the Soviet advance. Despite orders and safety regulations, people kept pushing and shoving, practically hanging on the side of the ship's rails just to be on it, frantic to get away from the Russians.

Edwina too, with baby in arm and Rebekka in tow, rushed to be on the first ship leaving, but came too late. The Wilhelm Gustlof had just left the Baltic port of Gotenhafen. The weather was poor, the wind was strong and it was snowing. The temperature was 10 degrees below zero when the large cruise liner began to push its way through the choppy, blustery Baltic Sea. Unfortunately for those who considered themselves lucky to have made it on board, the Gustlof never made it to safety. Russian torpedoes hit and sank the ship, taking thousands of people into their dark icy watery grave. Most would never see the light of dawn lift over the freezing waves of the Baltic Sea.

German Navy ships were then ordered to stand by, to protect and aid the rest of the ships. Edwina, her baby boy and Rebekka, among others, made their way to safety on the Hansa. None of them had knowledge of the ghastly outcome of the previous ship, Wilhelm Gustlof. For days the German officials raced to rescue the mass of terrified fleeing people, believing by doing so they had saved two million people from falling into the Russian hands. And it was none too soon, as within a week the railway tracks that had been the rescue line for many, were now overrun by the Red Army. By January 30, Danzig was cut off and surrounded. But what about those, deep in the heartland of Poland and beyond, that had been unable to make the escape?

51

The reports of Russian advances were now coming in more frequently over the underground radio. And after Hetti had not returned, she could only guess that her parents had followed through with their plan of getting their daughter out of Poland. Now she realized even more the urgency that they too should leave and go before it's too late. Frantically she was trying to convince Father Wendel that they should also pack up and go, but he just could not be moved.

"Where to should we go? I can't sit for days on the wagon in these freezing temperatures. My arthritis is killing me as it is. I tell you I won't survive and... what about the little ones? How can we shelter them from this dreadful cold and what about milk and food? I tell you Katina, this is not a good idea. We'll all be found frozen on the roadside and no one will come looking for us. No...No..." He shook his head. "I say we rather stay put. As I told you before the Russians, they are my friends. There's no need to worry." With that he hobbled off and sat down on his bed, close to the warmth of the cook stove.

Frustrated, she gave up. Yes, she could see his point and she knew the risk they would be taking, but from what she had heard, it was too dangerous to remain. He of all people who had listened all along to the news should understand the danger they found themselves in if they stayed here. She was stuck. She could not go alone with the children and she did not want to leave him behind, as she honored Johann's promise he had made long time ago in Mangalia, that he would always be there and look out for his father as long as he needed him. Now she felt she had to keep this vow in Johann's memory. She felt torn and so utterly helpless. What should she do?

As it was, Father Wendel was not her only deterrent. Living under the full gaze of Heinrich Schwarz was definitely to her disadvantage. The slightest move to show that she or any one of her neighbors was planning to leave was immediately noticed.

"If I see any one of you trying to leave, I'll report you immediately to our home group leader," he had warned again. She could still see the look that he gave her. His eyes were hard and cold.

It was only two days later, when she noticed Schwarz's place deserted. There was not the slightest movement. It seemed Heinrich and his family had done what he had told them not to do. Most likely he had quietly slipped away under the cover of darkness. Soon she and her friends discovered that all of the German authorities had also left without notice.

It was now that Father Wendel agreed to leave for Germany. Would they be able to make it? She had been packed and ready since the Kranzes had told her to go. All along it had been in her mind to meet up with her sister Edwina and Rebekka in Leslau, which lay to the north of Kutno, en route to Danzig, but for obvious reasons, she was unable to follow through with this plan. Now the moment had come and she started to collect the items that were to be loaded. Father Wendel quickly went to hitch up the coach. But by inspecting the horses he found that one of them had developed a big boil between the upper front legs.

Her heart sank. It was out of the question to make a sick horse pull a wagon. Pan Slovak had helped Father Wendel put on a special poultice, hoping that it would work and make this festering sore disappear, but to no avail. The only thing left was to put the horse out of his misery. That was another blow to their escape plan.

Considering the distance and this cold and unpredictable winter weather, they needed both horses. It would be ludicrous to go ahead with only one horse towing.

She felt let down. There seemed to be one obstacle after another delaying her plans to escape. Now they were stranded here indefinitely and there was nothing she could do about it.

"What's next, dear God?" she questioned with tears of hopelessness welling up in her eyes.

Her question was answered when on the next day word came around through the Slovaks, that most of those who had fled in the last days were caught. The men were reported to have been executed and their women and children each scattered to unknown places. Pan Slovak did not want to tell, that in most cases Polish vigilantes stopped the fleeing German families right outside of town. In some instances the women with their children were told to go on, telling them their husbands and fathers will follow later. But instead the men were hung, shot or beaten to death.

"I would advise you against going," he said in earnest after relaying the bad news to her and Father Wendel. "All the escape routes are blocked by the Russians. Cleverly they had circled in from the south and rushed up to Danzig, where they hoped to cut off as many fleeing civilians as possible. And I would not doubt, with this maneuvering, their main purpose was to cut off the last of the retreating German Armed Forces as well."

Pan Slovak stood his head hanging. He had heard of the disgruntled murmurs and whispers of revenge among his people. And it was gaining momentum even now as he spoke. He had heard and seen what had happened in his country before the war started. Now he and his family worried for Katina and her children, as well as Johann's father and some of their friends and families. Most of the young women were in the same predicament as Katina, as they too had lost their husbands, and now were left with children and their elderly parents or in-laws.

When he and his family saw the vision of Johann walking up the street and standing moaning in front of their living room window, they were terrified thinking it a bad omen. But now he understood, Johann must have been so worried for his family that he was trying to tell him, in fact he was begging him, to watch out for them.

With Katina, her children and her father-in-law still here, he knew they needed protecting and he was scared for all their lives. It would not be long now before this terror was upon them. He had to protect them as best as he could in honor of a dear friend and decent human being.

He looked up at her. He wanted to say more but it was best he kept quiet. This had to be in secret or he and his whole family would be subjected to the same wrath and it would come swift and harsh.

When Pan Slovak had gone, she stood for a moment, deeply shaken by this devastating news. She realized now they could not have escaped even if they had two good horses. Seeing no way out of this difficult situation, she and Father Wendel were resolved, they had no choice but to stay put. Either way they were doomed to face the consequences.

What Johann had feared had come to pass. The unthinkable was about to unfold. The Poles would be taking the opportunity of revenge on the Germans who had invaded their land.

--

The coming day in the early evening hour, Father Wendel walked to the barn as he did every day. The street in front of their house was normally busy as it was a major east to west route through to other towns and cities; yet today it was quiet. It was like an omen of something dreadful about to let loose. It gave him the chills and he did not like the feeling.

He wished now he had agreed to leave the first time Katina had wanted him too. But now it was too late and there was no going back to change the circumstances; as much as he wished it so. With lantern in hand he opened the door, but then hesitated. Something was not right. He felt it.

Slowly he made his way into the inside and looked around. Then cautiously he continued to do his chores, the shadows creeping long in the dim light of his lantern. He struggled to climb up to the hayloft to retrieve a bundle of hay for the horse. The faint odor from the last tobacco crop was still lingering among the rafters of the barn. Wistfully he looked around. Just then there was a stir behind him. He turned to lift his lantern from the floor. A gasp escaped his lips.

"What in heaven's name..." he mumbled in a half loud voice straining his eyes to see. "What are you doing out here in this freezing weather?" he questioned when he saw Klara Koenig, their neighbor from the left of their property, huddled in the hay.

"Herr Wendel!" she whispered with fear on her face. "Are you alone? You have to help me... please!"

After explaining her plight to him, he went as quickly as possible to the house and told Katina in quiet. Marianka and her father and brothers had gone home for the night, something about a family gathering, so there was no one else around. With uneasiness she looked about as she stepped out, making sure she was not seen, she proceeded to cross the yard. In her arms, she held a blanket and a basket full of food and a container with hot tea. Carefully, she walked into the barn.

She was shocked when she saw Klara's panic stricken face "What is it? What's wrong?" she asked in a hushed voice, wanting to hear firsthand what was going on.

"Please, for God's sake help me!" Klara came up from a sitting position, grabbing her by the arm. Her eyes open wide, Klara babbled on in a raging delirium. "They're after me day and night. I have nowhere to go..." she gasped her eyes portraying the terror she found herself in.

"They're trying to kill me. Please Katina, please help me. I have to hide. My home, it's not safe. Oh Katina, please look after my mother and my little girl, should something happen..."

Fractured sentences escaped Klara's mouth, overwhelmed by the horrific ordeal, her eyes clouded with tears. "I'm worried for them. How will they survive when I'm gone...?"

She was torn by Klara's dilemma and truly felt sorry for her neighbor. Yet how could she possibly help her as it is she and Father Wendel were just as vulnerable. But why Klara...? Suddenly she remembered the times when Klara had mistreated her assigned Polish workers. As a neighbor, she did not like what she had seen, but she could not intervene. It would have been perceived as siding with the enemy.

Now she wondered if those workers were the ones seeking retribution. Whatever it was, it was enough for her neighbor to leave her daughter and aging mother and hide in their barn.

"Please don't let it slip out, even to Marianka that you've seen me here," Klara begged.

"We won't. If there is anything we can do to help we will," Katina answered. "I'll be coming back with more food tomorrow evening after Pan Slovak has gone home."

Klara agreed. To leave her neighbor in this state was not easy on her and it weighed heavy on her mind. A sudden ice cold gust of wind took the barn door out of her hand as she opened it and stepped outside. She pulled the shawl tighter around her head and shoulders. "What a night to be out," she said in a half loud voice, alarmed by the thought of Klara's plight.

"Oh dear God... Please protect them... Protect us all," she prayed suddenly frightened.

Is this what will happen to all of them? She threw a glance over the frostbitten land. At times she had thought it inviting and beautiful, but now it lay foreboding in front of her. The snow crunched under her feet. Suddenly over come with fear, she trembled and looked back to where she had come from. Did she see the outline of men lurking in the shadows? Her steps hastened. She dared not look back again.

Where were all their dreams? She recalled the day when she and Johann stood and gazed over this land. How happy they felt. It all had changed so quickly. She almost missed the Schwarzes across the street. Now their place looked so forsaken. Yes, it was bad, him watching and reporting their every move, and the unjust treatment of Pan Slovak, as well as all the Polish people, from the German Authorities here in Quadenstadt.

But now with them all gone, and with what was going on, "Uh," she shuddered. It felt so dreadfully scary, almost sinister. "Oh God help us...help us all."

A few more steps and she reached the front door. Quickly, she opened and closed it, making sure the lock was secure. Father Wendel gave her a quick but surprised look, then continued to listen in on the latest broadcast.

"We did what we could and that's about all we can do." A shiver went through her, her eyes moist, she walked closer to the stove. "It's almost too eerie out there," she indicated with her head toward the barn. He nodded in agreement, as he felt the same way.

"I'll go and check all the windows. Oh, and can you check the door to the carriage house one more time? I want everything locked up tight tonight."

He nodded as he got up and made his way around the stove toward the side entrance.

When they both settled in for the night, they knew that sleep would not come voluntarily. Klara's plight lay heavy on both their minds.

In the morning when Father Wendel went to the barn, he found Klara Koenig gone. There was no sign of her the following day or the day after. Katina shuddered at the thought as to what could have happened to her. All their friends in the neighborhood did not want to speculate, but none ruled out that she was done in by the very same people she had mistreated. Her mother and her daughter were now left to fend for themselves. She had promised Klara she would look in on them. But how in the world could she tell her mother and her daughter about her last hours? She herself knew how painful and devastating it was to receive such news. Yet it had to be done.

She took courage and walked over to Klara's house. The elderly lady opened the door with her granddaughter by her side, her face pale, showing little emotion.

"Klara's gone isn't she...?" she stated so matter of factually. A deep groan suddenly shook her body, followed by a painful pent-up cry. "Klara... Oh God! My poor daughter... my poor girl," her face buried in her hands she wept uncontrollably.

Katina reached over to comfort her. Klara's daughter Anna stood bewildered, looking from one to the other. She too started to cry, reaching out to her grandmother.

Clinging to her granddaughter the older woman started to lament even more.

"What am I going to do now? All of my family is gone. I'm so scared Katina.... What will they do next...? I am so afraid for her... What if I can't look after her anymore...? What will happen to her...? Oh God! We shouldn't have come here..." she wept uncontrollably.

"I promised Klara that I'll be there for both of you and I'm sure Elisabeth Ruck and her two daughters will be more than willing to help..." She trembled at the heart breaking sight in front of her. Compassionately she reached out again and held the older woman and the young child, as tears streamed down her face.

She knew it would take some time to get over this shock. But then she did not have to tell this to a woman who had lost her husband, her two sons, a son-in-law and now her daughter. This war has brought many sorrows to so many people. A deep anguish rose inside of her. When will it all end... oh God... When...?

--

Now even more than before she looked to the Slovaks for refuge and protection. She gave them permission, knowing that she soon would lose control over all her belongings, to take whatever they needed from the homestead.

In the dark of night, quietly not to draw suspicion, the Slovaks did as told. They butchered pigs and canned the meat. There was no time to remove the bristles from the skin; that could be dealt with later. They took the horse and other livestock, wagon and coach, anything they possibly could use. They also took her sewing machine and stacks of fine dress material Johann had sent home from his last stopover at Kutno. The material had been a constant reminder of not being there on that day. And she was actually glad to give it away.

She gave to them most of the edible goods from the attic. Only the barest essentials she kept, including a couple of large milk cans filled with fried pork; they had prepared earlier in the fall. She had a good feeling giving to the Slovaks. With that she hoped, to the best of their ability, they would not abandon her and her family, just as she and Johann had done in their time of need.

Soon after, the thunder of war was drawing closer. In the distance they could hear heavy bombing to the east in the direction of Warsaw. Then saw the whole night sky light up from the incendiary bombs (referred to as Christmas trees), falling over Lodz. Father Wendel related to her in a somber tone, "The enemy is near... it won't be long..."

She nodded in defeat, her heart full of angst, for she dreaded the unexpected. "What will happen to all of us Father?" She looked at him but he gave no answer.

The next morning, Father Wendel went to the barn as he had always done, although these days there were no chores, no tobacco leaves that needed looking after, but he came anyway just to get out of the house. He had always enjoyed spending time alone up in the barn and still did, even though there was nothing left for him to do. Solemnly he hobbled along. The whole incident with Klara Koenig had left him weary and had made him hesitant at first to go back to the barn. But then he chose to remember the good things instead and that made these visits bearable.

Suddenly he halted his walk. He thought he heard something stir in the horse barn. Again uneasy he stood listening. "What in heaven's name is going on?" he mumbled under his breath. Cautiously he approached the door then opened it slowly. Suddenly the cocking of guns reached his ears. With hands up in the air he stood in the doorway expecting the worst. To his surprise he heard some of the young men talk German to each other.

"What should we do with him? If we shoot, we'll draw suspicion to this place. And if we don't, he'll run and tell others that we are hiding in here."

Father Wendel quickly intervened on his behalf. "Don't shoot, I'm a German."

When they heard him answer back in their mother tongue, a whole group of young German soldiers came out of hiding, glad to have met up with one of their own countrymen. Relieved they settled down again, resuming what they were doing before he interrupted them.

Pity suddenly filled Father Wendel's heart. He could only guess why they were here. And to hide out in this barn was simply too dangerous. "Why don't you just run out of here in the dark of night and make your way to the Fatherland?"

"Old man!" one of them replied. "It's too late. Don't you know we are encircled? It won't be long and they'll come and shoot us, but we are ready. See this...?" The soldier held up his rifle and a bottle of Vodka.

Father Wendel had noticed them drinking. He guessed their age to be about seventeen to nineteen years of age.

"This...!" the young soldier took a long sip from the bottle. "This is to numb our minds... And in here... the last bullet in each of our rifles is destined for each one of us..."

He started to cry.

"So you see, there is no way out... We drink, so the memories of our mothers... our fathers...our sisters and brothers won't be so painful... and... the task before us... easier to deal with.

"Oh God! We're too young to die... We don't want to die..." Overcome with sorrow, all were now sobbing, by the hopelessness and terror before them.

Father Wendel hung his head. He had no words of comfort for these poor desolate young men. He stood for a moment trying to think of what to say, but then... saddened and deeply affected he left them to their cruel and heart wrenching fate. There was nothing he could do for them, only to bring them something to eat. Suddenly he realized this fate could be theirs as well. His steps hastened as he hurried back as fast as he could, and when he neared the house he could hear the enemy tanks approaching.

"Quickly...! Everyone on the floor and don't make a sound."

He and Katina just managed to gather the children, and not a moment too soon. When a loud commotion and screaming was heard, followed by a scattering of gun fire. Shocked and scared they listened for more action... their hearts pounding... Fear-stricken they remained on the floor. Katina did not dare ask questions. The children started to cry, sensing something was wrong.

Suddenly the side door opened. They all stared in horror, holding their breath... Only to realize with relief that it was Pan Slovak with Mandek close behind him. Signaling to be quiet they joined them quickly on the floor, their ears perked, they listened fearfully. Suddenly the front door flew open, guns drawn, the home was overtaken by Russian troops.

By questioning if there were any Germans living here, Pan Slovak quickly answered back in Polish. "No sir, only my wife and children and my aged father," he motioned with a gesture of his hand toward them. Accepting that as the truth, the Russian officer gave orders to his troops to move in. He then ordered Pan Slovak and Katina to provide food and drink for them. She was grateful, but awestruck at Pan Slovak's quick thinking to pose as her husband. She gave him a thankful look as he and Mandek went about to gather the food. Suddenly Marianka also appeared and was at her side to help her in preparing the meal, while Father Wendel watched over the children. Heniek too, had come to assist and help watch the two little ones.

Now all their planning for provisions came in handy. For with a full stomach the soldiers were more even tempered. Every inch of space in the house was now occupied. Daily new troops permeated the house as they were passing through. After the first Russian troops left, others followed. At one time a whole group of young Russian boys, their age being no more than twelve years, came alongside an older Russian woman and a couple of seasoned soldiers, who seemed to be looking after them.

Katina felt pity for the young boys, to be tossed into this grueling, gruesome and gruff task before them. What would become of them once the army was through with them? Their minds trained to be ruthless and uncaring. Could they ever know and feel how to love and to be kind and caring? Or will their hearts be forever hardened? War has a way of producing this state of mind. Distraught she turned her thoughts to the immediate task before her. She tried not to think of these things, knowing that it was not in her power to change them.

Uneasily she went about her task in helping to feed the forever hungry troops, ignoring the stares of soldiers. It was as if they could sense that she and her family were not who they portrayed themselves to be. She felt so deeply indebted to Pan Slovak and his family, for without them... She shuttered to think what fate would have befallen them.

Quietly she worked alongside Marianka, focusing only on the task before her, hoping that their little scheme would not be discovered. Knowing very well that by doing so, Pan Slovak and his family had risked their very own lives to save her and her family. And for that she was truly thankful. Faithful they had remained to stay with her and her family, not leaving them out of their sights.

Across the street Elisabeth Ruck and her two grownup daughters had also been spared by their Polish family, who had done what they had experienced in their time of need. Next to them, to the right of the Ruck's property, the same was true for Jobina Greis and her daughter Maria. Yet unknown to the rest of her friends, Claudia Ebert and her family had not faired that well. Like so many other young German women she and her family had succumb and were exposed to horrendous acts of cruelty from ruthless uncaring Russian soldiers. And Klara's mother; the previous Polish owners of their homestead had taken over, letting her stay on to work for them, till such time when they could decide what to do with her and her granddaughter.

--

The dangerous circumstances of war and the cold winter weather had kept Father Wendel, as well as Katina and the children, housebound. With so many soldiers around they were scared of losing the small space that was still left for them; to sit or rest their tired bodies on. Often she fought not to cry, as she watched the home that Johann had so lovingly built, deteriorate in front of her eyes. Dismayed she looked on as the Russian soldiers; their pockets full of sunflower seeds, cracked and spit the shells all over the once beautiful wooden floor. A floor now mixed with all kinds of garbage and clumps of icy snow that was dragged in from under their boots.

One thing she had to admit, with their quilted coveralls, hats with flop downs to protect their forehead, ears and neck, their warm gloves and winter boots, they were much better equipped and prepared for the cold winter weather than their own soldiers. With sadness she remembered the light

I WILL REMEMBER ALWAYS

winter wear Johann had been fitted with. It was certainly no comparison to the Russian soldiers' outfits.

The thought of Johann's last letter came to mind, a sudden twinge stirred in her heart, bringing on again the overbearing grief. The whole ordeal of what had happened and what was happening, was unthinkable for her to comprehend and to deal with. What was in store for them next? She dared not to think anymore. It was out of her hands. She had to take whatever was coming and try to make the best of this hopeless situation; knowing all too well that she and her family were not alone in this dangerous and gloomy predicament.

After a day the young Russian infantry too had moved on and another troop followed. This time Polish soldiers and civilian men, whose job it was to dig and clear trenches. Along with them, came the previous owner of the property. In an instant the owner's wife confiscated all household goods, furnishings and other items that were left. Katina was glad to have had the foresight to have moved most of her belongings to the Slovak's house; as now she would have not been able to do so.

The only thing that was still in her possession and never left her sight was her large black handbag. In it she kept stored away some of her children's clothing and hidden underneath them, some of her important documents, pictures, her wedding ring, some jewelry and in particular, an old songbook. The songbook was a gift from her pastor in Mangalia, Reverend Freiman. It had his signature and the date of her baptismal inscribed on the front page.

She had not thought to store these things at the Slovak's, thinking they would be safe with her. But suddenly she had her doubts. Maybe she had thought wrong. She was especially aware of this when she noticed the prying eyes of the owner's wife looking. More than once she had eyed the handbag and the leather boots she was wearing. They were gifts Johann had brought home on one of his furloughs.

So far, and thanks to the Slovak's protection, she had felt safe, but for how long? As she was made aware, they would not always be able to be there for her and her family. This gave her great concern, especially now with the former owner's hostile takeover. She shuddered to think what would happen to them.

To quiet her hopeless and tortured spirit, she released all her fear and concerns to God, who is above all. In the end, He is and was the only source that could protect and deliver them out of this hellish predicament.

52

All day the sky had been overcast and the temperature outside was bitter cold. Their hard work of cutting and gathering wood and dried cow paddies had paid off, as now they had sufficient supply to keep everyone in the house warm all winter long. Katina thought, as she retreated to their small corner of refuge where her children had remained all morning, with Father Wendel watching over them. She was very thankful that the two little ones and Julia were content to just stay put in that small space. All along they had quietly watched the constant coming and going of strangers.

Suddenly, she noticed Elisa staring out of the window that overlooked the main street in front of the house, Katina's eyes followed those of her little one. She noticed them fixed on the frozen corpses of young German soldiers lying on the roadside; stripped of their boots and other valuables by the passing Russian Infantry. For days the endless stream of men and machinery had been pushing past en route to the west. Quietly, with empathy, she pulled Elisa away from the window and held her. She was concerned over the lasting impression this devastating picture would have on her little child. She herself had become numb to such tragedies. All she felt was an overwhelming hopelessness, emptiness and inconsolable sorrow, but no tears.

Ever since the takeover, the house had been in a constant turmoil from overcrowdedness with little room to sit or lay one's head. And she had found it hard to relax, never mind sleep at night. The same went for Father Wendel who had occupied a small space on the floor in the front bedroom beside Julia's twin bed, where she and the children had been fortunate to sleep on. More and more she realized how smart it was to have stashed most of her belongings at the Slovak's home. Even Father Wendel had planned ahead and wore two suits, one on top the other. One, it would keep him warm and two, it would last him through whatever lay ahead. So he had told her.

The next day though, and without warning, they were surprised to be suddenly taken out of the house. Along with friends, they found themselves in a small attic room not far from their homesteads. They were now prisoners with no rights. A Polish man, whom they had all known and seen collecting eggs from the farmers during the German occupancy, had now proclaimed himself as police chief, and this did not look favorable for the captured; most of them, young women with children and their elderly parents.

Within a day, like so many of the captured, Katina was brought before Russian officials for questioning. To her surprise Kazio Slovak, a relative of the Slovaks, who also had benefited from her and Johann's kindness; came to her aid. He was speaking out on her behalf, pleading for her and her loved ones' lives, saying..."What do you want with her? She has done nothing wrong. She was good to us."

The Russian official listened, indifferent to the man's pleading, waving for her to step forward. Seeing that she was trembling he spoke to her kindly, but with a military undertone.

"Don't be afraid, no harm will come to you. We only want to know where you and your husband were born."

Relieved, she gave a grateful nod to Kazio Slovak. Then empowered with renewed confidence and courage she answered the Russian official's question.

"I was born in Cogealac, Romania, and my husband was

born in Yevpatoriya on the Island Crimea by the Black Sea."

The official wrote down the information, then looked up and with a stern formality told her that she had to go back to where she came from. "But Sir," she quickly and suddenly came back. "I can't go back, all my extended family is living in Germany and I would like to be sent there!"

The Russian official squirmed in his seat, uneasy about this request. With a wave of his hand he told her, "That's all we want to know for now." With that she was escorted out of the courtroom. She was about to step outside when her eyes fell upon a man in the adjacent room near the entrance hall. He sat huddled against the wall to steady himself, his face beaten almost unrecognizable; near him Russian soldiers stood guard. Their eyes met. His look conveyed the horror of his ordeal. Shocked and trembling she walked on. It was pastor Freiman who had baptized her in Mangalia. She had recognized him and he her. By the looks of his swollen face she could only guess what horrible torture he had endured; but why him, what could he have done or known to be caught in this predicament? She would have liked to have known more, but that was not to be. It pained her to see him in this state and she wondered where his wife and family were. She had noticed him look at her, shocked but surprised to see her here, almost sad she had not escaped to Germany. Was he worried for her, to find her trapped here in this place?

The net that caught them did not discriminate between good and bad.

For a second, her mind full of questions, she had paused in her step, but did not linger. All at once she felt the cold barrel of a rifle poke against her back. "Move!" The gruff and uncaring reply came from the guard behind her. With haste in her step, she was taken away back to the makeshift prison.

Soon one by one, they all had been called and came back from the interrogation place, Father Wendel included, as he too had insisted to be sent to Germany. She was thankful that she and all the others in their group had not been detained and had come out unharmed, for now.

She had her doubts though about Pastor Freiman. She dared not to think what awaited him. She felt cold shivers going down her back. It was too much for her to comprehend; purposely she pushed the oppressive thoughts out of her mind. Her and her family's own safety in all of this was overbearing enough to deal with, to add to this would certainly wear down her mind and spirit. But try as she might she could not shut out the grave dilemma in which Pastor Freiman found himself in.

Sitting in the makeshift prison she now wondered about what Johann had told her the last time he was home on furlough. It was about Heinrich Schwarz and Thomas Backer and the land deal they were bidding for in Mangalia.

Both had been involved in shady land claims in Mangalia, and both had a hand in the disappearance of Herman Grundman, his family and the mysterious mishap of his servant. Some of the men in Johann's artillery division had known about this secret and confessed to him, of Schwarz's and Backer's ill dealings in Romania and here in Poland. She wondered of the whereabouts of Thomas Backer as she herself had not seen him since that day in Mangalia.

She thought again of Heinrich Schwarz and his family as she recalled Pan Slovak's story of those who had tried to flee and were apprehended. Were Heinrich Schwarz and his family among those captured? She had never dared to ask Pan Slovak if he knew. It would have done her no good anyway to know.

She had to admit she was very angry with Heinrich, especially for watching and reporting their every move to the authorities, showing no mercy for her and the children; hindering them in their escape.

'He, who had dealt so harshly with them, received his reward.'

Suddenly she caught herself by this thought, seeing herself cold and uncaring. It was not right to think this way and what of Pastor Freiman? What did he do to deserve this? Ashamed of herself, she put her misgivings aside. It was useless anyway to dwell on things that cannot be changed. She had to put it all behind her and focus on the things that were important now. Trying to stay alive and survive. "God help us all," she prayed, "Guilty or not."

53

The place she and all the prisoners found themselves locked up in was on the third floor of an existing old dilapidated three story building. It was not far from their original homesteads. The first floor was the smallest of the three, as each floor increased in size. And every time a heavy armored army tanks and trucks thundered past, it felt to her as if the lower part of the building was on the verge of collapse by the rumblings and swaying of the two upper floors.

Here she sat with her family and the rest of them in a cramped small attic; no room to stretch out or lay down. And if one had to use the washroom, they thought twice. It consisted of one large old pail standing outside in the freezing cold behind the house; protected only by a three-sided rusted piece of scrap metal. And if that did not deter them, a Polish guard with a rifle aimed at them surely would.

As it was, she had claimed one corner of the room with her children, with Father Wendel close beside her. Next to Klara's mother and daughter were other acquaintances with their elderly parents and children she had gotten to know while here in Quadenstad. There was also Claudia Ebert with her five children, who with her husband and father-in-law had occupied and managed the flour mill. Then Elisabeth Ruck with her father and two grownup daughters, Magda and Rosa. There was also Elisabeth's neighbor Jobina Greis and daughter Maria and her father-in-law.

At night when sleep did not come, she wondered about Rebekka and Edwina with her little one. Were they also captured and imprisoned, and what about her parents and other siblings, would she ever see them again? Tears of hopelessness welled up in her eyes. Her prayers were short, but often. She had no choice but to leave them and themselves in the Almighty's care.

With no blankets to keep them warm they all huddled together on the hard floor, scared for the unknown, unsure of what terror the next hour or day would bring. Knowing what had happened to the young German soldiers and to some of their neighbors, she feared the worst.

--

On the morning of the next day, they heard loud noises coming from the stairwell. They heard the rattling of keys against the lock and with a forceful bang the door flew open. Struck with terror, they stared into the hateful eyes of a mob of Polish men. If looks could kill, they would have all been finished off right then and there.

With an angry motion, their captors grabbed, pushed and separated all the younger women from the rest of the captives. They lined them up to be led down the stairs at gun point. Many were crying and the children were wailing for their mothers. The women struggled not to be separated from their children and parents. Only to find themselves knocked down with a sharp thrust from the butt of a rifle.

'This is it," Katina thought. 'We're going to be killed. One by one, they will kill us all.' "My children...! I don't want to leave my children," she cried out and reached for them, as other women followed to do the same.

Angered by this outbreak the Polish men cursed and shoved the gun barrels even harder into their backs. She fell and caught herself just in time, before tumbling all the way to the bottom of the stairs. Huddling together, the elderly and the children watched in horror as their daughters and mothers were led away. Thinking that this was the last they would see of them.

When they reached their destination, she, as the rest of the women, all expected to be killed. Instead they were forced to work and clean up the mess that had been left behind by the retreating German military.

Work was unbelievably hard and tedious, but at least they were still alive, but for how long? This constant thought kept gnawing on all of them.

An hour after the young women had been led away there was suddenly another commotion outside the stairwell. "What in heaven's name do they want now?" Father Wendel exclaimed angrily, but concerned. Just then the same self-declared Polish police chief and his self-appointed deputies unlocked the door, impatiently ordering all the old men to come with them.

Father Wendel was struggling to get up from the floor. The arthritis in his body had really been acting up, the cold, plus the hard floor, had contributed to the stiffness and pain. Julia felt pity and suddenly came to his aid. He looked at her with surprise. Here was one child he had disliked so much, yet now she was the one who showed kindness to him. Without further comment, he turned and hobbled behind the others down the stairs, with guns drawn at their backs.

Silently the old men walked along familiar streets. Once in a while when one of them could not keep up, a sharp poke of a gun barrel against the back, accompanied by some choice swearwords, hurried them on unwillingly. Many curious onlookers followed the procession, increasing as they neared the town's cemetery. Picks and shovels stood ready and were handed out to each of the prisoners, ordering them to start breaking the ground with the provided tools, to dig out a large hole.

Father Wendel and the other old men labored under this hard task, wondering why this had to be done at this time of the year, for the frozen ground was almost impossible to break. He tried to straighten out, to relieve the pain in his back, but immediately felt the barrel of a gun shoved against it. "Hurry up and don't waste our time old man," the self-proclaimed police chief yelled impatiently.

All at once a horrifying thought crossed Father Wendel's mind, now it all became clear why they had to do this backbreaking task. He had an uneasy feeling when he and the other men were led away. But never had he thought it possible that he might end up dying in such a cruel and horrifying fashion. Suddenly, he started to sweat profusely, his body trembled, partly from weakness, but mostly from the terror of what was awaiting him and the others. He managed to glance over to his fellow prisoners and noticed the fear expressed in their faces. They too had understood what was about to happen.

Suddenly it gave him concern for Katina and the children. What was in store for them? Agonizing thoughts of helplessness flooded his mind. There was absolutely nothing he could do to help them or himself.

Powerless against such a lynch mob, he and the others had no choice but to accept. All at once, one of his friends started to mumble the Lord's Prayer. He was sure now that they all felt and thought what he had perceived. Suddenly he was compelled to join in, where otherwise he would have rejected to do this.

"Shut up!" the police chief yelled and drew his gun, adding a few choice words. "Drop your shovels! You and you," he pointed to his deputies, "help them out of the hole." Startled, the prisoners looked with horror-filled eyes at their adversaries. "I want everything taken off, except the underwear... Jackets, shirts, pants, socks, shoes and boots," he yelled from the top of his lungs.

Once out of the hole, they were immediately stripped of all their clothing, in particular their wedding bands and gold watches.

With his hands tied behind his back, Father Wendel felt the icy cold metal of the gun barrel touch the back of his head. His knees began to buckle. An overwhelming fear of the unknown gripped his whole being. He could hear the moans of others beside him. Suddenly, he panicked at the thought that the bullet to his head might not finish him off completely, leaving him to die a slow and suffocating death as the frozen soil was heaved back over them.

All at once multiple shots thundered across the cemetery. Just as their unconscious bodies were about to collapse, they were quickly shoved into the hole, each one falling on top of the other.

Not all of the Polish town's people who witnessed the execution looked favorably on this type of retribution. Kazio Slovak happened to be there and saw the whole gruesome act. He had known most of these older men to be kind and giving when his family and friends needed help, but who could go against the likes of this self-proclaimed police chief and his deputies. If he would have said anything or tried to stop them, they would have charged him with siding with the enemy. The fate that had befallen these prisoners would have been his too. He had remained long enough after the shooting to see the police chief and his deputies tally out the loot among each other. With a sick feeling in his stomach, he turned to walk away.

--

Later in the evening, when under heavy guard the young women were brought back, they questioned as to where the old men were, but no one knew, even the guards were tight lipped.

Even though no one in the attic room said the unthinkable, they all knew they would never see their husbands, fathers or father-in-laws again. Bitter tears for their loved ones and for themselves were shed that night. They realized that it was only a matter of time when they too will be led away to face the horror of dying a torturous death.

'The children... Oh God the children. What if I'm killed, what will happen to them?' Katina cried out in her heart,

I WILL REMEMBER ALWAYS

with inconceivable grief.

She and the others would find out later that there were arguments between the Poles and the Russians over the German prisoners. The Poles eventually had won out and now were granted eight days in which they could revenge themselves. There was a deep resentment all over Poland going back to 1939 when the German Army first invaded and had executed many Polish men for no valid reason. After that the Polish and Jewish inhabitants suffered horribly under the German Authorities until the Red Army came.

Many Poles now seized the opportunity to revenge the evil done to them; thus unfolding on the unsuspecting German prisoner's unspeakable crimes and unutterable grief of torture and horror. It did not matter if one was innocent or not, just being of German descent was enough to be beaten, tortured, shot, or hung.

54

For days now, every morning, she along with the other women, were led away at gunpoint. Often mistreated and forced to work under indescribable stress and grueling, repulsive, harsh conditions at various workplaces. This was the eighth day and on this morning they had been taken to a place which in earlier years used to be a dairy factory, now the Poles had changed it to serve as a slaughterhouse.

So far in the past seven days, she and the others had been forced to do all sorts of cleanup jobs, yet by far, today was the worst they had encountered. With their bare hands they were ordered to pick up, scrape, scour and clean the ankle deep bloody mess. The stench of rotting flesh soaked into their skin and clothes. It was enough to turn their stomachs, which after so many days of starvation already felt weak and easily upset. She purposely did not look too close as to what she was touching. Quickly she discarded the pieces of decomposing flesh into the provided large trash bin; squeamish that she might discover more than just animal parts.

When the time finally came to go home, she and the others found the door to the outside suddenly locked. It was barred by a group of young men who were standing in front of the building wielding long knives and other sharp objects in their hands.

In an instant she and the rest of the women knew

what was before them. Inconsolable and distraught they all started to sob and wail. It was unthinkable to even comprehend or to grasp what hideous and torturous ordeal lay before them. Katina's anguish became even greater when she thought of her children. What will become of them? With a heavy downcast heart she cried out for deliverance.

Just then she noticed a group of Russian officials walking on the other side of the street. The young Poles had their backs to the road and did not notice them approaching. Immediately she made the others aware of this.

"Now or never, let's take a chance and knock on the windows and call out for help. Maybe, they will hear us and rescue us? It is worth the try. What have we to lose?"

Quickly they started to rap and pound against the windows and the door, raising their voices louder and louder. 'Now or never,' was in everyone's mind.

To their surprise, one of the Russians, who appeared to be of higher rank, stopped and called out to the young thugs, "Who do you have in there?"

Angered of being found out, they were reluctant to cooperate. But upon more outcries from the inside and a stern command from the Russian officer, they finally gave way and opened the door.

Immediately the women surrounded the officer, sobbing as they tried to explain their plight to him in all adopted languages. To their amazement the officer, a white Russian from Belarus, answered back in perfect High German with a Berlin accent.

"I understand German! You can talk to me in your mother's tongue." He did not have to say more. Instantly he was swamped by all of them. They told him of their fears of being killed and about being held captive with their children and mothers in an unheated attic. With no food and water, or blankets to keep them warm. They also told the officer about their coats, which the young Polish men had taken from them this morning.

He listened quietly to all of them, then walked outside and with a rigid command he reprimanded the young thugs. Then ordered a search for the coats, when found, he made them return each and every one to the women. With anger in his voice he turned to the young men again.

"If any harm comes to any one of these women and their children you will have to answer to me. Is that understood?"

Still fuming, they unwillingly agreed. "And furthermore..." The commander raised his voice even more. "I want each and every one of them returned to their former homes, and that's an order!"

Overwhelmed, she and the women poured out their gratitude toward this kind stranger, thanking him over and over. He gave his salute, nodding his head slightly in a gentlemanlike manner. He kicked his boot heels together then turned to continue his interrupted walk. The rest of the officers saluted politely and quickly followed. Unwillingly and still fuming, the young thugs gnashed their teeth in anger, but had no choice but to obey the order, at least for now.

Early the next morning a pale winter sun tried her best to unthaw the small window toward the front of the house. Katina and the others in the attic room had waited patiently for the Commanders order to materialize. Yet no one came to do so.

She stood up to take a look outside, scratching the ice from the window in order to see better when she noticed Heniek, Slovak's youngest son. He waved and smiled at her. She gestured to him that they were hungry and cold. Puzzled, he smiled and nodded understandingly, then walked away. Not long after, to her surprise, there was commotion in the stairwell. They could hear the same familiar Russian Commander's voice, ordering the owner to unlock the attic door.

As the door opened his eyes were filled with pity and disgust at the impoverished and deplorable conditions. His

I WILL REMEMBER ALWAYS

patience had been tested too many times, with anger in his action he tore the lock off the door and threw it down the stairs. "At once, I want to see that food and water be given to these women and children, and that each and every one will be returned to their original homes. And I mean, at once!!! If this order is not obeyed, I'll see to it personally that you'll be severely punished." He turned to the women and saluted politely, then turned to walk down the stairs, followed by his two assisting officers.

The women were surprised and astonished over the Commanders swift reaction; they could not believe what just had happened.

"Now there's a true gentleman, a cavalier," Elisabeth mumbled under her breath to the others.

"Aha, a son a mother can be proud of," Jobina added quietly, with a quiver in her voice.

Shaken with disbelief, Katina glanced up, only to look into the hate filled eyes of their captor. Angered by what he was ordered to do, he unwillingly stepped aside and let them go.

After the Russian Commander and his entourage had left many of the Polish people from the neighborhood had gathered to see the outcome of the confrontation. Heniek and Marianka were among the gathered, happy that their intervention had brought such a swift and just reaction.

When they escorted Katina and the children back to their original homestead, Heniek told her excitingly. "When you noticed me on the street this morning, I'd just come and delivered food for you and the children, just as I'd done over the past seven days without fail."

She was astonished and shook her head. "Never did we see or receive even a morsel of it."

"I realized something was wrong, when you signaled to me that you were hungry. When I told my family, they were all appalled at the audacity of this man. We knew him to be capable of many things, but this topped it all. Upon further investigation, we had proof enough to report him to the

347

Russian officer. He was outraged at the injustice, which then brought about this quick reaction."

"Thank you for standing by me and the children. Again I don't know where we would be without you and your family." She gave them both a grateful hug. "Tell your mother and father and all of your family a heartfelt thanks. But tell them also, as I tell you now, be careful, and don't put yourselves at risk," she warned and added with deep affection. "You are like family to me and the children and I wouldn't want to see you punished or worse yet, killed for our sake."

"We've already gone too far, and there are many who are after us and wish us ill. But we are also a large family with many friends and acquaintances, who would not hesitate to stand by us and fight, if need be," Heniek proudly proclaimed and Marianka nodded in approval.

Upon further talk, Heniek disclosed to her in quiet the sad news about Father Wendel and the other old men. He told her of what one of his relatives had witnessed. "Apparently all the men had been led to the town's cemetery where they were ordered to dig a mass grave," Heniek swallowed hard to steady his voice. "They were stripped of all their clothing and valuables, then bound and shot, then pushed into the open pit."

"We all had a feeling, when they didn't return that evening, that something had gone wrong. But never did we expect this," her voice quavered.

Shocked and saddened by this, she just buried her head in her hands and wept.

Now she feared even more what was in store for them once the Russian officer moved on and was not here to protect them. She knew that as long as they were here on Polish soil, their ordeal was far from over. And she was sure the Slovaks knew this too, that's why they stood by her, trying repeatedly to protect her and the children.

Once at their former home, Marianka had again chosen to

remain by her side, as she did not trust the new occupants. The moment they had entered the house, her hunch proved true; as all the other captives also found out. There was no home to come home to anymore. A lot of the belongings and their hard worked equities on the property had been looted, damaged or confiscated.

In all fairness, she could understand. After all, they had lost the war, they were strangers with no claim, no rights to any of these properties. The Russian officer had meant well and it sounded good in theory, but it was almost unfeasible to presume that most of the Polish inhabitants of this town, or anywhere else in Poland would back off and let their previous adversaries take back what once had belonged to them in the first place. Or did it? She suddenly remembered their plight back in Romania. As it was there, so it could be here. Had there been others that once had been the true owner of some of these properties? War had an ugly way of messing up people's lives.

Whatever the case, this was not hers anymore. This she understood and took it with grace. Her only wish, as well as the others caught in this dilemma, was to be free, to be able to go to Germany or anywhere their hearts desired. Yet again, she knew this was unreachable, and as far as she could see, an impossible request to wish for. For now she and all the rest of the German women and their families had to accept their fate; to continually live in fear and danger of being preyed upon or killed. Surviving this ordeal was on everyone's mind.

She was grateful that Marianka had chosen to stay with her to watch over the children as she and the other young women still ceaselessly were summoned to do hard labor from dawn to dusk. The children were left vulnerable to all kinds of danger. Aware of this, it made her realize again that by staying at her side and keeping watch over her children, Marianka, as well as her family were risking their very own lives.

For some of the Polish, the time of revenge allowed to

them by the Russians, in their minds and to their liking, had been too short. Their hate and vengeful hostility toward anyone that was of German descent had been spurned on by the atrocities done to them under the former Nazi rulers.

True revenge would pay back six years of equal amount of pain and an equal amount of time. The problem of revenge is that it did not provide healing to their community. It only traded one form of destruction with another.

Quadenstadt had good farmland, but with the consumption and looting breaking the fabric of their already fragile society, there grew shortages in food and supplies. Soon even the Polish inhabitants themselves were not safe from looters.

'It seemed like a vicious cycle with no end,' she thought. 'Evil is paid back with evil. Innocent people on both sides are usually the ones to be put out, victimized, tortured and killed. Where will all this end...?' She tried to calm her tormented mind. Again, she was very fortunate and felt indebted to the whole Slovak clan and their friends in this town. For without them, she and her children and many of her friends would most certainly not be alive anymore.

In the short time of their stay in her previous home, she felt degraded and humiliated by the audacity of the self-declared owners. With much defiance they refused to hand over anything that had once belonged to her. Willfully they did not budge or share. Without a care they slept in her bed, using her and the children's featherbeddings and feather pillows, while she, the children and Marianka slept in a bed next to them, with very little to cover with. And to top it off, the owner's wife had taken her silk nightgowns, which Johann had bought for her and paraded them spitefully in front of her.

When they had been apprehended and taken prisoner, she, in all the hurry and turmoil, had left behind her large black handbag. Now it was nowhere to be found. The only thing she recognized to be hers was the old songbook, which now the owner's children used and played with; scribbling in it and tearing the pages.

Dejected, she watched, nothing beckoned her to stay. Sadly she remembered the good times they had here as a family, but now so many things have changed. The house Johann had labored to perfect, as well as the furnishings and all the household goods, all had suffered from the constant abuse and neglect. She released a depressed sigh. Truly this was not her home anymore. Saddened over this fact, she felt even more disheartened and displaced. Only memories remained... painful memories.

For two long and dreadful days, Marianka and herself had tolerated and taken the abuse. Realizing there was no change in sight, the Slovaks decided to rescue Katina and the children and take them to their already small and cramped home. Here at least, so they thought, they would be safer and more protected.

Upon leaving the homestead, Marianka did her best to gather a few of Katina's personal belongings. But when confronted, the owner put up a fuss and refused to give her anything. Finally after Marianka threatened to go to the Russian officer with this, she gave in and handed the large handbag over. Inside were a few of the children's clothing, some pictures and the torn songbook. Most of the children's clothes, documents, as well as Katina's wedding ring, and jewelry had disappeared, and there was nothing Marianka could do to retrieve them.

Unfortunately, by taking them in, the Slovaks had left themselves vulnerable to constant attacks. Vengeful neighbors, who knew of them harboring Katina and her children; snitched on them to every passing vigilante, putting them all in great danger.

It happened one evening when Katina was brought back again from work duty. Cold and tired she stood near the oven to warm herself, when all at once the front door flew open. Three angry Polish men stood in the doorway demanding to hand over the German woman and her children. Pan Slovak and his two eldest sons intervened in trying to calm the strangers, offering them food and a bottle of vodka.

After a couple of drinks, two were persuaded not to pursue this issue further, but the third one, of Jewish descent, could not. His eyes, filled with hate and fury, were fixed on Katina. His jaw clenched, he jumped up from his seat by the table and raced over to where she stood; his raised bayonet poking her chest. She could feel the sharp point pressing against her breastbone. Weak and tired, she had no strength to react. 'Any minute now and the sharp dagger will pierce through,' she thought. Julia cried out, realizing that her mother was about to be killed, "No! No! No! No! You can't! You can't!"

Ignoring Julia's outcry, gnashing his teeth the man retorted... "They killed my family... my mother... my father... my sister, and my brother... I should kill you too."

Katina felt the point of the bayonet increase in pressure against her chest with every word spoken. A burning pain indicated to her the sharp bayonet had punctured her skin. Trying to shield the children Marianka and Pani Slovak held them back. Suddenly realizing the seriousness of this situation the other two men including Pan Slovak and his two eldest sons kept persuading the man in all earnestness, calling out to him. "Why don't you come and have a drink with us and leave her be."

"She has done no one wrong... she was kind to us... she is a good person," Wiktor added.

Enraged the man lashed out, "She is a German... Isn't she...? She doesn't deserve to live," continually he lashed out in rage.

Over and over the others tried to coax him away from her. Then finally, after some anxious moments, and to everyone's relief, the man gave in and lowered his gun. Still fuming, he came back to the table and sat down for drink, all the while not letting Katina out of his sight, cursing and swearing; expressing the wish to do away with her.

I WILL REMEMBER ALWAYS

The minute he had lifted the gun off her chest, Katina's knees buckled. In an instant Heniek was at her side catching her as she went down. To everyone's relief, as the evening wore on, they had the man so liquored up that he forgot what he had come here to do.

--

The invasions and attacks that were carried out against the Slovaks were not just about harboring Katina and the children. It also had leaked out through envious neighbors that Katina had given and stashed away a lot of valuables at their house. This had made their home even more susceptible to ransacking and looting. The police chief and his men found and uncovered items hidden in the cellar under a heap of potatoes. And upstairs under heavy draped tables and mattresses; in the attic or barn, nothing was safe. Resolved not to lose everything the Slovaks took whatever was left of their valuables and hid them at various homes of relatives.

55

Seeing that the order to return the German women and their families to their original homes had not been successful; the Russian commander designated the large unfinished hospital compound in the middle of town, that Johann had helped build, as their temporary stay. This was to be carried out until such time when he could sort out what to do with all the captives.

After more incidents of ransacking and the continued threats to all their lives, Katina came to the conclusion that she had no choice but to go. Her last place of refuge had become impossible to sustain. It brought only turmoil and danger to the ones who harbored her and her children. She, as well as the Slovaks, knew now that it was only a matter of time when they would separate. But when the final day would come, they also knew it would not be an easy departure on both sides, for the Slovaks felt a responsibility toward her and the children. They knew that by releasing them to that prison complex, their lives were even more in danger, as they would be exposed to beatings, kidnapping, exploitations, abuse, rape, starvation, and many other atrocities.

With this intent, she was and always would be grateful for what they had done, but she could not impose on them any longer. Besides, the Slovaks had to move out of their present home which they had temporally occupied when their own home was destroyed on the onset of war. They had done as

354

all the rest, looked for an unoccupied home and claimed it for the time being as their own.

Lucky were those where no one came back to claim the property. Yet being part of the unlucky ones where the owner returned, the Slovaks now found themselves out of a home again and looking for another, but to their misfortune, this time there was none to be had. Fortunately for them, Pani Slovak's sister made room in her house and took them all in, Katina and her children included.

After one night in their new quarters, sleeping in even a more cramped condition, Katina knew it was time to part. Tears were shed and the goodbye was bittersweet. Just three years ago they were strangers and now after all they had been through, they were more than friends. They were her adopted family, dear hearts, which she did not want to say goodbye to, or lose, for she had lost so much.

On the final day, because of the continuous forced work duties, she had no choice but to leave the children in the Slovak's care. An arrangement was worked out that Marianka would bring them later in the day to the compound. Julia then was to take over and watch her little siblings until she herself was brought there after work. With a heavy heart she parted from her children, trusting that Marianka will stay true to her word and everything will work out.

Upon arrival at the large complex, she found herself remembering Johann working on it. It stood only partly finished, with the red bricks still lying on a pile beside the main entrance, just where he and those who worked with him had left them, waiting for other craftsmen to skillfully finish the job. She felt a deep yearning in her heart. She missed him so much. It was as if it all had been a bad dream.

'At least the windows and the outside doors are in place... They would at least give some protection from the elements.' She sighed wistfully, thinking, if she would still be in her home she would not have to worry about these things. Johann had built it to withstand even the coldest winter.

There was also enough provision to keep the house warm all winter long. 'But for whom?' Distraught, she released another heavy, oppressive sigh.

As she and the others in her group were being escorted hurriedly across the yard by two of the police chief's men, she stole a quick glance around the compound and noticed it to be an enclosed area with more than one building. At the front entrance to the left of the yard stood an L-shaped structure, which would have been the intended hospital. It was the tallest of all the others, with a basement underneath the first structure. Then the same was attached to another building that had a raised second floor, but only at the corner. The rest of the attached complex seemed to have been designated for offices with a large drive-through garage. To the right of the enclosed yard, there stood two long barracks with sectioned off entrances. The tall building to the left and the first barrack to the right were joined together at the entrance by a wide tall wooden gate. To the far end of the whole compound, a small rat infested creek straggled alongside the intended office building and the drive-through garage. It enclosed the whole area toward the second barrack, creating a perfect oasis to keep the prisoners separate from the town's inhabitants.

She paused for a moment to look back, when all at once she felt the cold barrel of a gun pushed hard against her back.

"Hurry up and get going, we've no time to waste," one of the guards retorted, ramming the gun barrel even harder against her back. She suppressed a painful gasp then followed the others.

Once they had reached their designated building, the second one of the lower barracks, they were quickly escorted inside. As she and the others walked along the corridor of the structure, passing one room after another, it suddenly struck her as to how many women and children had been caught just in this vicinity alone. Surprisingly, there were also a handful of old men among them. After what had happened to Father Wendel and the older men in their group, she had not thought it possible that any German men would have survived.

She recognized some, but most she did not. Like sardines they were laying or sitting on makeshift metal army bunks, or in some cases, piles of straw. She noticed the horror and pain on their faces, the turmoil and hunger, the hopelessness and despair. All at once she had to steady herself, overwhelmed by the sight of the desolation and the musty smell that lay heavy in the corridor and beyond.

One by one they disbursed into different quarters and then finally she too had reached her designated place. To her surprise and relief, she found her loved ones waiting patiently, sitting on a familiar twin sized bed next to the entrance of a good sized large room.

"Mama," the children cried out, glad to be reunited, they surrounded her immediately and clung to her. Exhausted and with tear filled eyes she praised Julia for taking such good care of her siblings.

Marianka had kept her promise, and by some small miracle along with the children she had managed to smuggle in one of her daughter's single bed, as well as one of their twin feather duvet and two feather pillows. Upon further inspection, she discovered a freshly filled straw sack to sleep on. She was overcome with gratitude, everything had turned out better than she had expected.

"We filled the sack ourselves," Julia bragged, showing off what a good job she had done.

"We got the straw from over there," she pointed through the window, across the yard toward the large drive-through garage. Katina stood in disbelief.

"You did very well."

She gave all of them a grateful hug. "I'm so proud of you."

Julia beamed at her accomplishment.

Katina looked around and almost felt guilty seeing what others had to be content with. The feather comforter and the two pillows looked filthy and had no covers, but she did not care. It had her worried how she would keep the children and herself warm, but now she did not have to worry. Even though the cover was a little small for the four of them, it would have to do.

"It's better than nothing," she mumbled quietly to herself. She glanced around the room again and noticed Elisabeth coming toward her.

"Katina... I'm so glad to see you and the children unharmed and well. Welcome to our humble abode, wretched as it is," she said sarcastically. "Well what do you think?" she asked and gestured with her hand around the room.

"It is wretched indeed, but it'll have to do I guess. At least we have a roof over our heads," she gave Elisabeth a weak but weary smile, then sat down on her bed where her children quietly played with one another. It's just like Elisabeth to try and be upbeat, she thought. But then she herself had no right to think that she was the only one suffering. These women, her friends, had gone through hell and were stuck here just like her. So she better not make things worse for them or herself. They have been thrown into this mess together and now they have to try to help each other to survive. Her mood changed as she suddenly straightened up gesturing for Elisabeth to sit down beside her.

"It must have been some doing to achieve getting all those items," Elisabeth tried to change the subject in a little triumphant and joking manner as she took the place beside her; gesturing at the bed and the bedding.

"I could only think of one person who could've done this and that would be Pani Slovak's sister. Remember? She had a fiery spirit that could make her opponent's lives very uncomfortable." Katina's mood suddenly lightened by that comment and she found herself chuckling despite the gloominess around her.

"I remember!" Elisabeth laughed and nodded in

agreement, then added with contentment. "Isn't it a nice setup?" She turned and pointed around the room. "At least we're together and can help each other when need be."

Katina took a glance around and had to agree. "Yes, it's true... It is a nice setup and I'm glad we're together," she spoke a little more upbeat.

"See, right there next to your bed, is where Jobina took the lower bunk and Maria will share the upper bunk with one of Claudia's girls. I know it'll be tight but we have to make it work," Elisabeth paused putting her hand on one of the two tiered narrow bunk beds and gave it a little shake. "A little rickety, but then again we have to be happy we have them. They are left over from our own Armed forces. So I was told," she added then continued.

"We just have to be careful no one falls out of them while sleeping," she paused for a moment inspecting the beds more closely. "We'll definitely have to make each other aware of this. Well anyway..." she moved on. "Along the window wall there, Claudia and her youngest claimed the lower and her oldest boy and his brother are sleeping on the upper bunk. And on the opposite side of the entrance from you, Magda and one of Claudia's girls will sleep on the upper bunk while Rosa and I share the lower one.

And if you're wondering about Klara's mother, she has her quarters right around the corner in another room, where she has claimed a lower bunk for herself and her granddaughter. So you see it'll all work out good."

She had to agree with her friend, it was better than she had expected. These dear friends she knew to be like-minded and caring, very sensitive in helping and sticking together. They will look out for each other and strive for the same basic essentials, first shelter, then safety and food, all these and more; to survive this dreadful and horrifying ordeal.

Knowing this would be their daily struggle, she could not single out which one of these would be the greater to overcome. She was sure their endurance would be tested continually to withstand everything and anything that was laid upon them.

A cold March wind blew around the corners of the building as they settled in for the night. She listened in the dark to the sounds of her children breathing. To have all three children and herself sleeping in the twin bed, Julia and Elisa lay on the foot end of the bed, while she and Stefan slept on the opposite end. It was a tight squeeze and there was not much room to move about especially with one's feet. Purposely she had Julia sleeping on the opposite side from Stefan, while she slept across from Elisa. Just to have them close gave her comfort. It was good to know that Marianka had taken good care of them and had brought them here safe and sound.

She breathed a sigh of relief... another day done, but what about tomorrow and the next day. Anxious, she had to leave all her concerns in God's hands.

For a little while longer she listened. It was dark and without the warmth of a fire, the cool air was creeping into their sleeping quarters. She could still hear some people in the other rooms getting settled, but with the exhaustion of the day, she soon fell asleep.

56

Suddenly she awoke by noise coming from the outside. Dark shadows moved past the windows of their building. She could hear the front door being clumsily pushed open. Then heavy erratic boot steps made their way along the unlit hallway. Stumbling over something or someone as that person or persons seemed to be feeling their way around. Suppressed swear words followed. By now most of the captured were awake and listened in fear. To everyone it was apparent, invaders were in the compound and they were here helpless as sheep and the men were about to assault them.

She remembered the attack of the wolves in Romania. She wished now for more protection. She wished she had a dog like Mamuk to stand watch. She now felt vulnerable being so close to the doorway. And worse, Julia and Elisa were closest to the opening, but at least their room was not the first room from the main entrance of the barrack.

Suddenly, she heard the steps coming closer. They were wavering and unsure. There was a bang and again swearing in Polish. Whoever it was must have walked into a doorway. The boot steps continued again, they slowed down when they reached their doorway. It was as if he knew where to go. For a moment the man lingered.

Katina held her breath. There were no doors to the individual rooms, nothing to protect them. She prayed quietly as he entered into the room bumping against their bed, feeling his way. Of those who were awake, no one said a word. It was as if they all knew and understood the danger they were in. They all feigned to be asleep. Yes, they were sheep and the wolf was here, and he was drunk.

He came into the room and misjudged the location of the beds. Being so crowded, Katina's bed protruded into the normal pathway of the room. He stumbled and fell on top of Julia and Elisa!

They stirred. Julia awoke frightened. He swore again in Polish and kept searching through the room for a young woman to take. Now there was a commotion and several of the older women told him to go. Rosa was right in his path, in the dark she slid down and hid under the bunk. He fumbled around the lower bunk and tried to crawl over. Just then Elisabeth let out a scream. Shocked by the sudden noise and realizing that it was not a young woman he had in front of him, he swore again and unwillingly made his way out of the room. In the dark they could hear him searching and moving around in the next room, again bumping into things.

Katina and the others listened as the man continued to the next room. There was a struggle and then a scream of a young woman. Suddenly there were more boot steps.

With fear she and the others in the room remained alert. Panic stricken they listened knowing it was only a matter of time when the men would find their way to their room. And they could do nothing about it.

--

A few days later as they arrived back at the compound in the dark of the evening, they passed through the main door to their barrack. Katina took a glance at the door and realized there was no way to lock it. They were left vulnerable. In the past few days there were several instances where drunken and not-so-drunken Russian soldiers or their Polish captors came through at night looking for young women.

Elizabeth had come in through the door entrance after Katina. Behind them the others in their group followed.

I WILL REMEMBER ALWAYS

Walking along the darkened hall they hastily made their way each into their designated room. After a long and laboring day everyone just searched out their sleeping quarter and sank tired into bed. The children with hunger in their bellies by now were fast asleep.

While the others settled in she quietly talked with Elizabeth. "What can we do about the men coming in at night? I looked at the front door and it has no lock. If it would have a lock we could close it at night."

Elisabeth answered back in a hushed voice, "What of the people who need to go out to the toilet? I don't think a lock would work."

Katina thought for a moment then spoke again in quiet, "If only there was a door to our room. It's the third time some man has stumbled over our bed in the dark. I fear for Julia and Elisa, I hope they won't get hurt."

"I know," Elisabeth replied. "I know how it feels." After a moment in thought she spoke again. "I have a brilliant idea," her voice getting louder then intended. "Yes! There is an old zinc bathtub near the back of the yard. I think they were letting horses drink from it. We can clean it up as good as possible and bring it in here?"

Now excited they told the other women in their room, who had heard Elisabeth talking and were now standing around them.

"We could use it as a night toilet," Rosa exclaimed. "That would be safer than using the pit outside."

Katina winced, "Only for night, remember we have to sleep next to it."

So the next evening after they came back from work, they went out in the dark, carrying a pail with them. With the bucket full of water in hand, they located the zinc bathtub, poured the water into it then washed and cleaned it. They then carried it inside and placed it right up to their doorway. This would now become the door that had been missing to their room.

363

The tub as a night toilet became popular with some of the other women and children in the surrounding rooms also. It was much safer than going outside in the dark. Yes, there was a strong urine smell, but then there was a stinky musty odor hanging over the whole barrack anyway.

She remembered the stench the first time she was led through the barrack. It was no wonder with all the sweat and odor from all the unwashed bodies; not to mention the soiled from the old and very young who were unable to look after themselves. She had gotten used to the unpleasantness. With all they had been through that was the least of her worries. Just having the barrier there felt more secure even though she knew the tub could be stepped over or moved by a determined intruder.

It was only a week later when the tub's presence proved helpful. Another drunken intruder slipped while trying to cross over the tub and fell into the concentrated pool of urine. In his soaked state, he changed his mind and left them cursing. There was much rejoicing from the women in the room, but what about the others. She wished now they all could be helped.

As she had seen it, this new installment would serve two different purposes. For one, and as primitive as it was, it would hopefully deter unwanted intruders and another, it solved the need for an inside toilet. As it was, the one provided for them outside was too dangerous. Dangerous, because of what lurked for them in the dark, in the way of man. But also this unconventional toilet facility was only a large open pit with long wooden planks laid across, each spaced one foot apart. This flimsy contraption of an oversized hideous outhouse was surrounded by half finished temporary walls, with little privacy for anyone. Maybe it had been good enough for soldiers, but not for women with small children.

It was in her eyes, an ugly smelly, disease infested sight, that occupied a space to the far side of the compound near the creek. I guess their captors figured it good enough for their prisoners. Apparently it had been quickly erected and used by the German Armed forces and since then had served all the other occupying and passing through armed personnel.

"The place is an accident waiting to happen, especially for little children," Claudia Ebert exhorted. "In fact just the other day my little boy had a near mishap by stepping on a slippery board. He was lucky his sister caught him just in time."

"Yes a few days later the same happened to Elisa, when she slipped and hung by her arms. Fortunately, I happened to be beside her and rescued her. The poor thing was so shocked and frightened. I tell you, something has to be done about it," Rosa added with dismay.

"It's shocking at the possibility of what could have happened and I still shudder at the thought. We could have lost both of our children. But how do we go about it and who will listen to us?" Katina spoke with concern. "I think for now, there is little else we can do about it. I would caution for all of us to be extra careful and watch each other, especially the children."

They all agreed.

57

A mong all the dangers that surrounded them, there was the constant problem with lice and bedbugs. She and the others in the room had noticed these types of intruders when they first moved in. Tired from the grueling work load that was put on them they had no strength or the means to deal with these pesky creatures. Exhausted as they were, it had become so troublesome that they were waking up at night itching and scratching. She remembered the bedbugs from the old dilapidated two room hut when they first had moved here and she suspected the same here.

Woken by her children tossing and scratching themselves, tortured no doubt by the bites as she herself was, she heard the others as well tossing and turning. Suddenly she heard Elisabeth jump out of bed.

"These pesky bugs... I wish... Ugh..." Elisabeth stood flailing her hands against her body. Katina now slipped out from underneath her cover scratching herself.

"I'm itching too and can't sleep. I wish we had a light to see with."

"I'm plagued too," Claudia suddenly joined yet remained under her covers.

Elisabeth walked over to Claudia's bed.

"There's a full moon shining right through the window and onto your corner of the bed. Maybe it's enough to see...?" Curious Claudia now got up to also have a look. The illuminated spot was just enough to detect some movement of tiny creatures.

"Aha!" Elizabeth exclaimed, "Just as I had suspected, Bedbugs!"

Katina and some others in the room joined Elizabeth and Claudia to see for themselves. Realizing now what they saw in Claudia's bed was also in all their beds as well.

"What should we do? We have to clean," Jobina said resolutely.

"Clean with what? We have nothing not even soap," Rosa came crawling out of bed and was now standing with them.

"We can try. We have to try," said Elisabeth, "I can't sleep like this.

"We can boil water on the small potbelly stove." Jobina nodded with her head toward the hallway where the unused stove was standing. "We can dunk at least our under garments into the boiling water and dry them there by the stove. It would kill the lice, but I'm not so sure about the bedbugs."

"And how do you think we can achieve that? There are too many of us. And when do we have the time or the space to do all that? And who would go first? Remember we come home late and our wet woolen undergarments will take forever to dry," Claudia confronted the rest of them.

"Claudia is right. It is impossible in this short time and as she said there are too many of us. Just think if we have them in our beds, so will all the others in this barrack," Katina paused for a moment. "I think we have to try and come up with another solution to get rid of them."

"Ugh... I can't go back to bed and lay on top those... Ugh..." Elisabeth shook herself. "I can already feel them crawling all over me. Ugh..."

"I know! I feel the same way." Claudia shook herself agreeing with Elisabeth, as did the others. Reluctant they went back to bed, hoping that by some small miracle they will find a way to get rid of this infestation.

58

It was one late evening in the last days of April, as always before nightfall, the women would go one more time with their children to the open pit. Elisa was wearing one of the older girl's slip-on shoes, much too large for her little feet.

She was about to crouch when to everyone's horror she lost her balance and tumbled head first into the deep thick mucky rat infested mass!

Katina was beside herself ready to jump after her. She heard Elisa cry out several times, as she struggled to keep afloat.

"Mama... Ma... ma...!" she cried as she went down into thick disgusting waste.

Katina was torn not sure what to do.

If she jumped after her now she might land on top of her little girl and what if she herself could not get free of this thick slimy mess.

Then just as she was contemplating to jump in, Elisa's outstretched hand suddenly appeared again above the moving refuse. She leaned forward as much as possible and grabbed hold of her little one's hand.

"No... No... No... Oh God no...!" she cried out in shock and horror, just to watch Elisa's hand slip out of her hand, back into the thick smelly soup.

She contemplated again to jump in after her, but then her body felt weak, too weak...

368

"Oh God this is too much, I can't lose another one of my loved ones. I can't bear it..." she gasped in the middle of her cry.

There was movement in the thick waste.

There was Elisa's hand again.

"Ma... ma!" Her little one took one big gulp of air and as she struggled she took in a mouthful of the putrid mix of urine and feces.

By now it seemed all the imprisoned population of the compound had heard about this terrible plight and had come out to help and give advice. Others just stood in disbelieve and horror.

One more time Katina saw Elisa's arm stretch out high above the moving mass.

This time Julia was at her side.

Instantly they both reached down for Elisa. Once again Katina got hold of Elisa's arm and Julia managed to grab hold to her sister's long dress sleeve.

"Hold on, for God's sake hold on, don't let go...! Don't let go, hold on tight...!" Julia heard her mother cry out again and again, as they both struggled to hang on.

Terror filled Katina as she felt Elisa's arm slowly slip out of her hand again. The muck was giving her no grip.

"God help us..." her words spoken in defeat echoed over the crowd.

Julia braced herself and held on to her sister's sleeve hoping it will not tear from her hand.

Someone in the crowd gasped, mumbling a prayer, "Holy Mother of God... save her...."

The crowd stood fixed in horror holding their breath while watching Katina reach out again.

This time reaching farther she caught Elisa's other arm holding now also onto her dress sleeve.

There was a hush among the crowd. Everyone stood waiting and watching as Katina and Julia struggled and pulled until by a small miracle Elisa's almost lifeless and limp body was safe in her mother's arms.

With Julia in tow, she quickly walked over the plank and onto solid ground.

The onlookers gasped a sigh of relief, happy that the rescue had been successful.

Katina sat down and immediately reached into Elisa's mouth to clear it from all the waste. Again and again she repeated it until she was sure Elisa could breathe on her own. Trembling she wiped her little one's eyes and nose and stripped her tiny body of all the dirty clothes.

The minute she and Julia had succeeded in pulling Elisa out of the pit, Magda and Rosa were up and running carrying water from the well while Elisabeth was busy getting the fire going in the potbelly stove. The rest of her friends with their children, including Stefan, kept bringing the straw that was needed to heat the stove. Someone had managed to produce a piece of soap. Others from the barrack helped empty the old zinc tub and placed it outside for the warm water to be poured in.

Katina scrubbed and washed Elisa until she was sure she had done all she could.

While working to get Elisa cleaned up, the others around them were gagging at the stench. Yet she and Julia, still so in shock, did not smell anything nor had the urge to gag.

Later, when all was done, she lay in bed with her three children sleeping securely around her. She was retracing the near-tragic event. It was amazing to her how everyone had banded together and was willing to help.

By their own strength, she and Julia could not have managed to rescue Elisa, as they were, like the others, very weak and suffering from malnutrition. She was sure God had intervened.

She was suddenly overcome by tears at the thought of almost losing another one of her precious family. Oh how she missed Johann and Rebekka and Mama and Papa and all her siblings.

"God how long... How long...?" she wept, once again unlocking the special memories in her heart.

She missed Johann's strong arms around her and the closeness they shared. For a moment she envisioned his tender touch, his loving smile always cheering her on. She relished these moments. They renewed her strength to go on.

For a little while longer, she remembered, the sunny days and warm summer evenings by the sea. It seemed so long ago. Tired and exhausted from the day's events she tucked her memories deep into her innermost heart. Listening to the even breathing of her little boy beside her, and despite the crawling invaders that shared their bed, she soon felt herself drifting into a deep sleep.

--

Early the next morning the sun shone brightly. She and the other young women had long been gone, taken away to their various work places. It was the middle of spring and Mother Nature was trying her best to renew and cover up the devastation the war years had brought along. And so it was with little Elisa, yesterday's chaos almost took her little life. Today she was sitting by the open window, enjoying the morning sunshine, singing her little heart out.

The older inhabitants in the compound were asking, "Is this the little girl who fell into the open pit toilet?"

"Yes!" came Julia's happy reply.

They were all surprised and delighted to see the change from one day's tragic mishap, to another day's miraculous recovery. Many could not believe this was the same little girl, as Elisa sat all cleaned up with her hair curly and shining in the bright morning sunlight.

The warm rays of sunshine penetrated deep into the dark and otherwise gloomy corridors, and listening to the little girl's singing brought cheer to many poor and sick souls. Even for a brief moment, the unbearable devastating conditions of their fate was forgotten.

59

In the following month Katina's and the other women's work duties suddenly changed from the grueling cleanup chores to being farmed out to mills, stores, farms, restaurants, private homes and such. Anywhere their adversaries found work for them to do, they were forced, whether able or not, working long unrelenting hours of hard labor.

She thought often of the Slovaks and how they were doing. Were they still living at Pani Slovak's sister's place? Or had they found another home? She wished they could have had their homestead. Johann had built it so wonderful and strong.

And the land.

"Ah, yes, the land..." she released a deep sigh. It had been the most idyllic setting, one she really had become attached to. It was a beautiful property.

Many times she, Jobina, and Maria were led past their former homes on the way to work. In passing she stole a quick sideways glance, just to see how they looked. Her and Johann's former homestead was still occupied, naturally so, for who would not want to live in this place. It had big potential with the land and the house. She thought of the many hours Johann had slaved to perfect it, although if he could have had the time he would have expanded it to a much larger home. He had high hopes for this place.

'Poor Johann,' she sighed again. Deep profound painful

memories of what had been and all the trouble and pain they had endured surfaced.

The place did not look at all what it once had been. The land lay neglected, the house too had suffered and the once beautiful garden in the back, she could see from afar, had a lot of weeds growing. Once it had been a flourishing business in their time. And now…?

"Oh well… Don't look anymore…" she told herself in quiet.

Jobina and Maria had done the same every time they passed their place. Elisabeth landed work a few times in Ebert's former mill. It so happened that their former assigned Polish family, which had worked for them, had claimed the mill as their own after the collapse of the German Reich. As far as she knew the Slovaks had not been so lucky.

She had seen Marianka a few times when they were led past Pani Slovak's sister's place to and from their various workplaces. But for obvious reasons they could not talk to each other, exchanging only a quick glance. In that moment she could detect a sad look about Marianka's face. Obviously dismayed of what she saw.

60

Because of the scarcity of food and poor living conditions, sicknesses of typhoid and cholera, which Katina had not seen since the outbreak in Mangalia, suddenly surfaced in an alarming rate. To add to this, the battle against bedbugs and lice was neverending. Diligently she and the others in her room tried to keep these diseases and infestations at bay. As it was now with the warmer weather, they had succeeded boiling their undergarments now for the second time. She and her friends targeted these particular pieces of clothing, as worn so close to the warm skin they were a perfect breeding place for lice. As for the rest of their clothing there was nothing they could do. And forget the bedding, there were no covers to speak off. Besides if they could wash their clothes, there was no safe place in this compound to have them dry, inside or out.

Because of minimal clothing for the children, she had washed Elisa's soiled dress, stockings and underwear that night after she had fallen into the outhouse. Trusting as she was, she had hung them in their room to dry. The next day by evening when she and the others returned back from work, all of Elisa's things had disappeared. After that she had never dared to leave any clothing laying or hanging about. She was scared after this that people would go so far as to steal what she had hidden under her mattress. As here she had kept, among other things, one good set of clothing for each of the two little ones. Standing by her bed now thinking about this unfortunate incident, Elisabeth suddenly appeared beside her.

"Katina! What are we going to do? We did all we possibly could do…" Elisabeth paused, her stooped forward statue showing her exhaustion.

"The others are still busy boiling their laundry and it's late. And of all things it won't dry fast enough for us to wear again tomorrow morning. I don't know if all that work is really helping. I, for one, am at my wits end. We have slaved and done all we could do and before morning those pesky creatures are always back again." Tears filled her eyes, "Katina, I'm so tired I don't know if we can keep this up."

"I know Elisabeth. We all feel the same way, with the heavy workload and coming home so late? Believe me we are all ready to give up. I see it in all of us especially Claudia."

"Yeah… Have you noticed it too? As far as I know she has not been feeling well for quite some time now. In all the month's we've been together you'd think she would let out what's bothering her."

Elisabeth thought for a moment then spoke again.

"None of us have much food to eat. As it is we all have been eating from our army's leftover vegetable pile that's laying half-rotten down in the cellar. Which by the way is diminishing fast. And I would not put it past if that's what's making so many people sick? But now I'm getting away from what I wanted to say. I think Claudia is pregnant." She looked around to see if anyone was near listening range.

"Now that you mentioned it, I think you might be right."

"What do you mean… might be right…? Katina, I've been a midwife for many years… I know the symptoms of a pregnant woman."

Elisabeth sat down thinking.

"But how do we go about asking her? We can't just go ahead and confront her. We'll have to let her come to us in her own good time. I think that would be the best thing to do. What do you think…?"

Katina looked questionably at Elisabeth, but Elisabeth did not give her an answer, instead she jumped in with a deep sigh.

"Poor thing. Just think... In that condition and being forced to hard labor... It won't be good for her or the baby."

"How far along do you think she might be?" Katina asked again.

"Well, by the looks of it I figure about five months."

"Elisabeth. Do you know what you're saying? Our husbands have not been with us longer than that. Do you know what I'm saying?"

"Yes... I know... The poor thing. It must have been around the time when the Russian soldiers..." Elisabeth stopped herself right there. "We were lucky our Polish workers and their families stood by us. God bless their souls."

"Poor Claudia... and here she's been keeping it all inside and carrying the burden by herself." Both sat for a moment in quiet thought.

"Hey wait a minute?" Katina suddenly burst out. "What about birthing? What are we going to do? I know for myself the last time I needed a doctor present, and now going through all this with no food to sustain a healthy baby I don't know if she or the little one will make it."

Elisabeth's face suddenly lightened. "As far as delivering her baby, I've heard that Claudia had all five of her children without the help of a doctor. Besides I'm here! Have you forgotten that I'm a trained midwife?"

Katina waved her off. "You're right."

"Oh... on another note... What about those pesky bugs?" Elisabeth quickly changed the subject as the others came into the room. "What are we going to do about them? We know we can't keep up with what we're doing. We'll kill ourselves trying."

"You can say that again. I... and I think all of us don't have the strength or the time to do all this cleaning," Jobina spoke up. The others all agreed.

I WILL REMEMBER ALWAYS

"But what else can we do? It's now not just about the lice and bed-bugs but also these diseases?" Claudia sat on her bed tired.

"What could we do?" Katina thought for a moment. There was little hygiene practices among most inhabitants. The blame rested mainly on not having proper facilities and the means to keep up with them. Many of the elderly were too weak and too sick to even bother to clean up after themselves.

The stench of the barely living corpses could turn even the strongest stomach. She shook herself at that thought.

It was heart-wrenching and spirit weakening to be surrounded with these issues day in and day out. She, for one, found it oppressive and overwhelming to deal with. Besides all that, the subject on how to get relief from the tormenting infestation of lice and bedbugs was forever gnawing on her mind. Contemplating about this now, she suddenly spoke up.

"You know, here we are, slaving away with all that boiling, and all along the problem with these pesky creature doesn't go away. It just dawned on me, where do we get all the straw to fill our mattresses?" She looked at everyone.

"Yes, of course..." Jobina's face suddenly lit up. "We could go on and on with all the cleaning and it won't help," she thought for a moment. "But what else can be done to get relief?" she added.

Katina listened for a moment then went to her bed and pulled her large black handbag from underneath her straw mattress.

"I almost forgot about this. Marianka had rescued it and put it in the bag for me to wear. But who has time to change? To me it is useless, as we all are tired and have no time to change from our day clothes."

"What in heaven's name are you mumbling about?" Elisabeth said, curious about what Katina was getting at. All at once Katina produced this beautiful brand new white

377

cotton nightgown.

"Oh! It's beautiful!" Magda exclaimed.

"I haven't seen anything so clean and white for a long time..." Rosa added with awe in her voice.

"I'm going to try and barter this in exchange for petroleum."

"What, this beautiful nightgown? Katina you must be crazy. Are you sure you want to do this?" Claudia shook her head in disbelief.

"If it means getting rid of these terrible creepy creatures...? Yes, I'm quite sure."

"I can't believe my ears... and where will you go? I think most will just take it from you and not give you anything for it," Claudia replied a little skeptical.

"At least I can go and try. If it works? Good."

"And if it doesn't?" Jobina asked.

"Well if it doesn't...? At least I've tried."

"But you might lose it," Maria looked dismayed.

"Yes, Maria, I know, but it's worth a try. Remember we've lost much more than that."

"Yes, but that would be a shame. It's so beautiful..."

61

The next day, as usual, she and the women were picked up early in the morning. There was no time allowed for grooming or washing, and how could they? All they had was a dinged up pail and an old bowl, which they filled the evening before with water. It was enough to get one's hands wet and wipe across the face, then straighten the hair as well as possible, put it in a bun, and then tie the kerchief around it. No need for mirrors, as they had none anyway. It was better she and the rest of them did not see how they looked.

Tired, with the pain of hunger in their stomachs, she and her friends made their way along familiar streets, but it was not for her own wellbeing that bothered her most, it was the children she worried about. How long will she, her children, and the rest of them be able to go before they will all die of starvation, and if not from that, the diseases would surely finish them off. But as she had seen, it did not seem to bother these vigilantes that walked behind them with their rifles and whips in hand. It was as if they wanted to starve them out, or work them to death, whichever came first. Yet for some puzzling reason they as women had kept on going.

Suddenly she felt the butt of a rifle shoved into her back. "There that's where you'll be working today. Hurry up and don't doddle woman, we have no time for that." Puzzled she looked up. It was a private home... She sighed, already exhausted. Just then a woman opened the door.

"I have a ton of things that need washing," she said with an impatient tone in her voice. "So get yourself in here and start." Katina looked at the washboard and the laundry beside it. Her heart sank at the sight of the large heap. But she hid the displeasure of this job and mustered enough strength to go about this unpleasant task.

By the end of the day, with the laundry done, the woman seemed happy over what Katina had achieved. All of a sudden she showed a different side and started talking with her about ordinary everyday things.

Katina took the opportunity and mentioned the trouble with lice and bedbugs. When the woman mentioned petroleum, she took the chance. Unbuttoning the front top of her first dress, she pulled the nightgown out from behind it. She had always worn two dresses one on top the other. She did not want to wear out the newer one underneath and dared not leave one behind in the compound. Even though it would be hidden underneath the straw mattress, it most likely would be stolen and then what would she do? She definitely needed to protect the newer dress in case the older one wore out.

At first, the woman looked puzzled at her, at what she was doing, but when she produced this beautiful white nightgown, the woman could not keep her eyes off it.

"Please..." Katina started. "Would you please be so kind and trade a container of petroleum for this, for my children, please..." she begged. "I would be ever so grateful," she pleaded.

"You know I could just take it from you, you know that, don't you?" The woman looked at her with scorn in her eyes.

"Yes. But you're a mother yourself and surely you would do anything for your children." She guessed that it was so, as she had seen children's clothing in the laundry she had washed and hung outside to dry. From the size of the outfits they must be around the age between Elisa and Julia.

"Well... Certainly I would... What do you think...? I love

my children." A little put out the woman eyes were still on the gown. "Well... now that you put it that way... Hmmm..." She stood for a moment deciding, looking at her then to the nightgown. "Alright then, but don't let it be seen or known that I gave it to you, or I'll be in big trouble."

She went quickly into the adjacent room and came back with the petroleum.

"You had better hide it. My husband and children are due to come home any minute and they better not find out that I gave it to you."

Quickly Katina unbuttoned the top of her dress and placed the small container into the midsection of her body. The belted dress would keep it from slipping out from underneath. She thanked the woman again, but got no reply. Engrossed in her find, the woman was happy that she came across such a beautiful nightgown. In these times even for her, just like most Polish people, items like these were hard to come by.

In the evening she produced the container with petroleum and the others were astonished.

"How in heaven's name did you manage to get this...?" Elisabeth gasped in disbelief, her voice lowered not to make a scene. "I'm honestly surprised. I did not think it possible... Well... I can't believe it!" she exclaimed excitedly.

Katina just smiled at her. "Thanks to Marianka! If she would not have tucked the nightgown in my bag, there would have been nothing to trade with."

Now with the petroleum at hand she doled out for each person and child a small dab to rub into their hair. The older ones helping the children then repeated the same. They rubbed a small portion on their bodies and saved the rest for another time. With that they were hopeful the petroleum will do its job to deliver them all from their miseries.

At first it seemed their little experiment had worked. But to her and everyone's dismay they found it was only a temporary solution, one that had to be constantly reapplied

381

to make it work.

Disappointed, she came to the realization that without the means to get more of the petroleum, she and the others in the room were once again stuck to slave away at their tedious job of boiling their personal laundry.

In her opinion, it was a hard and tedious job that took effort and time, and unfortunately, time they had so little of. Yet she was determined not to give up and she was sure her friends were on board with this. As long as they had the strength and the means they would not give up and continue to fight the pests. They owed it to their children as well as to themselves.

62

After yet another hard and debilitating day, she, along with the rest of the women, entered their appointed building. She noticed the atmosphere subdued, almost too quiet. Walking along behind the others, she dragged herself to her room. Turning the corner she saw Elisa and Stefan playing with Claudia's two youngest boys. Not paying much attention she plunked down on her bed. But then something suddenly disturbed her. She looked around. 'Odd...?' she thought. 'Usually at this late hour everyone is inside the barrack.' Suddenly her and Claudia's eyes met, both realizing their oldest children missing.

"Where is Julia?" she leapt to her feet.

"Yes! And where are Benjamin and Lora and Lena?" Claudia called out.

"Mama...!" Elisa came running toward her with a scared and anxious expression on her face. "Mama, they took all of them!"

"Who did...?" she asked, now instantly alert. She looked at Elisa then around the room for an answer. There was a shuffle from the room across the narrow hallway.

Then Klara's mother's frail hushed voice was heard as she made her way to their room.

"They... They took them with the rest of the children to work... Down the hall..." The woman had trouble breathing. She pointed her thumb over her back and taking a deep breath she struggled to speak.

383

"A woman... from the 'Black Sea Germans... when her son... the same age as Julia was taken... she... she told them... that Julia was old enough... to go as well. Claudia... your three oldest... they were also taken," she lowered her head teary-eyed. "They... took our Anna too." A sniffle was heard, then a lamenting heavy sigh. The others in the room looked at each other shocked and sad that now their captors had gone so far as to involve the children in the slave labor.

Katina was filled with anger. "What right did that woman have to do such a thing?" she grumbled to the others in a half loud voice. But then she had a change of heart. 'Circumstances sometimes brought out the worst in people,' she thought, 'and maybe she had judged the woman unfairly.' But aside from that, she had been naive in trusting that all of her countrymen, or women in this case, were on the same level of truth and honor; especially those who had come from the east, where they and their forefathers had endured and lost so much. Would they not stick together even more so as people of a common heritage?

What bothered her most about this was that her small children were now left alone to fend for themselves. Without Julia, Elisa and Stefan were left exposed to all kind of dangers and that worried her. She was sure Claudia and the rest of the mothers felt the same way.

As she seen it, most of the children left behind were under six years of age, with Elisa being the oldest. There would be no one to look after them from the early morning hours until late in the evening. She and the other mothers were beside themselves with pity. But there was no relief or grace given to them by their captors on this matter.

This incident with the Black Sea woman made her aware that her adversaries not only existed on the outside, but were very much alive within the circumference in this compound. Now more than ever she and her friends had to be careful. She was grateful for the community of women she had in her room. They were people she could trust. But what of the children? Who was there for them?

--

Like all the mothers in the compound she feared now even more for her children of being mistreated, molested and kidnapped or even killed, and so it was with Julia. For days now she and the other mothers and grandmothers, had not heard of their whereabouts. Anxiously she and the others waited. Then suddenly one evening she heard Julia wailing. It came from the direction of the bridge. Quickly, she made her way down to meet up with her. One by one the rest of the children followed all glad to have found their way back home to reunite with their loved ones. Many told stories of horrible abuse and molesting. To her relief, Julia was unharmed and for that she was grateful.

By morning though the ordeal began anew, as she and the other women as well as the older children were summoned for work duties. It was hard to see Julia being taken away, crying as the rest of them. It left her deeply anguished. Yet her deepest sorrow came when she had to leave Elisa and Stefan behind.

--

The following evening Julia had told her that she was to be moved to a different workplace. To her relief, this one was only three kilometers away from town and she was very pleased.

'A little closer to home,' she thought triumphantly. At least it would be easier for Julia to come home. She was even more relieved to hear that the farmer's son was a very compassionate lad. Julia relayed to her that he missed his mother and sisters, who had just up and left for the big city. That was the reason why they needed someone to help out.

"He even went out of his way and told me, when you cook potatoes for the livestock, add an egg once in a while for yourself and take a potato home for your sister and brother. But when you do it, do it in secret and don't let my father see it."

Worried, Julia began to lament, "Mama I don't know what I'm supposed to do. I've no idea how to cook and clean or look after livestock. I've never done these things. I'm only eleven. I don't want to go Mama. I'm scared to be all alone out there on the pasture," she started to cry.

And like it or not, she had to go. Their captors did not show mercy. Her heart ached for her child. She wanted so much to protect her daughter, but it was not in her power to do so. The only thing she could do was to encourage her not to be afraid.

63

That day Marianka had seen Katina and Julia being led off with the other German women and their older children. Marianka had been, and still was, very concerned and worried for her and the children, and so was her whole family. Just to see the abuse of these vigilantes toward the captured made her blood boil. Many times they as a family wanted to intervene but could not. They knew of the hunger, the diseases, the abuse, and neglect Katina and her children had to endure. Marianka knew she had to do something, maybe talk to her aunt, as she lived so close to the compound. Maybe she could slip a piece of bread to Elisa and Stefan. She had noticed Elisa and Stefan venturing out of the compound on several occasions and it was not to her liking. She realized by doing so they were being harassed by young thugs from the neighborhood. She knew the thugs very well, as like their fathers, they too had taken on the vigilante mindset.

She pondered over this dilemma. She had to figure out how to get close to Elisa and Stefan. They needed her now more than ever and she knew Katina would be very grateful for that. One thing though, she would not be able to be here in town very often. As she and her family had found a place three kilometers west of Piatec and now resided there. It was again a small home, but it had more land for the livestock, and the soil there was good for gardening and growing crops.

They had agreed as a family to get seed for the land.

They would start a vegetable garden, just as they had helped establish for Katina. Many times they had sat in deep discussions, trying to find ways to help Katina. It had not been to their liking to let her go into the compound. But again the truth was they had little choice in that matter. Marianka's idea was to slip the two little ones bits and pieces of bread and they all agreed was a very good plan, even though it would not be enough to fully quiet their hunger. At least Elisa and Stefan would get some nourishment, and Julia and Katina would benefit from it as well.

They would also watch the border. Maybe, there was a chance to get Katina and the children out of here. But that plan was dangerous and it needed money, which even for them was a hard commodity to come by. There was no work to be found anywhere and even for them food was scarce. But in their case they had a horse as well as ducks and chickens; all left over from Katina.

They were lucky they had rescued at least some of the animals, among other things Katina had given to them. For this she and her family were forever grateful to her as now they could get by and would not go hungry.

Just this year her father and brothers had managed to grow some sugar beets. She remembered the children loving the sugar beet buns. Again her aunt would slip one or two of those to them.

She missed the children. After all the time they had been together she had become very attached to them, especially Elisa. She had always wanted a daughter of her own, but with this whole war business...?

As it is, there was a man she had liked and there was talk about marriage, but then the war came in between and he was taken to Germany. Well, she had never seen him since. She was 33 and there were not many men left in her own age. The war had been unkind to so many.

She thought of Johann... Katina had truly lost a good man. She had always liked him and thought of him as a good and kind man, very loyal and loving to his family. Those men were rare, although in her family all the men had this kind of nature, and her man as well, had a little of that in him. Unfortunately it was not meant to be, but then she was not alone in that. Her thoughts went to Katina. She had to help her, somehow...

64

Lonely for her mother and sister, Elisa decided on the following day, a rainy Sunday morning, to go and look for Julia. She had heard her sister telling Mama where she was working and she thought it would be easy to just follow the instructions.

She remembered Julia saying, "Follow the street that passed by the compound, then go across the bridge over the rat-infested creek, and just keep going along the same road."

Barefoot and skimpily dressed with only an old torn blanket for cover, she and Stefan set out, determined to find her.

Scared and unsure, Elisa only six and Stefan, only two years younger than her, kept following the same road, navigating their way north through town which today surprisingly seemed very quiet. Here and there they encountered some older women dressed all in black, apparently going to church.

Shyly, they both glanced at the women from underneath the cover of the blanket, but none of the women paid attention to what the two were up to and where they were going.

Soon she and Stefan found themselves all alone on the lonely country road, stopping only once in a while, but always keeping a watchful eye on their surroundings to locate their sister's whereabouts.

She had remembered Julia mentioning just the other

night, that she was herding the cows from noon to the late afternoon along the main road, and this was what she was looking for.

A good stretch later they stopped again and rested by a small shallow creek. Wading in it, Elisa discovered reeds growing to one side. She remembered way back when they were still living on their own property, She and Julia and friends of hers were playing at their favorite swimming hole when some of the kids plucked the reeds and ate the soft part on the end of it. Now she did the same and pulled some out for herself and Stefan. The reeds were still young and tender and very satisfying. And to wash it all down, she bent over; cupping her hands together she scooped up a good portion of water and drank from it, showing Stefan to do the same.

The creek seemed to be about a foot, to a foot and a half deep in some areas, but very clear. Not at all like the one that ran halfway around the compound. There the water was dark and murky and she definitely had not seen any fish swimming in there, only water rats. How different it was here. She and Stefan spotted many fish racing to and fro along the gravelly riverbed. And on occasion they spied a slinky eel gliding through the fresh cool water right in front of them. Playfully, they chased after it almost forgetting why they were on this journey.

Once on their way again the sky suddenly cleared and the sun was shining brightly. The warmth penetrating through the damp rain soaked blanket felt comforting and soothing to them, but soon the heat of the sun and the strain of the excursion began to take its toll on their already fatigued little bodies.

"It won't be long now," Elisa kept encouraging Stefan, as she now realized that she had overestimated her, as well as her younger brother's, endurance. Walking had suddenly become a lot more difficult and every step seemed to be more of a chore, rather than a fun-filled journey. Yet, despite it all, she kept pushing herself, as well as Stefan, to go on. The yearning to find her sister drove both of them onward. They took only brief stops to look over the surrounding meadows in hopes to see a glimpse of Julia and the herd of cows.

As it was, Julia had just stood up from her sitting position to move the cows over to a better pasture. It was at that moment that she noticed a movement along the road of something strange and unrecognizable. Scared at first she stared, straining her eyes to decipher what it was. As they neared her she recognized the blanket.

"What are they doing here so far from the compound?" she questioned and ran toward them, upset at her two younger siblings for venturing out so far.

"We were hungry and we missed you," Elisa sobbed. "We were scared we wouldn't find you," she added. Stefan looked sad and big eyed at her, ready to cry.

"Well, it was not a good thing to do!" she scolded them lightly. "But since you're here, we'll not think about it anymore."

She hugged them and led them toward the place where she had been herding the cows.

"You sit here on the blanket with me and rest a bit until it's time to bring the cows back to the farm. I'll have some explaining to do and hope the farmer will be understanding," she added concerned of what awaited her.

Elisa nodded with apprehension, a little scared, realizing now she had done wrong and put her sister in a difficult position. Sitting in the warm sun and tired from the long walk, she and Stefan curled up on the blanket. Suddenly, before Julia could say more, they were fast asleep.

"I guess the walk was a little too much after all," she mumbled quietly to herself shaking her head amused at Elisa's courage. For now she had no choice but to keep the two vagabonds with her for the rest of the day until it was time to go home.

"I hope the farmer won't be mad," she said again worried.

In the evening when she told her mother, Katina was

beside herself as she tried to bring it to Elisa's attention that it was too dangerous to wander away from the compound.

To see her mother so upset, Elisa promised that she would never do this again. Leaving it at that, Katina hoped this stern talk would be enough to deter her little daughter from venturing out again. It was all she could do, painfully realizing anew she could not be there to watch over them.

65

A couple of days later, Julia and Claudia Ebert's boy, Benjamin, were tending cows for different farmers on the same meadow.

Suddenly a group of men appeared from out of nowhere, not far from where on the previous day Julia had been tending the cows. Both she and Benjamin now stood horrified as the men came straight towards them. With a serious look about them they walked right up and started to asked questions.

"How are they treating you at the compound and around town? Are the conditions improving?"

Crying and scared, she and Benjamin did not answer; they stood not knowing what to do.

"Don't be scared," one man spoke gently to them. Seeing that they were very frightened and upset, he tried his best to make them understand that they were not here to harm them.

"We are your friends. We are on your side. We only want to help you," another man added.

Suddenly she and Benjamin understood and were relieved they were in no danger. They told them everything they wanted to know.

Still a little shook up and in disbelief, they both watched as the men walked off. For a moment Julia had turned and then glanced back to make sure she had not just imagined this strange encounter, only to realize that the strangers had vanished just as quickly as they had appeared.

"It's as if the earth had swallowed them up. Where did they go?" she questioned Benjamin, who just shrugged his shoulders in bewilderment.

"I don't know. I just saw them walking and then they were gone. It's just like you said, but we both know this is not possible. Maybe...?" He turned to look again.

Speechless both she and Benjamin stood in a daze, looking over the meadow, trying to understand what had just happened.

"The sooner we can get away from here the better it'll be," Benjamin warned.

"I'm scared. Why don't we just do it right now and move the cows a little closer toward the road," she urged him on.

Still shaken and excited they both reported the incidence to their mothers. Katina was shocked to hear this but grateful that Julia and Benjamin had not been harmed. She warned both of them to be extra careful, yet at the same time wondered who these kind strangers were, and why they were concerned about them. Had the Russian Commander and his entourage moved on? Was this why these strangers suddenly appeared and were asking those questions? Were they once again susceptible to more wrath and atrocities?

--

The next day she and all the other women in the room got a firsthand report from Magda, who had lately been summoned to work at the police station.

"At first I did not know what to make of all the chaos and why the place looked like a whirlwind had gone through," she said all excited. She took a deep breath then continued. "But I overheard the police chief talking to his men about strangers, out of town partisans to be exact, who had suddenly burst into the station the evening before and started rough-handling them."

"I tell you. Those men, whoever they were, had left quite a chaos behind. Nothing, I tell you nothing was left untouched. All the equipment was destroyed and the police chief and his men, well, they were so badly beaten, I think they'll not soon forget the visit, seeing how awful they looked. Oh, and I've also heard the police chief mock sarcastically about a warning from the strangers, swearing profusely as he spoke about it."

"'Who do they think they are, coming here and telling us what to do? Those...! The nerve of them... Telling us to stop harassing the prisoners... Hmm those...! We'll show them who is running this town. Next time they come, we'll be waiting for them and then we'll show them who's in charge. I told them I will send the Russians after them. Can you imagine they called us criminals...? The Russians are looking for them. I'll tell them they were here. Then we will see who the criminals are. Those...!" Magda mimicked the police chief, over which they all had a good chuckle.

"I just hope that after this they'll let off a little. It sure would be a relief for all of us," Elisabeth commented thoughtfully.

The others nodded in agreement. Happy and amazed that there were Polish partisans fighting on their behalf, against their own Polish countrymen who were creating their own rules.

Yet despite the good news, Katina and the rest of her friends knew it would take some doing on the strangers' part, or anyone else's for that matter, to deter this self-declared chief of police and his men from tormenting and torturing his captives.

Knowing this they decided that it was in their best interest to keep this information to themselves.

Secretly though, Katina was hoping and praying that these kind strangers would succeed in what they had tried to do. For now though, she and all the others in the compound would have to go on and endure what was put upon them. As prisoners they were at the mercy of their captors, for good or bad.

66

As it was the case now, her latest workplace had her digging out potatoes from huge earth mounds, which were used to keep potatoes from freezing during the cold winter months.

The farmer there was an understanding and caring sort who had told her in secret when no one was listening, "Take some potatoes home for your children, but do it in such a way no one else sees you." It seemed to her that he too was afraid of repercussion from the police chief and his men.

Grateful, she thanked him, waiting for the right opportunity near the end of the day. Not to damage her dresses, Elisabeth had given her a well worn light coat. It would come in handy, just the right garment for what she had planned to do. Thinking it over, she tied a twine from a potato sack around her waist and filled as many potatoes as she could in the inside of her upper dress. Tying shut the sleeves of the old coat she also filled them with potatoes. By doing this she succeeded to smuggle quite a few potatoes into the compound for several days. To her dismay though she had been putting them in the cellar where everyone, who had come down to look for food, also helped themselves to her potatoes. Realizing this, she got wise and hid the next batch under her bed. She did not mind sharing and understood everyone was hungry, but her duty was first to her children.

As it was, those who managed to smuggle the little food

they could get into the compound never shared, and those who could not, were at the mercy of whatever remains of old food that was left in the cellar, or whatever food they could salvage from the street. Katina this time chose to share, but only with those she knew. There were her children, Claudia's children and also Klara's daughter, that needed looking after. Many times she had purposely opted to abstain from eating so the children could have a little more to eat.

--

Soon rumors spread through the compound that the Black Sea Germans were to be shipped back to where they had come from in the Ukraine. This news apparently did not sit well with some of them. Yet others were happy to be going home again. But she wondered, after all that had happened to them was there really anything left to go back to? She had her doubts. She for one would not wish to go back and hoped that all of her family had made it to Germany, with the exception of Mark and his family who had decided to remain in Austria. It was Germany that she wanted to go to, God willing, if she and her children were to survive this treacherous ordeal.

--

The threats and warnings to the police chief and his men from the partisans seemed to have made little difference in the way they were treating the prisoners.

Just the other day and for unknown reasons, one of the older men from the Black Sea Germans was brutally tortured and beaten outside the barrack. The poor man had been screaming in agony for hours then suddenly there was a bone-chilling silence... Only the quiet sobbing, from a woman down the hall, was heard. No one had dared to take a peek or come to his rescue. Why this happened, no one knew, and those who knew did not say.

This was proof again to her and all the prisoners, that things had not changed and anytime day or night they were at risk. The stress and strain of the constant danger and upheaval, mixed with hunger and diseases, had manifested itself so deeply into their frayed minds and worn-out bodies, to the point where many a soul just gave up in despair.

She was especially burdened with all the abuse of the children who were taken so far away from the compound. The fear on their faces when they returned, were a haunting reminder of the horrors they endured each and every day.

She felt sorry too for the young women, especially Elisabeth's daughter who was forced to "serve" at the police headquarters. Already Magda had been through a miscarriage, but there was no letting off. So far Rosa and Maria had escaped this burden. But how long before they too, like so many young women, would have to deal with this unwanted burden?

Claudia Ebert, with her pregnancy fully underway, was falling into depression. That, combined with her weakened state, she no longer was capable of looking after herself or her children. She had noticed this as more and more Claudia's children were now left to fend for themselves. She and the group of women in the room did their best to help along and watch over them but it was not easy.

The horrific day to day experiences, day in and day out had left a lasting impression on herself and everyone's mind and body, especially the children. To most, hope had gone and what was left was a perpetual misery, like a thorn that could not be removed.

--

One evening when she had taken a moment to help Claudia with her children, Claudia suddenly felt compelled to talk. All this time she had kept it in. The traumatic events of that time had been too devastating to share. But now she felt she had to tell someone, and this evening when the others had gone for one last trip to the outhouse she took the chance and opened up to Katina. Telling her about the day when they as a family had readied themselves to flee, but were caught in the attempt when the Russian army had overrun the town.

Claudia sat now in the semi darkness of the room and

looked off into the middle distance.

"We were still on our yard when the Russian soldiers overtook our wagon." She paused and took a deep agonizing breath. It was still so painful to talk about it, but she felt she needed to share this. She could not carry this inside any longer.

"They shot my father-in-law in front of me and the children. Then they took the rest of us back to the house."

"There..." Claudia stopped talking and looked down at the floor. Tears filled her eyes but did not fall. "There were fifteen or more men that took turns every night having their way with me."

"It was brutal. I feared for my children. What a thing to witness. I feared my two girls... What if the soldiers...?" She could not finish, blinking back the tears. "This torment is forever in my mind and I can't shed the horrible images. They're like demons haunting my soul and there's no relief. Oh God help me... help my children... my poor children..." Claudia began to weep.

"Now look at me. I'm burdened with this pregnancy. How can I go on...? I wished so much that I could have aborted it." With the back of her hand she wiped part of the tears from her hollow cheeks." Then after a pause she looked up at Katina.

"I was almost tempted to do what some of the Romanian women had done. But then to push a sharp knitting needle into my...? Ugh... Just to think of it sends shivers down my back." She paused for a moment, then with regret in her voice continued.

"You know, I never had the guts to actually go through with it. For fear I might end up bleeding to death like so many back there did. Katina what am I going to do with this child...? As it is there is barely any food for the rest of my children. Never mind milk for the baby once it's here. How will we take care of it? Oh Katina I'm so tired, so tired of going on."

Claudia looked so distraught to Katina who had no words for her friend. She just hugged her quietly. This horrifying ordeal had definitely left a permanent scar on Claudia's whole family.

"I had no idea you've had to go through all this. Oh my God what a thing to endure… and for the children to witness… Claudia, did Lora and Lena ever confess to you that they were also…?"

Claudia cut her off.

"No… Oh no… If they were they never mentioned. Poor children…! I think they did not want to burden me…" She broke down crying as she tried to finish. "Seeing… that I was struggling with my own…" Claudia buried her head into her hands, sobbing.

"I… Elisabeth, Jobina and our families… we've been lucky. We were protected, but you?" she shook her head with deep sadness. "What a terrible plight to go through on top of all these other horrors." Heavy-hearted she stopped right there. It was too much. It pained her terribly. She wished she could do more for Claudia. Physically she and the other woman would not abandon her or her children. But as far as her mental state was concerned, only God could bring healing.

She released a deep sigh, as now she had to carry the burden of knowing. How many more had been caught in this…? 'Oh God… What hardship… What a dilemma…' she lamented in silent thought.

Suddenly a weary thought of Rebekka and Edwina entered her mind. She wondered now of their whereabouts. She prayed they were safe. It would be too much to think they were trapped somewhere in Poland like she and the rest were. How would she find out now? Would she ever know? That thought left her deeply troubled. It was all too much to think about… It was all too much… She needed to be strong for her children, for Claudia and her children as well as for Klara's mother and daughter. She needed to be strong.

67

Early one morning, the rumors about the Black Sea Germans came true. Suddenly large covered trucks made their way toward the prison compound to transport all of the Black Sea Germans to the train station in Kutno. Marianka, caring as she was, realized at once the danger Elisa and Stefan were in. Among all the commotion the two little ones would easily be swept along with the crowd and taken from the compound. She hurried quickly, and to her relief found the two playing in their room. She gathered them in haste and took them to her parent's place where they would be safe. Then in the late afternoon she brought them to Katina's place of work, where she was still working for the farmer. Katina was surprised to see Marianka and her two youngest suddenly show up on the farm. Upon further explanation, she was relieved and thankful for Marianka's quick action to protect her children; and it was here, in passing, Marianka whispered to her about an escape plan.

"As soon as the border patrol has eased," she said quietly upon leaving.

Katina prayed that it would be soon.

Now with the Black Sea Germans gone, the compound looked empty. It stirred a longing in her as well in all the others left behind to be free and go wherever they wished to go. But the reality was it was not theirs to be.

--

Not long after the barracks were filled again and this time with more inter-married Polish-German families. This again gave more opportunity for those in power to loot and seize property. After fleeing to Germany during the war, some of them had now returned back to Poland. Because of overcrowding and shortage of food in Germany, many had returned, thinking they would be safe here. Yet those in power had seen it differently.

To make room for all of them, the original group of captive women and their children were moved out of the barracks and into the main building. This building was mostly unfinished, just as Johann and his men had left it. Being unable to climb stairs Klara's mother and daughter opted to stay in the lower part of the building. Katina, on the other hand, along with her children, Elisabeth with her two daughters Magda and Rosa, Maria and her mother Jobina, as well as Claudia with all of her children, found themselves in the unoccupied attic. Here they discovered two unfinished rooms in the upper corner of the L-shaped building. The larger part of the existing space was still in its raw stage with open rafters and a minimal floor.

It seemed the biggest obstacle that deterred many to take refuge in the higher quarters, was the missing landings of the stairs. The only way up was to swing around the inside post to reach the upper staircase. Katina and the others admitted that it was simply crazy and very dangerous for anyone to dare, especially the children. Most of all they feared that in the darkness of the night someone might slip and succumb to injury or worse.

"If anyone does not pay attention, they'll end up all the way into the basement and that won't be good," she acknowledged to the others, as they stood inspecting the situation.

"Yeah... especially in the dark," Magda put in her comment.

"We will all have to memorize every step and twist of the

stairwell. We also have to watch around the top of the stair, for here the railing is missing," Elisabeth paused to think then spoke again. "One thing is sure. If we find it hard to climb around the stairwell, so will the intruders."

"Just think of it as a security measure, especially at night when this place won't be easily found. At least that's what we hope," Jobina encouraged everyone. "And even the rafters. We could hide deep in the back of the rafters were the men won't find us."

"Maybe now we can relax and sleep better," Maria added her say.

--

As expected on the second night in their new quarters, a drunken Russian soldier followed both of Elisabeth's daughters home from their various workplaces. Once in the building, the two quietly and quickly tried to lose him in the darkness of the corridors. But they did not realize he was following the sound of their footsteps. Not until he stumbled onto the stairs. Alarmed by the sudden noise behind them, the girls quickly headed for the high attic rafters to hide.

Suddenly a painful scream pierced the stillness of the night, followed by a heavy thump. Everyone in the compound held their breath and listened. Then more yells followed, along with the sounds of a body hitting the hard cement stairs all the way down to the basement.

At first she and the others worried it might have been one of their own. But they quickly dismissed it when they heard a man cursing and swearing; his voice echoing along the basement corridor and through the whole complex.

She, as the rest of her friends, had an inkling of what had just happened. For them it was sweet victory, but for the others in the complex, who had no idea what was going on, it sent cold shivers of fear through their bodies thinking that yet another beating or murder was in process, only to find out in the morning what really happened.

The next evening, their hideout up in the attic proved to

be not only dangerous to the unwanted intruders, but also to one of their own. As one dear friend, who tried to flee her pursuer in the darkness, in panic had miscounted the steps and fell all the way down to the basement, breaking both of her arms.

It brought home to everyone. They had to be extra cautious and familiarize themselves more with the dangers of their new quarters.

They also had to keep alert, especially after nightfall, when in the unlit corridors and hidden nooks, doorways and crevasses lurked not only infestations of rats, mice, bedbugs and lice, hunger and multitudes of diseases, but men. Men who took pleasure to hunt down their victims to molest, torture, or even kill, if it so pleased them.

--

Katina and the women in the attic owed it to themselves, but especially their children, to make sure they had all their toiletries. So there was no need to leave the safety of the attic at night, they managed to bring the zinc bathtub upstairs to use it for this particular purpose again. Now they had made the attic as secure as they could, but it was missing the one thing they had in the barracks, an oven to heat water on.

Katina remembered the way Johann and Father Wendel built their kitchen stove out of brick and clay so she decided to try to build something in their quarters. When the opportunity arose, some of the young girls went down with her to the rat-infested creek. There they dug up some clay from the edge of the creek. She then formed the clay into a makeshift stove on the concrete floor, then added a few of the red bricks for stability. They had found the bricks still lying on a pile in front of the main building just where Johann and his men had left them. Once finished, the makeshift stove was about a foot and a half high and two foot deep. It would be big enough to put a tightly twisted bundle of straw into it. After that was done she topped it off with a broken part from a heavy iron stove top which the women had found laying in the yard.

When Elisabeth did the honor to light the stove with some of the leftover straw they had lying about, they were all proud to have accomplished this task. It was not a perfect stove, but it would do. They managed also to salvage the pail and one good size pot from their previous barracks. They were set again to continue their routine of boiling their undergarments to control some of the insect infestations whenever time allowed.

--

Believing that the attic was a safe place was soon dispelled when their pursuers found out how to get around the unfinished stairwell. Frantically the young women and girls took refuge in their usual hiding place, the high attic rafters.

So it was not uncommon that every little stir and noise on the concrete steps was perceived as 'Take cover enemy approaching.'

It happened one evening when Elisabeth had proudly produced a candle she had found and used it to light up the dark attic. By dim candlelight, one by one the women and children took their turn to make the journey to the zinc tub; as it stood outside their rooms across from the open stairwell. While everyone had come and gone, Elisa was unintentionally left alone in the semidarkness to finish up.

Katina had not expected or given much thought on the effect all the previous encounters and mishaps would have on her little girl. But when her ear-deafening scream suddenly pierced the dark stillness of the night, she and everyone else thought the worst. At once the young women ran to the rafters to hide. She and the others braced themselves against intruders.

Elisa's eyes fixed in horror as a large monstrous shadow arose at the end of the hallway. She was traumatized by the sheer sight and was beside herself screaming uncontrollably. When suddenly to everyone's surprise, an alley cat came slinking past them, obviously on her nightly hunt for food.

The light of the candle had enlarged the shadow of the cat to ten times its size as it was coming up the stairs. Spooked by all the commotion, the cat high tailed quickly into a dark corner of the attic.

The effects of all the horrific and terrorizing acts of war had manifested itself so deep in everyone's mind. As she noticed that by the slightest sign of danger they all were easily spooked, just as it showed so vividly tonight.

For a long time after, she held Elisa, trying to calm her as the little one was clinging to her, trembling in fear. Her eyes still fixed bewildered into the eerie darkness of the attic.

The next day everyone in the compound was curious. They all wanted to know what had happened, for all had heard the screams and as usual feared the worst. Upon further explanation they all felt sorry for the little one. They could not help but chuckle when found out an alley cat had been the cause of all the commotion. It felt good for once to laugh and find a moment of lightheartedness amidst all the anxiety.

68

On an evening when the need for another cleansing was required, Katina and the others once again stood heating up water to continue their battle against lice and night crawlers. Again they soaked everyone's hair with petroleum, which Elisabeth had managed to bring home. And as it was their usual ritual they boiled their undergarments; appreciative to have a pot and the makeshift stove.

Yet after all that work of cleansing, Elisabeth was almost immediately infested again, scratching profusely. They were all stunned and dismayed, too tired to go through the whole ritual again. But it had to be done. Elisabeth had to go through the whole process once more, or they all would be reinfested again.

Watching, they all noticed Elisabeth had neglected to take off her knitted woolen bodice. By further inspection they discovered she was unknowingly contributing to the population of these pesky creatures.

"It's a perfect breeding ground, having them so close to your warm body," Jobina commented. "If you keep this up we'll never get rid of them."

"Ooh!" Elisabeth shook herself. "Just to think of it gives me goose bumps."

In disgust she lowered her woolen brassiere carefully into the pot, holding it by her thumb and her index finger, as if to shield herself from having them crawl up her arm. Quickly she proceeded to drop and push it with a wooden stick into the boiling water. "There," she said triumphantly. "I hope this will be the end of them for a while."

They all had a good laugh.

--

Painstakingly they had tried to keep on top of this unpleasant invasion as often as time permitted. Yet if one mother slacked off, like Claudia Ebert with her five children living in the room next to them, it spelled disaster. Especially for her two girls, ages ten and twelve, as the lice had eaten through the skin on top of their head and had created deep ugly puss-filled wounds.

Katina could not stomach to let the two girls suffer any longer and took it upon herself to rid them of their dilemma. And since Elisa had started with the same condition she included her too.

As she had learned from her father, when Johann had suffered from frost boils, she applied the same method here to the girls. But because of the scarcity of lemons she used saltwater. The salt for this Elisabeth had managed to get from her place of work. It certainly was not easy to bear the pain, and she felt bad to administer it, but the girls showed no weakness and held out. To everyone's surprise, within a week there was considerable improvement.

There was one problem though that she did not know what to do about. As it was, little Stefan had developed a black boil underneath his foot and it had become very bothersome for him to walk on. Not knowing how to go about helping her little one she asked the others in her room.

"I heard that it's a sign of typhoid, some call it a death boil," Elisabeth said as she came to take a closer look "Is it any wonder...? With all this rotten food, the poor children need better nourishment. In the barracks, I've heard some children have died just last week from this. And it's not just the children, many of the older ones have suffered the same fate. If that keeps up... we'll be next."

"Elisabeth you know what you're saying? You're telling me... my Stefan is going to die? That is not what I wanted to hear. I'm only asking if anyone knows what to do to get rid of this boil..." she stated teary-eyed, shocked by Elisabeth's statement.

"Well, I'm only telling you what I've heard. I'm sorry for being so blunt, but that's the truth."

"I know you only meant well. It's just... I wasn't ready to be told, or to accept that my son is going to die."

"I fully understand Katina and I'm sorry. But come to think of it, there was something... a home remedy... but I can't seem to recall..." Elisabeth stood looking at the boil.

Suddenly there was movement behind Elisabeth and Jobina came forward.

"I don't know if I should tell you. It might sound peculiar, but back in Romania during the 'Great War' when my sister had come down with the same. My mother was told to catch a frog and cut it open alive and place it on the boil?" Jobina came closer to inspect the boil. "Yes. I would give it a try if I were you. I know it helped my sister."

"Now that you mentioned it, I think that's it, Jobina. How could I have forgotten? It's an old remedy. It's said that frogs contain some special healing quality," Elisabeth came around.

"I'm sorry Katina I shouldn't have been so blunt. We'll help you find a frog tomorrow and try it. I'm sure we'll find plenty here by the creek. Thanks Jobina," Elisabeth acknowledged.

"Yes. Thank you. I really appreciate it," Katina too gave Jobina a thankful nod.

"No thanks necessary... I'm glad to be of help and I hope it'll work."

--

After arriving at the compound the next evening, the women immediately went on a frog hunt and found a large one. Once inside, they all stood around Elisabeth, a little squeamish watching her get ready to perform this delicate operation.

"All right now. I need a little bit more room."

Elisabeth, with an old knife at hand, started to slice into the frog.

"Ugh! You'd think after all we've been through it shouldn't affect me. Ugh!" Jobina shook herself. "I just can't watch. Tell me when it's over," she turned her head to the side.

"It's done Jobina. You can look again," Katina said, holding part of a torn rag ready to wrap around Stefan's foot the minute Elisabeth had placed the still jerking frog under it.

"There now it's done. Now we'll have to wait and see." Elisabeth stood up, proud that once again they had banded together as women. And hopefully again succeeded to beat the odds.

"All I can say, you have been great friends to have at a time like this. I think we have overcome and endured much. If we wouldn't have this bond, I think most of us couldn't have survived all the hardship. I just hope there will be an end soon to all this torment..." her voice broke.

Most had tears in their eyes, and that evening as they all bedded down for the night, there was a warm feeling in their hearts. They indeed had something special. It was the camaraderie that kept them going. Katina was right. Together they had been able to survive, but for how long?

Ten days later and to everyone's surprise, the boil had indeed retreated and disappeared from Stefan's foot.

'Thanks to Jobina for remembering the old remedy and to Elisabeth to perform the whole operation, but most of all thanks to the Lord Almighty,' she rejoiced.

Empowered, she and her friends were now ready to fight on.

69

After another hard day of labor, she and the rest of the women returned once again to their holding place. Yet as soon as they entered the compound, she heard an unprecedented commotion and wailing coming from more than one place. Entering their building she had noticed some women crying inconsolably.

In the lower floor there was an old man of Polish descent called Janke who had married a German woman. He and his wife were among those held here with their eight grandchildren. He had looked at her then shook his head. She had just seen him in passing but never spoke with him.

"A Russian truck came by today. The soldiers ran out and grabbed any young boys they could find and loaded them into the back of the truck. They drove away before anyone could do anything. You too have a young boy?" he questioned.

She could not answer. Fearing the worst she made her way quickly up the stairs and around the missing landings. The sound of wailing from the lower floor was strong in her ears. She could hardly breathe. The angst in her heart was overbearing.

At the top of the stairs she found her group of women talking heatedly. There was also Elisa and Stefan. She ran and hugged them both crying, relieved they were unharmed.

"I am so glad you are safe," she cried out.

"I saw the truck come and the men get out," Elisa spoke

excitedly. "I tried to shoo the other kids into the building but they would not listen to me. So I grabbed Stefan, and Karl and Albert came too. We were hiding down in the cellar till it was safe to come out."

Chills went down her spine when she realized that she too could have been one of the mothers who had lost their little boys. It was almost unbelievable that Elisa had sense enough to react so quickly to save her little brother and Claudia's two youngest. In awe over her daughter's quick reaction, she praised her and hugged them both, glad they were safe. Yet she was deeply saddened for the other mothers, who were in deep agony over this unbelievably cruel act.

She could not imagine herself being in their predicament. What sorrow... What unimaginable grief... How can one try to console and comfort such a loss? All she and others could do was to quietly be there and hold the sobbing and wailing mothers, who were beside themselves with grief.

For some reason, she suddenly thought of the young group of twelve year old boys that had been stationed with a couple of seasoned Russian veterans that night in their home. Who exactly where they? Could it be that they too had been kidnapped and were trained to become soldiers? She shuddered at this grim thought.

Now even more, she was worried for all of them. Had their rescuer, the gallant Russian Commandant, moved on? This thought gave her, as well as the others, great concern. All they could do now was to hope the partisan strangers, to the best of their ability, would still be there to help and protect them.

--

It was only a few days later when after returning late from work duty she found Elisa lying in bed trembling and shivering from excruciating pain. Her face was beaten unrecognizable and her little body covered with black bruises. Her heart broke at the sight of her little daughter. She could not contain the tears as they flowed down her face and onto Elisa's bruised body. Desperately she tried to ease her little one's pain by applying cold water soaked rags on her sores. The thought of an escape became more and more prominent. How she longed for an end to all this suffering?

"Somehow, somewhere God will open a door," she told herself, hoping, praying and believing that it will be soon.

Later old Father Janke informed her that while the children were playing outside some of the young teenage Polish thugs came into the yard harassing and beating the children.

"I told them to leave them alone, but they didn't listen," he said dismayed, then continued. "Elisa in her protective way tried to gather the children and urge them to run to the safety of the buildings. She stood between the children and these youth. But by doing so she took the brunt of the thugs' fury. I ran toward them and told them to stop. With their boots they kicked her viciously, until finally they left her alone and walked away. When I got to her she lay on the ground moaning in pain. I helped her up and aided her up the stairs to your room where she crawled into bed and stayed there."

Old Janke hung his head and turned as if to go, then put his hand on the wall nearest him.

"It's just awful, just awful," he shook his head repeatedly then turned again to face her and this time there was a fire in his eyes.

"But I tell you something Katina," his voice suddenly changed with gratifying conviction, waving his index finger as he spoke.

"This power the police chief and his men think they have will only be temporary. It will not last. And...," he pointed with his thumb over his shoulder toward the town. "In all seriousness, just wait and you'll see the full power of the Russians. In due time the truth will come out and the turmoil you see here is only the beginning." He wiped his brow as he spoke. This topic had him so aggravated that he had to wipe

414

more than once. After a moment of silence, he continued.

"Yes," he nodded with assurance. "Just wait and see. Everything I have told you will come to pass and then we'll see who's in control." He paused again to collect his thoughts. Then with a knowledgeable undertone he continued.

"I for one will probably not live to see the day. But then, who knows...?" he shrugged his shoulders. "It might come sooner then we think..."

She went away thinking about what old Janke had told her. Sadly she knew she could not protect her children from all the terrors of the day or of the future. The only thing left for her was to hope there will be an end to all of this soon.

70

One evening in the chill of October, Claudia's time to deliver had come. Elisabeth had asked her to stand by to aid her in the birthing, while Jobina and Magda boiled the water needed for washing and cleaning up. Maria and Rosa took care of all the children in the adjacent room. As Elisabeth had predicted, the little one came into the world with no complications. His little body looked frail and his skin very wrinkly, not what one would expect from a healthy newborn. This was understandable as Claudia herself, like everyone else, had lacked the proper nourishment. Elisabeth did what she knew best and cleaned up both of them as good as possible. Then she bundled the little one in a blanket and laid it beside Claudia. In her already weakened state Claudia looked at the tiny bundle unattached, as if it was a foreign object. When Elisabeth saw how Claudia reacted toward the baby, she gently coaxed her on.

"Claudia. Try to breastfeed the little one."

Claudia stared at the baby again then at Elisabeth with an indifferent lost look in her eyes.

"What are we going to do?" Katina asked, scared for the baby, as well as for Claudia.

"There's nothing we can do... We've no bottle or milk to give to this little one." She threw Katina a sorrowful look, shaking her head. "There's absolutely nothing we can do."

The others heard Elisabeth's comment, came near and stood at the doorway with tears in their eyes. Earlier on,

416

I WILL REMEMBER ALWAYS

Katina had briefly filled them in about Claudia's unfortunate story. Now they stood overwhelmed at the sorrow. Not just for Claudia and the little one, but for the rest of her children. As they, most of all, felt the burden and pain of their mother's indifferent state of mind.

Quietly Claudia's children slipped into the room and surrounded their mother looking shyly at their new baby brother who was crying.

"May I hold him?" Lora asked Elisabeth, who just nodded overwhelmed like the rest at this heartbreaking scene. When the baby continued to cry, Elisabeth coaxed her.

"Just let him suckle on your small finger," she encouraged. Maybe he'll quiet down a little," she said again, but then added a little distraught. "What he needs is his Mama's milk and that's... That as we all can see, is impossible considering her condition. So for now we can do nothing but to stand by and try our best to be there for both of them." With a somber look she gave a glance toward the other women in the room. They all knew what she meant.

Quietly Katina helped tuck in Claudia and laid the baby close to her for warmth. Just then Claudia reached over to Katina and held her by her arm with an anxious expression in her eyes. There were no words, but Katina knew the look. "Don't worry... Hush now and don't worry..."

Claudia gave a look toward the baby and held her gaze there for a moment, then turned away staring into the darkness of the attic.

One by one, they all had made a last visit to the zinc bathtub, then Elisabeth, being one of the last to go, blew out the candle they had burning near the stairwell. Settling in they all knew that with the babies cry and all that had been going on, sleep would not come easy.

Weary and worn Katina let her head sink deep into the musty smelling pillow. Despite its repulsive odor she welcomed to lay on it, hoping now they could get at least some time to sleep. Lucky for all of them after an hour of crying, exhausted, the little one fell asleep for half of the night.

In the morning when the women and the older children were picked up for work, Claudia sat at her bedside detached as the little one beside her kept crying, hungry for food and his mother's loving touch. Even their captors did not dare take her away to work seeing the state she was in. One of them signaled to the other, indicating with his hand to the side of his forehead that she had gone mad and to leave her. The lost look in her eyes was an indication and proof of this conclusion.

With every day the baby's cry became weaker and weaker until it finally faded away.

Soon after that the baby died.

The dead body of the baby was taken by the women and placed in a special room, where all the dead bodies had been gathered and placed. From there their captives took the deceased and buried them in unknown mass graves.

Sadly though, for the rest of her children, Claudia remained in her state of dejection.

It had been heart wrenching to hear the little baby's agonizing cries and they were all relieved to see him pass away, knowing that he was at peace. As for the rest of them, life as hard and bitter as it was still had to go on.

Katina, and rest in their group, now more than ever, felt the necessity to look after Claudia and her children, but that task was not an easy one, as they were all in want of food and whatever there was, was not enough for the whole lot of them.

It was to her relief when she was assigned to work in a kindergarten nearby the complex. Here, she was to help with cleaning up and serving food for the Polish children. When after a few days of observing a lot of leftover barley soup and crusts of unfinished bread going to waste, she took heart and asked the teacher if she would be allowed to take the leftover food to the compound for her children. The teacher, who had been kind to her, willingly granted her wish, but she warned it was to be done only under strict and utmost secrecy.

She promised and set out on her usual daily chores of drawing and carrying well water to and from the compound to the kindergarten. Hiding the pails high enough under the cover of her large shawl, she was able to transport the precious morsels back and forth without drawing suspicion on herself. In doing so, she soon realized that it took too much time out of her regular work schedule. She needed someone in the compound to help her distribute the food.

On previous occasions she had found herself talking often to old Father Janke. Today she met him and his wife standing on the front steps of the building watching over their small grandchildren. As she was about to enter the building they started to talk to her telling her of their own dilemma.

They told her of their daughter who had foolishly left with a Russian officer who apparently had promised her marriage.

"Sometime later we got a letter from her, begging us to rescue her..." Mother Janke was crying, overcome with sadness.

"As it was... after arriving in Russia she found herself abandoned far into the Siberian tundra, where she was forced into hard labor, working in a mine," Father Janke's voice quavered as he finished the sentence. "But sadly there was little we could do to help her." He paused to wipe away a tear. "Now we're left looking after all her children and you know how hard it is to feed eight hungry mouths. It is almost impossible, but we do what we can..."

Hearing this she suddenly felt compelled to help. "You know I have some leftover food from the kindergarten. And I was just about to go upstairs and give it to my two little ones as well as Claudia's two youngest." She paused, thinking.

"But as it is I'm pressed for time and I wondered... Would you...? I know it won't be enough to satisfy all their hunger. But could you take it upon yourselves and divide it evenly between your grandchildren and Claudia's two youngest, as well as my two little ones? There's the barley soup…"

She just lifted her shawl for them to see the pail with the soup in it. "If you have a pot to pour the soup in, that would be helpful. I need the pail to carry the water back to the kindergarten? Oh… and here are some bits and pieces of leftover bread. You can divide them also between the children."

Father and Mother Janke's mouth dropped at the sight of the soup and the morsels of bread.

"Yes, we'll gladly do this. Thank you for sharing this with our grandchildren. No need to worry. We'll make sure they'll get their share evenly."

"Keep it to yourselves though. I don't want others to hear about this. As you can see it's hardly enough for our children," she cautioned both of them to which they gladly agreed.

"We'll gather them all into our room, as there they'll be out of sight. I also have some bowls and spoons for the soup. The bowls are a little chipped but they'll do. Father, will you go and gather the children, while Katina and I go inside and put out the bowls?" Mother Janke asked her husband in a hushed voice.

Seeing that everything was under control Katina retrieved the pail from Mother Janke and made her way out again. In passing, with the children behind him, Father Janke thanked her again quietly. One more last hug to Elisa and Stefan as they ran up to her and then she was off again, trying to make up for lost time. She herself had dared to take only a few bites of bread. She wanted the children to have most of it.

--

This arrangement was heaven sent. But unfortunately it did not last, as after a month she found herself reassigned to another job.

This time she was told to work in the mill alongside Elisabeth and her youngest daughter Rosa. But here… there was no food to take home… not even a cup of flour.

To her dismay, Elisa and little Stefan found out where she was working. Repeatedly, against her stern warnings not to do so, they ventured out of the compound and sat in front of the mill waiting for her to come out. It broke her heart to see them sitting on the sidewalk, hungry and cold with only minimal clothing to cover their shivering little bodies. It was all that was left for them after the takeover. She worried now about the youths on the street and wanted Elisa and Stefan in the compound where at least they could be watched by the Jankes.

On occasion her work took her past the front window. From time to time she watched them as they scoured the area for morsels of discarded food. She herself was not given any food or drink. So she could not pass anything out to them or even acknowledge that she was aware of their presence. It was heart wrenching to see her little ones in this state. How she yearned to go out and comfort them, but she was not allowed to do so.

With a painful sigh she went about her work, worrying about them and praying for their safety. When she looked for them at closing time, she had noticed them gone. 'How terrible, deserted and lonely they must feel,' she thought, mournfully.

Once, she and the other women prisoners had returned from a grueling day at work, she found little Elisa again in bed, brutally beaten. With deep sadness she held her little daughter and tended to her as best as she could.

"Did they come into the yard again?" she asked Elisa while holding the cold compress on her bruises.

"No Mama... They were by the gate when Stefan and I came back. We were looking for you and couldn't find you," Elisa paused, and then changed the subject. Proudly telling her what she had discovered.

"Stefan and I and the other children were playing by the drive-through garage. I saw a hen walking around in the straw clucking. I watched her sit in the corner. We all went to play in the muddy creek and watch the water rats. After that I went back to the garage and found two eggs in the straw where the hen had been.

"Mama I took the eggs and ran with Stefan up to our room," Elisa told her all excited. "Then I took some of the straw that was lying outside our room and started a fire in the stove," she said proudly.

"You started a fire in the stove?" She could not believe what she was hearing. "With what...?"

"With the matches I found laying on top the rafters not far from the straw!" Elisa said so matter-of-factly, knowing that everybody knew where the matches were hidden. She just shook her head as Elisa went on.

"I cracked the eggs right on top the stove. Then I took the old spoon that was lying near the stove and scraped the eggs off." With a sheepish smile she reached down and produced the metal spoon from under the bed, still showing traces of the egg yolk. She then glanced over to the stove and saw remnants of baked on eggs.

"I gave Stefan one to eat and I ate the other. Mmm... it tasted so good Mama. I'm going to watch the hen again. Maybe I'll get more eggs. I'll leave one for you next time. Is that alright Mama?" she questioned innocently.

That's alright with me. But be careful and watch out for those boys. Don't let them see you take the eggs. She said with concern, knowing also with all the hungry people around the chicken most likely won't survive.

She had to smile at Elisa's ingenuity. She was surprised how her little one had all this time observed and learned from her and the others how to use the make-shift stove. How she had managed this without burning the place down was amazing to her. Concerned though, she gave Elisa strict warning to be careful.

"You know Elisa I would rather if you wait for us grownups to light the fire. With all the straw around, this place can go up in flames and then we have no where to

I WILL REMEMBER ALWAYS

stay and no bed to sleep on. And you wouldn't want that to happen, do you?"

"Uh-Uh... No Mama I don't. I promise not to do it again," Elisa consented with seriousness in her face.

Giving another cold compress to her little daughter's bruises she was amazed over Elisa's boldness. To go outside the compound despite the warning not to and it worried her greatly. She thought of Julia and the other older children. By now they would have reached the town and were well on their way to the compound. With this thought she quickly tucked the two little ones into bed and asked Jobina to keep watch over them. Then she made her way down to join the other mothers to meet up with their children.

It happened lately more and more that their original captors slacked off and let individual Polish farmers who wanted workers come into the compound and take children to work for them. Come evening most of them were left to make their own way back home. Yet what was even more worrisome, in some cases the children were held and kept for days. As Julia mentioned that the farmer she worked for repeatedly told her that she should stay overnight. But his son had warned her against it. Julia knew why and heeded the son's warning. She had also realized that on occasions the farmer had a tendency to become violent.

'It's no wonder his wife and daughters left him,' she thought as she recalled what Julia had told her. Knowing all this was another thing that laid heavy on her mind.

She and all the other mothers were concerned for their children, especially with all the dangers that lurked in the dark of night. Yet she was glad that Julia and Claudia's kids, as well as Anna, were among those who were still able to come home. As difficult as it was it felt good to know; once they arrived home they were safe at least for another night.

71

The weather outside had changed and the mellow sunny and rainy days of fall had long gone and another cold and harsh winter was upon them. Because of lack of proper food and sanitation she noticed more and more the prison population decreasing. The typhoid and other diseases were taking their toll on the sick and starving. But if she entertained the thought that things could not get worse, she was mistaken.

As she and the rest of the prisoners would find out the following night. What they had feared had come to pass. There had been a change in the Russian commanding position for this region. And the new commander was rumored to be more of a brutal and uncaring sort. This was a standard obviously adopted and passed on to his troops, unlike the ones of the previous gallant commander. And it was on this night when the prisoners in the Quadenstadt compound became aware of this change.

Just when everyone in the compound had settled in, she and the others suddenly heard a loud commotion of screaming and yelling. They could hear profanities that brought everyone to their feet. The loud commotion came from the lower level of their building. Then suddenly the screams and angry shouts moved outside to the center of the yard.

"What's going on?" she whispered to the others, scared as they all huddled together, each holding on to their loved ones. For hours screams of agony coming from a man were heard. The darkness and not knowing what was happening gave way to greater anxiety and everyone was praying for this ordeal to end.

Come morning the full damage was revealed. The Janke's room, the only room with a door and the closest located to the entrance of the building, had been targeted. Russian soldiers apparently had banged at their door to gain entrance. Old Father Janke, fearing for the women and in the room, held the door shut until they all had successfully escaped through the open windows.

To her surprise old Father Janke asked for her the next morning. Upon entering she noticed him brutally bruised from the beatings he had received. He had trouble breathing as he spoke. Still, he took great effort to tell her the whole story.

"Suddenly, a huge rock came hurling through, smashing a gaping hole into the door. In a raging fury, they beat me and tore my clothes off. They dragged me outside into the cold winter night, where I was beaten again and again. They plunged me over and over into the icy cold well water." With trembling hands Father Janke wiped the tears from his wrinkled face. Obviously, this horrifying ordeal had left him scared and very shaken. With a painful expression on his face, he spoke again.

"When they finally had enough... they left me... lying in the snow... where my wife and the others found me." Overwhelmed, he broke down in front of her.

She was shocked to see this dear friend in such a state, his face and body swollen to the point where he was almost unrecognizable. But why of all people had he asked her to come and see him?

"Get rid of your leather boots, at once," he told her, almost begging her.

"My boots...?" she was perplexed and stunned.

"Yes, they wanted to know where the woman with the

boots was. They apparently saw you yesterday." He held his stomach, as it gave him pain even to talk.

"Apparently... they saw you yesterday... when you were... coming home from work... wearing your boots. They beat me... again and again..." he lamented. "But I didn't... I wouldn't..." he spoke with defiance. "I wouldn't... I couldn't tell them..." he added with a quiver in his voice. "I had to protect you..."

"Oh my dear, dear friend..." Katina broke down sobbing, with much sorrow. "I can't bear to think..." she shook her head in disbelief. "Because of me you had to go through this hell. What can I say? I'm so sorry... so very sorry. I shouldn't have worn them. How naive of me to think no one would notice. You risked your very own life to protect me."

She cried.

"How can I ever repay you?" she said overwhelmed with grief and guilt over all the suffering she had caused this dear friend.

"There, there, don't be dismayed. God willing..." he took a deep but painful breath. "I will... recover soon... You've been kind... to our grandchildren," he paused for a moment, fighting to gain control over the pain. "I did no more... than any other decent... human being would have done," he spoke to her in a comforting way, seeing how distraught she was.

"Thank you... Thank you for what you've done for me," she said wiping her eyes with the back of her hand. "I'll do as you've told me. I'll get rid of them today! They'll never see me wearing them again," she solemnly promised.

As she made her way back to their room up in the attic, she thought back. The boots had been a gift from Johann, along with the dress material he had sent on that fateful day from the Kutno train station.

"Nevertheless it had to be done. The pain and suffering this poor man had to go through just because of these boots," she scolded herself. "I've got to get rid of them, but how?" she contemplated as she sat on her bed and proceeded to take off her boots.

On the way to their various work places, she hid them under her coat so no one could detect them. Elisabeth had kindly given her a pair of old shoes to wear instead, which she had kept all this time under her mattress for safe keeping.

Once at the work place, she tried her best to bargain with the owner of the mill, to trade her boots for some flour. But she was very discouraged when she saw how little she got in return. She had expected a little more than a handful of flour to come out of this deal. Upset, she swallowed her disappointment.

"Better a little than nothing, at least no one will be looking for them anymore," she said resigned.

72

The winter cold had come upon them. And with it she had noticed herself getting weaker and weaker. She was still restricting her food intake to have enough for her children. Yet that was not the only reason why she was eating less. Just smelling the stench from the dead and dying people around them and seeing daily their open puss-filled wounds, made her stomach turn and reject even the smallest morsel of food. The battle against all the infestations, hunger and unsafe living conditions never seemed to cease.

One case in particular she could not put out of her mind. Because of cholera, a sister of old Mother Janke had to sleep in the adjacent room, close to the main entrance. For weeks her strength had been fading and she had become bedridden and dependent on others. One could see the outline of her tiny almost lifeless body lying underneath a well worn wool blanket on top of a neatly piled up heap of straw. Because there was no door, at night her weak voice would echo through the corridors, as she was calling out to her sister for a sip of water. She remembered vividly the pleading almost begging calls that kept haunting her.

"Matilda... Matilda... I am thirsty... Matilda... Water... Please Matilda... A cup of water... Please Matilda..." It was heart wrenching to hear her begging in a painful agonizing voice, again and again.

Everyone was scared and dared not to come out of their

quarters in the darkness of night. Yet some brave soul always did just that and came to the poor woman's aid. A couple nights later, while she was calling, intruders in their drunken state attacked and beat her terribly. They threw her down the concrete stairs into the basement and left her there to die. The morning revealed her sad fate. To everyone's horror, a moving mass of lice covered her whole body as well as the straw heap she had been placed on. It was an unbelievably shocking site to see.

And these were the images she and all of the other inhabitants of this compound had to observe and deal with on a daily basis. It was very discouraging and almost next to impossible to keep one's spirit up.

As it was, Klara's mother now too was sick and lying among the almost dead corpses. She had tried to aid her as much as she could but had found it hard now in her weakened state. Whenever possible, she had shared the few meager rations with her and Anna, which she and Julia had managed to bring home. That was all she could do. She purposely kept most of the food for the children, as it was hard for her to see them go hungry to bed and not be able to do something about it.

Anna, the poor girl had begged her now that her grandmother was dying, not to forsake her. She feared to be left alone, to be taken away and no one will know where she was.

This plea lay heavy on Katina's heart, she felt for the girl. She had to help her. She had promised it to her mother and grandmother. She would have to make room for her in their upstairs quarters.

"Oh God help...," she prayed that Elisabeth and Jobina and their daughters would still stand by her and help her. I'm sure they would, she reassured herself, but still it was overwhelming.

She never thought that Klara's mother would die and leave her with Anna. She had her own and Claudia's children to consider. Now one more...?

"I don't know dear God... I don't have the strength to..."

Suddenly overcome with sleep, her tired mind, exhausted from all the responsibilities, just shut off. She felt herself drifting into a much needed sleep.

The coming evening the inevitable happened. After coming back from an exhausting day of work, she collapsed as she was about to enter their room in the attic. While she lay in an unconscious state on the floor, Elisabeth and Magda stood over her, massaging her till she regained consciousness.

"You were lucky this time Katina!" Elisabeth exclaimed. "Next time we might not be able to revive you and what will happen then to your children, hmm...? I have enough with my own. I can't take care of more!" Elisabeth said in a joking manner but with a concerned undertone.

"Come what may, I am going to tell them to let you rest," she retorted, talking about those responsible for picking up the women for work duties.

Morning came and after a lot of profound swearing, the men finally gave in. "But only for a day... that's it."

Elisabeth had succeeded.

Luckily, and thanks to Elisabeth, within a couple of days her place of employment had changed. This time she was called to work for a Polish doctor and his Russian wife. Both of them took pity on her when at mealtime they had offered her food and she could not eat. Away from prying eyes, the doctor gave her a small drink of vodka.

"Here..." he said. "A little of this everyday with a little bit of food and you'll soon feel better."

She was thankful. God had intervened again, with Elisabeth's help of course. He had made it possible for her to come to this place. Grateful, she thanked both the doctor and his wife for their kindness. She could not believe that once again, among supposedly bitter enemies. There were people like she and Johann, who went against the orders and showed compassion.

--

It was the twenty-second of December and thoughts of Christmas were on everyone's mind. The town's people were all getting prepared for a joyful Christmas with family and friends. The prisoners perceived that things were beginning to look a little brighter for the Polish inhabitants. So in the spirit of the season, the women and their children up in the prison attic rooms also tried to make the best out of this situation and prepared to celebrate. They had been given a few days off from their drudging work routines and that in itself was a reason to celebrate. It was indeed a welcome and much needed rest to everyone involved.

The young girls had made it their task to bring a little Christmas tradition into their quarters. All excited to have found a dry old branch from the yard they began to decorate it with eagerness. As they had seen it, it seemed to have been lying out there throughout the years, just waiting for this special moment. Now it would shine and bring hope and joy to the seemingly forgotten and forsaken.

Upon leaving, the German Army had thrown all their leftover office papers into one particular room near the drive-through garage. Stacked up to the ceiling it was an unimaginable untapped treasure. To the delight of the children, one window had been tampered with by a previous intruder, and that made it easier to climb through and retrieve this immeasurable find. With a pair of scissors the girls created all sorts of toys for their younger siblings. That, to everyone's relief kept them occupied and playing contently for days.

The art of converting these plain sheets of paper into beautiful crafted three dimensional Christmas stars was taught to the younger ones. These ornaments were then hung with much joy and enthusiasm on the dry branch until it was totally covered.

On that holy night, they had brought Claudia into their

room with her children and Anna, too, had joined them. Sadly her grandmother had died and she was now alone. They all sat around on their beds or straw heaps. Hungry and without a morsel of food to quiet the overwhelming gnawing in their bellies, but celebrate they did. The makeshift stove in the room gobbled up more straw than intended. They had hoped it would last at least long enough to warm their otherwise cold and damp quarters, but that was wishful thinking seeing how quickly it burned. Their lowly Christmas tree heard the old familiar songs and carols resound throughout the hollow attic walls. Familiar songs they all knew so well, among them 'Silent Night'.

Suddenly one by one, overwhelmed by grief, their voices faded, instead of singing their room was filled with sobbing. Even the older children were affected and started to cry.

Remembering their sorrow and grief over lost loved ones and missing the togetherness of family was just too much to take. Without their husbands, fathers, mothers, siblings, grandparents and some of their children, there was no joy in celebrating. It was a painful reminder that brought home again the desolate state they all found themselves in.

This was the first Christmas since the Russians swept through Poland. Although to them it seemed like such a long time ago.

Long after the embers in their makeshift stove had ceased to glow. And everyone had gone to bed; the darkness of night once again engulfed the rooms in the attic. Katina lay awake. The air in their quarters had dropped to an uncomfortable frigid level. Everybody had bundled up with whatever they could find and crawled into bed or straw heaps trying to keep warm. She could feel Stefan cuddling close to her, the same with Julia and Elisa. To add more warmth she had thrown the old coat and her large shawl over the existing small feather comforter. It unfortunately barely covered her and her children. To have Elisa in bed was a definite plus in this cold winter weather. Her warm and often sweaty body felt like a hot water bottle to the rest of them. Although in the heat of summer no one wanted to sleep next to her. She smiled at that thought as now they were all appreciative of her warmth.

She could hear Elisabeth turning, thinking that she too must be lying awake. But she dared not to ask for fear of waking the others. Outside, a cold wintry wind blew snowflakes against the window, adding a new fresh layer over the already deep piles of snow. It would make it even harder to walk through, especially with their scarcely covered feet.

'Elisabeth's shoes will not be the best or warmest to walk through the snow. It was too bad what had happened. It would have been great to have the boots now. They would keep my feet nice and warm, but...' She stopped herself abruptly, almost scolding herself, to think this way.

'Stop thinking about it...' she reprimanded herself again. 'What was...was. And besides, it had to be done. At least now nobody would be hunting for them, and no one would have to go through what my dear friend had to.'

But the thoughts did not cease and sleep reluctantly evaded her tormented mind. She tossed her head back and forth, recalling the events of the evening and how it affected everyone. In all this time of imprisonment they had endured work from early morning until the late hours of the evening and there had been very little time to think or reflect. She, like the rest of the women, had done what was forced upon them and worked, 'like zombies,' she thought. How they had survived all this time was a miracle in itself.

Her heart ached for her children and all the other children, as they too, like the rest of them, had suffered much. She nestled closer to them, smelling the pungent odor of the petroleum stained bedding. That was mixed with the stinky sweat of unwashed bedding and clothing and the heavy layer of dust from the disintegrating straw. She could feel her side of the pillow cold and uncomfortably wet from the tears she had shed.

Once again she unlocked memories of happier times, which she had kept tucked away in her heart. She recalled Johann's gentle voice, when he had whispered words of comfort to her the last time they had spent together. She relished in this thought a little longer, gently overcome with sleep she closed her eyes.

The snow that had fallen during the night had left a foot deep layer on top of the existing one. 'It would definitely make the necessary chores even harder,' she thought to herself. 'And anyone, especially the children, had no business venturing outside unless they had to. It was best to stay inside where the cold was not quite as harsh.'

While the children played with their paper cutouts. The women busied themselves heating water for boiling and washing everyone's under garments and hanging them around the stove to dry. 'It felt good to get at least partly cleaned up for the New Year...' she sighed, hoping it will bring changes and relief from their desperate situation.

--

On New Year's Day, news swept like wild fire through the compound. It was said that in the early morning hours, right outside the prison compound, heavily intoxicated from partying all night, the police chief and his wife had been on their way home and when crossing the bridge the horses suddenly spooked. He apparently was thrown out of the coach and under the wagon wheels where one of them crushed his neck.

Most of the prison inhabitants saw it as an act of God and rejoiced in this revenge. For he and his sons had been part of the Polish men terrorizing them since the beginning.

Days later the report came again through Magda, that the official's sons were very shocked and sobered up by this tragedy.

Everyone in the compound now hoped that this mishap would bring about a change in their adversaries behavior and relieve some of the miseries and sufferings they had caused to so many of the captured.

73

The winter months dragged on and Katina found it hard to cope with the daily grind of work. On one icy wintry morning she was pushed and fell on the slippery entrance stairs of the prison complex. It happened when she and other women were again forcefully and maliciously escorted out of the complex to their various workplaces.

She remembered vividly how the Polish man stood enraged as he cracked his whip angrily over her. She had expected it to hit hard on her already weak and painful body, but for some reason the furious man had held back. Instead he lashed out in indignant and hateful curses. But try as she might all the fury of his words and actions could not bring her to her feet. Left on the stairs, she dragged herself to her quarters and with Elisa's help she tended to her wounds as best as she could. Unwillingly she prepared herself mentally and physically to face the same hostility the next morning.

Since that day, the sores on her knees would not heal and had made the slightest movement unbearable. Her overall health had been in a rapid decline and the fear for her children had become more profound. As without her they would be left in the hands of merciless strangers. Or did she dare to hope that the Slovaks would rescue them and take them into their home? But even this thought did not ease her concern. She tried her best to hide her anguish and fear from her little ones. At night, when she thought no one was watching and listening, she let her tears flow freely into her pillow.

Overwhelmed by her weakness and helplessness, she was provoked again in seeking for an escape. But she knew in her heart that this was only possible with God's help. She would also need the Slovaks help to escape. But she had to rely on God, for without His protection and guidance all attempts of going ahead with this plan would be in vain.

The fear for her children's safety and wellbeing had haunted her from the onset of imprisonment. It was her greatest agony not to be able to be there for them. Prayers were the only solace she had to be content with. She especially worried for Elisa and Stefan. As now more than ever, when left alone, they were still in this dangerous habit of wandering out of the premises in search for her, Julia or any familiar face.

More than once she was made aware that they had been at Pani Slovak's sister's house, near the prison compound. To Elisa it had become a familiar place, where over the last few months she had ventured to beg for food and came back with slices of bread or on occasion even a small loaf of bread tucked under her torn and tattered garments.

She was dismayed over this and had warned Elisa not to do this but felt powerless to enforce it. She knew of the loneliness and hunger her children had to go through. It was a force so strong that her determined little girl would repeatedly risk being caught and exposed to cruel beatings from the youth in the town.

In her weary mind she often pondered how this child of hers, who had endured more than her share of punishment and mishaps, could dismiss all danger to herself in order to look after her and her little brother's needs, as well as other children in the prison compound. It was of great relief to her, that whenever Elisa and Stefan had wandered out of the compound, Pani Slovak's sister had lately taken it upon herself to keep the two at her house until she, herself, was released from work duty.

Without her knowing, God in His ultimate wisdom had a plan. She soon realized, because of this contact, there was hope in establishing secret communication between them. It proved true, when she received the news the following day that the border patrol was still under heavy observation. A little dismayed about this information, she reserved herself to be patient and not to let this report get her down.

--

Winter had given way to spring and once again the warm sun penetrated the dark and musty corridors of the prison complex. She felt her spirit lifted and sensed the same in others too. She could even see a slight change in Claudia's depressive mood, as on occasions she showed to be a little bit more positive. But it was not enough to fully take charge again of her family.

It was the first day of May and the sun shone bright. The sky was blue and not a cloud was seen. Katina let out a long and heavy sigh. How beautiful it would be just to take the day off and spend time with her children, with no one to order her around.

It would be absolutely wonderful, so carefree. It had been so long. She would not even know how it felt to relax and do nothing, absolutely nothing. She let her mind drift... to dream. A sudden noise of a door closing interrupted her. Reality sank in that it could only be a dream. Dismayed and unwilling, she pushed herself to do the chores before her.

She heard the May Day parade pass by and stole a look out of the window. The entire town's people seemed to be out on the street. They marched in their colorful native costumes with much fanfare in music and singing. She watched with delight and remembered the same jubilation and celebration in times gone by.

Suddenly she stopped in her gaze with disbelief, for there among the merry crowd walked the woman from her former homestead. She could not help but release a chuckle. Of all things, the woman was wearing one of the silk nightgowns Johann had given Katina.

"I guess it looks beautiful enough to be worn at this time of day and what better way to show it off. Well whatever tickles her fancy," she chuckled again shaking her head at the audacity of this woman to be so bold. No doubt she was proud, holding her head up high. She walked along with an air of certain haughtiness.

"At least she's happy," she sighed, indifferent to see her property paraded on someone else's body. What did it matter anyway? It was of no importance if they were or were not in her possession. The situation as it was she would gladly trade them in for her and her children's freedom. How lovely it would be to join in the gaiety of this moment. Painfully... she took a long drawn deep breath then surrendered it with a downcast heart.

For her and the other prisoners, not much had changed, as it was still the same grind, day in day out, of enforced labor. Yet ever so slightly she noticed an unnerving change within the prison walls, as more and more women with their children were taken completely out of the compound to be used as slave labor on large farms and homesteads. It would make it much harder, or next to impossible, for anyone to escape.

With this move, she as well as the others around her felt the loss of the many familiar friends. As a group they had supported and encouraged each other often. Instead now, their empty rooms were filled more and more with interracial families. And to add to their displeasure, because of the safe location of their attic rooms, she and the other women and children who had sought refuge there were forced down to the more unpleasant dark and unprotected musty smelling quarters in the basement.

Again they found a large room that was big enough to house all of the women and the children from the attic. As depressing and dank the location, they were comforted that at least some in their group of friends with families were still here. Only Anna, who, to everyone's horror and dismay, had not come back to the complex a few nights earlier. This worried all of them as they had no idea what had happened to the child. Was she still alive? Katina especially was very concerned for her.

But there was absolutely nothing she and the others could do but to keep on going. It was enough to worry for one's family, never mind worrying about others. As painful as it was, they just had to leave Anna, as well as themselves, in the hands of the Almighty.

There was only one thought in her mind and that was not to lose hope, but to carry on as best as she could. Mechanically, she and the others went about the usual ritual to protect themselves against unwanted intruders, which especially here in this dark basement felt more foreboding than in their attic hideout. Their trusted large zinc tub once again found its use and was placed at night across the doorway.

Unfortunately, here again she found her and her children's sleeping spot near the entrance. She knew it would make it a very dangerous and uncomfortable place to be, but she was not about to argue.

As usual, late in the evening after work, she and the women, who had children taken away to work for farmers, still continued to band together and slip quietly out of the compound under the cover of darkness to meet up with them. Scared and terrified, most of the children started to cry when their mothers came in sight. Quickly they were comforted and hushed to be quiet. She too shushed Julia, who started to wail.

"How long Mama... how long?" she sobbed.

"I promise you it won't be long," she comforted her, purposely hanging back a few steps from the others.

"I will tell you a secret, but you have to keep it to yourself."

Julia nodded eagerly. She was twelve years now and

understood the consequences and the dangers of being found out. She had seen enough to know.

"We are going to leave here. We are going to try and escape to Germany," she said in a hushed tone.

Julia listened intensely to her mother and asked again, "When Mama?"

"As soon as the borders open," she whispered quietly into her daughter's ear. She drew her close then moved quickly forward to keep up with the others.

It was always a relief to her and the others involved in this nightly vigil, to reach their quarters safe and unharmed. One after the other they slipped away into their familiar spaces. She found it amazing how they all had adapted to find their way in the dark foreboding shadowy corridors of the compound.

"Thank God we made it," she said quietly to Julia, and she wasted no time and quickly tucked her into bed. But before she did the same, she leaned over where Julia had cuddled in beside Elisa, and whispered once more into her ear.

"Remember not a word."

"Yes, Mama," Julia was elated and proud that Mama had entrusted her into her plans and she was determined to keep that promise.

A pale moonlight lit the room enough for her to see that the others had settled down as well. Time was so precious and everyone knew, that before long the night will give way to another tiresome and treacherous day. She was about to follow suit and put herself to bed when she felt a hand on her back. She held her breath in panic. Elisabeth, who had her bed closest to her, shushed her quietly.

"It's me," she whispered. "I could not help but overhear. Are you planning something?"

She was shocked that a whisper in the dark stillness of the night could be heard by others.

'I have to be more careful,' she scolded herself in thought. On the other hand she had known Elisabeth for a long time now and somehow she was compelled to tell her plans to her. They both stood close, while in a hushed voice she told her friend of the escape.

Elisabeth listened intensely, she was almost ready to join in and do the same. Yet she felt she did not have the guts and dared not put herself and her daughters into more danger. She revealed to Katina, that she too had plans to leave this place. The miller and his wife, whom she had worked for, told her they had a room to spare and offered for her and her two daughters to move in with them. An offer she could not refuse. There, she was told, her daughters would be safe from being harassed and molested.

"It'll be better than staying here. Or worse yet be split up and taken to who knows where," she said with a worried undertone.

She had to agree with her friend and was glad for Elisabeth and her daughters, but she also knew, no matter where they were taken, they would be used as slave labor and never be free. For that she was truly sorry. She sighed, but did not tell Elisabeth about her concern.

"Katina! You can count on me. I'll be there to help you in any way I can. This is my solemn promise to you and I earnestly hope you'll succeed."

"Ugh…" she shook herself. "Just to think about it gives me goose bumps. You sure you want to go through with this?"

"I've no choice but to go along with Marianka's plan. To stay will surely kill me and what will happen then to the children? Elisabeth, I'm so scared for them. What if you can't revive me the next time I go unconscious? I can't leave them behind."

"I know, I know," Elisabeth acknowledged. "You don't have to remind me. But promise me to be extra careful…. Will you?"

"Yes!" she gave her promise. With that they quietly parted each to their own sleeping quarters.

Long after, she could hear Elisabeth tossing and turning.

Probably this news had come as a shock to her friend. Maybe it started to make her think. Was she planning to join her? Suddenly she found herself engaged in a lot of questions. But there were no answers.

Quietly and deep in thoughts, her eyes fixed on the moonlight, as it reflected the outline of the small basement window against the wall.

How peaceful it looked, she thought. Peace. That's what she needed. Ever since the news from Marianka, her mind was tormented and troubled. What had she gotten herself in to? Would she be able to pull it off? Would she be strong enough to make it? What if they were caught? What will happen to them then? Was it worth the risk, to go ahead with this dangerous plan?

"Oh God help me," she prayed quietly in her mind. "I'm so scared and troubled. If we stay here, I don't know what'll happen to all of us. If we dare to go, there are many dangers also. Give me peace to know what to do and strength and protection for all of us to see this through."

For a moment longer she watched the reflection of the moonlight. It felt calming. Gently, ever so gently she felt herself relaxing. Reminding herself that even in this seemingly forgotten place, the God of her forefathers was near. Comforted by this thought, she gave one more glance toward the moonlight. She did not want to think what, or who was lurking in the dark stillness of the eerily silent corridor. Purposely she kept her eyes from peering beyond the ominous foreboding doorway. She was sure if she did her mind would get the better of her and....

'Don't even think about this now,' she scolded herself. But too late, she felt the eyes of strangers staring at her from the near darkness. Quickly she turned. She could not have her back toward the opening, just in case.

'Why was it that she and her children always were the ones sleeping next to the doorway?' she questioned herself. 'Well hopefully it won't be long and they can leave this horrible place for good,' she comforted herself with this thought.

'At least they had the zinc tub as a barrier,' she thought thankfully. Just to have it there gave her a secure feeling. Tired, she tried to shut all these uneasy thoughts from her mind. She needed to calm down, she desperately needed to rest. She gave one last look toward the moonlight. She listened to the sounds of her children and others sleeping in the room. She was glad she was not alone and that comforted her.

She closed her eyes thinking of Mama and Papa and all her siblings. It had been a long time since she had seen them. Suddenly she recalled the melodious sound of harmonicas, mandolins, and zithers. Her heart ached. She remembered the harmonious singing. Will they ever be together again? Quietly she held this thought, straining her mind to reanimate the sound of the instruments. It soothed her troubled mind.

74

Summer had come and gone and she still had no news as far as the border's patrol was concerned. As for work... she found herself again for the second time at the daycare center. She was happy to be able to work again so close to the compound. Here she had a chance to see her little ones a few times a day. She also was able to again bring more food into the compound for the Jankes to share between the children. It felt good to be around to check on them from time to time when she carried water from the prison well back to the kindergarten.

She knew that this would not be enough to deter the new danger Elisa was facing. Just the other day old Father Janke had brought it to her attention that Elisa had been chased by a large German shepherd. The dog belonged to a Polish farmer, who wanted to take her away to work for him on his farm.

"I heard her screaming and came out to see, when I saw this beast of a dog chasing her into the basement," Father Janke said with excitement in his voice, angered by what he had witnessed.

"After some time of talking to the farmer and seeing that she did not stop screaming, he finally gave in and left her alone. I wish they would stop harassing the children and let them be," Father Janke said hanging his head in disgust.

With this news she felt even more indebted to this kind old man and thanked him over and over again for his thoughtful actions.

What if he wouldn't have been there? She shuddered. It was unthinkable to her how anyone could do such a thing to an eight-year-old child. Now she was even more anxious to leave.

By habit, she always took the same street and crossed the same yards to make her route to the compound and back to the kindergarten as short as possible. It was here on one of the back roads near Pani Slovak's sister's house, where Marianka caught up with her. She finally conveyed to her the message she had waited for so long. Quietly and not to make it too obvious she was told the good news that the border patrol had eased and to be ready to leave within a day.

Her head spun. She had waited so long for this moment, but now the excitement suddenly turned to profound fear. How could she pull it off and not get caught? So many things had to be done. How could she get Julia away from her work place without being too obvious? She had to concoct some excuse to have her daughter here with her when the time came. What about the two little ones? Who would bring them to the place of rendezvous? She could not be seen walking together with all her children along the road. Even walking along the back alleys, which Marianka had told her to take, would arouse suspicion. There were eyes watching every route. It had to be done inconspicuously. She also needed money! Suddenly all the weight and responsibility of her task unnerved her.

"Calm down and think Katina," she told herself out loud. She had planned out many times in her mind, how and what. But now it was real and it felt so absolutely frightening. It was agreed upon that she had to do her part on this end, while Marianka and her family did theirs on the other. After a lot of prayer and with much apprehension, she decided that it was time to ask for Elisabeth's help. She had to trust her and hope that she would stay true to her promise.

But as soon as she mentioned it to Elisabeth, every one

of their friends also seemed to know. Had the others in the room overheard them talking? Uneasy, she felt herself pressured by Claudia to include her and her children in the escape. Although Claudia had not quite come out of her complacency, their captors had seen fit to force her to resume the daily drudgery of slave labor.

She felt for her and wanted to help her but it was impossible. How could it be done with her friend not fully recovered? All the weight of looking after all the children would rest on her shoulders. She recalled the many times when she had taken it upon herself to help Claudia and her children. There was one occasion when she had worked for the Polish doctor and his Russian wife. Claudia's oldest son was brought in one day to have his hand treated and bandaged, and she was allowed to look after him and take him home back to the prison compound. The poor boy had endured much just like the rest of them. It happened that the farmer he had worked for had caught him stealing an egg. In his anger the Polish man had taken an axe and chopped into the boy's hand. A caring sort, the farmer's son, had taken pity on him and brought him to the doctor.

The dilemma of the poor children was very real. And she found it troublesome to deny Claudia this request especially after she suggested taking the children without her. Poor Claudia, how could she make her understand that this was not possible..? How could she take the children away from their mother...? Claudia definitely had not thought this through. What was she thinking? The children needed her. It would be devastating to them to go without their mother. It would leave them forever yearning for her and afterwards Claudia herself would miss her children dearly. She would always regret this decision. No, this was not a good idea...

Katina thought as she wrestled with this heart wrenching and burdensome request. No, she had to let it go and tell Claudia that this was not feasible. On the end this was not her decision to make anyway, as it rested solely on Marianka and her family. She took a deep breath. Her heart was heavy with the burden before her. She had to tell Claudia... She wished she did not have to, but she had no choice.

As it was, Claudia was not the only mother who pleaded with her to take the children away from their often dangerous and oppressive work places. And then there was Anna, who had come back from time to time to the compound.

When the girl heard what she had in mind, she begged, almost pleaded with her, "Please Auntie Katina..." as she had often called her that. "Please take me with you.... Please don't leave me here all alone... The farmer and his wife, they treat me terribly... There's never a day when I'm not beaten... I have to work hard from early morning until late at night with little food... The farmer and his son... they abuse me and the farmer's wife does nothing... I run away and come home to the compound, but they always find me and take me back... Please... if all of you leave one day... I'll never know... And those I have to work for, they wouldn't care.... I'll be forgotten... left behind and no one will come looking for me... Please Auntie... Please don't leave me here... Take me with you... Please let me come along..." Anna's cry resounded mournfully in her mind.

With a heavy heart she had turned down each and every one, except Anna, she didn't have the heart to tell her. It pained her to do this, especially after she had promised to Klara that she would be there for her mother and for Anna. Oh! The anguish of it all... She felt so tortured that she was forced now to go back on her promise. How could she tell Anna that she can't keep her promise...? How can she help them all...? Oh God, what a dilemma... She agonized with deep sorrow in her heart.

She realized that most of them had no one on the outside to help them with the actual escape. Besides everything else, there were the necessary funds that were needed to pay for the transport. And this she realized was a sacrifice even for the Slovaks on her behalf... It was unthinkable how all the mothers thought this possible as she was physically not well herself. How they perceived to have her leave with so many children was mind boggling to her. They surely would all be caught.

Now she feared that some would turn envious and squeal on her and the Slovaks, as they too would be punished to have aided her in her escape, but then she calmed herself to know she had good friends and none of them would find pleasure to do her in. At least that's what she perceived.

She wished she could help them all and it was very hard to see their disappointed and sad faces. She had not expected to create so much turmoil within the hearts of these dear souls. Nor had she prepared herself of the impact this heart wrenching situation would have on her, as well as them. She tried to put it all out of her mind and reminded herself that her hands were tied. It was not in her power to help each and every one. Heavy-hearted and with much anxiety in her heart, she continued to plan.

From her place of work she had many times taken a short cut through a small and unkempt yard. The Polish woman there often stopped her and talked to her. In conversation more than once she had mentioned that she was in need of warm bedding for her children. This knowledge and the need for money, made her think.

She had to bring her feather comforter to this woman and sell it as quickly as possible. At least then she would have some money in her pocket to buy things that were necessary for and during the escape.

She contemplated when and how to bring this about. For as far as she seen it this opportunity was heaven sent and she could not let it go. The short conversations she had with the woman from time to time had brought her to believe she could be trusted. At first a little apprehensive, she presented the sale of the feather comforter to the woman and told her that she needed money to buy food for her children.

To her relief and without hesitation the woman agreed. Again in times like these a good deal was hard to come by. And as far as the Polish woman was concerned, it did not matter who the seller was as long as she and her family were the benefactors.

Quietly and quickly Katina sold the feather comforter and came back to the compound with the money.

--

The final day was coming tomorrow and she was frantic. She had kept Julia home, knowing full well that by now the farmer would have discovered her not showing up for work. He would surely come looking for her, if not today then early tomorrow morning. She had to do something to keep Julia with her when the time came to leave, but at the same time she had to be careful and not raise suspicion. Suddenly, while carrying water back and forth, an idea presented itself as a perfect scheme.

She remembered the practice of cupping, the placing of a specific type of round tumblers that were heated and cupped onto the sick person's back. As the air cooled inside the glass it would create a vacuum and suck itself tight to the skin. After releasing the tumbler from the skin a particular kind of healing ointment was dabbed lightly onto the raised skin. It was an oriental treatment known to cure a long list of sicknesses. An eastern tradition her father and her father's father had adapted and practiced. She though had intended not to go all the way with the cupping. She just would go to the point where the skin reddened and then she would remove the tumblers. Hoping with this it would be enough for the farmer to see that Julia was not well. She prayed it will work.

She had seen old Father Janke use this treatment and went to him to borrow the whole kit for the cupping. Old Janke was skeptical at first as to why she needed it. Trusting him, she took heart and told him of her plan to escape. He had been there for her in so many instances and almost lost his life with the incidence of her leather boots. For that she would always be indebted to him.

Concerned that she might not know how to properly do the cupping he explained to her in detail how to go about it and supplied her with all the necessary items. With all this in hand she had to let Julia in on what was to happen. Later in the evening she told her; also that she had to be a brave girl to make this plan work.

Surely if the farmer sees her daughter's back swollen and inflamed, he would not force her to go to work. At least that's what she thought and hoped. It was a chance she had to take.

So far she had only told Elisabeth, old Father Janke, and Julia of tomorrow's plan to escape, for she still feared repercussion.

It may have been the lack of the feather comforter but that night she did not sleep well. Tomorrow... It will all happen tomorrow.

75

The next morning Katina and Elisabeth both reported for work. Then as strategized while running errands, they both made a detour back to the prison compound. Everyone in their room who was able to work had been summoned. Only Julia, Elisa and Stefan had remained. The Jankes had promised to look after Claudia's two youngest boys, Karl and Albert, so there would be no problem to carry out the plan. Upon arrival she quickly went about to prepare Julia for the treatment, while Elisabeth dressed and watched the two little ones. Everything that she owned she had packed beforehand in the large black handbag.

As it was she had always worn two dresses one on top of the other, wearing the good one underneath the shabby one; the same with Julia. She made a quick check around the room. Then she followed to do the same underneath her bed and straw mattress, where she had always kept and hidden all her belongings. She had sold the comforter the day before, and all that was left were the two shabby looking pillows which she had promised to Elisabeth.

All in all she was ready. Her hands were shaking as she uncovered Julia's back. She started to prepare the special glasses. She lit a candle and took the thin long wooden stick with tightly wrapped cotton gauze on one end. She then dipped it into a small alcohol filled bottle and held the soaked cotton over a burning candle. As she was told by Father

452

Janke; the flame it produced was then twirled a few times around in the inside of each tumbler to heat it up. She then quickly cupped it onto Julia's back. The heated glass sucked itself tightly on and pulled the skin up inside of it, just as it was supposed to. She continued feverishly, hurriedly applying each glass.

Her hands trembled while her mind raced from one thing to another. Will she be able to pull it off? Will someone squeal on her? Will Elisabeth take good care and succeed in bringing her two little ones safe to the secret meeting place? Will she and Julia be able to sneak out of this compound without being seen? Will...

"Ouch!" Julia winced.

"Oh, no...!" Katina let out a gasp.

In her excitement she took too much alcohol onto the cotton swab, which had produced a bigger than intended flame. Upset and in panic now she released the rest of the tumblers. Frantically she looked around for something anything to cool Julia's burning back. Her eyes fell on a piece of pork rind that was lying by the windowsill. Julia had brought it home the day before. Flustered she rubbed the inside of the rind over Julia's burned skin.

She had just finished packing away the tumblers with the rest of the kit, when the farmer came fuming around the corner. Angry and upset, he threatened to use his whip on her daughter.

"Why did you not show up for work?" his face turned red in anger as he questioned her. Full of fear she quickly intervened.

"Please ... She's very sick, but she will be back as soon as she recovers..." She then went even further and told the enraged man. "Julia loves to work for you and your son. She will be back at work as soon as her back heals." But no matter what she said the man was not convinced.

She could almost feel the whip on her own back as the man in his angry state shook it dangerously close, swearing profusely. In desperation she uncovered Julia's back and showed it to him. As by now it was truly red and blistering.

"I promise, she will be back," she stated again in a shaky voice.

He took a step backwards and swore repeatedly, "I'll give you until tomorrow...! She had better be there tomorrow...! Or I'll come and get her myself!" he yelled, waving his whip in the air as he left the room. All the way along the dark basement hallway his loud indignant swear words could be heard.

Katina broke down sobbing. The children too were crying and Julia especially had reason to wail. She apologized again and again to her for burning her back and tried her best to comfort her.

Elisabeth stood wiping away tears as she tried her best to compose herself.

"I'd better go. Marianka is probably waiting for the two little ones by now. And then I have to hurry back to my workplace before I'm missed," she spoke quietly. She hesitated and took a quick glance out of the basement window just to see the still fuming farmer drive past the compound.

"He is driving over the bridge. He is out of sight," she reported to Katina. "We have no time to waste."

Katina gave a tearful hug to her little ones then to Elisabeth. She thanked her for everything and wished her and her two daughters the best in their new place at the Mill. She let out a deep sigh at the thought of all the other dear souls.

"God be with you and keep all of you safe. I will never forget you."

"You too Katina... Take care..." Elisabeth answered wiping tears in haste from her face as she gathered Elisa and Stefan.

"I'll take the two little ones now and be on my way."

"Yes, and Julia and I will follow later in the afternoon. Hopefully no one will stop us and ask questions," she added fearfully.

"Again, say goodbye to the others for me and wish them well, once we're gone," she swallowed hard. "Oh, by the way there's one more thing Elisabeth… Could I ask for one more favor?

"What is it Katina…?" Elisabeth stood waiting.

"It's Anna, Elisabeth…" she answered with concern. "I feel so terrible leaving her behind. She has no one. Will you…? Could you help her…?" She struggled to speak overwhelmed by guilt. "Somehow be there for her…? I feel so bad leaving her like this, but I have no say who I can take with me. Please Elisabeth…?" Katina pleaded now in earnest.

"You know it'll be hard when we're not in the compound anymore. And I don't know if the miller's wife would want another one there." Elisabeth shook her head. "I don't know Katina. I just don't know… I can try, but that's just about all I can do…"

"Thank you Elisabeth. I would appreciate it. Thanks for all your help." She gave one more hug to Elisa and Stefan and finally to Elisabeth.

"Take care…" she said for the last time.

Taking the two in hand, a teary eyed Elisabeth disappeared with Stefan and Elisa into the semi-dark hallway. Katina listened to their fading footsteps; their fearful eyes had left an uneasy feeling in her heart.

"God help us," she prayed.

Anxious, she gathered the two empty pails and told Julia to stay put and wait for her. She then rushed to return with water filled pails to the kindergarten before she caused suspicion.

After the noon hour, when it was her usual time to fetch more water, she walked past the well and entered the compound with much caution. It was hard to pass some of the rooms without being noticed. But she kept her nose to the ground, rarely looking up, trying to act casually. She was scared that if she did, somehow the anxiety she felt would show and give away her true intentions.

At last in her quarters, Julia who was anxiously waiting for her return was relieved to finally see her. Suddenly she felt strange to step out for the last time, never to set foot in this 'God forsaken' place again. She took one more look around. She remembered in a flash all the horrifying days and nights she and her children had spent here with all the others.

'What will happen to them, God only knows' she thought. And in His care she had to leave them, as well as herself and her children.

She instructed for Julia to go out of the compound before her. Then wait for her beyond the entrance gate, so as not to draw too much attention. After Julia had gone she left the two pails in the room and then made her way up the stairs. She was about to reach the front door, when she remembered the 'cupping' kit in her hand. As she turned to knock, Janke's door opened.

"Katina…" The old Janke was now standing beside her. "Take care and thank you for everything," he whispered… "May God's protection be over you and your children."

She nodded, nervously looking around, just to see his wife standing in the doorway.

"All the thanks go to you, my friends. I can never repay you for what you've done for me…" she held out the kit and the old Janke took it from her, as he waved her off.

"That's all behind now, you just take care…" She turned and nodded a silent good bye toward Mother Janke. With tears in her eyes she quickly made her way out of the compound. The large black handbag she carried high over the right shoulder underneath her oversized shawl. This way it will be hidden from prying eyes. It was the same shawl she had converted from an old blanket and had always worn whenever the weather was cool. Anyone who had seen her carrying water earlier would identify her with this shawl and think nothing of it. It would look like she was doing her job.

Once she caught up with Julia she pulled her kerchief more forward into her face in order to conceal her identity as much as possible. She told Julia to do the same. Carefully they walked along familiar roads they knew so well, not making eye contact with anyone. Not once did they dare to turn to look around. Not until they came close to the cemetery. In passing both she and Julia stole a look over the burial grounds. She remembered the terrible fate of Father Wendel and the other dear friends. A cold shiver went through her whole body. The thought was too overbearing and depressing. She felt a deep pain in her chest, but no tears, just indescribable shock and sadness. Quietly, she said her goodbyes and then they moved on with urgency in their steps. They needed to put as much distance between them and this place of horror.

Cautiously they followed the route around the graveyard. Then they walked hastily along the dirt road which encircled the outskirts of town. They passed the fruit orchard with the land and homestead Johann had acquired and fixed up for them to live in.

The orchard had mysteriously been swindled away from them at that time by someone in the German community. Try as they might, both she and Johann could not find out who had been behind this. They could only have guessed that it might have been none other than their long time adversary, Heinrich Schwarz. But that was all in the past now. Sorrowfully, she looked over the land.

So many thoughts passed through her mind as she gave a quick glance toward the homestead. With mixed emotions she recalled the few happy times they had as a family. And she could almost see Johann running after little Elisa, who was always trying to escape from having her hair washed. Then her pleasant thoughts again were overshadowed by the sad and terrifying events.

Her steps suddenly increased in speed. She wanted to get away from here as fast as possible, but then the pain in her knees gave way to a slower and steadier pace. She had to be content to hobble along the dusty country road.

Julia too had glanced over the familiar harvested flax fields. She recalled the warm summer days when she and her friend would pass these fields to take a little dip in the deeper part of the small creek that ran through their property.

"Mama," she suddenly interrupted the silence. "The time we had here was not all bad."

Katina stopped for a brief moment to catch her breath. She looked again over the land, then toward the old homestead. How strange it looked. It did not feel like home anymore. Johann had big plans to make it into a beautiful place.

"Yes, Julia, we had good times here, but they were much too short." She gave a deep sigh. "We'll always remember and treasure them."

Again a deep pain stirred within her heart. With heaviness in her voice she concluded… "And they will always be there for us to draw on whenever we feel the need to do so."

Julia nodded quietly in agreement. "Will we ever feel at home anywhere?" She looked up and noticed the tears in her mother's eyes. Suddenly she could not hold back her own. The sad and tragic memories always pushed themselves to the forefront. It was all too fresh and too painful to deal with.

"Come, Julia." She took her daughter's hand. "We have to push on. The quicker we get away from here the better." She hastily looked around and then both started to walk again, their eyes fixed mainly on the road before them.

--

"It's amazing that we've made it this far, with no interference," she mumbled to herself, laboring in pain to keep up with Julia. In the distance they had noticed farm workers working in the fields, but so far no one seemed to have noticed them.

The sun stood high and shone warm on their backs. She welcomed the warmth, but Julia started to wince and complain. The heat of the sun made her back burn in pain.

"Should we stop over there for a moment?" She pointed to a large tree which stood by the road side ahead of them.

"No, Mama, if you can keep walking I can bear the pain on my back." She was determined not to complain, seeing how Mama struggled to keep going.

"You are so brave and strong." She gave Julia's hand a squeeze in appreciation.

It was a beautiful autumn afternoon. The birds cheerfully sang among the trees and bushes, while the long grass beside the road bent gently to and fro in the breeze. In the fields the wheat stalks too were swaying in waves over the field. Nowhere had she seen them stand as tall as in this region. It was a fertile, good, crop-bearing land, which they had discovered when first resettling here to this region. The same was true with the vegetable and fruit gardens.

Suddenly her walk came to an abrupt halt. In an instant she reached over to Julia and signaled for her to be silent. There, about a hundred feet away, she had noticed a group of field workers dangerously close to the road. Quickly both of them ducked down and hurried to crawl under some sheaves stacked up on the side of the road.

She calculated their hiding place was a safe distance away, so they would not be discovered. They could hear the farmer hollering to the workers, to hurry along. She could see the workers. And she knew in an instant by the wasted and gaunt looking bodies of women and children that they were from the prison compound.

"Poor people..." she exclaimed in a deep painful sigh.

She waited until the group had turned and moved a good distance away from them, then she gave the okay to crawl out from underneath their hiding place. Yet, as soon as they had stepped out onto the road she noticed in horror that the farmer had turned and was staring right at them. Her heart sank. An uneasy terrifying feeling gripped her whole body.

"Keep walking and do not act suspiciously," she advised Julia, who started to panic.

"Just keep your eyes on the road and stay calm. Oh Lord, we have made it this far... please help us now. God protect us," she prayed. She felt weak in her knees. She tried to steady herself and leaned on Julia's shoulder, who winced in pain.

"Mama, hold onto my arm."

She quietly apologized and did as Julia told her.

She glanced back to the field and noticed the farmer walking toward them.

"He is coming toward us," her voice quavered as she spoke. An unbelievable body and mind weakening angst crept into her. She could feel her heart pounding hard and fast against her chest. The fear of being caught was so overwhelming that her legs suddenly threatened to collapse from under her body. She fought to gain control and held on to Julia's arm to steady herself, she had to be strong for her daughter's sake.

A scared and desperate cry escaped from deep within her soul. "Oh God, this can't be happening. I can't do this anymore. I'm tired, so tired and weak. God, my children what will happen to them, to all of us? I have lost so much, I can't lose any more. Please help."

Uncontrollably the tears ran down her face.

Julia also quietly sobbed beside her. She understood her mother's pain all too well. Quietly, she tried her best to aid her.

Suddenly they heard a commotion on the field and as they looked back they could see the farmer stop his pursuit. Unwillingly, he gave one more glance toward them and then turned. The commotion on the field had drawn his attention toward his farm workers.

She could only guess that somebody had injured themselves, or had recognized them and had known of their plan to escape and now were purposely doing this to distract the farmer from going after her and Julia. Whoever it was, she was ever so thankful to them, but in the same breath she prayed for their safety, knowing very well what awaited them.

I WILL REMEMBER ALWAYS

"God help the poor souls," she muttered under her breath. Julia nodded, as she wiped tears off her cheeks. For a moment they stood stunned looking back in disbelief. The stress and anxiety was too much on their already frail and weak bodies.

"This was too close, let's go quickly before he changes his mind," she muttered under her breath.

Julia turned toward her. "God has heard your prayer, Mama. He has saved us."

She nodded in agreement, her body still trembling.

They took one more glance back and hastily went on their way. They had been spared and for that she was grateful. But what about those poor souls back there? What will happen to them? Only God can help them now. Willfully, she forced her thoughts away from what was behind and tried to focus on the task before her.

"It won't be much farther." She encouraged Julia as well as herself. "I can see the roof of the farm house further up in the distance." Knowing that the first part of their journey would soon be reached was of great comfort.

The sun had disappeared for a moment behind a cloud and the air had cooled considerably. Relieved and rejuvenated they pushed on toward the secret meeting place. She knew the area well. The homestead lay secluded and hidden by a grove of tall trees along the main road to Kutno, about three kilometers from Quadenstadt. But would that be far enough away from her pursuers? This fearful thought hovered constantly over her.

At the farm house, Marianka too was uneasy as she waited nervously for Katina and Julia. Anxiously, she paced the yard and was relieved when finally the two came in sight. When she heard of the incident with the farmer, she became very worried and hastily ushered the two into the house. Searching, Katina looked around, but Marianka read her thoughts.

"Don't worry, the little ones are safe. They had just finished half of a fresh baked sugar beet bun and downed a half a cup of milk."

Overcome with emotions, teary eyed and with a faint quiver in her voice, Katina managed a humble, "Thank you." All the pent up worry and stress of the past few days had left her terribly weak and exhausted. As they entered the house, the rest of Marianka's family was there to greet them. It was a relief to all that they had finally managed to get her and the children out of that oppressive place.

"So far all went according to the plan. Now we hope for the rest of the journey to be without obstacles." Pan Slovak was by her side, seeing that she had a difficult time.

"Come."

He aided her to a chair by the kitchen table, which Wiktor had courteously moved for her to sit on.

"This will help you get some strength back," Pani Slovak spoke positively as she served them the delicious smelling sugar beet buns. And Heniek hurried to pour them a steaming cup of his mother's own prepared herbal tea.

She was speechless and overwhelmed by the outpouring of kindness. It was like coming home. They were all she and her children had, true friends. They had always been there when she needed them most. Gratefully, she reached for a piece of a delectable bun in front of her, but realized after she had chewed on her first few bites; she could not eat anymore. After all those years of starvation and passing most of the meager morsels of food to the children, her stomach had shrunk to the point where it now rejected even the smallest portion.

At first look they were all shocked at the sight of her and the children. The years in the compound had worn them down, especially Katina. Her eyes were hollow, her stature thin and frail looking. Her once graceful smile was replaced by a hardened, overwhelmed look, one that witnessed much tragedy.

Seeing that she had a problem eating, Pani Slovak encouraged her, to at least drink her tea and that she did.

Slowly she sipped and felt the warmth of the tea radiating throughout her whole body.

"Oh, it feels so good," she commented with a satisfying smile toward Pani Slovak.

"I remember those buns," Julia commented with delight, as she bit into the piece her mother had left. "Mmm... They're so delicious. Your grandmother used to bake them," she looked over to Marianka.

"Yes, she still does once in a while," Marianka replied. "Although, these days she would rather sit back and let us do the work," she finished with a chuckle.

"How's everyone?" Katina inquired thoughtfully.

"There is not much of anything around these days, but then we can't complain considering what you and the children have endured. Times are still hard, as you can see.... but we've all survived. And even though it's not much, we've enough to eat to keep from going hungry, for that we're grateful... We do what we can to stay alive," Pan Slovak added with a smile. Katina nodded in agreement.

"And yet you have... and still do so much for us."

"That's repayment for all you and Johann had done for us."

With tears in her eyes, she again released a faint, "Thank you".

Reunited with her children and good friends, for the moment brought a little comfort to her tormented mind. But she knew that this was only temporary, as she would only be safe and at peace once she and the children had crossed the Polish/German border. For now though they would have to be on guard.

Behind locked doors and blanket covered windows, in a dimly lit room, they sat around the table. They spent the early evening reminiscing and sharing stories of past and present events, experiences they had all gone through. With tears in their eyes they recalled memories of good times. But also sad and troubled times which they all wanted to forget and put behind them. Destiny had brought them together. Out of the terrible circumstances, once strangers and supposedly foes, love and respect had flourished into a beautiful friendship. She considered them more than friends and she felt the Slovaks reciprocated that feeling.

The conversation was hushed several times, as the men went outside to inspect the surrounding premises. Nothing was taken for granted. They all felt vulnerable because of their involvement in the escape. The incident with the farmer today especially heightened the danger. Pan Slovak was the first to come back into the house, followed by Wiktor and Mandek.

"The sooner we get you onto the truck and gone from here the better it'll be for all of us." Pan Slovak spoke softly as he walked hastily over to the stove and helped himself to another cup of tea.

"One doesn't know what will happen next. We can only hope their search is delayed until tomorrow. By then our plan hopefully is successful and we'll have you and the children safe and sound on the road to Kutno."

They all agreed, while once again they discussed all the steps for the final escape, so there would be no last minute mishaps, which most definitely would ruin this whole undertaking for all of them.

After all was said and done, she and the children, finally bedded down for the night. The attic was chosen to be the safest place for them to sleep. Here they would be out of sight from unexpected prying eyes. The Slovaks had thoughtfully provided heaps of fresh straw for them to sleep on and a small blanket for Julia to cover. She used her well worn shawl to cover the two little ones. For herself she had to make do with what she had on and was grateful that she still had her pair of long stockings. That at least was left to her and each of her children. They would now come in handy for the cooler season ahead. She snuggled closer to Stefan to keep warm. Marianka too, bedded down next to Julia.

Over the years a very strong bond had developed between

Marianka and Katina and with the children, but most of all to Elisa. In her heart Marianka knew that tomorrow's parting would not be easy. So she made it a point to relish every moment they still had together.

Exhausted from the day's event, the two little ones were soon fast asleep. Julia took a little longer to settle down for her back was still inflamed. Earlier in the evening Marianka had used her mother's homemade ointment to relieve some of her discomfort. In the Slovak household this ointment was used for generations and all of them could attest to its quick healing and soothing quality.

Katina could vouch for it, as she had experienced many of their home remedies to work wonders. But for the open sores on her knees, unfortunately there was no short term cure. She knew that besides ointment and medicine; it would take time and plenty of rest and proper nourishment to hopefully bring the healing she so desperately needed.

At this very moment she was in agony and could feel the coolness of the night air working on her pain ridden body. Tossing back and forth she could not find a comfortable spot. Afraid that her restlessness would wake the children and Marianka, she forced herself to keep still; but to no avail.

Besides her bodily discomfort, she was also tormented in mind and spirit by this whole situation she found herself in, as she knew the Slovaks were just as much in danger. If caught in aiding her escape, they too would be punished and executed as traitors. The more she thought the more edgy and anxious she became, causing her body to become more painful.

Suddenly her mental and physical torment was interrupted by the rustling sounds of rodents crossing the attic floor. When she felt the rodents running over her body, she quickly tucked the lower end of her two layered dresses tight around her knees for protection. Normally she would have been squeamish over these ghastly creatures, but her time in the prison had left her numb to those feelings. To her surprise she felt their presence even comforting.

She reached for the shawl blanket and pulled it a little higher, listening to her children's soft even breathing. Julia stirred slightly and moaned, then went back to sleep. She then proceeded to cuddle even closer to keep herself and little Stefan warmer. Elisa lay between Stefan and Julia and as usual her warm body felt cozy to cuddle on, especially on a cool night like this. She wished for a moment she could have some of that warmth. But knowing that it was not possible she nestled a little deeper into the straw.

76

It was early before dawn the following day, when Marianka woke her, gently touching her shoulder.

"It's time," she whispered quietly.

In an instant a profound shock went through Katina's mind and body. The task before her suddenly overwhelmed her. She struggled to get up, her heart pounded strong against her chest. Stiff and painful, she forced herself up.

"I feel as if I had just fallen asleep. I'm so tired," she spoke softly to Marianka, who nodded in agreement, while helping with the children. Suddenly she felt weak and faint and she had to steady herself against the attic wall.

'Oh God, I can't go weak now,' she thought to herself as she fought to overcome it. Marianka noticed and came to her aid.

"Come, I'll help you down the stairs. What we all need is something warm to drink and eat."

She gently aided Katina, while Julia and the two little ones followed with fearful eyes. It was not the first time they had seen Mama in that sickly state and it worried them.

After a warm cup of tea and a bite of homemade bread, Katina felt a little stronger. Pani Slovak watched with amusement as the children each downed a warm cup of tea, along with a small slice of bread topped with rosehip jam.

"Now that feels better, doesn't it? Good that you finished it all." Pani Slovak smiled, pleased that the children had enjoyed their breakfast.

"Yes," Katina agreed, for she knew all too well that they

will have to wait a long time before they will eat again. She also knew that the Slovaks shared from their meager rations. Humbly she accepted their kindness.

The time had come to say their last goodbyes, as hugs were freely given. Tears flowed as they wished each other well, knowing that this would be the last time they would ever see each other. Then Marianka reminded everyone that it was time to go.

"We only have twenty minutes to get to the junction." she spoke in haste. "The truck driver is not a patient man. He's always in a hurry. So we had better be there a little earlier."

Katina agreed, as she listened once again to Marianka's last minute instructions. Wiktor and Mandek had walked around the yard and over to the junction to scout out the surrounding area. Upon their return they confirmed of no suspicious characters to be seen anywhere.

Pani Slovak had packed a few slices of bread and some of the leftover sugar-beet buns and passed them to Katina.

"Just in case the children get hungry..." she mentioned and gave the little ones a quick peck on their cheeks.

Katina gave one more look around the room and for the last time as if to capture their faces into her memory she nodded a farewell.

"Have a safe journey," Pan Slovak called after them.

"And God's protection, be over you," Pani Slovak joined in.

"The same to you my friends..." her words trailed after.

Relieved, but cautious they started to walk. She and Marianka each took hold of one of the children's hands, while Julia followed. Wiktor and Mandek brought up the rear, but kept their distance, so not to draw suspicion.

"I'll pay the truck driver and purchase the tickets in Kutno. Remember what we spoke of last night when someone inquires where you're going. All you have to do is pretend that you are a Polish woman with children who wants to join her husband in Stettin," Marianka reminded her again.

Then Marianka looked at the children and drove home to

I WILL REMEMBER ALWAYS

them the importance to play their part.

"Now, do not slip up and talk German. Just keep on talking Polish," she looked questionably at Julia who nodded in agreement.

"I know Stefan and Elisa are too small to understand. But I think they will be just fine," Katina agreed with Marianka. She thought back how quickly and fluently they had learned to speak the Polish language.

"Here, let me help you with this..." Noticing that Katina had a hard time walking, Marianka relieved her of her heavily-packed large handbag.

"Wow... just to think, there're only a few pieces of bread and buns," Marianka exclaimed surprised.

"Yes, along with the children's clothes, the pictures and the old songbook." Katina added giving Marianka a weak but grateful smile. "I'm so glad you've retrieved them for me Marianka. The book and the pictures, they're the only memories that's left for me... I'll always be beholden to you for that, and everything else you and your family had done for me and my children. I can never thank you enough," she said. Her voice quavered as she labored, hobbling alongside her Polish friend.

Marianka just waved her off. "No need to thank me Katina. Again, it's the least I could do." She was proud now to have rescued these items. "I wish I could have done more... But things don't always work out the way you want them too and for that I'm truly sorry..." Marianka said ruefully, still a little put out not to have succeeded in retrieving more items for Katina.

"Still I'm grateful... Thanks again..." She was truly glad that these treasures were once again in her possession. She looked down at herself, hoping she looked presentable and not too shabby. Earlier she had shed the dirty and tattered looking top dress and left it and the worn-out blanket shawl behind. Her shoes, yes they could be a little bit better, but she was happy that Elisabeth at least had another pair to spare

469

even though they were old and needed repair.

She gave a glance to the children as they walked beside her and Marianka, their faces washed and their hair combed. She was glad she had saved some of their clothing for this occasion. Although not being able to wash themselves properly, she hoped it would not be too noticeable, but then she comforted herself that not too many people had the luxury of soap these days. 'Well, whatever, there's not much she could do about that now...'

Just then a faint whiff of petroleum passed her nose from a soft breeze that blew from the back of them. 'Well at least I don't have to worry about body odor.' A smile crossed her lips.

She thought back to the time when she had obtained the first petroleum jar. One has to know how to go about achieving things. Of course it helped that she had this beautiful nightgown in her possession, but then it had been a better swap than what she got for her leather boots. Oh well, it's all in the past and for now she had to focus on the things before her. 'Now what were the things Marianka had told her and the children to do? She thought a little worried, hoping she and the children would not slip up and give themselves away.

The little money she had received from the sale of the feather bed was safely tucked away in her large bag which Marianka was now carrying. She only planned to use it when needed to buy food and drink for the children once they were well beyond Kutno. She would have loved to pitch in for the truck and train fares. But then the little she had wouldn't even make a dent in the actual cost.

Again it was incomprehensible to her that the Slovaks would do this for her and the children as they had so little for themselves. She felt a deep appreciation and so indebted to them, knowing that she will never have the chance to repay them.

--

The morning air was cool and crisp as they hurried toward the junction. Now she wished to have kept the blanket shawl or at least the old coat from Elisabeth but then they were not fit for this journey. It was important to her that she and her children looked presentable and no one could single them out. Or worse yet detect them to have come from the prison compound. She gave a quick glance around when they arrived. Suddenly a suppressed gasp of disbelief escaped her. For there among the crowd stood Jobina and her daughter Maria. Questions upon questions crowded her mind.

How in the world did they manage to come here to this place? Did they have outside help like her, or had they done it on their own? Who's to know? Perplexed, she now wondered how many more had followed to do the same? Would those left behind suffer the consequences and endure punishment for concealing information about her and other escapees?

She recalled the incidence with her leather boots, when Father Janke nearly lost his life for concealing her identity. She hated to think that this again would be the case. She sighed with heaviness in her heart. She thought again about Claudia Ebert and her poor children and Anna... who would help them now? Yesterday, when she and Julia passed the field and the farmer had turned to come after them, who had caused the diversion? Was it maybe Benjamin or his sisters? Poor children, she felt so bad for leaving them behind. She hoped if they had been the ones, they did not have to suffer the consequences or succumb to worse. It was just as well not to know she consoled herself. To know would only bring more grief to her already tortured mind. As for Jobina and Maria, who knows, they might have chanced it on their own to escape the same day and stowed away in the nearby fields until this morning.

She would have loved to know more, but had to restrain herself and not give away that they knew each other. Just in case someone recognized either one of them to be one of the German detainees from the compound. She gave another glance toward them and wondered now why Jobina had a scarf tied around her mouth and over her head. 'Hopefully the poor woman was not in any discomfort,' she thought compassionately.

Anxiously she looked along the road from where the truck was supposed to come. The wait felt like an eternity. Panic suddenly filled her anxious heart. Maybe the authorities in town were on to their escape and had stalled all the transportation out of the area. Chills went over her back, her heart started to beat heavily. She noticed Marianka also nervously pacing back and forth, checking and rechecking her wristwatch. Maria threw a questionable look at her, as did her mother. She could see fear in their eyes. Overcome with angst, she prayed for mercy.

Julia sensed the tension and moved herself and little Stefan closer to her. Suddenly there was a stir in the crowd. Someone had detected the vehicle in the distance as it was racing with great speed toward them.

With mixed feelings Katina watched to see if there were any officials on board, or following behind the vehicle. But to her surprise and relief the only occupant was the driver. As Marianka had foretold, he hurried everyone into the back of the truck and impatiently collected the fares. Then, just as quickly, jumped back into the driver's seat and accelerated to speed away, regardless of the safety or comfort of the passengers. But despite the rough ride, she was glad and relieved to finally put some distance between them and the place they had come from.

'So far so good,' she thought, as she watched the familiar scenery change and move past her into the distance. The years of warfare had left the land brutally devastated and like the people, it too, struggled to recover.

'What a senseless war,' she sighed. 'It had brought nothing but heartache and suffering.' Tears welled up in her eyes as she thought back.

A sudden sharp turn in the road made everyone fly

off their seats. One passenger swore in disgust, while he struggled to regain his former place, as did all the others. So far conversation among the passengers was minimal, for the road noise made it next to impossible. Most of the people just settled in and held on to the primitive benches they sat on, while the unfortunate ones, who had to stand, braced themselves against the rough wooden side rails of the truck.

All at once it came to her, as she glanced over the other passengers. There actually might be more escapees on board. It was hard to distinguish from one person to another, especially if they all spoke the Polish language well. She had heard from Marianka that German detainees in the Lodz area had their heads shaved to be more visible and thus more easily detected. She was thankful that this had not been the case in the Quadenstadt compound, for it certainly would have been a far greater deterrent and next to impossible to escape.

With every stop to take more passengers on board, she held her breath and prayed that no officials were among them. She wanted so much to already be in Kutno and on the train or better yet past Posen and beyond, the farther the better.

Thoughts of Johann suddenly filled her troubled mind. The agony of that day still haunted her. And she wished not to have missed the chance to have seen him one more time. It pained her now, as she was soon to be at the place where he had waited for her and the children. How lonely, how forsaken he must have felt... She caught herself utterly overwhelmed by this thought. She struggled in anguish to hold back her tears. The pain in her heart was profound and crushing. She felt so terribly guilty.

He's gone... and there is nothing I could do or change to... she stopped herself, thinking... How cold and painfully distant these words sounded.

O Johann! She fought to gain control of her emotions. If only... if only I could have been there.

The pain, like a dagger pierced her heart. It's too much...
O God... It's too much to bear. Help me... relieve me of this
torment, she quietly cried out. With profound emptiness in
her heart she released a deep heavy sigh in silent defeat.

Suddenly a strange and unexpected thought made her
look at Marianka as she held onto little Elisa. She had put all
her trust in her. But, would she stay true to her word and not
suddenly change her mind?

All at once she was upset with herself, to let a thought like
this enter her mind. Marianka had done so much for her and
the children. Why would she now have a change of heart and
turn against her?

No! That's absurd! She willfully rejected that thought.
Marianka had never given her the slightest hint or gesture
that would make her think otherwise. She had to get a hold
of herself before this thought got the better of her. She had to
trust Marianka, for she was their only life link to freedom.

"Kutno, we're here!" someone called out. The driver made
his final loop and came to an abrupt halt in front of the train
station. As they stepped off, she looked anxiously around,
noticing that the station was heavily guarded.

"Stay calm, and let me handle everything," she heard
Marianka's quiet warning as she set out to purchase the
tickets. She and the children did as told, trying to stay hidden
among the crowd. Maria and her mother followed to do the
same.

Puzzled, she looked on, when Marianka returned with all
the tickets in hand, realizing now that she was also involved
in their escape. Of course she had not seen them pay for their
fare on the truck. Marianka must have had a hand in this too.
Again there were so many questions, but they had to stay
unanswered for now. Quietly and inconspicuously, Marianka
handed two tickets to Maria and four to her.

Taking the transport slips, she knew this would be the last
time Marianka could intervene for them. From here on they
would be on their own.

Anxious, but at the same time with gratitude to have made it so far, but it was all because of Marianka. If it would not have been for her and her family, she and her children, and who knows how many other captives, would not have survived those dreadful years during their incarceration, and now in the escape.

"We have an hour wait," Marianka announced after she had slipped them the tickets. "I'm going for a quick walk around the area, but I'll be back to see you off before you board the train." She excused herself and started to walk away.

"Oh, by the way, do you mind if I take Elisa along? Then you don't have the worry of watching two little ones."

Katina nodded. "Yes." She agreed, for she was in no condition to run after two little ones or occupy them for that long of a time. And it would be too much for Julia as she would have her hands full with Stefan.

She watched the two, as Marianka led her little one through the train station. Suddenly she felt uneasy, but again she dismissed the thought. After all, Marianka had been so kind and faithful to her, how can she think otherwise? Yet a moment later, despite reassuring herself into trusting Marianka, she suddenly felt an overwhelming fear.

"Julia, quickly go and bring Elisa back. They shouldn't be far." Without question, Julia ran off toward the direction she had last seen them. When she caught up, Marianka was just about to take Elisa into a store.

"We are going to buy candy," Elisa beamed.

"Elisa, Mama wants you to come back." Julia spoke calmly.

Marianka hastily pulled the little one close to her. "There's plenty of time. Tell your Mother that I'll bring her back and not to worry."

"Elisa! Come with me," Julia's voice took on a demanding tone as she took Elisa's hand and pulled her toward her.

"But I want candy," Elisa protested wiggling herself free of Julia's hand and ran toward Marianka.

"Just leave her with me. We won't be long," Marianka spoke, annoyed at Julia's interference, but tried not to show it. Firmly she took hold again of Elisa's hand and started to walk.

But Julia was vigilant in her pursuit. Relentless in her task she followed close behind them and did not give up, coaxing her sister to come back with her. She had noticed a difference in Marianka's attitude the minute she had caught up with them and suddenly realized what she was up to. Fear gripped her heart and it gave her great concern she might lose her sister if she did not do something about it. She lunged forward and grabbed Elisa by her arm and pulled with all her might.

"Elisa... Mama wants you back right now," she pleaded. "Come, otherwise Mama will be very sad if I come back without you."

"Elisa, don't listen to Julia. I'll buy you lots and lots of candies," Marianka still kept her cool and tried to convince the little girl. Elisa stood for a while tempted by that offer, but Julia pulled on her arm and did not let go of her.

"Come Elisa, we have to go back before the train leaves. We can't take the chance." Suddenly a voice behind her interrupted their tug of war.

"What's holding you up?" Maria was beside them. "Your mother is worried sick over you."

"Elisa won't listen to me because Marianka promised her candies."

"Where is Marianka?" Maria asked searching for her.

"She is right..." Julia turned back. "She was right here a minute ago." Bewildered she looked around, but Marianka seemed to have vanished.

"Come you two, we better hurry back before both our mothers panic and think the worst."

"I tried so hard to make Elisa come back with me, but she just wouldn't listen," Julia cried.

"Good thing I came along," Maria comforted Julia. "Well,

I would've never thought..." she mumbled to herself as she took the girls by the hand and led them toward the station.

Katina was beside herself when she heard about the whole ordeal. She could not believe that Marianka would do this to her.

--

Marianka walked along the street near the Kutno train station. Dismayed, she let out a deep sigh. "It would have been so easy," She spoke to herself, "if she would not have interfered, I could have succeeded."

Dark thoughts entered her mind, but she knew she could not go through with it. For it would bring danger to her whole family and they would all face punishment.

A tremendous sense of guilt filled her mind now. She definitely could not let her family know what she had planned to do. It would be her secret until her dying day. Her family had been very devoted to Katina and Johann. They had done everything to repay the kindness they had received from them in their time of need. Oh, it would mortify them to hear about her deceitful plan. She felt so deeply ashamed and was disgusted now over her actions.

She never had intended to take Elisa, but when the opportunity presented itself, the thought came into her mind and she acted upon it. She had always loved and adored this little girl. It had been far from her to do this underhanded act, until she left the station with Elisa in hand. It felt so right and for a moment she had let her selfish feelings take over, not thinking of the grief she would cause Katina. She felt so terribly ashamed. She certainly could not go back to the train station now and see them off to say goodbye. She suddenly felt so alone.

--

Katina did not know what to think of this whole ordeal and felt betrayed and scared that Marianka would now turn against them. Fearfully, she and the others kept to themselves among crowds of people. Nervously, they waited to board the train to Posen and beyond to Stettin.

With great anxiety in their hearts they lined up to board the train. Maria went first with her mother and then Katina followed with her children. As they passed the security patrol, the attendant stopped Katina and looked at her questionably. At that moment Maria had glanced back. "Good God," she gasped quietly. "They're onto us," she whispered to her mother.

"What's going on?" Her mother was about to turn to have a look.

"No!" Maria grabbed her by the arm. "Just keep walking."

"They stopped Katina," she spoke in a hushed voice again.

"Oh no," Jobina whispered, her voice quavering.

"Must have been Marianka's doing," Maria mumbled under her breath. "I would never have thought she would stoop to this."

Katina felt her knees go week, panic suddenly overtook her whole body as she fought to put on a calm face. She felt the guard studying her. Any moment she expected to be taken away. She felt so weak, so utterly helpless. Stefan squirmed in her arms and her handbag seamed to weigh a ton.

Julia stood beside her and held Elisa's hand tight in hers. She had noticed her mother's face go pale. The man looked down on her and then to Elisa, then to Stefan.

"Going to be with your husband?"

Katina nodded with relief and gave the man a weak smile.

"It seems every woman is going to Stettin these days," he said with sarcasm and waved her to go through.

She felt as if a big load had been lifted off her. Maria assisted her quickly and huddled the children onto the train.

"Oh...! That was too close," she whispered to Maria, still shaken from the encounter.

"I know... for a minute I thought Marianka might have changed her mind and turned against us, but..."

"The same crossed my mind," she jumped in, exasperated

I WILL REMEMBER ALWAYS

by the thought, "but I guess she had not."

As expected, the train was packed with passengers, only a few empty seats where left. Maria and Jobina took the first, while she found a space near the window. She tried to seat all her children around her, but there seemed not enough room. Dismayed she looked around, when a man opposite her offered to have Elisa on his lap. At first she hesitated, but then gave in, seeing she had no choice. Julia found room on the next aisle beside other passengers, who graciously had moved together to give her a corner to sit on.

"Are you going to visit your husband in Stettin?" a woman suddenly asked her. Lucky for her she remembered what Marianka had told her to say.

"Yes," she quickly answered in Polish and smiled vaguely at the woman who returned the smile. In further conversation the woman told her that she was also going there to meet her husband. Suddenly, others nearby joined in the conversation, which was of great relief to Katina, as now she did not have to answer further questions that could endanger her position.

She took this chance of diversion and quietly pulled herself back into the seat. She needed time to come to herself. That dreadful incident with the security guard had left her unbelievably weak. She tried to make herself comfortable and cuddled little Stefan close to her in hopes that he would fall asleep. It would give both of them a little time to recuperate. She gave another quick glance through the window and discovered Marianka standing forlorn amidst a small crowd of farewell wishers.

Suddenly, her heart gave an extra beat, and she felt a twinge in her stomach. She noticed Marianka's look fixed intensely on the train, her eyes moving from window to window. Katina realized that she was searching for her and the children. Mixed emotions filled her heart. She had been infuriated over Marianka's deceit and still harbored resentfulness toward her. It was unfortunate that the

479

circumstances had brought their friendship to such a drastic and dramatic end.

Although now, when she saw her standing so desperately alone, all the ill feeling in her heart suddenly left her. Her bitterness changed and she felt only pity toward her Polish friend. She wished so much to go and tell her that she was willing to forgive her, but it was not in her power to do so. There was no way she could leave the train car and risk being exposed. Quietly, she watched as the train gave a jerk and started in forward motion.

"Farewell my friend," she whispered with deep remorse. "I will forgive you and will always remember your kindness above all." With tearful eyes, she watched until Marianka was out of sight. Another part in her life had come to an end, as she would never see Marianka and her family again.

She felt so incredibly drained from all the conflict and danger she found herself in. She wished this tormented journey to be over. With much fear and anguish, she cuddled little Stefan closer and kept her eyes ever so watchful on her two girls.

What will happen to all of us once we reach Stettin? What dreadful circumstances await us there? Will we ever reach Germany? Is the rest of my family safe, or had they been caught and dragged off to unknown parts of this war-torn land? Or worse, had they succumbed to a terrible cruel end, as had Johann and his father and so many others. Oh God, I hope not. The heaviness of the moment made her take an extra deep breath.

It suddenly dawned on her that she was going to a place she had little knowledge of. Her brother Robert was the only one in her family who had been familiar with the Fatherland. For a moment, she had concerns of what awaited them there, only to realize as she considered, that it was futile to think so far ahead, when at any given moment, all she had planned could be jeopardized and take a turn for the worse.

Quietly, she observed the passengers around her. Some

still in conversation with each other, while others sat, each to their own thoughts. She wondered where they had come from and what circumstances had brought them here. There was this man, who held little Elisa on his lap, he seemed to be kind and caring, but was he?

And then there was this woman, who claimed to have a husband waiting for her in Stettin. Was this really so, or was it just a ploy, an excuse to disguise who she really was? Just like her.

Katina looked now at everyone. Who really knew who was for real and who was not. Katina even considered the woman beside her, next to the window. Was she really who she appeared to be? It was mind boggling not to know. For this reason, it was best to keep to oneself, in order not to be exposed.

All at once, the conversations stopped, as Posen came in sight. With much anticipation everyone was watching as the train rolled into the station. There among large crowds and heavy Russian security, venders stood ready, calling out their goods.

Stefan suddenly awoke from the noise and commotion and to Katina's horror, called out in perfect German, "Mama, I want a drink of water." Shocked and terrified she glanced around to see if anyone had noticed. She felt her blood pressure rise dangerously fast through her body and into her head.

Surely now she was done for. Across from her the man who had offered Elisa to sit on his lap, gave her a quick smile. Katina believed he understood what it meant. She felt her blood drain from her face. She called for Elisa and Julia in Polish to join her. Suddenly the man stood up and opened the window, then ordered a beverage for himself, as did the woman next to him. Katina nervously waited to have her turn.

Lucky for her, among the noise and commotion, not many passengers seemed to have caught on. Or did they? It was hard to know what was going on. The seat by the window suddenly became vacant and she quickly claimed it for her girls. The little money from the sale of the feather comforter now came in handy. She had kept it divided in small amounts and in different locations in her bag, and now used some of it to purchase a drink to share among themselves. After that, she portioned the sugar beet buns into two meals, one for now and the other for later. As usual, she herself held back and took only a sip and a small bite of Pani Slovak's buns.

She glanced one more time out of the window and heard the conductor give the all clear whistle for the train to leave, when she noticed two Russian officials jump aboard at the last minute. Nervously, she pulled her kerchief deeper around her face. Were they after her? Did the woman, who sat next to her by the window, squeal on her? Fearful, she braced herself to expect the worst. She noticed the same apprehension in the man across from her, who also had seen the officials come on board.

Just as the train had reached its normal speed and resumed its westward quest, the officials entered their rail car. The man across from her suddenly stood up and hastily moved toward the opposite exit. The officials followed suit. Pale, and in shock, Katina stared after them. She glanced over to Jobina and Maria, who looked just as shocked and bewildered to what had just happened. Will they be next? She braced herself. Then, just as the train was speeding through a tunnel, a scream was heard. There was silence among the passengers. No one dared to speak. A little while later the officials entered the rail car again. She huddled her children close to her. One glance at Maria, told her that she too was scared. Jobina's eyes reflected the same emotion, and she noticed her quietly pull her kerchief further over her face.

Had someone tipped the authorities off after they had heard Stefan's cry for water in perfect German, or was this just a routine check? It seemed to be just that, she reassured herself. Suddenly, she noticed the officer's searchingly going from person to person. Her heart pounded heavy against her chest. All at once, she felt faint, as one of the officials stopped right in front of her.

"May I see your train pass?"

She did not dare to look up. The shocked expression in her face would have given her away. Quickly, she scrambled to look for the tickets.

She put them in my bag after going through the check point, but where are they now? Frantically she searched her bag.

"May I inquire to where you're going?" the Russian officer asked politely in broken Polish.

"Stettin, Sir... My husband is working there and I'm to join him with my children."

Finally she found the tickets and was about to hand them over to the officer, when her kerchief slipped off her head and revealed her face. As she looked up, their eyes met. She saw an expression of surprise in his look. Then his expression changed back to an official demeanor. He ordered her to come with him.

"But sir... My children," she held her kids close to her. "They're frightened. I can't leave them."

"Just do as I say and they'll be fine," he commanded.

By now everyone sitting in the rail car had their attention. The officer waved to his colleague to stand guard, while he escorted Katina out of the carriage. Her legs felt weak. She steadied herself and walked slowly toward the exit, in hopes to prolong what was coming beyond the exit door.

Am I next to be thrown off the train? It must have been that woman who heard little Stefan's call for water, or...? Her thoughts left her as her head began to spin. The officer caught her just in time.

"Katina!" he suddenly called her name, as he closed the door to the outside behind him. The noise of the moving train almost drowned out the word that was spoken.

"Don't you remember me?" Puzzled, she looked at him,

when he again reached out to steady her from the swaying of the train.

"Remember? I'm Stefan's friend Duza!" He spoke to her in Romanian now.

She suddenly came to realize that she was not in danger. The man in front of her did not mean her harm. All the anguish and tension released tears of joy and relief.

"What about that man?" she motioned with her head off the train.

"What man?"

"I expected to be thrown off the train, just like him."

"Oh, that man!" Duza exclaimed. "We did not throw him off. He jumped off before we could... Oh... and you thought..." He gave her a vague smile and shook his head.

She steadied herself again and held onto the rail of the car, then studied his face for a moment.

"Is it really you? How can this be?"

"I'm stationed here with my platoon to patrol this area. I'm a Lieutenant in the Russian army." Proudly, he showed her the insignia on his uniform. Then just as quickly his face expression changed when he realized that this was not the time to boast. He looked at her suddenly with great concern. She had aged. Her demeanor displayed a gaunt hollow-eyed sickly looking woman. Unlike the young and beautiful one he had met years ago on the train to Anadolchioi.

"What in heaven's name are you doing on this train?" he questioned her with concern.

Briefly, she told him of her plight. Compassionately, he reached out, "I'll see to it that no harm will come to you as long as you are on this train," he spoke to her gently. "But sadly, after Stettin you're on your own. I wish we could have met again in better circumstances." He clicked his boots and slightly nodded his head forward.

"Take care of yourself Katina. I will always remember the time we had on the train to Anadolchioi. As for now, I wish I could do more for you, but..."

I WILL REMEMBER ALWAYS

"I understand. Thank you Duza." She gave him an appreciative smile. "You have done more than enough."

With that he clicked his boots again. His face expression was that of great concern for her. He nodded respectfully, then opened the door to the rail car and led her back to her seat.

"Everything's in order," he bellowed to his fellow officer, resuming his role as an army officer. He gave one more farewell tap to his hat, then excused himself to Katina and proceeded to follow his comrade out of the rail car.

She stared after them. She felt it all to be a dream.

The girls swarmed around her, relieved to have her back. Julia was in tears and started to sob quietly as she hugged her mother.

"Hush now Julia, don't cry," she comforted her, knowing very well how utterly devastated she must have felt to witness her mother being taken away. Maybe never to see her again as it happened with Father Wendel. 'Poor girl...' she sighed.

"We thought we had seen the last of you... what a fright." Maria talked quietly, but kept a very composed demeanor, knowing others were listening and watching. "We had moved over to take care of the children. The fear in their faces was just too much."

She leaned over and lifted Elisa onto her lap to make the conversation inconspicuous and then moved even closer to Katina as she played with Elisa, again to distract from the conversation.

"We'll talk later," she added in a hushed voice.

Katina smiled vaguely. She was still in disbelief and had not fully recovered from the ordeal. Grateful, she welcomed to be left alone with her thoughts. She again cuddled little Stefan close and gave Julia a reassured smile. Then for a brief moment she closed her eyes, in her mind she replayed the event.

'I can't believe... Duza... here on this train... what a

485

surprise. What a dramatic event. It could have gone the other way... Oh...' she shuddered to think what could have been.

She settled back and took a quick look out of the window as the train pushed westward. Towns and villages had come and gone and the landscape had changed ever so slightly. Her thoughts went back to that day on the train to Anadolchioi, when Stefan Hartig first had introduced her to Duza and his friend Marika.

'Poor Stefan,' she thought, as she remembered how smitten he was over her and how desperately he tried to win her over, but could not deal with her rejection. She suddenly felt a cold shiver creep over her body. The tragic event of that visit in Anadolchioi still haunted her and she wished it would have never happened.

All at once, the further west they traveled, the more she felt the separation from Johann. She longed so much to hear his tender voice once again. Her eyes moistened by that thought. In her weariness she closed them and tried to recall the time of his last furlough. It was as if he tried to take in every moment and store them in his heart, then draw on them whenever he needed to, out there on the battlefield.

She recalled the deep sadness in his eyes as he sat polishing his gun to keep it in top working condition for his return to the front.

She still could hear the sad songs he had sung as he worked, soldier songs, yearning songs for home and loved ones.

'Oh, Johann! How can I go on without you?' A deep silent cry pierced her anxious heart. Overwhelmed by grief, she pretended to adjust her kerchief and with the same motion quickly wiped away her tears. A deep heavy sigh escaped her chest. Lovingly, she looked at her children, they were all she had now. For them she had to forget and move on. She embraced little Stefan and held him close to her heart. For their sake, I can't lose faith now she reassured herself. O God, give me strength, she prayed in her battle-scarred soul.

The train was slowing when they approached a small town en route to Stettin. And when it finally rolled into the station, she glanced out of the window. It was packed with people and it did not escape her how heavily patrolled it was by Russian soldiers, more so than in the previous stations. She recalled the meeting with Duza and wondered if he was still on the train. She strained to see if she could see him among the soldiers, but to no avail.

Just then, she noticed some of the Russian soldiers enter their rail car. She warned the children to stay quiet. Slowly the soldiers walked along the aisle, again searching and studying every face. She busied herself to give her children the last morsels of Pani Slovak's food. All the while dodging eye contact with the soldiers, as she again feared that the angst in her eyes would give her away.

Suddenly, one of the soldiers stopped. She could see his polished boots from the corner of her eyes. She felt his piercing eyes upon her, but she did not dare to look up. She tried to stay calm, remembering Duza's promise, yet could she rely on his word? Her heart was racing. She felt so utterly, devastatingly uneasy. It was as if the man could see right through her and could read her innermost thoughts. Finally, and to her relief, the soldiers moved on and resumed to walk out of the car.

Still shaking, she gave a quick glance toward Maria and Jobina. She did not have to ask, for the terror was still vivid in their eyes, as they probably perceived in hers. A cold shudder went through her body, stunned once again from the unnerving and dangerously close encounter. They all sat silently in a daze, no one dared to move or speak.

'It was strange though,' she thought. 'It was as if the soldier knew something.' Silently she took a look out of the window, as the crowd moved to and fro in the station. For her liking, there were too many Russian soldiers about. Anxiously, she wished for the train to move on.

After what seemed like an eternity, the train finally

started and kept its course in the direction of Stettin. Stefan and Elisa, both exhausted from the long journey, were now sleeping protectively, one on Katina's lap and the other on Maria's. Julia too was resting her head on her mother's shoulder, tired from all the commotion. Again, she understood what was at stake, every time their escape was in danger.

"When will this all be over?" Julia spoke in a hushed voice, her eyes still portraying fear.

Katina gave her a weak smile.

"Only God knows, my child," she whispered and leaned her head on Julia's to comfort her, but also to let her know she understood her frustration.

"I hope it will be soon," Julia replied solemnly.

77

The devastation of war was even more evident the further west they traveled. During their long years in seclusion, while enduring their own torturous and painful existence, they had not been aware of all the monstrosities this war had produced. In the process to gain control and power, many innocent lives had paid the ultimate price. Now in hindsight, had it really been worth it?

'All this turmoil and upheaval,' she sighed, her heart burdened by the senselessness of it all. It was inconceivable for her to comprehend the vast devastation of land and dwellings, and unfortunately, as they too had experienced, human fatalities.

Her disbelief and shock increased when the train rolled into Stettin, once a large and majestic city, now mostly a pile of rubble. Numb and dazed, she and the others stared out of the window. Even the children stood in awe of the destruction. As far as they could see there was hardly a building left standing which could safely be used as living quarters. Most of them lay in ruins with only a chimney or a partial wall remaining in an upright position, ready to topple by the slightest rumble.

She thought of the many poor souls who must have endured horrendous anxiety, as well as torturous suffering during the devastation of this beautiful city that now resembled that of a graveyard. It left a very disheartening and hopeless impression and she was sure the others felt the same. Was that what was to be expected for the rest of the journey? Shocked and scared, she did not dare to imagine anything better.

The train had slowed and finally came to a complete halt, unable to go further, because of the city's damaged infrastructure. There, in front of them, the massive train bridge lay broken in half like an injured giant. The broken bridge separated the numerous train tracks. Before being destroyed this bridge carried many a fine train far from the east to the west and vice versa.

Confused and scared of the unknown, Katina gathered her belongings and the children. She then lined up to follow Maria and Jobina, out of the train. Most of the people seemed to know where they were going, unlike her and the others in her group who suddenly found themselves lost and alone beside the train tracks with no one to help them.

"What do we do now?" Jobina asked with a quavering voice.

Depleted of all the essentials in mind, body and spirit, they just could not stomach any more obstacles and disappointments.

Twilight had set in and they were in desperate need to find shelter, to get out of the bone chilling evening air. Most of all, they had to find something to eat and drink, especially for the children, but how and where?

"If someone asks questions, remember what Marianka told us to say," she warned everyone.

Huddling close together, they stood contemplating on what to do next, when a scratchy voice from an old woman suddenly interrupted their concentration.

"Are you looking for a place to stay?" Surprised and startled, they looked around. Here of all places they would have never imagined to hear someone address them in their native tongue. Was it so obvious that they were Germans? Shocked and baffled, they could not believe that this was so noticeable.

The old woman, recognizing the perplexed and questionable look, said with a sorrowful smile, "I saw that lost and forlorn look in your faces..." she sighed and then added with pity in her voice. "I just knew..."

Looking at her, Katina perceived her to be on a scavenger hunt, for in her hands she held what looked like a slightly dinged cook pot and a dusty old tea pot.

"Just keep in mind not to speak German, not even a whisper, for even the walls of these ruins have ears." The old woman pointed to the damaged buildings as she spoke with warning in her voice. Then looking around to see if anyone was within ear shot, she proceeded with a quiet whisper.

"Tomorrow morning, if you want to eat, you'll have to go and register with the authorities in town. There you'll be properly integrated and most likely be called for work duty."

"What?" Maria retorted. "Then we are right back where we came from."

"Yes! Yes!" the old woman hushed Maria down. "But this time it's different. Don't forget you are Polish women, and even they must go through a process of registration if they want to reach their final destination."

"How long will that be?" Katina asked, with a defeated undertone. "I don't know if I can go through any more hard labor." She released a heavy sigh. The others in her group agreed.

"It won't be too long, at least that's what I understood," the woman stopped thoughtfully. "Let's see," she spoke to herself. "It's the second day for me now. If all goes well, we'll hopefully be transported out of here soon."

After a few more words of advice between them, the woman then told them where to go to find shelter. She pointed with her scraggily hand to walk over the bridge, then to go straight ahead.

"There, on the other side you'll find some of the houses that are not totally demolished. There you can search for a place to stay for the night."

Grateful, they all thanked her again and again and wished each other well as they parted. Eagerly, they did as they were told and struggled to walk down and then up again over the partly demolished bridge. They then proceeded along the rubble filled street, until they found what looked to them to be a stable house.

Once inside, they found two rooms unoccupied, the rest had been claimed by two other Polish women with children. One of the mothers there had pity on Katina and felt compelled to give her two of her pillows and a few morsels of bread for the children.

"In the morning you'll be going in this direction to receive your food rations," she pointed south and then added quickly, pointing in the opposite direction. "There is plenty of fresh water over there, not far from here." Grateful Katina thanked the woman for the gift and the advice.

"There is an hour of daylight left," Maria suddenly spoke up while the little ones chewed on their last bite of bread. "Julia and I have decided to go out and scout around for some pots, so we can bring water home for us to drink. And maybe, if we're lucky we'll find a bowl to wash ourselves in." She stopped for a moment, straightening her clothes, she added. "I don't know about you, but I could use a little freshening up."

Julia was on her feet and ready to go with Maria, when little Elisa started to cry. "I want to go with you." Seeing how hard it was for their mothers to look after both of the little ones, the older ones agreed to take Elisa along on their scavenger hunt.

"Be careful! And don't be too long!" Katina warned in a hushed voice, as the three left the room.

It could not have been more than twenty minutes when they returned with their treasure. Julia held a perfectly good aluminum cook pot in her hand. "And it has a lid too!" She proudly presented it to her mother. Little Elisa showed off a white enamel teapot she had carried protectively all the way back.

Maria too had found what she had wanted. "Now we can at least have a drink of water and wash ourselves too." She said triumphantly, holding in her left hand a good sized battle scarred tin bowl and in her right an old pail filled with the most delicious, thirst quenching water. "Drink up," she encouraged everyone. "There's plenty more where this came from."

Elisa's small teapot was initiated to serve up the fresh drink of water, to which they all agreed, had never tasted better. Satisfied, and tired from the long nerve-racking journey, they finally settled in for the night.

Not familiar with their new surroundings, they decided to stay together in one room for protection. While the girls had been away, Katina and Jobina had done some scouting of their own. They had found some torn dusty rags of clothing and blankets in the ruins nearby, which would come in handy to sleep on and for covering up.

Before long darkness filled their primitive quarters, huddled together, most of them were soon overcome with sleep. Not Katina. Her body was aching from the cool dampness that crept through the open windows and doors and along the dusty rubbish scattered surface of the floor. Once in a while she heard Jobina tossing, but in general the children seemed to be able to sleep.

Suddenly, she sat up, alerted by some rolling debris outside. All at once there was a shadow hovering in the open window. She felt a hand from behind. Trembling and in shock, a gasp escaped her lips. The years in the compound had left her scared and horrified at the slightest sound and confrontation of danger.

"Sh-h-h... It's me," Jobina whispered, as she too had seen the dark figure.

For the longest time it stood silent, outlined by the pale autumn moonlight. Katina felt shivers going up and down her spine. What was to be done? She felt helpless. She reached quietly around her, searching for a weapon she could use for protection, but there was nothing. Her heart nearly stopped when she noticed the dark figure crawl through the window and quietly step into the room. Luckily, they had chosen to bed down away from the window. Protectively, she held her hand over the children. She readied herself for an attack, and so did Jobina. Both sat quiet, not to alarm the children.

The figure suddenly stumbled. A suppressed moan escaped his mouth. Katina's mind raced, as she braced herself. They would have loved to find a more protective area on the second floor, but it had already been claimed by the others. An overwhelming uncomfortable feeling came over her, with her weakened state and sore knees she was in no condition to fight back. Jobina was not much better off. Maria was sixteen, a prime target for sexual predators. Had the girls been followed back to this place after their scavenger hunt?

Suddenly, a scream pierced the room. Elisa had woken and had noticed the large dark silhouette of a figure moving from the window towards them. In bewilderment and surprise the man leaped out of the window, again releasing an agonizing moan as he hit the uneven rocky debris below.

She quickly took Elisa into her arms, quietly talking to her to calm her. The poor child she thought. The years spent in that God forsaken compound had left her terrified of anything and anyone unfamiliar, especially in the dark hours of the night. Julia and Maria, woken by Elisa's scream, now stood trembling and ready for action. While she and Jobina quietly explained to them what had happened. Oddly enough, little Stefan had only stirred for a moment and went right back to sleep again.

She could feel Elisa's whole body tremble as she held her close. The little one jerked repeatedly to look back toward the open window where she had seen the dark figure. "Poor child," she sighed again mournfully.

After some time Elisa finally calmed down. Safe in her

mother's arms, she felt protected, releasing a few more heavy sobs she nestled in and soon fell asleep again.

No one dared to move. Quietly, they listened for any movement, but not even a trickle of debris could be heard. Had the man left or was he still crouched underneath the window, waiting to attempt the same again?

When after some time there was no movement, they reluctantly resumed to settle down. Tired, the others were soon fast asleep. To Katina though, the much needed sleep did not come, again and again she tossed and perked her ears, but all she could hear was the deep even breathing of the children and Jobina.

Once in a while Elisa coughed. 'Probably from the dust...' she thought to herself, as it hung thick in the air whenever someone stirred or turned. She tried to quiet herself and relax. For a little while longer she lay listening... But then, like the others, she too was overcome with sleep.

--

A misty cool morning greeted them the next day as a cold breeze sent a chill into their quarters, making it uncomfortable to remain lying on the damp ground. There was a lot of talk about the intruder among the other squatters in the building. As they too reported to have heard someone creep around the premises.

"The sooner we can get away from this place the better it will be for all of us," Katina retorted to Jobina, who agreed whole heartedly.

Quickly she and Jobina gathered the children and their few belongings, then joined the long lineup of the displaced masses of hungry people down the road, not far from where they had spend a cold shivering night.

As they neared the registration and distribution area, she noticed the Russian delegates questioning the people before they went on to receive their food rations.

"Remember... let Maria do the talking," she whispered to Jobina, who nodded in acknowledgment and pulled her scarf tighter across her face.

She reminded Jobina, knowing now that the kerchief around her head and over her mouth was to avoid being asked questions, as she was not fluent in Polish.

Julia understood the warning her mother had given to Jobina. She knew they all had to be careful and not let their guard down.

With the two little ones, Katina had purposely kept up speaking Polish to them so they would not lose the language, and at this moment she desperately hoped it would work and there would not be another outburst from Stefan, like the one they had experienced on the train.

Recalling the incident, a gripping fear suddenly swept through her. They had come so far and it would be devastating to be caught now. She prayed this would not happen. Quickly, she pulled the two little ones aside.

"I have to speak to these men over there. You stay close to me and Julia and do not say a word! Understand?" Elisa and Stefan nodded. Their faces portrayed a fearful look. They only had heard Mama speak this way when there was danger. Quietly, Elisa held onto her mother's hand, while Julia took hold of little Stefan's hand, as they approached the Russian officials.

Katina tried to muster up enough confidence in mind and body as she stood in front of the officers. He looked at her and the children for a moment, as if to study them."Where are you from?" one asked while the other sat by watching her and the children.

"Piątek," she answered in perfect Polish.

"Do you have any proof or identification?" The officer spoke Polish with a heavy Russian accent.

"None sir," she said with a clear voice. "I lost them during the German invasion."

He nodded. "I understand. And where are you and your children going?"

"To Germany sir, my husband is in the workforce there,"

I WILL REMEMBER ALWAYS

she spoke, surprised at herself how assured her voice sounded. It felt strange to lie, and yet there it was and she hoped it was convincing enough.

"It seems to be the thing to do these days." The officer turned toward his comrade, giving him a questionable look. Then the two talked for a moment.

"Are you absolutely sure you want to go to Germany?" the officer asked again.

"Sir, I've nowhere else to go," she pleaded, but stood firm on her request.

The officer looked straight into her eyes and thought for a moment. Yet, to her it felt like an eternity, when finally he seemed to have come to a conclusion.

"Okay!" He nodded in approval toward his fellow comrade, who then handed her a temporary pass.

"Do not lose this!" he warned with a stern commanding voice. "Tomorrow, there will be a train leaving for Germany, between six and eight in the morning," he said and waved her to move on, turning his attention to the next person in line.

She could not believe that she had managed to get past the authorities. Still in a grip of fear, her body trembled. Her knees threatened to buckle. She steadied herself, determined to succeed in her quest. She walked on with her children in tow to stand in the next lineup. As she received her ration of bread, she was told where she had to work, just as the old woman has warned them about.

"Of all things," she retorted quietly to Julia. "I have to go and help with the preparation and cleanup for a wedding. Can you imagine? Here, among this chaos and need, people are getting married and carrying on as if nothing had happened." She shook her head in disbelief as she glanced back and noticed that Jobina and Maria too had made it through the check point, and past the breadline.

Desperately she waited to tell them of her dilemma, but upon speaking to them she was informed that they too had been farmed out to work. She had hoped that at least Maria

497

would have been exempt from work duty, to help Julia with the two little ones.

"I guess I have to leave you then to look after Elisa and Stefan," she turned to Julia, now very worried for their safety.

"We'll be okay Mama," Julia reassured her and did not let on that she too was scared. "I'll try to be very careful. You don't need to worry."

She calmed herself with that and handed the bread over to her daughter, as she took a bite for herself. "If you go for water, be sure to go right back to the place where we stayed," she warned Julia, worried and dismayed that she had to leave them.

--

Julia put on a brave face, holding back her emotions. She had to be strong for her little siblings. Mama would have wanted it that way. Just then, Elisa started to cry. Quickly, she tried to distract her by offering her a small piece of bread. On the way back she detoured to walk past the train track, where yesterday she had noticed apple trees with some of the apples still hanging on the branches. Now upon closer inspection and to her delight she found her hunch to be true. What a treat that'll be. Mama will be so proud, she thought to herself.

Like a treasure she hid most of them in her coat pockets and kept one to share with her siblings. Then she walked the little ones back to the place where they had stayed for the night. She was happy to find it still the way they had left it. Taking the pail in hand, she told Elisa and Stefan to stay close beside her as they set out to get more water. All along she kept a watchful eye about her surroundings, stopping once in a while for her little siblings to rest.

--

Work was plenty and steady as Katina found herself assigned to prepare twelve freshly slaughtered hens for the wedding feast. Though while working on them she suddenly felt ill from the smell and look of raw fowl guts and it made her stomach turn. To her surprise the Polish woman who was in charge had noticed and offered her a shot of vodka. "It'll make you feel better," she said with a smile.

She tried a little, but on an empty stomach the brew acted twice as strong. Very calmed and relaxed now, she came to understand what the woman meant by 'feeling better.'

It was in the early evening hours when she was finally released from her place of work. The sun had gone down and twilight had set in. Here and there people hurried past her and then one by one disappeared in the shadows of the scarcely livable dwellings. All at once, she looked around. Had she taken the wrong turn? Suddenly she was unsure. Thick fog had started to set in, creeping quietly along the ruins, portraying the standing chimneys as ghostly objects.

"What a wretched time to be out," she said to herself, dismayed over her dilemma. Straining her eyes to make out the direction, she suddenly noticed a group of women coming toward her. Relieved, and to her surprise, she recognized Maria and Jobina among them.

"I'm so glad to see you," she called out to them in Polish. "I've just about given up ever finding my way back to our home base."

"Then we've just come at the right time," Maria called out to comfort her.

"Come along then, none of us is a hundred percent sure, but if we stick together we'll be able to find our way back..." A woman, unknown to her spoke up, as they busied themselves to keep on walking.

After they had gone a block, they surprisingly found themselves in familiar territory at the train tracks by the damaged bridge. Looking back now, their work places had not been too far from here in the first place. In the twilight, she had to admit, distance can be a little deceiving.

Tired, she struggled to keep up with the rest of them. She had been worried all day for her children, thinking the worst, but as soon as they had reached their home base, her anxious mind was quieted, for upon arrival, and to her surprise, she found them all safe and well taken care of.

In the semidarkness of the room, they sat down as a group and shared the few morsels of chicken feet and other discarded and leftover food that she had been allowed to take home. Hungry, they chewed off every bit of skin and soft cartilage and sucked dry the bare bones. It was barely enough to quiet their hunger, but they were grateful to have had what they had been given.

During the night she felt very restless. Nervously she kept listening for strange noises, but to her relief, there were no repeat visits from the intruder.

Anxious not to miss the train, she and Jobina woke early at dawn to get themselves and the children ready. They feared the train would be even more overcrowded than the previous one. That gave them the urgency to be there earlier, just to make sure they would make it out of here. She especially had no desire to stay behind another day in this stark, uninviting and forsaken place, and she could see it in the others too.

78

As they reached the makeshift train station, they encountered what they had feared. Hordes of people had already gathered, all anxious to be the first on the train. Most sat or lay huddled together for warmth, claiming a spot on the dirt floor. Her heart stirred with pity and anxiety as she looked over the lumps of seemingly motionless bodies.

Desperate, she looked for an open spot. 'The closer to the train tracks the better.' She thought. Careful not to step on the masses of cold and shivering people, they followed each other, maneuvering themselves toward a small opening. Here they settled to join the rest of the destitute. An old wool blanket, which Jobina had found among the ruins, came in handy. It gave them a little protection from the cool and moist fall air as they waited.

A pale sunrise greeted them when finally a long freight train approached from the east and slowed to a halt. Suddenly, the lumps of people came alive with a flurry of pushing and shoving, everyone was rushing toward the train to be first.

Maria and Julia had managed to jump on board one of the freight containers. Struggling not to be pushed off, they fought to pull the rest of their family on board. All around them people were panic stricken, screaming, yelling, pushing and shoving in desperation to get onto the train; each holding on to their loved ones for fear of losing one another.

Far in the corner of the freight container, away from the door, they finally found a spot and nestled into the straw covered floor. The air inside hung thick with dust from all the commotion, but they did not mind. They had made it, and that was all they cared about.

More and more people filed in, among them the old lady who had helped them when they had first arrived here. Quickly, they aided her to settle in beside them. Gladly, the old woman accepted. Surprised to see her all alone, Katina wondered what tragedy she must have endured to find herself in this predicament.

People were still struggling and pushing to get into their container, but there was no more space left. Suddenly, just as an official came by to shove the huge container door shut, a mother with a baby in her arms came running by, calling for her child that she had lost in the shuffle. It was heart wrenching and painful to hear her agonizing and terror-filled cry. Everyone sat awe struck.

"Someone, help the poor woman," another woman's voice suddenly emerged from their crowded freight container.

All at once a timid voice from the opposite far corner was heard and became louder. The lost child recognized the voice of his mother. Quickly, those closest to the door, hastily helped the poor woman and her baby join her lost child. Relieved and thankful, with tears flowing down her haggard looking face, the woman retreated to a corner, huddling her children close around her. Moved by this scene, Katina treasured to have her own children safe beside her.

Suddenly, the huge door slammed shut and she heard a leaver interlock from the outside. 'We're locked in like cattle and at the mercy of strangers,' she thought to herself, releasing a quiet sigh. A shrill whistle was heard, signaling that the train was ready to move out. Then, with a few bumps and jerks, the wheels started in forward motion. Struggling at first under the load it was carrying, the train picked up speed and moved along with great ease.

Holding onto her children with worry in her heart, she leaned back against the wall of the container. Tired, the little ones fell asleep, their heads resting on her lap while Julia leaned against her shoulder. Next to them sat Maria and her mother and right beside them, the old woman. Katina and Jobina had agreed to keep their few belongings between them, away from prying eyes and long fingers. As they all, especially Katina, had learned a valuable lesson not to let even a pair of socks lying about.

Crowded, and unable to move around, everyone in their group settled back, as did the other inhabitants in the container car, with each cuddling close to their loved ones for warmth, for the cool air from outside seeped through even the tiniest cracks in the walls. The familiar rhythm of the bump-bump of the train rolling along the tracks, soon lulled many of them to sleep.

Katina found herself suddenly daydreaming, remembering again the time when she had taken the train to visit her sister Tara. Her thoughts went freely from one event to another, revisiting carefree times. She almost could smell the fresh sea air that drifted over the land from the nearby Black Sea. All at once she felt herself getting drowsy and before she knew, she too had dozed off.

Suddenly, her snooze was interrupted as the train came to a halt. Loud commanding voices coming from the outside were heard. All at once their container door flew open.

"Everyone quickly outside!" a Russian officer commanded as a group of soldiers stood guard to watch each passenger as they stepped out of the train.

"Women with children go on this side! Men line up on this side!" the officer bellowed again.

"What is going to happen to us?" Julia whispered terrified as she moved towards her mother, each holding onto the little ones. Jobina and Maria also gathered close, as did the old woman. Frightened, they stood and watched as the officer, with a group of his men, walked slowly past the row of women and children, then in the same manner past the men who were mostly older in age. It seemed whatever or whoever they were searching for was not among the people standing.

"Search the containers!" the officer bellowed once again. Quickly a large group of soldiers swarmed into the emptied freight containers.

Suddenly, there was a big commotion of shouting and shuffling. Then to everyone's horror, the soldiers dragged, what appeared to be a young man, out of one of the containers. His eyes were hollow and full of anguish. His clothes torn and ragged looking from years of wear.

"An escaped prisoner... My God..." In a silent gasp Katina was holding her breath. He was tall in stature, but his haggard looking demeanor portrayed years of hunger and abuse. From what he was wearing, it was hard to know where he was from or who he was. She could not stomach to watch and tried to shield her little ones from witnessing what was to come. The fugitive was led away into the wooded area nearby. Then shots rang out. She, as well as her children, trembled in shock at the sound.

Pale and scared, they stood to await their own frightful fate. But the only order that came again from the same officer was, "If anyone has to relieve themselves, go and do so now before boarding the train." He pointed in different directions as he spoke, "Men go on this side and women with children to the opposite side."

Once on board the train they were locked in again, as the journey continued westward. For a long time, she, as the rest of the women in her group, sat huddled together each lost in their own thoughts, when she suddenly interrupted the silence. She leaned toward Jobina and spoke with a hushed undertone.

"Could he have been the intruder from Stetin?"

Jobina, without hesitation, agreed. "You know, the same

thought went through my mind. He had the stature of the shadowy figure. I wonder if he was a German soldier," she added, with a painful expression on her face, shaking her head with pity.

"He could have been a deserter or worse yet, a traitor. I've heard, if caught, most of them end up dead," the old lady whispered. "I've seen it happen even in our own army."

"Poor fellow," Katina sighed. "So young, it's a horrible way to go."

"And his family, if he had one, would never know what happened to him," Jobina whispered, distraught. Thinking of her own husband, of whom she had not heard from since the Umsturtz. She pondered often if he was still alive or dead. It was a torment not to know. Johann and he had served together in the same battalion on the Russian Front.

"At least you know that your Johann is dead, unlike me, I don't know where my Robert is," Jobina looked at Katina and started to cry. This dreadful event had reopened painful memories in Jobina, as well as Katina, for she too now had tears rolling down her hollow cheeks.

"At least you have some hope that your Robert is alive," she spoke up, a little miffed at Jobina's remark. "There isn't a moment where I too have thoughts of doubt that Johann is dead. In my heart I feel, and want to believe, that his comrades may have made a mistake and that he is still alive. I've heard from the Slovaks that many German soldiers had ended up in prison camps, far into Siberia. Maybe, just maybe…, one never knows." Her thoughts trailed. She was suddenly quiet as more tears welled up in her eyes, her mind full of anguish. "This war has brought nothing but heartache and pain," she mumbled mostly to herself. Her voice broke as she struggled with her emotions.

"The future had looked so promising back in Romania," she continued in a hushed voice, releasing a heavy sigh. "Now look at us. There are only a few of us women with children left, barely surviving. Most of our men are dead or missing in action or in prison camps. God only knows where. Our families scattered, who knows if we will ever see them again. Who is to know if they all made it to safety or if they are still alive, and who is to know what is awaiting us the next time the container door opens?" Again, she was overcome with tears, as was Jobina, while the old woman sat silent.

"Mama, you have us, don't cry Mama," Julia comforted her mother, as did Maria hers.

Katina dried her eyes quickly. "Forgive me. I shouldn't have said all those things. It's not good to dwell on them anyway. There's nothing any of us can do now but to hope for the best." Tired she leaned back, wiping away more tears. 'What was she doing? She had to be strong and not give in to these thoughts,' she scolded herself, knowing how upsetting it was for the children to see her cry.

"Get a hold of yourselves...," the old women spoke in a low voice. "I understand the pain, for I too have lost a husband. My two sons are missing somewhere in Stalingrad and my younger daughter... Oh God, it pains me still to think about it. She...." The old woman stopped for a moment to contain her emotions. "She... my poor girl... repeatedly the Russian soldiers had molested her, and after carrying an unwanted child she went into difficult labor. Oh God... what pain..." The woman's voice broke, as she fought to gain her composure. "My daughter and the child did not survive," She added with deep anguish.

Pausing for a moment to muster enough strength, she quickly added. "But we can't give up. I know! I know!"

She waved off the surprised look from the other two. "I know it isn't easy and you may think why go on...? But look at you two, you both have children to live for, and for them you have to have courage and not give in to the depression and sorrow."

"You're right!" Katina agreed, a little ashamed. "What have I to complain, at least I have my children, when you have lost so much?" With this she drew back. The old lady was right. She had at least her children for comfort. With that she had to be content. She closed her eyes. 'I will overcome... with God's help... I will overcome,' she battled with herself.

Julia and Maria both, had taken it upon themselves to distract the two little ones from the sad conversation and started to make straw dolls from the straw around them. Content, the little ones watched with delight and played for hours with their new toys; while the freight train rushed along, squealing occasionally by the slightest bend on the seemingly endless stretch of rails.

A hush had fallen over of the occupants in the freight container. Exhausted from the lack of sleep, and deprived of food and water as well as fresh air, most had resigned themselves to conserve what little strength there was to carry on.

Suddenly, a braking screech of the wheels brought everyone back to consciousness. Startled, Katina looked around the semi darkened container. The little ones were still sleeping on her lap. Julia and the others in her group were also alerted by the sudden jolt. How long they had been sleeping, no one knew, for none had a watch to verify the time.

"What now?" she heard Maria exclaim. Jobina as well looked alarmed.

"Maybe just another bathroom break," Katina spoke quietly.

She heard someone in the crowd mumble something about the border. Could it be that this was the case? Everyone was alert..., with eyes wide open they listened intensely for anything or anybody that could verify what was going on. With a final jolt, the train came to a halt, but no one came to open the door.

Maria took it upon herself to peek through a tiny crack in the wall of the container to observe what was going on, but to no avail, the crack was too small. Suddenly, she discovered a small lever, not far from where she had tried to peer through the small opening.

"Look at this!" she exclaimed quietly. "A peephole... I should have known about it sooner." Looking out now, she was disappointed at the scenery outside. "Nothing but trees as far as I can see.... It's hard to tell where we are."

"Let me see!" Julia whispered beside her. "Why, look at this..." she spoke in a hushed voice as she peered through the hole. "There are soldiers in the forest. I wonder what they are up to?"

"How come I had not seen them? Let me have another look..." Maria moved toward the opening. "It looks like a whole battalion..." she reported quietly back to the others. "They're unloading something from the train and carrying it into the forest."

"We're probably on a supply train. Remember, only selected freight containers were made available for all of us people," the old woman contemplated.

"That would make sense," Katina agreed. "They're probably guarding the border."

"Then we must be very close to the German border," Jobina added thoughtfully.

"Yes, I would say so," Katina spoke again in a hushed voice.

"Aren't we glad we are not escaping on foot?" the old lady whispered. "I certainly couldn't." She thought for a moment. "Who knows how many more are hiding in the thick of the forest. Oh, I get goose bumps just to think of being captured again and go through all the suffering and torture, or worse yet, being killed."

"Children, come away from there and close the opening, the less we are seen the better," the old woman warned. "It'll be a relief for all of us to finally cross the border and be free from all this torment."

"Well, I tell you what else is tormenting me," Jobina spoke in a hushed and bothersome voice. "I thought we had left them behind when we fled the compound. Can't you feel them? This dumbfounded straw is infested with lice. Uh, what a torture! I'll be glad when we finally can be free of them."

"I had noticed it soon after we boarded the train," Katina remarked casually and suddenly felt the urge to scratch. "The poor children," she sighed, and looked at them. "Hopefully on the other side of the border we can get relief from these pesky creatures. Just the thought of them, nesting and crawling all over our bodies... Oh!" She shook herself. "It's sickening!"

"Come, come now, let's not talk about lice," the old woman cut in. "There's a lot worse things to be concerned about than lice," she waved it off.

"I'm thirsty Mama," little Elisa suddenly awoke.

"Soon, hopefully soon, we'll get some water and food," she stroked her gently. "Go back to sleep, it'll help you not to think about it." Elisa listened and laid herself back down on her mother's lap.

She knew it would not be long before she would hear the same plea, and it bothered her deeply not to be able to help her child, as they were all in need of food and water.

"You're right," she resumed again, acknowledging the old woman's earlier comment. "It's true. There are far more dangerous and life threatening situations, but I still can't stand them."

Jobina nodded in agreement.

Both suppressed a quiet chuckle as they settled back, turning to their own thoughts, all the while listening to hear what was going on outside. Suddenly, Katina became aware that it was easier to sit in the train when it was moving then when it stood still. First, there seemed to be a little more airflow in the container, another, the rhythm of the wheels bumping along the tracks felt calming to one's mind.

Suddenly, a loud rushing sound from another train sped by them, blowing its ear-deafening whistle, and just as fast as it came, it faded into the distance again toward the east. They heard footsteps, distinctively those of soldier's boots hitting the stony ground with certainty and force as they passed by the container.

"Maria...! Take another peek and see what it going on, but be very careful," Katina cautioned.

Just as Maria had shown her face through the small opening, some of the soldiers suddenly became aware of the cargo inside that particular freight container. Noticing it she immediately pulled back and shut the opening.

"What's in the rest of those containers?" The soldiers questioned the other soldiers near the train. "I could swear I saw a beautiful young girl looking through an opening on that container over there," one soldier exhorted, as he pointed in their direction.

"Bah! They're just Polish women and children and a few old men, nothing to get excited about. Most of them are on their way to Germany to be with their husbands." One of the soldiers remarked, sarcastically.

But those who had detected Maria were sure of what they had seen. Suddenly, there was a commotion among the soldiers as they decided to see for themselves and moved in the direction of their train car.

"What's going on over there?" The officer, who was overlooking this operation, bellowed. "Get back to your assigned stations at once and if anyone dares to disobey my orders, they will be severely punished." Reluctantly, the soldiers moved away and resumed to carry on with their duties.

"I think we had just been spared by the officer," the old woman suddenly spoke. Born in Russia, she understood what all the commotion was about and what the young Russian soldiers were after. She knew all too well, if let loose, their brutal actions would know no mercy or boundary.

"If I were you," she motioned toward Katina and Jobina. "Yes, especially Maria, for she is the most vulnerable... I would wear the kerchief even tighter into the face and hang a big coat or shawl over myself, so not to be easily sought out for being young and attractive... And for goodness sake, stay out of sight and try not to draw attention to yourselves..."

Katina, as well as Jobina, understood the old woman and took her advice seriously.

"It was my fault to ask Maria to look out. It will not happen again," Katina apologized.

"Yes, we better stay low and not draw too much attention towards us, otherwise the other folks in the container will get suspicious too," Jobina warned quietly.

Jobina's warning provoked a sudden uneasy feeling in Katina and she started to pray silently that the train would soon be on its way again. For she knew she could not keep her little ones quiet once they awoke. It had been too long since they last had a drink of water or a bite to eat.

She sat now contemplating, looking over the people in the semi-dark container, some huddling in groups, some by themselves, the thought came to her again... 'Who is to say if they were all what they proclaimed to be?' In this situation it was safer to be cautious and not presume otherwise.

Suddenly, they heard the train whistle, and with a few heavy thrusts, the locomotive once again started. Slowly it moved the wheels of the freight containers into motion, and then increased to resume its speed westward. She had fallen asleep as did the rest. Suddenly woken by someone's cough, she stirred then stared into the semi-darkness of the wagon. Again not knowing how long she had been sleeping.

Her body ached from sitting so long in the same position, but she dared not to move for fear the little ones would wake. She closed her eyes to relax, she started to daydream, drifting back to more pleasant times, of sunny days by the seaside as she and Johann walked arm in arm along the shores of the Black Sea. She could almost feel his warm embrace. His tender voice filled with compassion and love, a love that was not easily found again.

'Life without you my darling will be so hard to bear.'

She fought to keep from crying, but the tears that did

escape rolled undetected into her kerchief. 'Oh Johann, you were my anchor, my rock I could lean on.'

Suddenly his smiling face flashed before her. His last words resounding in her mind, 'I hope we'll be together until the sunset of our days... together... together...'

Suddenly, an unexpected jolt and the sharp braking of the wheels brought her back to reality. She sighed, her heart filled with a deep oppressive emptiness.

The train kept on, moving slowly along the tracks.

"I wonder if this is it?" she heard Jobina's voice suddenly filled with heightened anticipation, and just as Jobina had finished speaking, the train gave a final jolt and stopped all together.

They all listened intensely, voices were heard, and suddenly the container door was thrust open again.

"Everyone out and line up," a man called out in German.

Surprise and disbelief, that they had finally made it, flooded over her. It was inconceivable to grasp. All the torment and anguish of the past two years were suddenly no more. 'Was this it now... or was there more to come...?' she pondered. 'How will their supposed countrymen accept them...? Would there be unforeseen problems ahead...?'

Her eyes fell on soldiers of a different army standing off to the side, watching intently, studying all the people as they filed out of the freight containers.

'More soldiers.' In an instant this thought provoked not so pleasant memories. Mistrusting, she questioned what torment was awaiting them now. Her head was spinning. She had lost all of her important papers. How can she prove that she and her children were German citizens? Full of anticipation and angst... yes mind and body paralyzing fear... She could not believe... here she thought they were finally among their own kind... Now seeing this unnerved her greatly. She tried to calm herself, but to her dismay, the fright did not leave her.

Fear had been an unwelcome companion since the onset of

the war and still, here again, it was haunting her. What was one to do? There was nothing she could do to rid herself from this numbing torment.

'Steady, Katina... Get a hold of yourself... Be strong... You can't give up,' she encouraged herself. Her weak body trembled, but she managed to gather the children and her few belongings and with great difficulty followed the others off the train.

"Where are we?" Julia asked with apprehension, as they stepped off the train and onto the grounds of a small station.

"Well, according to the man's language we must be in Germany," Maria acknowledged jokingly.

"Keep together so we don't lose each other," the old woman cautioned everyone.

Suddenly they noticed a big banner over the station, written in German.

"FRIEDLAND WELCOMES YOU."

"We have made it, it is for real, we are in Germany," Maria said as if to convince herself. She could hardly contain her joy. The others looked at each other in disbelief.

"We are free. Katina we are free!" Jobina spoke hushed and teary-eyed. Her voice broke as she removed her kerchief. "At last we don't have to be scared anymore."

Overwhelmed, and not quite convinced, Katina looked around as tears welled up in her eyes. The two and a half years in prison camp had left a permanent scar.

"Jobina, will we ever be free? Will we ever forget and find peace in our souls? Will the longing pain for our loved ones and the emptiness in our hearts ever go away? Oh Jobina... I hope to God it will."

"Come along now and don't stall," a scruffy looking man hurried them along.

"Men line up over here and women with children go over there," he ordered, as they were then led separately away.

Bewildered, they looked at each other, as they wondered what this was all about. After all they had gone through, it was not easy to blindly trust any order, even if it came from a fellow countryman. At least that's what she believed and she was sure the others who had gone through the same were like-minded. Cautious and still very suspicious, she and the rest of them reluctantly followed.

But as soon they had gathered in the large chamber, the purpose of this whole maneuver was made clear to them. They were to be deloused. Relieved, they followed the orders of a young man who stood ready with the necessary pumping device.

"Okay ladies, untie and unbuckle everything that is not hanging loose around the body, then line up in rows, and that goes for the children too!" he ordered with authority.

Quickly, they did as they were told. Katina watched dumbfounded with dismay as the young man started to pump white powder over every woman's and child's body. Lifting up skirts he pumped a heavy dose underneath and all around each individual and their belongings. Then, for extra precaution, she noticed him giving each of the woman two hefty pumps from the top down into their bra section.

Some of the women swore, humiliated by the treatment, while others laughed and joked about it. When it was their turn, Julia, not knowing what to make of this, stared wide eyed at the man. Just as he was administering the white powder over and onto her clothes and skin, Elisa started to cry as he presumed to do the same to her and then to Stefan. Detached and unemotional, the young man continued to do his job.

After he was through with Katina, she unintentionally brushed herself off. Angry, he scolded her, and before she knew what was happening, he had given her another double dose all over her body. Powdered from head to toe she stood bewildered, daring not to move.

"I don't think you'll ever need another delousing again!" Jobina burst out into a wholehearted chortle, pulling the others along into a roaring laughter over Katina's ghostly appearance. Little Elisa cried even louder. The young man did not understand what the fuss was all about. He just shook his head and proceeded to do the same to the next woman in line.

79

As citizens of Friedland, the town's people had taken it upon themselves to help feed and house all the destitute that came daily across the border. Burdened with the understanding in knowing the hardship, danger and sorrow those poor souls had endured, this was one way to let them know that the Fatherland cared.

After spending some time in the Friedland refugee camp, and going through intense interrogation by the authorities, it was in her favor that she had in her possession the old song book with her baptismal place and date. She also had a family photo with Johann in uniform and the small picture of his graveside. With his name, date of birth and death engraved on a wooden cross. It was enough to get her accepted as a German refugee. She was then briefed by the Red Cross to reunite them with loved ones and relatives.

Full of anticipation and longing, she found out that most of her family, including Rebekka, along with Edwina and her little one, had made it to safety and now resided in Unterfranken. And that her sister Tara and family had settled in Hannover. But the thought of seeing them soon was short lived, as she was told there would be a long process to go through, and that meant more refugee camps in various places in Germany before they would be reunited.

Anxious, but a little disappointed by this news, she had no choice but to go along with the authorities' decision. After all, they had the burden of dealing with all the displaced people. And whether she liked it or not, she and her children were among them.

Jobina and Maria, who had no living relatives, decided to tag along with her and her children claiming that after all the time they had spent together and the shared hardships, they might as well, for the time being, stay together and help each other out.

Sadly though, when the time came to leave, the old lady decided to stay in Friedland. She said her goodbyes to Katina and Jobina, as well as the children. They had become close in the short time, bound by the same fate that had befallen all of them.

"Maybe one day, God willing, we'll meet again under better circumstances," she sniffled.

"There's a soft heart underneath that tough demeanor after all," Katina whispered to Jobina, as they walked onto the waiting train.

"Aha," Jobina agreed with tear filled eyes.

"She reminds me so much of my own mother," Katina spoke again with fondness in her voice. Her eyes took on a faraway look, her heart longing, she sighed, "I can hardly wait to see them again..., I've missed them all so very much... especially Rebekka, my oldest..." her voice quavered.

Seated next to each other, they settled in. The interior of the train was by far more pleasing and definitely more comfortable than the previous one. She gave a last glance out of the window, thankful and relieved that they had made it this far, unharmed.

Earlier in the refugee camp, they were told that three allies had army personnel stationed here in Friedland, and the part of Germany they were heading to was under American control. Confused, she sighed. 'More soldiers. When will this all end?'

Suddenly the door of their train carriage opened and two American soldiers entered, slowly walking through the aisle. Elisa looked at them scared, her eyes open wide. In her little mind, soldiers had always been associated with danger. Then unexpectedly, one of the soldiers stopped right in front of her and gave her a big smile. Searching through his rations, he pulled out a chocolate bar and reached it down to her, gesturing for her to take and eat it. Shyly, she took it, and gave it to her mother. Surprised, Katina acknowledged the soldier's kindness. He smiled and saluted in return, then went on to continue his patrol.

"Well, after this I believe anything is possible," Jobina exclaimed.

Katina smiled and nodded in agreement. Quietly, she drew back to ponder this very thought, and then added a special prayer to her many treasured memories. Deep in her heart a relentless yearning, "Until we meet again my love," she sighed with deep heart-stirring emotion.

THE END

Epilogue

After nine meager years in Germany, Katina and her children journeyed again, following most of her family far across the ocean to their new adopted North American homeland. Here she spent her remaining years enjoying life to the fullest with her children, grandchildren and great-grandchildren.

Yet, in quiet times, one could observe a wistful expression in her eyes, as they took on a faraway look. Throughout the years in Germany, whenever there were reports of released prisoners of war far from the east, she held her breath, hoping that Johann would be among them, but it was not to be. In all the years this yearning torment never left her. Only special memories remained, especially of the beautiful and carefree times they had shared, but also memories of those devastatingly painful years.

Regrets? There was one in particular she had mentioned often in conversation, one which still haunted and tormented her into her later years. It was that of the orphan girl Anna, who had begged her before the escape not to leave her behind.

"I should have taken her along. My God the poor girl... I should have taken her with me," she lamented whenever she thought and talked about her.

Another regret? Not to have let the Slovaks know that she and the children had made it safely out of Poland. But on that subject she knew this was not possible as she still feared for their safety.

Many times she thought about all the dear friends left behind. Where were they now? She knew that a few years after their escape the German government negotiated for all German prisoners to be released from the east. But she had not heard if they had all survived and made it out alive.

Yes. She had never forgotten those years. They were part of her existence and were deeply ingrained in her mind and soul. She reminisced and talked about them often whenever someone lent a listening ear.

Living well past her ninety-fifth year, she had stayed unwavering and true to the God of her forefathers, who had delivered and guided her. A treasure she passed on to her family.

Elisa favored to take notice of all the stories and it was upon her mother's passing, that in a dream, she beheld a most wondrous sight. It was as if a veil from a narrow window had been pulled aside for her to see. Her father and mother walking hand in hand, young and carefree, along a peaceful and sun-drenched meadow. As she strained to see more, a large tree suddenly obstructed her view. Upon waking, she pondered over this beautiful, yet comforting scene.

Katina and Johann were together again.

About The Author

Irene Steinhilber

Irene Steinhilber was a creative author, painter, and poet. She also was a beloved wife, mother, grandmother, and great-grandmother. She cared deeply for everyone she touched. She passed away in 2013.

Made in United States
North Haven, CT
12 May 2024